MOSQ

SHEPHERD GRAHAM

MOSQ

PLOT THICKENS PRESS
WWW.PLOTTHICKENSPRESS.COM

Plot Thickens Press
www.plotthickenspress.com

Printed in the United States of America
First Trade Edition: June, 2010

The Library of Congress has catalogued this edition as:

Graham, Shepherd
MOSQ / Shepherd Graham
ISBN: 978-0-615-36769-9

Library of Congress Control Number: 2010908335

Cover photograph and book design by Ronda Birtha, www.rondabirtha.com
Back cover photographs by Sherry Carter and Ronda Birtha

DEDICATION

To all the readers who wonder, question, and think for themselves,
I thank you.

PART I
THE UNITED STATES
MAY, 2007

CHAPTER ONE

Professor Jonathan McKenna walked into his university office and dropped a stack of computer printouts on the guest chair, signaling visitors were unwelcome to sit. He sensed something off and, turning to his desk, saw an envelope not there before. One sent by courier.

When his eyes moved to the logo in the upper left corner, time imploded and his past caught up with his present. He stood motionless, breathing fast, the wall clock ticking minutes.

Finding control, McKenna slowed his breath and threw the unopened mail into a drawer, kneeing it shut.

The professor switched on Vivaldi and sat down to doodle. His doodling was not ordinary, but involved the rapid creation of complex computer code, his way of bringing his mind into unobstructed focus.

His telephone rang and broke his concentration. He lifted the receiver, immediately detecting the subtle airless tone of a call made from a secure line. He didn't bother speaking.

"Mac?" The caller's voice, all too familiar but sounding older.

McKenna clenched his teeth. "What do you want?"

"You got my letter," the man said, making it a statement.

The professor didn't respond.

"You read the message."

"No."

"I'll hold on."

McKenna swore, but cradled the phone against his shoulder and retrieved the envelope from his drawer. He tore it open and pulled out an encrypted note. He began deciphering the code but stopped himself and pushed the paper aside. "Why don't you just tell me."

"We've lost three operatives in the past four months."

"How?" McKenna asked, instantly regretting the question.

"Taken out, all of them. A couple were made to look like accidents, of course. The usual."

"So what do you want from me?"

"I want you to come in."

"No."

"I need you, Mac."

"No."

"You're the only one left."

"What do you mean, 'the only one left?'"

"Those men were all from Operation Hard Place. That leaves only you from that group alive."

McKenna closed his eyes and pressed the heel of his hand to his forehead with a groan.

"And PASCAL," the caller said, "you were the best."

"That was a long time ago. And don't call me PASCAL. That's over. Besides, I have commitments here."

"You're taking a teaching sabbatical in a couple of weeks."

"How do you know that?" A foolish question. "Anyway, I have plans for that sabbatical."

"Come in," COBOL said. "I need you."

"No."

"I'll tell you the rest when I see you. I sent airline tickets. You'll have them today."

McKenna said nothing.

"And Mac?"

"What?"

"Bulk up."

COBOL disconnected, the click loud in McKenna's ear. He replaced the receiver and stared at the phone, jaw muscles tight, adrenaline on the rise. His old personality pushed to emerge and he worked to refuse it.

The last chords of Vivaldi faded into silence. McKenna sat for a long time in their wake, looking out his campus window without noticing the new Michigan spring or the coatless students sitting in the quad.

Footfalls at the door brought his attention back into the room.

A pretty computer science intern walked into his office tucking a lock of shiny jet hair behind her ear. "Dr. McKenna?" She smiled, gazing at him from under long lashes. "This just came for you." She moved in close and put an envelope on his desk.

Airline tickets.

The professor nodded once.

The intern sighed and turned, giving him a final glance over her shoulder before leaving the room.

McKenna shoved the flight packet and COBOL's message under his blotter and resumed doodling.

CHAPTER TWO

Mark Hughes thought it interesting he didn't dread the upcoming meeting with Reeves. A year ago he would have.

He put on a sweater over his shirt in spite of the warm weather. It seemed he felt cold all the time lately. A glance in the mirror, an old habit of checking his appearance before going out in public, now yielded little response.

Hughes picked up his car keys and went to the front door. He looked at the dog bed across the room, its emptiness paining him. *Don't think about Hercules,* he told himself, his eyes filling with tears. He wiped them before they fell down his face and stepped outside, pulling the door shut with a thud as if determined to keep the sadness from following him to his car.

He keyed the ignition on his BMW and drove from his D.C. townhouse, rounding Dupont Circle to New Hampshire Avenue. Clouds sliding in front of the late-day sun created a contrast of light and dark on the buildings and curbside trees. Pots filled with lilies, petunias and impatiens lent splotches of color to the passing scene, like impressionist oils on canvas. Though he'd traveled this route hundreds of times before, he'd never been so acutely aware of his surroundings.

The evening rush hour over, Hughes took M Street through the heart of Georgetown, noticing after-work shoppers and dinner patrons coming and going from stores and restaurants. Once on Canal Road, he headed toward the abandoned monastery and his meeting with Reeves.

Reeves. Mark had watched him on C-Span yesterday when the debates on defense spending aired. It shocked him to see the senator so fat and jowly, the result, no doubt, of glutting on the fine food and expensive cognacs his lifestyle afforded. The camera's close-up showed eyes of a man with no soul, flat and black as obsidian.

He tried to remember a different Reeves, back when they were young. No, even in the early years the signs were there. What he'd done to those kittens, to the little girl down the street, the cruelty he'd shown toward his own brother.

Hughes continued his drive.

He arrived at the monastery to find the senator already there, hands in pants pockets, walking in small, impatient circles in ankle-deep weeds in the abbey's decaying parking lot.

A cold fear shot up his back. So, perhaps he dreaded this encounter with Reeves after all.

Mark got out of his car and walked toward the man he'd seen on C-Span, fully aware of the irony of this meeting.

CHAPTER THREE

Raised voices echoed off the stone walls of the monastery that had lain in ruins for some time now.

"Rumor, that's all it is." Reeves Sjoda spat. He turned his back on Mark Hughes and walked to a rocked ledge that surrounded the abbey, shielding his eyes from the setting sunlight shimmering on the Potomac River below.

Mark trailed after him. "No, it isn't," he said. "I have proof."

Reeves snapped his head around. "What proof?" he asked, his voice low and gravelly.

"I saw the laboratory."

"Which one?" Sjoda saw Mark's surprise and realized his question had just given something away. It didn't matter.

"The one in Zambia."

"What the hell were you doing there?"

"Monitoring the effects of soil erosion," Mark said.

"And?"

"I met a woman who worked at the lab…." Mark hesitated, seeming afraid to say more.

The senator narrowed his eyes and jutted his chin, signaling him to continue.

Mark took in a breath. "She told me the disease didn't come from monkeys. And...." He paused.

"Say what you came to tell me," Reeves said.

"She showed me names," Hughes said in a rush, "of the people and governments involved." He looked at Sjoda, a plea in his eyes.

The senator stood unmoved.

"Damn it Reeves! Millions of people are dying. My friends are—"

"Yours was not the target group," Sjoda said, his voice barely audible.

Mark lifted his brows in question, but Reeves ignored him and took a pack of unfiltered Camels and matches from his pocket. He drew out a cigarette and lit it, dropping the live match to the ground. The flame ignited a tuft of dry grass; the senator left it unattended.

Hughes reached with his foot to snuff out the fire.

Sjoda inhaled deeply. He eyed the man in front of him and squinted. Something about his appearance rankled. His sweater hung loosely on his too-thin frame, the long sleeves reaching to the middle of his hands. A day's growth of beard made his skin look gray. Mark had always been so fastidious.

Hughes spoke. "I know, too, about the vaccine. And why it's not being released."

"Fuck." Sjoda spit out a piece of tobacco clinging to his tongue.

"You're in bed with them, Reeves."

"You're the one's been in bed." Sjoda scoffed. "You still with what's-his-name?"

"Phillip," Mark said in a whisper. He lowered his head. "No. He died."

Reeves said nothing, though his silence was not borne of sorrow or respect. He flicked his cigarette to the ground and reached into his suit jacket to grab what he needed with a firm hand.

The senator's next movement came swiftly. The upward thrust of the knife met its target. Hughes slumped forward, the weight of his body pushing Reeves against the stone wall, causing a jagged rock to cut a gash in his hand. Sjoda lost his balance and both men fell to the ground.

Winded, the senator pushed Mark off him and got to his knees. He slid his hand into his victim's back pocket and removed a wallet. He took the drivers' license and, reaching into the bills' section, ripped away the safe deposit box key taped inside.

Reeves snorted. Mark, always so predictable.

Sjoda stood, wiped his fingerprints from the wallet, and dropped it to the ground. Then, leaving his brother's body pooling blood in the dust, he walked away without any thought of looking back.

CHAPTER FOUR

Reeves Sjoda pressed a pudgy thumb on the remote door opener and eased his Mercedes into his townhouse garage. Exiting the car, he removed his blood stained Armani summer suit jacket, silk tie, and shirt, and wrapped them around the knife used to kill his brother. He stuffed the bundle in a garbage bag for trash, the loss of expensive clothing meaning nothing to him. He didn't worry about being caught with blood on his clothes on his drive home from the monastery. He was well known to police, and none would dare stop him.

The senator entered his home and washed his hands in the kitchen sink, watching the soap bubbles turn pink from a mixture of Mark's blood and the small-but-deep gash in his own hand. He thought about putting an anti-infective on the wound, but that could wait.

Opening the door to his warming oven, he looked at the meal his chef prepared for him, but left it untouched for now. Instead, he walked to the bar in his den and poured a hefty measure of Cardinal Mendoza, gulping half where he stood.

Reeves carried the remainder of the drink to a nearby recliner and dropped into it with a grunt, the chair's new leather creaking under his weight. He drained the rest of the brandy meant for sipping, and thought about calling the escort service. He'd ask for Martina—expensive, but worth it. She'd do it all and wouldn't complain when things got a little rough.

Looking at his empty glass with annoyance, Sjoda heaved himself out of his seat and poured another drink. While up, he pulled his lobster Newberg from the warming oven and returned to the chair to eat in large mouthfuls but with less importance than getting down the liquor.

He belched and rubbed his crotch, thinking again of Martina. No, he wouldn't get his money's worth tonight. He'd had a long day, starting with having to sit through that early senate meeting with a whopping hangover. He'd just have a few more drinks instead, and go to bed.

CHAPTER FIVE

Detective Maggie O'Neal wondered if she'd ever get used to the raw, meaty smell of a recently-stabbed body. The drying blood, sticky in the morning sun, attracted flies. Their incessant buzzing and the stench of the corpse made her lightheaded, and she fought the urge to vomit.

O'Neal looked down at the balding head of the medical examiner as he went over the body of Mark Hughes in the weeds of the abandoned monastery. Whistling tunelessly, the ME pushed up the long sleeves of the victim's sweater and shirt and made a note of what he saw on the skin underneath.

Heavy-steps signaled the arrival of Sergeant McClusky, and Maggie turned at his approach. He nodded to her as he lifted the yellow tape over his bulk to enter the crime scene.

"Robbery?" he asked, his voice gruff.

O'Neal shrunk in his presence. She made an effort to answer succinctly, knowing the sergeant lacked patience for over-long responses. "No, um, that is, apparently not. There's money in the wallet, and, ah, credit cards, but no driver's license." She felt her cheeks get warm. "Looks like his wallet's been gone through, though. There are blood smudges inside."

McClusky turned to the ME. "Can you stop whistling long enough to tell me what you've got?"

The man peered up at the sergeant and frowned. "Perp knew what he was doing, I'd say. Single stab wound to the aorta. The victim's been dead more than twelve hours. Rigor's passed off."

Maggie heard the squeal of the Latex gloves as the medical examiner peeled them off his hands. He dropped them into a small plastic container marked for medical waste, and, snapping his bag shut with a click of authority, stood and brushed dust from his trousers.

"Anything else?" McClusky asked.

"Yeah, Sergeant," the ME said. "Your murderer killed a dying man."

CHAPTER SIX

Maggie O'Neal parked her yellow 1977 Volkswagen bug at the curb in front of her family's aging brownstone.

Her brother Brian sat on the stoop reading a *National Geographic,* and he looked up when his sister got out of the car.

"Hi Mags!" he called to her. "You're home early."

"I testified in a prelim murder trial this afternoon. Court recessed at three-thirty," she said, climbing the steps.

Brian, seeing her face, said, "Another dead body today, huh?" He frowned.

"Yes, this morning." She came alongside and tussled his red-blond hair, something she'd done since his toddlerhood.

"How come you got assigned to DC Homicide anyway?"

"Brian, you know I can't talk about it."

"I know, but how long do you have to work there?" He wrinkled his brow. "You come home looking green-faced almost every day."

"Well, I'll be there until I get assigned someplace else," she said. "And stop wrinkling your brow. You'll have permanent lines before you're fifteen."

"I'll be fifteen next Christmas."

"I know. That's what I mean. You'll have an old-man's forehead by then."

Maggie glanced at the front door and knit her own brow. "Is Mother home?"

"No. She and Aunt Mary went to the hospital to see Dad. And Aunt Mary's brought dinner, so you don't have to cook tonight. She and Mom are going to church to play bingo after we eat."

"Oh, good." O'Neal heaved a sigh of relief and entered the home. Out of habit, she eased the screened door closed behind her. She'd learned as a child to move through the brownstone quietly.

An aged orange cat jumped down from his sunny spot on a window ledge and came to greet her.

"Hi, O.J." Maggie let him stretch before picking him up. She hugged him close, feeling his throaty purr. "Catch any mice today?"

"O.J. hasn't caught a mouse in years." Brian's voice preceded the loud slam of the screened door.

"Oh, I know," Maggie said, "but it makes him feel good for me to ask." She scratched her cat under his chin; he purred louder and squeezed his eyelids shut in feline pleasure.

"Maggie?" Her brother looked at her with eyes the same green-gray color as her own. "When's Dad coming home from the hospital?"

"Friday afternoon."

"He'll start drinking again, won't he, as soon as he gets here?"

"Yes, he will."

A shadow crossed Brian's face, and his sister stood with him in silence a moment.

O.J. wiggled to get down and Maggie put him gently on the floor. He went into the kitchen in search of supper, and O'Neal watched as his orange fur disappeared around the doorjamb.

Brian looked up at Maggie and asked, "You going to run this afternoon?"

"When will Mother and Aunt Mary be back?"

"About five-thirty."

Maggie glanced at her watch. Not quite 4:00. "Then I will."

"Your running clothes are on your bed. I folded laundry after Mom left. I can do stuff around here, too, you know."

"Yes, I know." Maggie rumpled her brother's hair. "And thanks."

"Sure." Brian's expression turned hopeful. "You going to compete in the New York Marathon again this year?"

"Yes. That is, I plan to. I registered."

"Good. I'm glad."

A plaintive meow came from the kitchen.

"I'll feed O.J.," Brian said. "You'd better get your run in before Mom comes home."

* * * * *

Maggie O'Neal ran like the wind. She ran to give freedom to her strength, and to define herself as other than the non-person some saw her to be, with no voice or presence. And sometimes, if she went fast enough, she could almost outpace those undefinable feelings that plagued her.

Her usual running route took her through nine miles of D.C. streets that included and adjoined her neighborhood. Smells from car exhaust and garbage bins placed curbside accompanied her as she breathed the city air. Ahead, late-June heat rose from pavement in shimmering waves.

Maggie's neighborhood, once blue-collared but neatly kept, began to decline more than a decade ago. "*Gone to hell,*" her mother'd said. Her father had bought their brownstone in his mid-twenties when people of Irish ancestry lived in the surrounding homes. Now foreign-language lyrics and rhythms of different cultures spilled from open windows as O'Neal went by.

She reached her halfway point and circled back home, passing familiar old women fanning themselves on stoops, their dresses hiked high above their knees, exposing fat, dimpled legs. Smells of dinner spices, meats-on-the-grill, and occasionally marijuana, wafted by her nose.

Low-income-family children played on the sidewalk and in the street. Maggie felt sorry for the kids in her neighborhood. Seeing their oft-despairing faces summoned dark clouds from her own childhood, and those undefinable feelings arose in her again, like a foreboding in reverse.

She increased her pace.

After almost an hour, Maggie returned to her block and slowed to a walk. She glanced at her watch as she neared her brownstone, glad she'd have time for a short bath, and reprieve, before her mother got home.

CHAPTER SEVEN

McClusky sat at his desk in the squad room with his head tilted down, snoring softly.

"The sergeant's cutting z's again," he heard one of the detectives say.

"He can't help it," a female cop said. "He's got a condition. It's called narcolepsy."

The detective snickered. "He ever fall asleep over a dead body?"

"No, he seems okay if he keeps moving. It only happens when he's sitting, I think."

"Nice to be able to sleep on the job and get away with it."

"Oh, give him a break, will ya? He works all the time. He's been here every shift I've been on, and you know how they've got me rotating around the clock. Sometimes I think he never goes home."

"He doesn't have to. He does all his sleeping here. How'd he get a job in DC Homicide as one of our sergeants anyway?"

"I heard he has connections..."

The voices faded as the two left the room.

Through almost imperceptible slits in his eyes, McClusky observed his computer monitor. *Come on,* he thought, willing what he awaited to appear on the screen.

The clock in the squad room read 4:00, quitting time for the day shift, and most of the detectives were preparing to leave. McClusky watched through seemingly-closed eyes as cops walked out the door that read HOMICIDE DIVISION in backwards letters on the interior's side of the glass. Other squad members were coming on duty for the night.

He returned his attention to the computer. *Come on. Nothing in ten days.* His frustration grew.

He sensed the change before it occurred. The screen flickered, and McClusky increased the volume of his snoring.

Finally.

He had only seconds. He opened his eyelids a fraction and scanned the data on the computer before it disappeared. He heard the distinctive noise of a laser jet coming to life and his eyes went to the sound.

As before, a detective named Jaffey moved quickly to the printer and lifted a single sheet of paper from the bin. He folded it into quarters, looking furtively around the room. When Jaffey came back to his desk, the document was out of sight.

McClusky made a snorting sound and scratched his stomach. He yawned, stretched, and labored to get out of his chair. Feigning stiffness in his legs, he walked to the water cooler, passing Jaffey's desk.

"Working overtime again, Detective?" McClusky asked.

"Yes, sir, but only long enough to finish this report." Jaffey tapped a form on his blotter.

The sergeant nodded and went into the men's locker. When he emerged four minutes later, Jaffey was leaving the squad room. McClusky followed him to the parking lot and watched as the detective headed toward the food truck that serviced the police department around the clock.

McClusky's car was parked just outside the rear entry of the building. He stood near the driver's side door, biding his time digging through pockets for keys, his back to Jaffey. He turned to see the detective leave the concession, a Styrofoam cup in his hand.

Jaffey raised the cup to McClusky as if to offer a toast. "Coffee…one for the road," he said, walking toward a new-modeled SUV, pricey for a low-salaried detective. "Maybe you should try it, Sergeant."

McClusky watched Jaffey open the driver's side door of the SUV and slide in. The detective held the cup atop the steering wheel with his left hand, and started the ignition with his right. Nodding to the sergeant, he backed out of the parking space and drove from the lot.

McClusky got in his vehicle and followed. Staying several cars behind, he tailed Jaffey through the streets of D.C. and into the Virginia suburbs.

Come on, Jaffey, give me something today.

His plea went unanswered as the tail ended uneventfully at the detective's apartment complex. The sergeant knew better than to keep watch outside the place. During previous stakeouts, Jaffey'd made no contacts.

A recent covert search of his apartment revealed no coded printouts or pertinent transmissions to or from his home computer. His taped telephone conversations yielded nothing either. Yet the information was getting out. *How?*

McClusky drove past Jaffey's complex without stopping and headed to his own destination.

CHAPTER EIGHT

The hot water soothed Maggie's muscles as she soaked in the tub. The cat O.J., positioned on the closed toilet seat next to the bath with his legs tucked under him, kept her company.

She smiled and reached out a wet hand. "What would I do without you, O.J.? You're my best friend."

The animal's ears twitched at the sound of her voice. He squeezed his eyes in a long blink as if to relay his understanding of what she'd said.

Maggie withdrew her hand and leaned against the back of the tub. She looked up at the ceiling and frowned at the peeling paint.

The wallpaper, too, was coming away in sections above the three-quarter tiled wall. A pattern of green ivy climbed a darker-green trellis against a once-white background, now yellowed with age and decades of her father's cigarette smoke. Dried water streaks from years of steam marred the surface.

Maggie hated that paper; the same pattern embarrassed the walls in the kitchen. When she'd saved enough money, she and Brian would get a place of their own. *Soon,* she told herself. *Soon.*

Her mind drifted to her recent assignment in D.C. Homicide and the body of Mark Hughes. It seemed she could never get away from death.

She thought of the crime scene, and an image of Sergeant McClusky appeared. Something about him didn't jibe, like put-together pieces that couldn't quite make a proper whole.

Maggie sunk deeper in her bath and her knees poked out of the water. She drummed her fingers on them as she tried to figure what bothered her about McClusky.

His dark-brown hair seemed at odds with the color of his skin, which gave the impression of having been freckled in boyhood. He moved like someone not used to his weight. His arms and legs were thick, but his fingers and face were not. And the way he smelled—like soap, or laundry dried in the sun. That clean smell didn't match his appearance, which bordered on sloppy.

She shifted in the bath. Why did the sergeant unnerve her so? Why, in fact, did most men affect her that way? A picture of her father popped into her mind and she slid down into the tub, submerging her head beneath the water as if attempting to wash the image away. Memories threatened, and she stayed underwater until her lungs felt like they would burst. She surfaced and sucked in air.

O.J. looked relieved.

On the floor below the screened door slammed, accompanied by determined footsteps. O.J.'s eyes opened wide and he pricked his ears.

O'Neal's mother screamed, "Magdalene!"

Maggie counted, *One, two, three.*

"Magdalene!"

O'Neal took a deep breath and slipped under the water again, grabbing a last moment of peace. Her hair floated on top like seaweed.

* * * * *

The smell of corned beef, cabbage and boiled potatoes greeted Maggie as she entered the kitchen.

"Hello, Aunt Mary," she said, smiling. She turned to her mother. "How's Dad?"

"Not that you care," her mother said. "You couldn't even take the time to visit him today. You ran, didn't you? Instead of visiting your father in the hospital, you ran."

"I saw him yesterday, Mother—"

"I cannot believe such a selfish, ungrateful daughter came out of my own body," Mrs. O'Neal said, her voice pitch rising. "After what we've sacrificed for you? And in return, all you ever do is run and shoot your stupid bow and arrows."

Maggie mentally grit her teeth.

Mary Levy rolled her eyes ceilingward and put an arm around her niece's shoulders, giving her a squeeze. "How are you, dear?"

"I'm okay, Aunt Mary. How are you?"

"Just fine." She patted Maggie on the back and went to the stove. "Sit down, Maureen. I'll serve the food."

Mrs. O'Neal sat at the table, her lips pressed into a thin line.

"Please tell your brother supper is ready," Mary said to her niece.

Maggie walked to the front door. She peered through the screen and saw Brian sitting on the stoop saddle-soaping his baseball mitt.

"It's time to eat," she said.

"Okay." He stood and came inside.

Maggie returned to the kitchen with her brother, and they took turns washing their hands at the sink before joining their mother and aunt at the table.

Brian forked into a potato. "Hey, Mags, guess what? I think I'm getting Mr. Scarletta for biology next year."

Maggie looked at her mother and saw it coming. She tried to warn her brother with a gentle kick on his shins, but she missed. He jumped, then, when his mother yelled, "What good is biology going to do you when you're a priest? That public school is filling your head with garbage! I told you you're going to a *catholic* high school. Then on to seminary!" She slammed her hands on the table, causing dishes and silverware to rattle. "YOU ARE GOING TO BE A PRIEST. A *PRIEST*, I SAY!"

"Now Maureen, leave the boy alone," Mary said, her tone calm.

Mrs. O'Neal turned her ugliness on Maggie. "Some day you're going to get raped running through this neighborhood."

"Naw, Mom, Maggie runs too fast," Brian said. "Nobody could catch her."

A smile played on the lips of Aunt Mary and her niece.

Maureen O'Neal opened her mouth to speak, but got trumped by the ringing of the home's single telephone in the hall.

"I'll get it," Maggie said, jumping up and moving for the phone. She reached on the third ring and brought the receiver to her ear. "Hello?"

The voice on the other end of the line was deep and resonant. "Maggie?" Her boss. "Sorry to bother you at home."

She knew he wasn't.

"I need you to come in tomorrow. Ten o'clock, my office. You're being reassigned."

He hung up without saying goodbye. Maggie knew this wasn't rudeness, but theatrics, for which her boss was famous.

CHAPTER NINE

Jonathan McKenna sat across a large, highly polished mahogany desk from Nathan Shoemake. The desktop was bare except for a single manila folder.

Nathan Shoemake, code name COBOL and Directorate of Operations for the CIA, was in his mid-forties, tall and fit, with sailboat-tanned skin. Silver hair enhanced deep blue eyes that twinkled with humor as if he were in on some joke. Like McKenna, he wore no glasses, surprising, considering the long hours they'd both spent in front of computer screens in the early years.

"You out partying all night, Mac? I tried calling you until four o'clock this morning, at home, on your cell, and at work."

"My cell phone service's been spotty lately. The provider said they're working on it," McKenna said, giving only a partial explanation for his being unavailable.

"Well, I'm glad you got my message." Shoemake linked his fingers together and stretched his arms and hands, palms outward. "I've never asked you, you like your digs?"

"The place has bugs," McKenna said. "I hate bugs." He shifted in his chair. "What's this all about?"

"Let's wait so I don't have to tell it twice."

"Twice? Who else do you need to tell what to?"

As if on cue, Shoemake's secretary opened the door to admit another person.

"Thank you, Claudia," Shoemake said. "Come on in, Maggie."

A woman in dark pants and a shapeless white blouse walked into the office, her hair pinned in a bun.

McKenna's jaw dropped in recognition. "Detective O'Neal?"

Maggie's head turned sharply. "Sergeant McClusky?"

Both looked at Shoemake, who smiled broadly. "I think you two know each other." His eyes danced as he bobbed his head from one to the other in mock introduction. "Mac, Maggie. Maggie, Mac."

"It's actually McKenna, not McClusky," McKenna said to her.

"Sergeant McKenna?"

"No, Detective O'Neal, just McKenna." He paused. "It *is* Detective O'Neal?"

"Yes, well uh, no. It's not Detective. It's just O'Neal...that is, Miss O'Neal...that is, uh, Maggie." She blushed and turned away.

Nathan Shoemake grinned.

McKenna crossed his arms and glared at him across the desk.

Shoemake put a hand out in a stop gesture. "Okay, I'll explain." He leaned forward. "I put both of you undercover in DC Homicide for our Operation D-Tech, but I thought it best that you not know about the other. I wanted you each working independently on this investigation."

The Directorate of Operations said to McKenna, "I put Maggie in Homicide so she could use her position as a woman to get close to the men in the squad room and see who might be passing our secret defense technology to foreign interests."

Maggie squirmed.

Shoemake turned to her. "Mac's been on an extensive leave of absence from the Agency. I called him back because—"

"Not leave," McKenna said. "Retirement. You brought me out of *retirement.*

Shoemake frowned. "I called Mac in from *leave* because he knew those three operatives we recently lost. He worked with them in an Iraqi field op in the nineties called Hard Place. You may have heard about it during your training. It became declassified about the time you were at Camp P."

Maggie nodded.

Shoemake continued speaking to O'Neal. "It's possible, of course, that these officers' deaths were connected to Operation Hard Place, although that mission ended eight years ago. Mac, we believe, was targeted in Iraq during that same op, but the assassination attempt failed."

Maggie turned to McKenna and raised her eyebrows.

McKenna ignored her. He glared at Shoemake, his mouth set in a hard line.

"After Hard Place," Shoemake said, "our three officers were given a subsequent assignment in Iraq. They came back to the States four months ago and were put on Operation D-Tech. Soon after, they lost their lives. Either they were killed because their covers were compromised during D-Tech, or because whoever wanted them dead waited for them to return to the States for easier access.

"These operatives got far enough along in their D-Tech investigations to discover our defense secrets were being relayed, via computer they believed, to a man in DC Homicide. I thought Mac could help determine who's been passing our technology overseas, as well as flush out the people responsible for the deaths of our CIA officers."

By being a sitting duck," McKenna said.

Shoemake ignored him. "Mac is highly proficient in computer technology. While undercover at Homicide, he established that our defense tech is, in fact, being sent to someone by computer. So with him back from leave—"

"Retirement," McKenna said, his voice steely. "And now that I've learned who at Homicide is receiving this classified data, I'll soon be heading back to Michigan where I belong."

"You know who it is?" Maggie asked.

"Yes, Miss O'Neal," McKenna said. "It's Jaffey. And I also discovered what defense secrets are being compromised, because I wrote a program called *Spider Web I* that duplicates, on my screen, all information coming into every Homicide computer."

"However," Shoemake said, "we don't know who's passing the technology to the detective."

"We'll know soon," McKenna said.

"Good," Shoemake said. "When?"

"As soon as the next block of data is relayed to Jaffey. I wrote another program called *Spider Web II* to determine the location of the sender. That's what I was doing until after four o'clock this morning," he said, looking pointedly at COBOL. "My initial program, *Spider Web I,* also saves all Homicide's incoming information and sends it to an off-site system. Tonight I'll print what's pertinent for hardcopy evidence and bring it to the Agency."

McKenna got up from his chair and stood with his back against the wall. He said, "I feigned narcolepsy at Homicide because it afforded me the opportunity to watch my computer monitor when those in the squad room thought I was sleeping. The incoming defense data, which is encrypted, by the way, only appears on screen for a few seconds. First, Jaffey gets notification on his computer that the sender is ready to transmit. When he acknowledges that he's at his desk, the data is relayed. The detective then clicks the print icon, and the information immediately disappears from his monitor and goes to hardcopy. If someone were to get to the printer before Jaffey, it wouldn't matter unless he or she knew code. The transmission just looks like garbage, or like a printer glitch."

"If the encrypted data only appears on screen for a few seconds and Jaffey gets the hardcopy, and you haven't printed your *Spider Web I* file yet," Maggie asked McKenna, "how do you know it's the defense technology?"

Shoemake explained. "Mac has a photographic memory. A few seconds is all he needs. And, he recognizes encryption because he was one of our top decoders before he went on leave." He looked at McKenna. "It's good to have you back, PASCAL."

"It's temporary, COBOL."

Maggie swiveled from McKenna to Shoemake and knit her brow. "PASCAL? COBOL?"

"PASCAL and COBOL were popular computer languages when we were in school together in the eighties," Shoemake said. "We took them on as code names. I'm COBOL, Mac is PASCAL." He pronounced it PAS-KAL, with the emphasis on the KAL.

Maggie turned to McKenna. "*You're* PASCAL?" she asked, her normal reticence gone. "I thought PASCAL was supposed to be dead." She looked at him as if he ought to be.

Shoemake said, "Yes, that's what we wanted everyone to believe, which is why he's undercover in Homicide using the name McClusky."

Maggie ran her eyes over McKenna, her expression hinting at disgust or disappointment.

"Can we get on with this?" McKenna asked, conscious of the fat belly and extremity padding he wore under his sergeant's uniform. He came slightly away from the wall and stood taller. "Why'd you bring us in?"

"Mark Hughes's murder. I know from your daily e-mail reports to me that you both went to the crime scene yesterday morning. Last night I received this by courier." He handed a copy of a typed letter to Maggie.

McKenna didn't move from his spot near the wall, so Maggie read the correspondence aloud.

"Nathan Shoemake, Directorate of Operations, CIA, Langley, Dolly Madison Boulevard, McLean, Virginia.

"Dear Mr. Shoemake:

"This letter is being sent to you upon my death, as per my prior instructions to an associate. It is imperative you act immediately.

"The HIV/AIDS virus is man made. Different strains have been injected into a large percentage of the African population, as well as American gay men and individuals in Thailand, from various sera created in a lab in Zambia and other locations.

"Vaccines effective against HIV/AIDS are available, but are not being given to most who have the disease.

"High-level officials in several governments have implemented a massive depopulation program. United States military and government personnel, including some on the president's staff and an individual within your own agency, are party to this scheme.

"The exact location of the Zambian lab and the names of the countries and governments involved are detailed in documents in my safe deposit box, number four-oh-eight at the main branch of the First Washington Trust, DC. The key to this box is taped inside my wallet.

"I saw, but was unable to obtain, a list of names of the specific depopulation plan participants kept in an off-line computer in the Zambian Laboratory.

"Time is of the essence, because the viral infection program is escalating. United States citizens are being targeted. Please investigate and bring those responsible to justice, as these activities constitute acts of terrorism.

"Sincerely, Mark Hughes."

McKenna came away from the wall and took his seat. He moved his chair closer to Maggie and speed-read the text over her arm, not willing to accept what he'd just heard without seeing it for himself.

He looked at O'Neal. "You said yesterday that no money or credit cards appeared to be missing from Mark Hughes's wallet, but there were blood smudges inside. Did you find a safe deposit key?"

"No, I didn't but—"

"I'd like to get my hands on that wallet," McKenna said, "to see if there's any evidence of something having been taped there."

"There was," Maggie said.

McKenna raised his eyebrows.

"There were tape marks and sticky tape residue inside the bills' section. It's in my report."

"I didn't read your report," McKenna said. "Though I'm undercover as a short-timer in Homicide awaiting retirement and perform the same in-house duties as the other sergeants on staff, my real focus is on Operation D-Tech. I only went to the crime scene yesterday to fill in for Detective Diaz who called in sick."

Maggie nodded her understanding.

Shoemake punched a button on his desk phone. "Claudia!"

"Yes, sir?"

"Get Isaac Greenleaf at the First Washington Trust on the phone."

"Yes, sir."

Shoemake released the intercom. "If the content of this letter is true and US Citizens are being targeted with a deliberate viral infection program, we have to get access to that safe deposit box. Since Hughes's murderer probably stole the key from his wallet and got to the box first, we'll most likely be too late to retrieve the documents, but we might be able to get forensics."

Claudia buzzed in after a moment. "Not there, sir. I left a message."

"Okay, but if he doesn't return the call soon, try him again. It's important."

"Yes, sir."

Shoemake let go of the intercom and asked, "How long does it take to get fingerprint identification back on murder cases in your police division, Mac?"

"Well, those people are as slow as sh..." He glanced at O'Neal. "... molasses."

"Because of the possible terrorist connection to the Mark Hughes murder, I'm bringing the CIA in on the case, now," Shoemake said. "We'll get our forensics team to investigate. Mac, finish up at Homicide as soon as you can. See if you can zero in on how Jaffey's getting that information out, and to whom."

"The food truck," Maggie said, her voice barely audible.

"What?" Shoemake and McKenna asked in unison.

"The food truck," O'Neal said, a little louder. "I've seen Detective Jaffey hand paper to the vendor. I assumed he was giving him a sandwich or drink order. He volunteers to get stuff for the other detectives sometimes."

"I'll bring Zach Ellis in on D-Tech," Shoemake said, "and have him in position to follow the vendor the next time Jaffey receives an encrypted message. Ellis is only a year out of training, but he's good.

"Maggie, you're off DC Homicide. Finish up what you need to there this afternoon. Beginning tomorrow, I want you on the HIV/AIDS terrorist plot investigation. Start by finding out all you can about Mark Hughes."

"I know he had AIDS," Maggie said.

Both Shoemake and McKenna looked at her in question.

"It's in the medical examiner's scene-of-crime report." O'Neal shifted in her chair. "Do you think it's true, sir?" she asked Shoemake. "Do you think it's possible that individuals within our government could be involved in the creation or spreading of HIV/AIDS?" She returned Mark Hughes's letter to her boss. "And someone in the CIA?"

"I don't know," Shoemake said. "If proof exists, though, we have to get it. The very idea of a deliberate viral infection program is unconscionable."

"What about Homeland Security?" McKenna asked. "Or the FBI's Counter-Terrorist Group? Aren't they supposed to have primary responsibility for terrorists threats?"

Shoemake scoffed and mumbled something under his breath.

McKenna looked at him a moment with pursed lips. "If what Mark Hughes wrote is accurate and you're suggesting we pursue this as a formal investigation, you're asking us to spy on our own government."

"Ours and others," Shoemake said.

"It's not the CIA's job to spy on its own people."

"No, it isn't," COBOL said. "Welcome back, PASCAL."

CHAPTER TEN

Maggie sat in her VW outside the health department, prepared to report her morning's findings. She took out her CIA-issued cell, punched a number sequence to line-secure the call, and phoned the Directorate of Operations' office.

Shoemake came on the line.

"Sir? It's Maggie. I have some information on Mark Hughes."

"Good. What do you have?"

"Um, for one thing, he was Senator Reeves Sjoda's half brother. They had different fathers. The senator's biological father ran off with another woman when Sjoda was eight, and a divorce ensued. His mother quickly remarried and became Mrs. Willa Hughes. The following year, she had Mark."

"Senator Sjoda's brother, huh?"

"Yes, sir. I tried to see Mrs. Hughes but she wouldn't talk to me. She slammed the door in my face, actually. Then I went to Mark's townhouse near Dupont Circle to see if anybody in the neighborhood could give me information, and a man came out of the next-door unit with a dog, so I asked him if he knew Hughes, and he said he did." Maggie mentally chastised herself for rambling. "In fact, he said they'd been good friends. So

I went with him while he walked his dog. His name is Derek Weisner. The neighbor, that is."

"Did you tell him you worked for the CIA and were investigating Hughes's murder?"

"No, sir. He just started talking so fast, I didn't get the chance."

"Okay. Go on."

"Well, um, he was, uh, gay sir. Mark Hughes that is. And, oh, the neighbor is, also. And we already know this from the ME's report, but Derek told me Mark had AIDS. It was advanced, too. Oh, and that Hughes's, uh, lover recently passed away from AIDS."

"Okay, what else?"

"He said Mark's dog died of Parvo, and that Hughes was convinced his dog got Parvo because he had AIDS, and that the two diseases are related."

"I've never heard of any connection between Parvo and AIDS."

"No, sir, neither have I."

"Did the neighbor say when Hughes told him about the Parvo-AIDS connection?"

"Yes, the night before he was killed. Derek had friends over for a coming-home dinner party for Mark, because he'd been away for several months."

"Okay. What else?"

"Well, he told me that Hughes worked for a private agricultural consulting firm here in DC called AgriSolve, Inc. Then Derek had to get ready for a gallery opening so he couldn't talk to me anymore. But he invited me back tomorrow for lunch, and to show me Mark's collection of antiques, because he said they're worth seeing. He has a key to Hughes's townhouse. When I'm there, I'll look around to see if anything stands out that might point to his murder."

"That's a good idea, Maggie," Shoemake said. "And, it sounds like you and Derek got along very well."

"Yes, sir. Next I went to AgriSolve and met with Hughes's former secretary. I told her I was investigating his murder and showed her my CIA ID."

"Was she cooperative?"

"Yes. First, she told me a little about AgriSolve. They're agricultural specialists providing low cost, efficient farming solutions to both national and international clients. I asked her about Mark Hughes's job, thinking maybe it was connected to his murder."

"And?"

"She said he was an agricultural engineer working as a consultant in Zambia, Africa. On soil erosion."

"Hmm. Hughes's letter mentioned a Zambian lab location."

"Yes, sir."

"Anything else?"

"Only that Mark was in Africa for three months and she didn't see him when he got back. He was supposed to come into the office on Wednesday, but that's when his body was discovered.

"Did you locate Hughes's biological father?"

"He's deceased, sir."

"All right. Anything more?"

"Well, that's all I have so far on Mark Hughes. But I went to the health department to get some information on AIDS, and they gave me some pamphlets. On how you can get it." She didn't want to elaborate and hoped he wouldn't ask. "And how it's a fragile virus."

"Well, keep digging and see what else you can find. Also see if you can learn of any connection between Parvo and AIDS."

"Okay, sir."

Maggie disconnected and checked her watch. 1:49 p.m. Her father was due home from the hospital this afternoon and she might not be able to get a run in after work.

She grabbed her duffle bag from the back seat, reentered the health department, and changed into a T-shirt and shorts in the ladies' room. She'd put in a few miles now, and eat the lunch she'd packed in her cooler when finished.

O'Neal drove to a path along the Potomac River and exited her vehicle. After a few warm-up stretches, she took off running and built to a racer's pace.

CHAPTER ELEVEN

The phone rang on McKenna's desk in the Homicide Division's squad room as he sat watching his computer screen. He lifted the receiver and said, "McClusky."

"Anything?" Shoemake asked.

"You'll be the first to know."

Shoemake told McKenna about the connection between Mark Hughes and Reeves Sjoda.

"Senator Sjoda's brother?" McKenna kept his voice low.

"Yes. Maggie also said Hughes just came back from Zambia, Africa."

Africa, McKenna thought. An image of his wife flashed into his mind. He pushed it out. "Anything on Hughes's safe deposit box?" he asked.

"Empty. I've got forensics working on it, seeing if they can raise any prints."

"Is Ellis on the job?"

"He's out there now," Shoemake said.

"He alone?"

"No. He has backup."

"Okay. I'll keep my eyes opened."

"You mean closed." Shoemake laughed.

"Yeah. I mean closed."

* * * * *

McClusky a.k.a. McKenna a.k.a. PASCAL sat slouched at his desk in the squad room with his arms crossed over his chest and his head bobbing in a snooze. After a brief nap, he raised his eyelids and blinked as if trying to come awake. He stretched, and went to the coffee pot. The brew wasn't as good as what the concession offered, but it would do.

Coffee in hand, McKenna returned to his desk and absently opened the thin file on Mark Hughes. He kept his monitor in peripheral view, blank now except for a black cursor flashing in the upper left corner of the light-gray screen.

The medical examiner's report stated that Mark Hughes had AIDS. According to the ME's estimate, the knife that severed his aorta shortened the man's life by about nine months.

McKenna assumed that Hughes's murder had to do with the information he'd locked away in his safe deposit box. He thought about Mark Hughes having his letter sent post mortem to the Directorate of Operations of the CIA. The Agency's charter is to collect foreign intelligence, so the "*high-level officials in several governments*" statement in the courier-delivered text might warrant a CIA investigation.

But it isn't the Agency's job to spy on U.S. citizens, unless, as in the case of Operation D-tech, the purpose of the domestic spying is to gather intel on other countries whose activities threaten national security. Although, the "*U.S. citizens are being targeted*," statement, if true, does represent a terrorist threat to our country.

If Hughes's killer, or someone associated with the murderer, was interested in the contents of the safe deposit box, how did he or she know about the key in the victim's wallet? How did Hughes find out about the HIV/AIDS infection plan and the involvement of those he alluded to in his letter? Did it have anything to do with his having the disease? Maybe he simply happened upon the scheme during his stay in Zambia.

Did the person who had the letter delivered to COBOL know of its contents? Nathan said the envelope arrived with a wax seal on the flap embossed with Mark Hughes's initials, an old-fashioned-but-effective way to protect confidentiality.

McKenna realized he'd been thinking about the Hughes case and stopped himself. He picked up his cup, still warm to the touch, and took a sip of coffee. He wanted to finish Operation D-tech and return to Michigan and the reason why he'd planned a sabbatical. Working for the Agency again was unsettling. Too many reminders of the past, of his wife and son, his fellow officers in Operation Hard Place, now dead, and of Nathan Shoemake, who'd once been his closest friend.

Friends. He didn't have any in Michigan. Only his sister-in-law Constance and nephew Jason were there. A woman professor whom he'd twice turned down for dinner dates accused him of being more interested in computers than people. "*Code. Ones and zeroes,*" she'd said. "*With computers you don't have to feel. With people, you do.*"

He glanced at the empty desk that'd belonged to O'Neal. Her job had been to get close to the men who might be receiving and passing American defense technology to foreign interests. She hadn't done that. In fact, thinking back on her behavior, she seemed to have avoided the men in the squad room. He shook his head at COBOL's using her on D-Tech for that purpose. He wondered, even, if she were CIA material.

True, she'd been a thorough and competent homicide detective, and in her short time in the Division, had a high-solve rate for those murders to which she'd been assigned. Her observation and investigative skills were keen—it was O'Neal who'd figured out the defense secrets were most likely being passed to the food truck vendor.

She sure didn't have much of a personality, though. He'd never seen her interact with any of the other detectives in the squad in a social way. She always brought food—cold leftovers, it looked like—and ate lunch by herself when in-house. He assumed she dined solo while out, also.

A loner.

A cord of truth tugged at his gut. He could just as easily be describing himself.

His mind went back to the Mark Hughes case. Hughes's letter indicated some highly placed individuals in the United States government, even those close to the president, were in on the HIV/AIDS infection program. Did the president, now is his second term, know about this depopulation plot? And who within the Central Intelligence Agency is involved?

If COBOL got proof enough to justify an investigation, he'd have to get it approved and funded. How could he do that without involving Homeland Security and the FBI, or if U.S. government and military officials, and even someone in the CIA, would be incriminated? He'd figure a way. Nathan Shoemake always got what he wanted.

McKenna saw a flash on his computer screen—encrypted defense technology. *Spider Web II* would identify the origination of the transmission and send it to his remote computer.

He watched Jaffey move quickly to retrieve the printout, doing a poor job of acting casual. Immediately after, the detective left the squad room.

With a keystroke, McKenna deleted his *Spider Web* programs from Homicide's system. He put Mark Hughes's file in his briefcase and exited the building to the parking lot.

Jaffey, heading toward his SUV with a Styrofoam cup in his hand, called out to him, "Hey, McClusky. You done for the day?"

"Yeah, Jaffey, I'm done."

McKenna walked to his car and nodded almost imperceptibly to a man across the street tinkering under the hood of an old pickup.

Zach Ellis nodded back.

McKenna got in his car and drove away from D.C. Homicide for the last time.

CHAPTER TWELVE

After spending the afternoon at CIA headquarters in Langley, Maggie came home to find her father at the kitchen table in a sleeveless A-shirt that did little to hide his beer belly. At 5:18 in the evening, Paddy O'Neal sat hunched over a half dozen cans of crushed Icehouse empties that littered the table. A cigarette burned in an ashtray overflowing with tan-filtered butts.

The absence of Maureen O'Neal meant she'd be upstairs lying in her bed with the shades drawn. The palpable tension in the brownstone gave evidence there'd been another argument. *Or one-sided tirade, more likely.*

The vitality had gone out of Paddy O'Neal nine years ago when his son Patrick died.

Maggie put cheer in her voice. "Hi, Dad."

Her father grunted in response.

"Hi O.J.," she called to her cat.

The orange feline jumped down from a window ledge to greet her, and went to sit in front of his empty dish on the floor. Maggie opened a can of food and O.J. came to rub on her legs. She could feel the boniness of his body through her slacks and thought, as she often did lately, of how old he'd become. She put a freshly-filled bowl on the floor and picked up the used one. Small bits of caked cat food clung to its surface smelling faintly of fish.

O.J. bit into his meal delicately, chewing on the right side of his mouth with his few remaining teeth.

Maggie reached to the crock-pot and lowered the temperature, deciding she would get in a quick evening run after all.

"Go to the icebox and git me a cold one before ye go a-runnin,' daughter," Paddy O'Neal said.

Maggie obliged her father and went quietly up to her room to change her clothes. She managed to get back down the stairs and to the screened door before her mother yelled to her.

"Magdalene? Magdalene! Don't you dare go off running—"

Maggie fled out the door. She broke into a fast pace and didn't slow down until she'd gone two blocks. Those unidentifiable feelings were rising in her throat and threatening to choke off her air. She stopped and leaned against a construction dumpster recently placed on the street, taking away two more neighborhood parking spaces.

"Ugh!" she shouted skyward, bringing her fists into the air.

Two men unloading drywall from a GEORGETOWN RENOVATIONS truck stared at her.

Embarrassed, Maggie took off running again. Thirty minutes later, she circled back and slowed her pace to walk with Brian, coming home from a softball game.

"Hi," she said, barely out of breath.

"Hi, Mags! I hit a homer today! You should've seen it! It was a two runner!" He did a victory pump in the air with his bat. His baseball cap was turned backwards, and his mitt, looped around his belt, bumped against his hip as he walked.

"Looks like you did a slider," Maggie said, brushing his T-shirt.

"Yeah, and it was real close, but the ump called me safe."

Maggie smiled.

They walked along in silence for a moment.

"Someone's fixing up that place," Brian said, pointing to a run-down brownstone.

They'd come to the dumpster sight. Maggie, glad to see the GEORGETOWN RENOVATIONS construction truck and workers gone, paused with her brother to look at the home undergoing renewal.

After a moment, they started walking again.

"Hey Mags, is Dad drinking?"

"Yes, Brian, he is."

"Are they fighting?"

"I'm sure they were. Mom was lying down when I got home." Maggie put her arm around her brother's shoulders. "We'll get our own place soon."

Brian leaned into his sister. "I know," he said with a sigh.

CHAPTER THIRTEEN

McKenna walked into Shoemake's office, still wearing the fake belly and fat padding under his sergeant's uniform, his CIA badge clipped to a pocket. COBOL was putting papers away in his file safe, getting ready to leave for the weekend. Claudia had already gone.

"Got something?" Shoemake asked.

"Yup. A plane ticket to Michigan."

Nathan frowned. "Sit down, Mac." He waited until McKenna complied. "Zach Ellis brought in the concession vendor. Name's Ahmed Yousef. He's being interrogated now."

"Good."

"Ellis also got some background on Reeves Sjoda."

"Our young officer's been a busy boy."

"Yes, well, when I learned from Maggie that Sjoda was Mark Hughes's half brother, I asked Ellis to do some checking." Shoemake pulled a file from his drawer. "Seems the good senator has quite a history."

"Why doesn't that surprise me?" McKenna'd had some dealings with Reeves during Operation Hard Place. The man'd been a military cryptologist before entering politics and used his position on the Senate Select Committee for Intelligence to try to tell McKenna how to do his job.

"Senator Sjoda was investigated for allegedly taking bribes to support legislation favoring large corporations," Shoemake said. "He was cleared and, let's see..." He opened the file and skimmed a pen along the text. "Brought up on rape charges in college, twice, then again in the Navy, and—"

"Let me guess. Also cleared."

"Yes, and oh, this is interesting. It seems he makes frequent and large contributions to children's charities. Well, that's a good thing, at least. And, okay...there are some ethical violations noted here, and several sexual harassment complaints lodged against him since he's been in the senate. The harassment complaints were—"

"Dismissed. And all complainants were either paid off, threatened, or they're dead," McKenna said.

"Yes. And according to our intel," Shoemake taped his pen on the open file, "Sjoda frequents prostitutes and likes it rough. Has a reputation for beating them. He's real dirty. Once—"

He cut his sentence short to answer the telephone ringing on his desk. "Shoemake."

COBOL listened a moment. "Okay, go on." He cradled the phone against his shoulder and grabbed a pad from his drawer. He wrote a list of countries, thanked the caller, and hung up the phone.

"Well," Shoemake said, "it seems the food vendor, Ahmed Yousef, gave it up right away. Each piece of the defense technology's been going to the highest bidder, exclusively. It's being relayed through various computers to individuals within these countries whose identities he doesn't know. He's given an e-mail address and told to go to different locations to scan the encrypted data into designated PC's."

McKenna read the list on Shoemake's pad upside down. "North Korea, China, Iran, Libya, Afghanistan..."

"Yup." Nathan slowly nodded.

"How does Yousef know which countries are receiving the technology?"

"He said he researched recipients' Internet service providers to determine general locations."

"Why?" McKenna asked. "Job security? Evidence for future blackmail? Just for curiosity?"

"Don't know." COBOL looked up from his notes. "You get the originator of those transmissions yet?"

"That's what I came to tell you. The information's being routed through numerous ISP's."

"Of course."

"So I'll have to trace it. It may take some time."

"All right," Shoemake said. "I'll put Yousef back into place at the precinct's concession. He'll work for us now and continue to pass along what he's getting from Jaffey, and let us know the locations of the PC's he's using for relays."

"Good. Tell him to e-mail us from each PC to an address we'll set up for that purpose, and immediately delete the e-mails afterwards. That way, I can get into the systems Yousef's using for sending the technology, and track the individual buyers. And, I'll intercept the data that's being sent to Jaffey, encrypt bogus defense information, and route it through to the detective's computer at Homicide, so what's going out to the buyers will only appear to be real."

"Excellent." Shoemake put Sjoda's file back in his desk drawer. He dipped his head, but not quite enough to hide a sly smile, as if pleased to have gotten his old friend back in the game.

CHAPTER FOURTEEN

Maggie rang the doorbell to Derek Weisner's townhouse just before noon. A few notes from *Phantom of the Opera* chimed, and Derek opened the door. He hugged her as if they were longtime friends, and O'Neal returned the hug.

"Here," she said, handing him a box. "I stopped by Zarelli's Bakery and picked up chocolate éclairs for dessert."

"Oh, thanks, girlfriend. These are a favorite of mine."

A small white poodle wagged its tail at Maggie's feet, panting at her expectantly. She bent over and gently petted it on the head. "Hi, Priscilla," she said, remembering the dog's name from having been introduced yesterday. The poodle gave a happy yip in response, and followed as Derek led Maggie into an immaculate kitchen designed for entertaining.

Dishes, bowls and small appliances sat neatly displayed behind glassed-door cabinets, and an eight-burner stove, two ovens, and a grill provided cooking options. A countertop bar, holding two wine racks and a variety of glasses hanging upside down, bordered a pass-through from the kitchen to a formal dining room.

"May I get you something to drink?" Derek asked. He put the bakery box on the counter. "I have wine," he gestured toward the selection, "red, white, pink, or amber. We're having crab salad for lunch, if that helps you decide."

"Just water, thanks."

"Sparkling?"

"Oh, yes, that would be nice. May I help with anything?"

"No, girlfriend, I've got it covered." Derek flitted around putting finishing touches on lunch. He looked up from the task and asked, "Would you like to see the rest of the townhouse?" He waved a hand toward the other first floor rooms. "You can give yourself a tour. It'll be a few minutes before we eat."

"Okay." Maggie left the kitchen and went into a generous-sized living room, drawing in an appreciative breath at its beauty. Overstuffed sofas, love seats and club chairs, all in a soft cream, were set against copper-colored walls. Candles burned inside an off-white marble fireplace and reflected light onto a highly-polished hardwood floor. Throw pillows in a variety of subtle hues, along with simple watercolors and well-placed baskets, added texture to the space.

Classical music played, and O'Neal followed the sound to the back of the townhouse where Derek had set up an art studio. Finished paintings were propped on floor and shelves, and abundant light from tall windows illuminated an easeled work in progress—an English garden bursting with flowers.

Maggie recited the names and medicinal purposes for each of the flowers in her head: *Columbine, Aquilegia Canadensis, the roots, seeds and leaves of which are used to relieve headaches and treat lice. Black-eyed Susans, Rudbeckia hirsa, taken internally to expel worms and treat colds, and applied externally as a wash for snakebites. Purple cornflower, Echinacea purposa, an immune system stimulant, its leaves and roots beneficial in treating colds and flu.*

"We'll be eating on the patio," Derek called from the kitchen.

"May I help you carry anything outside?"

"No thanks, girlfriend. Just go on out."

Maggie found her way to the patio and sat at a round table set for lunch. Fresh purple irises and blue lilies in a crystal holder complemented cobalt-blue placemats, violet napkins, engraved silverware, and china patterned with flowers matching those in the vase.

Derek stepped outside to deliver her sparkling water in a fluted glass with a wedge of lime on the lip, and put his white wine at the head of the place setting opposite hers. He went back into the kitchen and returned with a tray of serving dishes.

"Help yourself, girlfriend," he said, transferring bowls and a breadbasket to the table. After setting aside the tray, he took his seat and put a few small bites of seafood on a dish, placing it on the floor for Priscilla.

Everything looked and smelled wonderful. Maggie spooned crab salad and minted mixed fruit onto her plate, passing each in turn to Derek. She broke a piece of wheat bread from a warm loaf.

"Girlfriend," he said, taking the breadbasket from his guest, "I haven't even asked you your name. I've been so overwrought about Mark's death and my gallery opening, that I'm afraid I was abrupt with you yesterday."

"No, not at all. I'm Maggie O'Neal."

"Maggie," he said, as though tasting her name. "Is that short for Margaret?"

"No, Magdalene." She took a bite of crab salad.

"You must be Catholic."

O'Neal patted her lips with her napkin and smiled. "Yes."

"Did you go to parochial school?"

"No, public."

"You're lucky. I went to Catholic school and the nunzies beat my hands black and blue with their rulers." He frowned. "I came to regard rulers as horrible things. So now I use a measuring tape or a straight-edged-anything-else as a substitute."

Maggie offered a sympathetic smile and changed the subject. "So how did the opening go last night?"

"Divinely. I sold three paintings."

"Oh, good for you! I looked at your artwork. You're very talented."

"Thanks. I love to paint." He reached for his wineglass. "So, what do you do for a living?"

"Oh, I meant to tell you yesterday. I work for the CIA. I'm investigating Mark Hughes's murder."

Derek took in a breath and stared at her as if dumbstruck. He withdrew his hand from his wine. "To whom do you report at the CIA?"

"The Directorate of Operations, Nathan Shoemake."

Derek gave a small gasp. Maggie looked a question at him but he didn't respond. He seemed preoccupied, and no longer the enthusiastic person who greeted her at the door. He picked up his fork and ate in nervous silence.

After a few minutes, he dabbed his mouth with a napkin. "I guess you'd like me to tell you what I can about Mark."

"Yes. Please. Anything may help."

"All right." Derek placed his napkin back on his lap and spent the rest of the meal telling Maggie about Mark's passion for antiques, his grief over the loss of his lover, Phillip, his job as an agricultural engineer, and his affection for his dog, Hercules.

O'Neal listened carefully and filed the information away in her head, but nothing shed immediate light on Hughes's death.

When they finished dessert, Derek flapped at the air and said he'd clean up later. He went to get the key to Mark's home, and Maggie met him at the front door. Priscilla curled up on her dog bed in the entrance hall for a nap.

Minutes later, they entered Hughes's townhouse in respectful silence and began touring the first floor, starting in the living room. The layout seemed a mirror image of the Weisner home. Here, though, walls were painted in neutrals and the rooms furnished with an eclectic collection of antiques, including some in a primitive style.

Judging from the powder covering furniture and woodwork and from the opened drawers exposing things in disarray, the home had been dusted for fingerprints and searched for other evidence as well. Weisner frowned at the mess, and, mumbling something Maggie couldn't hear, rushed to close the drawers.

They continued through the townhouse and Derek recited the age, origin and a short history of each of Mark's antiques as they went along. His mood darkened.

"Oh," he said, pain evident in his voice. "It's such a shame. Mark's mother is getting all of this." He swept his arm to indicate the scope of her inheritance. "The townhouse, the antiques, everything except the paintings. Those he left to me. It grieves me that Mrs. Hughes doesn't care about his precious things. She's well...I don't like her very much. Mark made me executor of his estate. He didn't trust anyone else to handle it."

They returned to the living room, and Maggie noticed a well-used dog bed in the corner. She went to it and saw foam peeking through a worn section on its side. Dog hair was matted into the fabric of the indented center.

Derek came beside her. "Hercules died four months ago," he said, "but Mark kept this old thing right here, dog hairs and all." He sighed. "It's all so sad."

Maggie reached and touched Weisner's shoulder.

His eyes pooled. After a moment, he sniffed and looked at his watch. "I have to be getting along to the gallery soon," he said.

Maggie nodded in acknowledgment. She took a final glance around the home and went toward the entry.

They left the townhouse and Weisner locked the door behind them. O'Neal hadn't seen anything on the cursory tour that would provide a clue to Hughes's murder.

She stood with her host on the sidewalk.

"Maggie?"

"Yes?"

"I may be needing to call you, well, about...something," Derek said, his expression sober.

"All right," Maggie said, looking at him with concern. "I'll give you my cell number." She took a pen and paper from her fanny pack, wrote her number, and handed it to Derek.

"Thank you for lunch," she said. "Everything was delicious. And thanks for showing me Mark's antiques."

"Sure," Derek said, but he stared off into the distance.

She waited.

After a moment, he turned and hugged her absently.

Maggie got into her car and drove away wondering about the change in Derek's mood, the change that occurred when she'd revealed she worked for the CIA.

CHAPTER FIFTEEN

McKenna pinched the bridge of his nose. He'd been working at this for two days and still hadn't found the source of the coded transmissions to Jaffey. So far, he'd traced the message routes through Internet service providers, or ISPs, in Germany, France, Great Britain, Japan, Australia, and the U.S.

Leaving his computer on task, McKenna went into his apartment's kitchenette to make coffee. He'd just spooned instant granules into a cup when he heard a bleep.

He walked back to his computer and peered at the screen, now revealing a D.C.-area ISP. He typed a few commands, and his program searched for a name. It got a hit.

I'll be damned.

He printed his findings and instant-messaged COBOL at his home.

GOT THE ORIGINATOR, he wrote in code.

He waited. No response.

Come on, Nathan, be there. He stared at his monitor. No answer.

McKenna went back to the kitchenette and put water on to boil. He shifted from foot to foot whistling a Wagner tune until bubbles began to rumble in the pot. He turned off the stove and poured steaming liquid onto instant granules, the water hissing and spitting against the inside of the cookware. His computer bleeped just as he placed the pot back on the burner.

Coffee in hand, McKenna slid into his seat in front of the monitor.

TELL ME, COBOL'd texted in code.

McKenna put his cup on the desk and typed, SJODA.

There was a pause before Nathan responded, THAT SOB. TEN A.M. TOMORROW, MY OFFICE. I'LL CALL IN O'NEAL.

CHAPTER SIXTEEN

McKenna, still in fat padding and sergeant's uniform, sat in front of Nathan Shoemake's unattended desk with Maggie O'Neal at 10:05 a.m. Neither said anything since their mumbled greetings to each other when Claudia showed them into the office. Shoemake, uncharacteristically late, presumably got delayed in his Monday morning meeting with the Director of the CIA, Kenneth Berns.

McKenna scanned the room and noted the same medium-gray carpet and light-gray walls as when the previous Directorate occupied the space. A credenza sat under the wide window behind the desk; a picture of the President of the United States hung on the wall to the right, the CIA emblem to the left.

At 10:12, Shoemake walked into his office and nodded to his officers. He placed his briefcase on the credenza, opened it, and removed an envelope before taking his seat.

"The meeting in DCI Berns's office ran long," he said, not sounding happy. He turned to McKenna, "Have you told Maggie yet?"

"No."

"Mac found out who's been sending the defense technology to Jaffey," Shoemake said.

O'Neal looked at McKenna and raised her eyebrows in question.

Shoemake answered for him. "It's Senator Sjoda."

"Oh, my gosh," Maggie said.

Shoemake leaned forward and folded his hands on the desk. "There's going to be a dinner at the Magnolia Ballroom in honor of two retiring senators Friday night. Reeves Sjoda will be there." He put his fingers on the envelope he'd removed from his briefcase. "The CIA has twelve tickets to the event. My wife and I are going, as are some of the other directorates and their wives." He shifted in his chair. "Mac, you'll be going as Jonathan McKenna, no disguises."

"I'm flying back to Michigan Friday."

Shoemake ignored him. "You'll be recognized, of course. I want to see who'll be interested in your coming back from the grave."

"You mean you're setting me up. That gives me a warm feeling."

"And Maggie, you're going to the function as Mac's date."

Maggie turned first to Shoemake, then to McKenna, a look of panic on her face.

McKenna asked, "What's O'Neal's role in all this? Why does she go as my date?"

Shoemake answered by speaking to Maggie. "I want you to try to get close to Reeves Sjoda."

"What!" McKenna exploded, coming partly out of his seat. "Nathan, you can't!"

"Maggie, the senator fancies pretty women and he likes to chase. That should keep him off the serious stuff for a while."

McKenna doubted it. And it was one thing to make a sitting duck out of an experienced officer like himself, but to put O'Neal on the line was sacrificial. He shoved out his chair and went to the wall near the president's picture. He leaned back and folded his arms across his chest.

"You'll need to dress to the nines." Shoemake said. "A tux for you, Mac, a gown for you, Maggie."

McKenna saw O'Neal lower her head. She rubbed her left thumb over the nails of her right hand as if inspecting them for flaws. He could see from where he stood they were unpolished but well groomed.

He moved his eyes to Maggie's face. Her skin was clear, almost dewy, and bare of makeup. As Detective O'Neal, she'd worn her hair pinned up behind her head. Now, it fell to her shoulders. Shiny, the color of a desert sunset.

Rather than her usual dark pants and plain blouse, O'Neal wore a sleeveless white cotton dress, clean but old. The edges at the shoulders were beginning to fray, and something about that tugged at a place inside McKenna he didn't want touched.

"Of course," Shoemake said, addressing O'Neal, "the Agency will pay for your gown, shoes, the whole works. My wife will take you shopping, and believe me," he said with a smile, "she knows where to shop." He leaned back in his chair. "And Mac, pick Maggie up at her house in the limo."

"No!" Maggie said.

They looked at her in surprise.

"I'll meet you there," she said in a lowered voice.

"Maggie," her boss said, "you can't pull up to this kind of a political function in that old rattrap Beetle of yours."

Her eyes went to her lap again.

Nathan regarded her, a thoughtful expression on his face. His features softened, and he said, "On second thought, let's book you into the Washingtonian Hotel. Hobnobs coming in from out of town for this shindig will be staying there. Maybe you'll see or hear something of interest.

"And Maggie, between now and the retirement dinner, I want you to schedule time at Camp P. We don't know where all this will take us, so sharpen your skills, especially at the shooting range. Do your running there."

Nathan turned to McKenna and said, "Spend some time this week getting into shape. You're too fat." He barked a laugh.

McKenna glared at him.

Shoemake's eyes held a twinkle as he pressed his phone's intercom button.

Claudia answered, "Yes, sir?"

"Is my wife here yet?"

"She's just coming in now, sir."

"Bring her right in, will you?" He released the intercom without waiting for a reply.

The door opened and Suzanne Cinque, five-feet, eight-inches tall and dressed in tan linen slacks and a bittersweet silk blouse, came into the room. She wore flat, navy pumps and carried a matching slim leather bag. The tan, bittersweet and navy colors in her paisley scarf completed her attire. Her hair, glossy-black and thick, ended in a shoulder-length, straight-line cut. A hint of expensive perfume followed her as she went behind the desk to kiss her husband on the cheek.

"Hello, darling," she said, her voice cultured and throaty.

She retraced her steps and extended her hand to Maggie. "I'm Suzanne Cinque." She pronounced it SIN-CUE, and McKenna always wanted to say, "you're welcome" when he heard it. "Most people call me Zann."

Suzanne turned to McKenna and a look of surprise came over her face. "Well hello, Mac. I didn't recognize you at first in that police uniform. It's wonderful to see you again." She gave a brilliant smile.

"Hello, Zann. Long time."

"I understand you're going to the senators' retirement function."

"So it seems."

"Good. I'll see you there, then." She turned back to Maggie and said with delight in her voice, "All right, my dear, let's go shopping."

Zann moved toward the door. "Bye, darling, bye, Mac," she said, finger waving over her shoulder and trailing her expensive scent in her wake.

Maggie stood to follow.

"Miss O'Neal," McKenna said.

"Yes?"

"I'll pick you up at the Washingtonian at seven-thirty on Friday night. I'll phone your room when I arrive at the hotel."

"Okay," Maggie said, her cheeks getting pink. She stepped away quickly.

Zann held the door for her. "Let's have lunch before we shop. I know a marvelous cafe..."

The door closed, leaving the men alone.

McKenna returned to his seat. "I don't get it, Nathan," he said. "Using O'Neal for these assignments? She hardly seems qualified. She's so... awkward."

"She's just socially shy, Mac."

"Since when do socially-shy people make good operations officers?"

"What kind of homicide detective did she make?"

McKenna leaned back in his chair. "A good one. Professional, though I could see she was queasy around dead bodies."

"Few wouldn't be. It takes getting used to."

"How'd she do in her training at Camp P?"

"Top of her class, actually." Nathan pulled a manila file folder from a drawer on the right-hand side of his desk. He opened it and started reading. "On her final course test she came in first, so she outran and out climbed everyone, including the men.

"Less proficient with a firearm, though. Archery is her forte. Won three regional championships in bow and arrow in her late-twenties. It's noted here she split her own arrow in the target."

McKenna found himself impressed, although his better judgment fought it. "I thought that was only done in movies."

"Yes, well... She graduated in the top ten at university." Shoemake skimmed his index finger over a page. "Majored in criminology, minored in botany and entomology. Has her masters in—"

"She has a master's degree?"

"Yes, a double. Botany and entomology. Plants and bugs."

McKenna mentally grimaced at the word "bugs." He loathed the things. "Operation D-Tech her first field assignment?"

"Yes," Shoemake said. "Before that she worked at our Domestic Resources Branch, overseeing the US citizens recruited to spy in other countries while traveling there for pleasure or business. They reported any gleaned threats to our national security directly back to her."

"What about her psychological profile?"

"You know that's confidential, Mac, even for you."

"I know. I'm not asking for explicit details. I'm just trying to get a feel for this woman. I can't read her."

Shoemake pursed his lips and flipped over some pages in the file. After a few minutes he said, "All right, Mac, I'll tell you this much. The staff psychologist reported that her profile indicated evidence of serious childhood trauma, particularly of a specific nature." He raised his head and met McKenna's eyes.

McKenna regarded COBOL a moment. He slowly nodded and said, "It fits, what little I know of her. It explains her unease around men. How old is she?"

"Thirty-two."

"Lives alone?"

"No, with her parents."

"Still?"

"There are extenuating circumstances."

McKenna steepled his fingers and tapped them against his lips. "Okay, so other then avoiding the men you wanted her to cozy up to, she demonstrated a notable level of competence at Homicide. I concede that. It's the other side of her that concerns me, the side that seems to lack a certain kind of maturity. She's too ingenue...too innocent, something."

McKenna read a look on Shoemake's face and arched his eyebrows. "Nathan, that's why you want her at the retirement dinner, isn't it? You know Sjoda is attracted to her type. To pursue and ruin."

"Yes. I know the senator will be drawn to her."

McKenna exploded, coming out of his chair. "That's unconscionable!"

COBOL put his hands on his desk and leaned forward. "You're losing perspective, PASCAL."

"Am I?"

Shoemake raised his voice. "I don't risk my officers. I don't deliberately send them into situations over their heads. You don't know as much as you think you do."

McKenna turned and made for the door. He put his hand on the knob and said through a clenched jaw, "I damned well know a sacrifice when I see one."

CHAPTER SEVENTEEN

Maggie heard a knock at the door. *That'll be Zann,* she thought with a sigh. Shoemake's wife had said she'd come to the hotel early to help her get ready for the retirement dinner. O'Neal hadn't wanted Suzanne's assistance, but didn't know how to tell her so. She felt nervous about the upcoming evening and wanted to be alone.

The knock came again, louder this time.

"Coming," Maggie said, though half-heartedly.

O'Neal opened the door and drew in an admiring breath at Zann's beauty. She wore a full-length, cobalt-blue gown of obvious designer origins, accented by what appeared to be a diamond and blue-stoned necklace with coordinating drop earrings. Her hair was swept and pinned high on her head, with curled tendrils falling softly around her face. Her strapped silver heels matched the bag she carried.

"Wow, Zann, you look stunning."

"Thank you," she said, stepping inside the hotel suite. "You will too when we get you out of that robe." Zann touched the sleeve of the worn material. She frowned. "They don't pay much at the Agency, do they? Her eyes swept the room. "Where's your gown?"

Maggie went to the closet for her dress, still covered in the store's protective opaque bag. She carried it to the bed almost reverently and gently unzipped the plastic. She didn't want to disrobe in front of Zann, but thought going into the bathroom to change too obvious.

"Nice view, isn't it?" O'Neal nodded to the window, hoping Shoemake's wife would turn and look out at the city.

"Yes, it is," Zann said, walking toward the cityscape.

Maggie shed her robe and slipped into a simple spaghetti-strapped, Caribbean-green raw-silk gown. She removed hot rollers from her hair, putting a towel over her shoulders so loose hairs wouldn't fall on her dress when she brushed.

"How long have you known Mr. McKenna?" O'Neal asked, taking a cosmetic bag from her suitcase, opened on the bed. She went to the mirror and started putting on makeup.

"Mac?" Zann turned away from the window. "Eighteen years, give or take. Why?"

"It's just that I'm suppose to be his, uh, date tonight, and I don't...um, anything you can tell me might help."

"Well, let's see...." Zann sat in a chair by the window and crossed her legs at the ankles. "According to Nathan, Mac's one of the best officers the CIA's ever had. Very professional and competent. He was a master code breaker in Iraq during Operation Hard Place. The Hard Placers, as you know, gathered intelligence on chemical and biological weapons' deals. Nathan was in charge of that mission." She paused.

Maggie stopped applying makeup and turned from the mirror toward Shoemake's wife, who seemed to be off in some memory.

After a moment Zann said, "He saved Nathan's life once. Mac almost died doing so."

"Wow," Maggie said softly.

Zann uncrossed her ankles and rose from the chair. "I came here to help you get ready. Shall I assist with your makeup?"

"Oh, no, thank you. My aunt sent me to finishing school the summer before college, 'to round me out as a lady,' and I learned how to apply it there."

Zann nodded and retook her seat.

Maggie turned back to the mirror and resumed putting color on the apples of her cheeks. When she finished applying blush, she dipped a lip brush into a pot of soft peach gloss.

"Mac and his wife used to be our best friends," Zann said.

Maggie swung around. "His wife?"

"Yes."

"Oh. I thought...um, I didn't know he was married."

"Yes. Well, no, not now. His wife was killed eight years ago in Iraq during Operation Hard Place. His son, too. That's when Mac left the Agency."

"Oh." Maggie finished putting on the gloss, recapped her lip brush, and returned it to the cosmetic case.

"Mac changed a great deal after he lost his family," Zann said. "He became distant. Hard." She paused, and Maggie turned to her again.

Suzanne remained silent. After a moment, she smiled. "Mac used to be such fun. He and Nathan played practical jokes on each other all the time. They'd howl with laughter at the other's cleverness." She sighed and her smile faded. "They were so close. We all were."

Zann stood and came to sit on the bed. "Mac became a shell of his former self. He believed he was the real target when his wife and son were killed. When he subsequently wanted to resign from the CIA, the Agency invented his death, and he relocated. Nathan didn't see him again until he flew here from Michigan at the end of May."

"He and your husband don't seem like friends now," Maggie said. "Does McKenna blame Mr. Shoemake for the death of his wife and child?"

"No, he's just angry. Not at Nathan, I don't think, but at what Nathan represents."

Maggie gave Zann's response thought while she leaned over and brushed her hair from underneath to give it loft. She straightened, and it fell softly around her face. She finished styling it with a comb.

"How old is McKenna?" O'Neal asked.

"Let's see." Zann paused before answering. "He'd be forty now."

"Oh, I thought he might be—"

The phone rang, and Maggie jumped. She went to it and lifted the receiver. "Hello?"

"It's McKenna. I'm in the lobby."

"Okay," she said, a slight tremble in her voice. "I'll be right down." She replaced the receiver.

"Don't hurry," Zann said. "Men expect to be kept waiting. Besides, Nathan is in the bar. The two can have a drink."

Zann got up from the bed and went to her purse, left on a table by the door. She opened it and removed a rectangle of gray jeweler's cloth. "Here," she said, returning and handing the item to Maggie with a smile. "Wear this tonight."

O'Neal unfolded the material and revealed an exquisite necklace of gems that matched the color of her gown. A round center stone the size of a nickel, with four smaller stones on either side, were set in white gold.

"Oh, Zann, it's beautiful."

"Here, I'll help you." Shoemake's wife grinned. "Maggie, you'll have to take that towel away from your shoulders."

"Oh, yes. I forgot."

O'Neal removed the towel, pivoted in her stockinged feet, and lifted her hair so Suzanne could fasten the necklace.

"There," Zann said. "Now let me see how you look."

Maggie moved to face Suzanne again.

"Oh, my dear. You're beautiful. You'll certainly turn heads tonight. Perhaps you'll even bring Mac out of his eight-year malaise."

Maggie felt the color rise in her cheeks.

"He's very handsome, wouldn't you agree?" Zann smiled. "I've seen females of all ages quite swoon over Jonathan McKenna."

Maggie looked at her doubtfully. She slipped her feet into a pair of three-inch heels.

"Perfume?" Zann held a small bottle out to Maggie.

"No, thanks. I'm allergic."

Zann nodded in understanding and returned the bottle to her purse. "Ready?"

No, thought Maggie, her face warming again.

Suzanne looked at her. "Are you blushing? Your face is quite pink."

"I can't seem to control it. Especially where men are involved."

Zann inclined her head and regarded Maggie a moment.

O'Neal went into a deeper flush. She put her room key in her purse and opened the door for Shoemake's wife.

The women rode the elevator in silence.

Maggie was too nervous to speak and felt herself becoming short of breath. She remembered the advice her friend Francie had given her. "*Take three slow, deep breaths, and center yourself.*" Maggie did, and calmed a little. She even felt her face cool.

That is, until the elevator door opened and she saw Jonathan McKenna standing ten feet away.

* * * * *

He wore a black tuxedo with cummerbund and bow tie against a ribbed white shirt, his dress shoes highly polished. He stood fit and trim within his six-foot, two-inch frame.

Maggie drew in a breath.

McKenna stared at her with eyes the color of faded denim, an unfathomable expression on his lightly tanned face. His hair seemed muted, as if it was once a brilliant red, but had, over time, suffered the fate of too many washings.

Out of the corner of her eye, O'Neal saw Shoemake's wife appraising McKenna too.

Suzanne leaned toward Maggie and grinned. "Oh my," she whispered. "Very handsome, indeed. What a pair you two make. And apparently," she said in a louder voice, "Mac and my husband didn't meet. I'm going to the bar to find Nathan. See you in a bit." She finger-waved over her shoulder.

"No," Maggie croaked through a dry throat, but only in time to see Zann's cobalt gown disappear around the near corner of the lobby. Her heart thundered and she tried to swallow, but couldn't. *Oh God,* she thought.

McKenna bowed to her slightly.

Oh, God.

CHAPTER EIGHTEEN

Maggie O'Neal stood outside the elevator door, seemingly frozen to the spot. McKenna heaved a sigh and, finding a smile, approached her.

"Miss O'Neal?"

Maggie stared at him, saying nothing.

"Would you care to take my arm?" he asked.

"Okay," she rasped. She slipped her hand tentatively through the crook in his elbow, and McKenna guided her toward the door.

"The limo's waiting," he said.

"Okay." Maggie pivoted her head toward the bar.

"If you're looking for Nathan and Zann, they're going to meet us there."

"Oh, okay."

McKenna turned to her, letting her arm slip out of his. Her face was in high flush. "Miss O'Neal?"

"Huh?" She spoke into his chest.

"Since our jobs require us to act like we're on a date, perhaps I shouldn't be referring to you as 'Miss O'Neal' tonight. How about I call you Maggie?"

"Oh, okay."

She said nothing further, but continued staring at his chest.

Is she memorizing every square inch of my shirt? He said to her, “You may call me McKenna. Or Mac if you like.”

“Oh, okay.”

They stood facing each other, O’Neal’s eyes fixed on his sternum. He waited.

What she asked next took him by surprise. “Does anyone call you Jonathan?”

“No!” he thundered.

Maggie drew back.

“Let’s go,” he said, his voice hard. He turned and walked out of the hotel, leaving O’Neal to trail behind.

The limousine driver held the door open, and Maggie passed by McKenna and got in. He followed, sliding into the backseat alongside her.

The driver took his place behind the wheel and pulled away from the curb without speaking. That suited McKenna; he hated chatty chauffeurs.

He felt irritated. Hearing his first name spoken by a soft female voice brought up memories he wanted to keep buried. He knew that blaming the lady beside him for his foul mood was unfair, and decided to try to dispel the awkwardness between them. He took a breath and put on a smile.

“I saw you run the course at Camp P this week. You’re fast, Maggie.”

She didn’t respond.

“You ever run a marathon?”

“Yes.”

McKenna waited for her to say more. She didn’t.

“I watched you scale the wall. You climb well, too.”

“Thanks.” She looked out the window on her side of the limousine.

He attempted amusement. “Did you climb trees as a kid?”

She half turned to him. “Yes.”

With that, the exchange died, and McKenna didn’t try again. He leaned his head against the back of the seat and rubbed his eyes with his thumb and forefinger. *Oh, boy, this is going to be a long night.*

He turned slightly and looked at O’Neal in silhouette. Nathan was right. She was pretty. More than that, she had the budding quality of a rare flower. Her dress was form-fitted around the bust and waist and revealed an exquisite firm figure not apparent in the baggy clothes she'd worn at Homicide.

He felt terrible about subjecting her to Reeves Sjoda. It was like leading a tender lamb to slaughter. He again questioned Nathan's judgment.

McKenna closed his eyes. *Uch,* he thought. He wanted this job to be over. He wanted O'Neal to go away. At least he'd be going back to Michigan on Monday on his rescheduled flight—

"Sir?" The driver held the door for him. He must have dozed. McKenna shook off sleep, wishing he could shake his mood as well.

He exited the limo and took Maggie's hand to help her out of the seat. Then, tentatively arm-in-arm, they walked up the marble stairs to the Magnolia Ballroom, looking anything but like a happy couple.

CHAPTER NINETEEN

Reeves Sjoda went to the open bar, his drink in hand. He made it a habit to return while some brandy remained in his glass in case he had to wait in line. He threw back the rest of the liquor and placed the empty on the countertop, signaling the bartender for another. He'd not yet reached that mellow state and pushed to get there.

Brandy refilled, Reeves strolled to the buffet tables of international food and scanned the offerings. Not bad. Caviar. Russian, of course. King crab. Jumbo shrimp. He looked to where the chefs stood ready to carve the roast beef, lamb, and pheasant, mild steam rising to their faces beneath pleated, puffed-white hats.

The senator turned and saw one of his employees coming toward him. He went to meet the man and pulled him aside.

"Did the information get through?" Sjoda asked.

"Smooth as silk. No problems."

The senator nodded and swirled amber liquid in his glass. He took a large swallow. "Any changes in personnel?"

"Yeah, funny you should ask. Those two who transferred in recently got transferred out."

Reeves frowned. "What's that about?"

"Don't know. Rumor says they were caught doing something unholy."

"In Homicide? What'd they do, kill somebody?" Reeves snorted at his own joke.

"Don't know."

"Well, find out. I don't like personnel changes."

His employee nodded and headed toward the door.

"Julian!"

The man turned.

Reeves walked over to him. "You have a description of those two?"

"Yeah. Sergeant's a big guy, bulky, out of shape. Dark hair. The detective's a mouse of a thing. Frigid, old maid type. Never said nothing."

"Names?"

"His is McClouski or something. Don't remember hers."

"Well lay off the cocaine and get your brain back in gear. Get me those names."

His man grunted and left the room.

Reeves went for a refill, and, fresh drink in hand, strolled around the room, weaving in and out of dining tables acknowledging acquaintances. Occasionally, he joined small groups of people standing and talking so he could keep abreast of the subtle goings-on in D.C. He paid special attention to the women, of course, trawling for one he could get on to.

The senator circled back to the bar and out again to the buffet. He reached for a plate and halted, feeling a shift in the room. He turned toward the entrance and saw her.

Instantly, he felt himself get hard. *Oh, sweet. So very sweet.* He maneuvered closer, beads of perspiration forming on his face. He licked his lips.

A man appeared at the woman's side and cupped her elbow. Reeves couldn't believe his eyes and glanced at his drink as if it tricked him. He looked up again and squinted. But there was no doubt.

PASCAL.

His final prey, right here.

He almost climaxed.

Reeves never did believe that crock-of-bull story about McKenna being dead. He would get both of them tonight, PASCAL and that sweet little treat he stood next to.

Oh, life is so good.

The senator walked to the side of the room and removed his cell phone from his custom-tailored tuxedo jacket. Holding his drink in his left hand and the phone in his right, he punched a number with his thumb.

When his employee came on the line, Sjoda turned his back on the retirement dinner crowd. "Julian?" He kept his voice low. "Our last bird has come home to roost." He paused, listening. "That's right, McKenna." He took a swallow of his drink and said to the man, "Kill him. This time, make sure he's dead."

Reeves disconnected and replaced the phone in the pocket of his tux. He took a long pull on his drink, emptying the glass. *Yes, life is excellent, indeed.* This would be more delicious than killing his brother Mark. He could never, ever, remember feeling this good.

CHAPTER TWENTY

Maggie stood at the entrance to the ballroom, a crawling sensation traveling up her spine as Reeves Sjoda closed in.

When Shoemake had privately briefed her on her role as McKenna's date for the retirement dinner, he specifically warned her about the senator's predatory tendencies. So accordingly, she'd practiced for this night, planning what she'd say and do. Still, nothing could have prepared her for the reality of Reeves Sjoda. She felt as if she were watching a slow motion movie through a blurred lens, her feet stuck to the floor.

Minutes ago, McKenna had left her by the door to sign the guest registry and hand in their tickets. He now reappeared by her side and took her elbow. It surprised her to be glad he was there.

"Maggie," he said, bending toward her. "Try to smile."

She did, but her lips formed a grimace.

"Let's go to the bar."

She didn't move.

"Maggie, walk."

McKenna gave her a nudge and she moved her feet. Moments later, she found herself standing in front of the bar, her co-worker still holding her elbow.

"What do you want to drink?" he asked.

"I don't drink," Maggie said.

McKenna let out a sigh. He said to the bartender, "Two Perrier's, please."

"Oh." Maggie hadn't thought to order anything nonalcoholic. Her face flushed, and she turned momentarily away.

McKenna handed her a glass of chilled Perrier and she took a sip. It moistened her throat and the cold of it helped snap her back to herself.

"I'm sorry, McKenna." She lowered her chin.

"Maggie, look at me."

She raised her eyes to his face. His expression was unknowable, and it bothered her that she couldn't discern what went on in his mind. She could usually read people; it's how she navigated through life.

"How's it going?" Shoemake asked, coming alongside with Zann.

"Nathan, I don't like this," PASCAL said.

"I'm alright now," Maggie said in a low voice to McKenna.

She looked away and mentally chastised herself. *Get yourself together. You have a job to do. This is what you've trained for.* She remembered the advice Francie had previously given her: "*When faced with a circumstance you feel unequipped to handle, think about someone who'd be good in that situation and assume his or her persona.*"

She almost smiled recalling these words, because the person she most often pretended to become, especially during her CIA training, was the highly reputed PASCAL. Now that she actually knew him, she suspected that devise would no longer work.

"Maggie?" They were all looking at her.

"Yes, well." She straightened her spine. "I'm going to the buffet. If I'm to be available for Senator Sjoda, I shouldn't stay here with you all night." She gave her Perrier to McKenna and made her way to the international food tables.

It didn't take long. Reeves intercepted her as she reached her destination.

"Hello," he said. "I'm Senator Reeves Sjoda." He held out his hand.

Maggie picked up a plate to avoid taking it. She put on a smile. "Hello. I'm Maggie O'Neal." Her heart thundered.

"Your name is familiar. Have we met before?"

"I don't believe so." She kept her smile.

"You're here with Jonathan McKenna, I see."

"Yes, do you know him?"

"Oh, indeed. We go back a long time."

Reeves turned and looked toward the bar. "May I get you a drink, Ms. O'Neal? Mine seems to be empty." He moved closer to her.

Maggie felt lightheaded and leaned a hand on the buffet table. "Oh, a Perrier, please."

Sjoda left to get the drinks.

O'Neal looked at McKenna. He stood about twenty feet to the side of the bar watching her closely, his expression still unreadable. Nathan and Zann were speaking with another couple.

Moments later, the senator returned. She shivered at his approach.

"So, how long have you and your date been seeing each other?" Sjoda asked, handing her a glass of sparkling water.

Maggie looked again at McKenna. He gestured for her not to drink the Perrier. She placed it on the buffet and busied herself putting food on her plate while she answered as rehearsed.

"Just a few months."

"Where did you two meet?"

"At a professional function. Actually, a friend introduced us."

"And *do* you make a nice *couple,* Ms. O'Neal?" He leaned in, his face close to hers. She smelled alcohol and cigarettes on his breath. He sweated heavily, and the hair combed over his bald spot sat wet against his head. He stood slightly shorter than Maggie's five-foot nine in three-inch heels.

The senator fired more questions at her, not waiting for answers. "What's McKenna up to these days? Where's he been? Out of country? I've not seen him for years. Why's he in DC?"

Sjoda's face almost touched hers. Maggie's head started to spin and she fought the urge to vomit. He stepped back and grinned at her lecherously.

McKenna appeared at her side, not excusing the interruption or acknowledging Sjoda in any way. "Maggie, there's someone I want you to meet," he said. He took her elbow and began leading her toward the center of the room.

Reeves grabbed her arm, almost knocking food from the plate she held in her hand. "Don't forget your drink," he said, giving her the Perrier. "And, I'll be seeing *you* later."

McKenna nudged her away. She walked with him to a clearing in the crowd.

"Don't drink that," McKenna said.

"I know." She put the Perrier and her plate on a nearby table and said to McKenna, "He inquired about us as a couple, and fired off a number of questions about you, but for all his supposed interest, he didn't ask much about me."

"He doesn't usually bother, Maggie. Let's go out to the porch and get some fresh air."

"Okay." Maggie looped her arm through his. He looked at her and raised his eyebrows. She smiled at him a little, then turned away as she felt her face get warm. She was glad, therefore, to see that the veranda was dimly lit when they stepped outside.

Maggie removed her arm from McKenna's and gratefully sat in one of the chairs. Not accustomed to wearing heels, she took one shoe off and rubbed her foot.

McKenna walked to the edge of the veranda, unbuttoned his tux, and leaned his left elbow on the railing, his body sideways to Maggie. She studied him as he stared off into the distance, his profile silhouetted against the soft glow of a candle lamp.

The conversation she'd had in the hotel room with Zann about McKenna's wife and son being killed in Iraq replayed in her mind. He seemed sad, and a resigned kind of alone.

He looked out over the grounds and Maggie continued to watch him, wondering what went on in his mind. She wondered, too, what he felt about her. His disapproval of her was evident. And, though he was professionally cordial, he didn't seem to like her much.

A rustle in the bushes disrupted her thoughts. McKenna turned his head toward the noise. *Rats, probably,* Maggie mused. *DC is full of them.*

She returned to thinking about her co-worker, and her mind drifted back to her days at Camp P. The trainees had heard stories about the legendary PASCAL, and some of the females openly shared their fantasies about him. Her dream was to *be* PASCAL, so she endeavored to do as well as he did, according to his reputation, in all her CIA-related skills.

Oh, there were some romantic notions about him too. She found this interesting, because it didn't fit with her usual reaction toward men. In her daydreams, though, PASCAL was different, and she was at ease around him. Their partnership was equal, their relationship ideal.

She smiled at the irony of the infamous PASCAL being across the veranda from her now, and the fact that she'd been working with him for several weeks in D.C. Homicide without knowing it. Well, so much for fantasies. McKenna-in-person proved that real life is never as good as life-imagined. In fact, it could be darned disappointing.

Maggie sighed and stood, wiggling her foot back into her shoe. She stepped across the veranda to McKenna.

"I should go back in and spend more time with Senator Sjoda," she said.

McKenna's reply was cut short by a disturbance in the bushes and the distinctive 'thwap' of a bullet fired from a silenced gun.

A second shot followed.

Both Maggie and McKenna dropped to the floor.

CHAPTER TWENTY-ONE

Moments passed, McKenna lying on top of Maggie, neither moving. Floodlights illuminated the lawn below the veranda and Secret Service agents swarmed the area.

McKenna lifted his head and surveyed the scene. His attention turned to O'Neal. "Are you all right?" he asked.

"Yes. That is, I think so," Maggie said. "I don't feel anything."

McKenna raised himself into a half push-up and studied her. "Are you numb?" Concern showed in his voice.

"No. I mean I don't feel like I've been shot." She grunted. "How about you. You okay?"

"Yes."

"Then, McKenna?"

"Hmm?"

"Could you get off me now, please?"

"Oh, sure."

He rolled away from her and jumped to his feet. His eyes moved around the area.

Maggie turned her head toward the lawn. The Secret Service agents seemed to have everything under control.

She sat up, and McKenna reached his hand to her. She took it and stood.

"Your dress is ripped," he said, pointing to a tear along the side.

"Oh." She frowned.

Shoemake appeared and rushed to his officers. "You both all right?" he asked.

"Yes," they said in unison.

A man sprinted from the lawn onto the veranda and pulled their boss aside. The two engaged in brief conversation.

Shoemake returned to O'Neal and McKenna. "Let's go," he said. "My limo." He speed-dialed a number on his cell, and spoke to his driver as they walked quickly through the ballroom and out the front door. The limousine arrived a few minutes after they reached the curb, and the chauffeur hurried to assist his passengers.

Shoemake said, "Get in. I'm going back for Zann." He instructed the driver to close the door.

Several minutes later, Zann and Nathan climbed in opposite McKenna and O'Neal, who were sitting on the jump seat.

Someone tapped on the window, and Shoemake lowered it about four inches. A man handed him two discs and left.

Nathan raised the window and keyed the intercom as the driver slid behind the wheel. "The Washingtonian Hotel," he said. He released the button and checked to make sure the privacy window was closed. He then turned on the overhead light and leaned forward to inspect his officers.

"Well, PASCAL, how many is that you've used up?"

"How many what?"

"Lives." COBOL reached across and put a finger through a bullet hole in McKenna's lapel near the vicinity of his heart.

Maggie's eyes went wide. She remembered him opening his tux on the veranda.

Shoemake said, "There's a guy lying dead in the Magnolia Ballroom's bushes. Name's Julian Gundry. He worked for Senator Sjoda. He's the one who shot at you."

"Who killed him?" McKenna asked.

"One of ours."

"Timing could have been a little better," McKenna said, fingering the hole in his jacket.

"Yes, well, things happened pretty fast. Our man didn't have time to get into position to spare your...lapel."

"How'd you know to have someone watch Julian Gundry?" Maggie asked, knowing she could speak freely in front of Zann, who revealed during their pre-shopping lunch that she, too, worked for the Agency in the Foreign Resources Branch, recruiting non-U.S citizens as spies for the CIA.

Shoemake pushed a button on the console to his right and a CD player slid out. He selected one of the two discs he'd just received and placed it in the unit.

"The answer to your question is on this CD, Maggie. We had a pen mike trained on the senator at all times." He pushed the PLAY button and both the in-person and cell-phone conversations Reeves Sjoda held with Julian Gundry audioed from the unit. "Now we know who's interested in your return from the dead, Mac."

"Yup," McKenna said.

Shoemake removed the first disc, inserted the second, and pressed PLAY.

The greeting exchanged by Maggie and Shoemake's wife at O'Neal's hotel door came on the player.

Maggie's face showed surprise.

Zann put a hand on Nathan's arm and shook her head.

He gave her a knowing nod, hit STOP, and switched to earphones. He pressed SKIP FORWARD, listened a moment, removed the earpieces, and increased the volume. The CD played the beginning of the conversation between O'Neal and Senator Sjoda at the buffet.

"How did you...oh," Maggie said, placing her hand on her necklace.

Shoemake nodded and turned off the CD player. "We put a microphone under the center gemstone."

Maggie thumbed the backing of the jewelry and popped out the largest stone. She opened it with her fingernail and removed a small round microphone. She gave the mike to Nathan and replaced the gem in her necklace.

Shoemake looked pointedly at McKenna and said, "We didn't throw either of you to the wolves. We had you covered."

"How many?" McKenna asked.

"In addition to the Secret Service guys already assigned to this function, four of our own."

"The bartender," Maggie said.

"Yes. He saw Sjoda put something in your Perrier and let another of our men know to intercept you if you went to drink it."

"McKenna signaled me not to," Maggie said.

"I figured it would be Sjoda's style, is all," PASCAL said.

The limousine stopped, snagged in D.C.'s Friday night traffic. A horn blew in the distance.

"The recording shows that Sjoda and Gundry discussed the personnel changes at DC Homicide," McKenna said. "It's only a matter of time before the senator discovers it was O'Neal working at the precinct. Could even be before the night's over."

"Yes. Doesn't matter Gundry's dead. Sjoda will put someone else on it." Shoemake reached into his tuxedo and took out a folded sheet of paper. He opened it and handed it to McKenna. "I want both of you to look at this."

Maggie leaned across McKenna's arm to see the report.

"The fingerprints in Mark Hughes's safe deposit box belong to Julian Gundry," McKenna said. "Pretty sloppy of him."

"Well, yes and no," Shoemake said. "Yes, because his prints are in the system from his having a police record—Sjoda tends to hire less-than-intelligent grunts at exorbitant pay so he can get people to work for him, given his undesirable reputation—and no, because Gundry, or whoever sent him to Hughes's bank with the key and stolen drivers' license for ID, probably wouldn't have thought anyone else knew about the safe deposit box."

"Good point," McKenna said. "Maybe the bank personnel didn't check the ID picture or signature too closely when they let Julian into the safe deposit vault. I don't know what Gundry looked like, but perhaps he resembled Hughes."

"Could be," Nathan said.

"I wonder if the person Hughes instructed to courier the letter to you in the event of his death knows about the box and the information it contained?" McKenna asked.

"A good question," Shoemake said. "And we still don't know who that person is. We raised fingerprints from the letter and envelope, but the only match is from Hughes, obtained post mortem. The other prints aren't in the system. I only touched the corners of the original paper, and what I gave Maggie to read was a copy."

"It sure took them long enough to get the forensic information from the safe deposit box to us," McKenna said. He handed the report back to Nathan.

"Yes, well, I looked into that. Seems our forensics guy lost the fingerprints data, then resigned without giving notice. A large deposit was made to his bank account the day after he quit. I had someone I trusted redo the prints in Hughes's box and got the report you just read late this afternoon. I was going to show it to you in the bar at the hotel, Mac, but you never showed."

"Yeah, well, I got delayed. I would've been late picking up O'Neal if I'd stopped in the bar."

Maggie looked first at McKenna, then at Shoemake. She leaned forward a bit. "It seems this is what we have so far. Mark Hughes was Reeves Sjoda's half brother, and the senator's man Julian Gundry's fingerprints were found inside Hughes's safe deposit box. That probably means either Sjoda or Gundry killed Hughes to get the key and drivers' license ID.

"And we learned there were no fingerprints on Hughes's wallet because it had been wiped clean. There were two different blood types found at the scene of Hughes's murder. Gundry's dead, and we have his DNA available for testing. If it's not a match, we'll need to obtain a sample of Sjoda's."

"I hope you're not going to ask O'Neal to get hair or saliva from Sjoda somehow," McKenna said, his tone sardonic.

"We'll get the senator's DNA when we bring him in, which will be soon." Shoemake said. "As important as solving Hughes's murder is, we're leaving Sjoda alone until D-Tech is closed, because we don't want to tip off anyone in the chain of defense secret buyers." Nathan looked at Maggie. "Mac's working on identifying these individuals, but he's not there yet. That's why Jaffey's been left in Homicide. He's now unknowingly passing on bogus technological information, because Mac's been capturing the real data, and modifying, re-encrypting, and relaying false data to the detective's computer. It's also why Ahmed Yousef's still involved."

Maggie acknowledged her boss's explanation and continued her summary. "We can assume that either Gundry or Sjoda has the documents from Hughes's safe deposit box. I wonder if the senator knew what his brother had secreted there and killed him because of it? And if he did, why? Unless Sjoda is connected to this alleged HIV/AIDS terrorist plot.

"Also, in his phone conversation with Gundry tonight, Sjoda said, 'Our last bird has come home to roost,' meaning you, McKenna. Then he ordered Gundry to kill you. Who were the other birds? The operatives from Hard Place? If so, might that indicate the senator was involved in the chemical and biological weapons' deals in Iraq?

"Perhaps Sjoda had the Hard Placers terminated when they got back to the States, and ordering McKenna killed would've finished up the group." She rambled some, but got there.

"That's what I'm thinking, too," Shoemake said. "But we have no proof of the senator's involvement in the Iraqi business or any intel yet on who eliminated the other three Hard Placers. We never discovered from whom those biological and chemical weapons' deals originated, though our intelligence indicated they were connected with someone in the US."

The limousine continued to inch its way through traffic. No one spoke for a couple of minutes, everyone seemingly deep in thought.

Zann broke the silence. "Would anyone like a drink?" She pressed a button on the console to expose a small bar, and recited the refrigerated selections. "We have Bailey's Irish Crème, champagne, and white wine." She withdrew the white and read the label. "A Chardonnay."

Everyone declined.

She replaced the Chardonnay, took out the champagne, and removed an unchilled bottle from the other side of the bar. "Let's see, also red wine—a lovely Merlot. And we have bourbon, vodka..."

"Maggie doesn't drink," McKenna said.

"I'll have some Merlot, please," Maggie said.

McKenna gave her a look and frowned. "Bourbon, neat," he said. He sounded annoyed.

"Same," Shoemake said.

"And I'll have champagne. Open this, will you darling?" Zann handed her husband the bottle.

Nathan finessed the cork until it gently popped. He opened the Merlot, next.

Shoemake's wife assumed the role of hostess, taking glasses from the bar and pouring drinks. She handed each in turn to her companions, her movements smooth and practiced.

Maggie leaned back in her seat and took a sip of Merlot. She'd had wine once before, at her confirmation into The Immaculate Conception Church. She remembered it being sickeningly sweet and wondered why anyone would want to drink anything so vile. This wine tasted clean and dry, and flowed gently into her stomach. She took a few more sips and found the sense of relaxation pleasant.

The four passengers finished their drinks as the limousine pulled up in front of the Washingtonian.

"Let's go in for a nightcap," Shoemake said.

The group exited the limo, and Nathan went to speak with occupants of a black sedan on security detail, pulled up behind. Shoemake returned moments later, and he and Zann walked into the hotel arm and arm.

McKenna took Maggie's elbow. She was feeling independent and wanted to pull away, but didn't. She clutched the ripped seam of her dress hoping no one would notice, and stepped away from the limo with McKenna at her side.

CHAPTER TWENTY-TWO

The wine had gone to Maggie's head, and it seemed as if the sidewalk rose up and hit the bottom of her feet rather than her stepping on the pavement. She resisted the urge to giggle.

McKenna appeared irked.

They entered the hotel bar and Maggie saw Shoemake whisper something to a cocktail waitress as he handed her a twenty-dollar bill. The woman nodded and led the foursome to a booth against the back wall. The few other patrons were sitting in the front area of the lounge near a piano player, who finished a tune and left the room.

The waitress gave them time to settle and took their drink orders, starting with Maggie.

"I'll have a Merlot, please."

McKenna gave her a disapproving look.

She grinned at him.

Zann ordered next. "I'll have an equal part of Grand Marnier and Courvoisier in a brandy snifter, heated."

"Same," Nathan said.

"Same," McKenna said.

Maggie considered changing her order to what the others were drinking, but didn't. She liked the Merlot in the limousine and stayed with wine.

No one from the group'd had an opportunity to eat at the retirement dinner, so Shoemake asked the waitress to bring menus.

When the server left, Nathan took a round object from his jacket pocket and placed it at the outermost edge of the table. Maggie recognized the device to be a SECS, a CIA-issued Small Electronic Conversation Scrambler designed to prevent anyone from overhearing their words.

The foursome engaged in general conversation until the waitress brought their drinks and menus. Zann, McKenna, and Shoemake swirled their snifters, and Maggie tasted her wine. It wasn't as good as the Merlot in the limousine, but almost.

Nathan switched on the SECS.

"Maggie, I'll arrange for a guard to be posted at your hotel door. I want you to move to a safehouse in Great Falls, Virginia in the morning. You too, Mac. Go tonight, since an attempt's been made on your life."

"I'll have to get my equipment from my apartment first. I've got hacks into various systems to collect data so we can close D-Tech, the bypass from Sjoda's to Jaffey's computer, and my programs to divert, modify and re-encrypt the defense technology."

"All right. You know to be careful."

McKenna nodded. "I didn't know the CIA had a safehouse in Great Falls," he said. "That's a rather expensive address for the Agency's budget, isn't it?"

"I'll give you both directions," Nathan said, ignoring PASCAL'S question.

Maggie took another sip of her wine, only half now remaining in her glass. "I have plans tomorrow at noon," she said.

"I'm assuming they can be cancelled." Shoemake said.

"Not really. I'm meeting a friend for lunch and she's traveling and temporarily without her cell phone. I have no way of getting in touch with her, and I don't want to worry her by not showing."

"I'll have someone go with you, then."

"No, thank you. I can take care of myself, Nathan."

All three of Maggie's companions looked at her in surprise. Shoemake moved his tongue to an inside cheek and smiled. His wife pressed her lips together to keep the corners from turning up, but her eyes shimmered with amusement. McKenna simply glared.

"Perhaps we should get some food," Nathan said, turning off the SECS. He flagged the waitress and when she came to the table, they ordered sandwiches.

Afterward, Shoemake reactivated the SECS. "Maggie, can Brian stay with your aunt while you're at the safehouse?"

"Yes. He's there now. And O.J.'s with him."

McKenna looked at her. "O.J.?"

"My cat."

McKenna puffed his cheeks and expelled air. He gave a slight headshake. "As in O.J. Simpson?"

"No, as in Orange Juice, because he's orange. And he's old—sixteen, so I named him before all the O.J. Simpson publicity."

McKenna stared at her for a beat before excusing himself to the men's room. His colleagues talked of things in general until he returned.

The sandwiches came and the four ordered another round of drinks.

When the waitress left, Maggie giggled, and the others looked at her in question.

"I just got it," she said.

"Got what?" McKenna asked. He sounded irritated.

"Operation Hard Place. Iraq. As in between a rock—I-raq—and a hard place."

"Yup," Nathan said. He and Zann smiled broadly. McKenna rolled his eyes and turned away.

The piano player returned and performed some easy-on-the-ears music, and the group listened while they ate their sandwiches.

Maggie's mental edges, usually sharp, were getting fuzzy. Something nagged at her, but she couldn't identify what.

McKenna did it for her. "Nathan, why'd you put O'Neal undercover in Homicide using her real name?"

COBOL looked at PASCAL but didn't respond. Instead, he said to Maggie, “We have enough on Sjoda so you won't have to get close with him, after all.”

“Better late than never,” McKenna said.

CHAPTER TWENTY-THREE

McKenna asked the chauffeur to drop him several blocks from his apartment. From there, he walked in shadows and slipped into doorways, alert to the possibility of being followed.

He reached his address and slid a key into the outside door of the apartment building. Entering, he tuned his ear for anything different from the usual noises, the drone of window air conditioners, sounds from muffled televisions, yips from his neighbor's Chihuahua. He heard nothing out of the ordinary.

Avoiding the elevator, McKenna removed his shoes and walked the hall to the first floor stairwell. He entered and, keeping his back to the banister, climbed the steps slowly, stopping at intervals to listen.

When he reached the second floor, he opened the door a crack and scanned the entire length of the corridor. No one. He continued his ascent to the third floor and canvassed the hall toward his unit. Empty.

Knees bent and walking like a cat stalking prey, McKenna approached his door. When he got to it, he froze. The inch of dental floss he'd wedged there, a ritual he'd practiced for the past fifteen years, lay on the floor in front of his apartment. He detected the faint smell of gunpowder. And something else. Plastique.

A door bomb.

He backed down the corridor and descended the steps quickly.

Reaching the street, McKenna slipped on his shoes and disappeared into the night.

CHAPTER TWENTY-FOUR

Reeves staggered into his townhouse, lifted the telephone receiver, and speed-dialed a number. The battery on his cell phone had gone dead.

"Security," a man said on the other end of the line.

The senator gave the man slurred instructions.

"Yes, sir. Right away."

Reeves replaced the handset and went to his bar to pour a drink. Even in his alcoholic stupor, he felt a beaut of a summer cold coming on.

He sat in his recliner and used the remote to bring his sixty-inch plasma TV to life. He surfed the channels until he found baseball.

His mind wandered from the game and he replayed the night's events in his head. Julian. Just as well he's dead. Too many screw-ups. There were plenty of young pups to take his place. Reeves paid well, and there were fringe benefits too....

He focused briefly on the ineptitude of a few of his men, but lost his train of thought and moved on to something more pressing. PASCAL. Still alive. What brought him out into the world again? Pure cockiness, probably. Well, his life would soon end. Julian didn't get him at the retirement function, but when McKenna entered his apartment, there wouldn't be enough pieces of him left to interest a shark.

Reeves chuckled at this and the laugh brought on a coughing spell. *Shit.* He spit up phlegm.

His cough subsided and he turned his mind to Maggie O'Neal. *Damn. She's fine.* He rubbed his crotch. He'd have her. And soon. And with this sweet treat, he wouldn't waste his time on a chase.

Sjoda lit a cigarette. He blew out smoke and returned his attention to the television. He watched the baseball game a few minutes and scowled. "Goddamn umpires. Fuckers're paid off."

CHAPTER TWENTY-FIVE

O'Neal awoke in her hotel room with a hangover. Her brain was fogged and her body slow. She wanted to keep sleeping but felt too awake. She debated taking a shower but didn't seem up to the task. Maggie wondered how her father'd gotten out of bed all those mornings after drinking so much the night before.

She forced her feet to the floor and went to the minibar for bottled water. She took a long pull, but it didn't satisfy. What she really needed was caffeine. And food.

Nathan (had she really called him by his first name last night?) told her to order room service. She picked up a menu from the desk.

Fruit and yogurt. Iced tea. Yes, that might work. She dialed the number and placed an order. It would be thirty minutes. She'd have time to bathe.

The shower felt luxurious, and Maggie let the hot water bead down on her head. Some of her brain fog cleared and her headache eased. The hotel soap and shampoo emitted a subtle, clean fragrance she found pleasant.

She turned off the water and, stepping out of the tub, dried herself with one thick towel and reached for another to wrap around her hair. It was then that she noticed the bathroom wallpaper—fresh and clean and richly textured. She let go a sigh.

Eschewing her own threadbare robe, Maggie donned the plush terrycloth one the hotel provided and went to the couch. She sat in its comfort, put her bare feet on the coffee table, and wiggled her toes.

My my my, she thought. *A nice hotel, a beautiful gown, new shoes and purse, an expensive necklace, a limousine. A "date" with the infamous PASCAL, drinking wine, breakfast brought to my room—*

A knock at the door caught her attention.

"Room service," a voice called.

O'Neal got off the couch and peeked through the security hole to see a man in a hotel uniform standing with a tray in his hand. When she opened the door, the waiter wore a look of displeasured surprise.

"You must be important," he said, bringing the tray in and placing it on a table. "That guy in the hall just frisked me and inspected all your food."

"Sorry about that," Maggie said. She smiled, and wrote a generous tip on the room-service ticket.

The waiter, seeming appeased, thanked her and left the suite.

O'Neal took her breakfast to the couch and sat, placing the tray on the coffee table. The phone rang just as she spooned into her yogurt. She went to it and lifted the receiver. "Hello?"

"Maggie, it's *Nathan,*" he said through what sounded like a smile.

She brought her hand to her forehead and closed her eyes.

"Any problems?" he asked.

"No, sir."

"Good. I want you to be careful today." He didn't wait for a response. "I can't raise Mac. Tried him at home, on his cell, even in the computer lab at Langley. He didn't go to the safehouse. Have you heard from him?"

"No, sir." *Why would I have heard from him?*

"Well, let me know if you do."

Maggie opened her mouth to say, "Yes, sir," but he'd already disconnected.

CHAPTER TWENTY-SIX

"Do you get to keep the dress?" Francie's intense brown eyes focused on Maggie as they sat in a restaurant in Georgetown, awaiting their lunch order. Her dark curls bobbed up and down on her shoulders as she spoke.

"Yes, but it's ripped. The tear's on the seam, though, so I can fix it."

"And?"

"And what?"

"How was *he,*" Francie asked.

"Francie...."

"Come on, Maggie, you used to fantasize about him. And there you were with him. So how was he?"

"Oh, I don't know. Moody, I guess." O'Neal took a sip of her iced tea.

"Girl, you really have a problem with men."

"Francie, don't start—"

"Well, I'll say it again. You ought to find out why you're so uptight around the opposite sex."

"It's just—" Maggie stopped speaking as the waiter approached with their food. He set their meals in front of them, asked if there was anything else they needed, and left.

Francie looked at her friend's plate and made a sound of disgust. "How long have we been coming to this restaurant?" she asked.

O'Neal thought a moment. "Oh, fifteen years, I guess. Why?"

"Because you *always* get the same thing." Francie reached across the table and poked her fork in Maggie's food. "Chicken with peanut sauce, sesame noodles, broccoli on the side, iced tea, and that same ol' chocolate dessert ordered *with* the meal. And, you'll have one refill on your tea and no more. God, that's so boring."

"Well, they ran out of this torte once just before we ordered dessert, remember? Besides, I like this meal," Maggie said, taking Francie's ravings good-naturedly. "It's my favorite."

"How do you know it's your favorite when you never try anything else?"

"I try new things," Maggie said. "I had wine last night."

"Wine? You?" Francie's eyes opened wide. "And?"

"And I'm hung over today."

"Not that *and*. I meant what else happened."

"Nothing I can talk about. The rest is all on-the-job stuff."

"Oh." Francie took a forkful of pasta. "How much wine?"

"About two and a half glasses."

"That's a lot if you're not used to it."

"Uh-huh."

The waiter came to check on them and topped Francie's coffee. When he left, the friends filled each other in on news since they were last together. Eventually, the conversation came back to men, and Maggie's issues surrounding them.

Francie leaned forward on her elbows and looked Maggie straight in the eye. "I really want you to consider seeing Eli," she said. "You need therapy."

"You know my financial constraints," Maggie said. "And besides, Eli's in Seaton, Georgia, and I'm in DC."

"Well, I'm in DC, too, and I've gone to see her. She does fly-in's."

"She does what?"

"Fly-in's. People who come from out of state to have therapy with her. And, from out of the country, too. She's that good, Maggie."

"I can't afford it, and I can't take time from my job to go to Seaton." O'Neal finished her entree and took a bite of chocolate torte.

"You can afford it. By now, you probably have more money than God."

Maggie shook her head.

"Maggie!"

"What?"

Francie leaned across the table and grabbed her friend's wrist. "You're thirty-two years old. You live at home. Your mother controls you something God-awful. You drive a car that's older than dirt and you haven't bought yourself anything new in years. The only money you spend is on Brian and these rare lunches with me. And you don't date. Maggie, there's something wrong with that."

"I've dated."

"Oh, what, a couple of guys in high school? You went out with them, two, maybe three times?"

"They got out of hand."

"You mean they tried something. Most guys try something."

Maggie put down her fork. "You know why I live at home. I'm saving money to get a place for Brian and me."

"You pay enough rent to your mother to live in Great Falls. Move out."

"I need to build up a nest egg. It takes a lot of money to support a teenage boy. They need stuff. School stuff and sports stuff and doing things with friends stuff. And college. That costs a fortune."

Francie's eyes drilled into Maggie's. "There's something dark and unholy in your past. I think it's time you found out what it is."

O'Neal looked down at her plate. "I can't afford it," she said to her torte.

Francie said, "You can't afford not to."

CHAPTER TWENTY-SEVEN

Maggie drove her 1977 Volkswagen Bug down M Street thinking about her lunch discussion with her friend.

She couldn't deny the changes in Francie since she'd been in therapy with Eli. Before, her friend had become bitter, self-destructive, and depressed. She'd gone to several psychologists in D.C., but they'd not been helpful. Upon entering counseling with Elizabeth Dansk, however, Francie'd begun to care about herself again and her happiness and vivacious personality returned.

"*I got back to my true self,*" is how her friend put it. "*And it didn't take me years of counseling that most people believe is necessary for change.*"

"*But Eli's expensive,*" Maggie said.

"*No, she isn't,*" Francie said. "*Her therapy is so effective, that one hour with her produces better results than years with other professionals.*"

A few notes of Johann Sebastian Bach ringing from Maggie's cell phone interrupted her thoughts.

She answered. "Hello?"

"It's me, girlfriend." Derek. "I have something I need to give you. Right away if possible." He sounded anxious. "Where are you?"

"I'm about to head over Key Bridge to Virginia. Where are you?"

"At home."

"Okay. I'll circle back and meet you at your townhouse."

"Maggie?"

"Yes?"

"They're all gone," Derek said, his voice breaking. "Mark's wonderful antiques are all gone."

CHAPTER TWENTY-EIGHT

O'Neal's meeting with Derek lasted only minutes. Immediately afterward, she called Nathan on his cell.

"Shoemake."

"It's Maggie. I have another envelope from Mark Hughes. Derek Weisner just gave it to me. It has a wax seal identical to the one you described to be on the letter sent to you previously."

"I'll meet you in my office at three-thirty. Watch your back."

"Yes, sir."

Maggie drove to Langley, now understanding why Derek had become so preoccupied after she identified herself as a CIA officer working for Nathan Shoemake. It was Weisner who had the first Mark Hughes letter couriered to her boss.

O'Neal arrived at the Directorate of Operations' office simultaneously with Shoemake. Both wore Saturday casual slacks and shirts.

A disheveled man sat in a chair facing Shoemake's desk, his back to Maggie and Nathan as they came through the door. From behind, he reminded O'Neal of the homeless she'd seen on the streets of D.C. An unpleasant body odor permeated the room.

"Let's sit," Nathan said.

Maggie took her chair and moved it to the corner of Nathan's desk, away from the malodorous man. She glanced his way and did a double take.

"McKenna?"

"Hi Maggie. Latest fashion." He gave a grin.

O'Neal sat and looked a question at him.

"I found my apartment door rigged with explosives last night, so I hit the street. I traded my tux to a homeless man for his clothes."

"You stink." Maggie wrinkled her nose.

"Smelling bad can be an important part of a disguise," McKenna said.

"Then how come you smelled so good when you worked at Homicide?" she blurted. She took in a breath and felt her cheeks get warm.

Nathan's eyes twinkled with amusement and a smile played on his lips.

McKenna stared at Maggie for a beat, his expression unreadable. She dropped her eyes to her lap, her face in high flush.

A moment of awkward silence passed before Shoemake cleared his throat and said, "Let's see what else we have from Mark Hughes." He reached toward O'Neal.

Without looking directly at either man, Maggie handed the envelope across the desk to Shoemake. He slit it open and read the enclosed correspondence aloud:

"Dear Mr. Shoemake: This second letter is insurance against the possibility of your not being able to gain access to my safe deposit box and the documents contained therein regarding the HIV/AIDS mass depopulation plan. The information is duplicated in papers hidden in the false bottom of an antique African chest, located to the right of the fireplace in the living room of my townhouse. Mr. Derek Weisner has the key to my home. Sincerely, Mark Hughes."

"I saw that piece of furniture," Maggie said, "when Derek showed me Mark's antiques."

"Both of you, go immediately to Hughes's townhouse and get that chest," Shoemake said to his officers. "Have Derek let you in."

"Oh no!" Maggie said.

The two men looked at her.

"The antiques are gone. Mrs. Hughes had all of Mark's things removed from his home. I guess when he wrote that second letter to you, sir," she said to Shoemake, "he didn't anticipate his mother disposing of his possessions so quickly. Derek doesn't know what she did with them."

"And Mrs. Hughes wouldn't talk to you when you went to see her," he said to O'Neal.

"No." Maggie turned to McKenna and said, "She actually slammed the door in my face."

"Mac," Shoemake said, "why don't you pay Mrs. Hughes a visit and learn the location of those antiques. Charm your way into her home. You've always been good with the ladies."

O'Neal made a face.

"I'll clean up first, Maggie," McKenna said, misunderstanding her look.

Shoemake slid Hughes's letter into a file on his desk. "I sent our explosives experts to your apartment to diffuse the bomb," he said to McKenna. "When you get your computer equipment out of there and when you're finished with Mrs. Hughes, go to the safehouse. Maggie, I want you to drive directly there from here. Claudia is on her way in to get your list of what you'll need her to buy for your stay, because it isn't wise for you to go home to get clothing and such."

"Yes, sir."

"Nathan, about my going to the safehouse..." PASCAL said. His cell chirped. He reached into his ragged clothing and flipped the phone open as he pulled it free. "McKenna." He listened a moment and his expression clouded. He mumbled an, "All right," and closed the phone.

"What was that?" Shoemake asked.

"My super." He put his cell back in his pocket. "There's been an explosion in my apartment."

"Anyone hurt?"

"No. It seems the damage is contained to my place."

Nathan grabbed his desk phone and speed-dialed a call. He held a brief conversation with someone on the other end of the line. A look of relief filled his face, and he disconnected.

"Our explosives' guys are okay. They removed the door bomb, but as they headed down in the elevator, they heard an explosion. Seems whoever wanted you dead planted a double."

"My computer equipment is probably dust. I'll have to start over again with everything I've been working on."

"We'll set you up at the safehouse in Great Falls."

"No. There's somewhere else I'd rather go."

"Where?"

"The Dungeon."

Maggie raised her eyebrows in question, but neither man explained.

Instead, COBOL looked at McKenna a moment. "All right," he said. "I'll make the arrangements."

"I'm here, sir." Claudia stood at the door to Shoemake's office.

"Maggie will give you her purchase list in just a few minutes," Nathan said.

"Okay, sir." Claudia came into the room. "What about you, McKenna?" She made a face at his homeless disguise and brought her hand to her nose. "Can I get you anything?"

"Yes," McKenna said. "First, I'd like a dress. Make it a red one."

CHAPTER TWENTY-NINE

McKenna stood outside Mrs. Hughes home in Fairfax, Virginia, dressed in tan slacks, white shirt and navy blazer, his hair platinum blond. He wore wire-rimmed glasses of no magnification.

He'd been unable to reach Mrs. Hughes yesterday afternoon or last night. Now, Sunday at 1:00 p.m., a pudgy, bitter-faced woman in her mid-seventies answered his knock, her resemblance to Reeves Sjoda striking. A large-print, blue-flowered dress covered her girth.

McKenna flashed her an ingratiating smile. "Mrs. Hughes? My name is Richard Stanton. I'm an antiques dealer." He handed her a computer-generated business card. "Please accept my condolences for the loss of your son."

Mrs. Hughes squinted at him.

"I understand Mark had a lovely collection of antiques," McKenna said. "I may be interested in purchasing a few of his items."

"You're too late. I sold them already."

"May I know the name of the buyer? Perhaps I could contact him or her." He smiled again.

Mrs. Hughes grunted and disappeared into her house. McKenna waited at the threshold, looking into the living room.

If Senator Sjoda shared any of his wealth with his mother, it wasn't apparent in the furnishings, which appeared old and cheap. Curio cabinets, tabletops, and bookshelves were filled with gimcrackery. A faded rug centered the floor, surrounded by chintz-covered sofas and chairs in prints similar to that on the owner's dress. The house had an old lady's smell.

Mrs. Hughes returned and handed McKenna a business card. He thanked her and started to repeat his condolences, but she closed the door mid-sentence.

McKenna got into his car and dialed the antiques dealer's number from his cell.

A man answered.

"Mr. Threlkeld? My name is Richard Stanton. I understand you're handling the Hughes antiques, and I'm interested in purchasing a few pieces."

He listened to the dealer's response.

"Oh, I see. Well, thank you anyway."

McKenna disconnected and called Shoemake at home. He relayed the conversations he'd had with Mrs. Hughes and Mr. Threlkeld.

After he hung up from COBOL, PASCAL drove to a deli for a sandwich and went to where he'd asked Nathan to relocate him—the Dungeon.

* * * * *

Maggie's cell played notes from Bach.

"Hello?"

"It's Nathan. Meet me in my office tomorrow morning at ten. Pack a bag of the items Claudia bought for you and bring your laptop. You're going on assignment."

CHAPTER THIRTY

"Seaton, Georgia?" Maggie said, her voice incredulous.

"Yes," Shoemake said. "Mrs. Hughes sold her son's antiques to a man who resells at auctions around the country. Mark's pieces will end up at Perry's Auction House in Seaton."

Maggie's eyes widened.

"You're flying to Atlanta immediately," Shoemake said. "A limo is on its way to take you to the airport. Claudia set up a contact for you in Seaton. Name's Betty Ann Almon, and she's a dealer of sorts—small collectibles, mostly. I know you could go to the auction on your own, but it'll be better for your cover—a new dealer who needs to gain buying experience—if you accompany someone who's a regular at Perry's. She'll meet you in the lobby of the Pine Grove Motel at six o'clock Wednesday night, and you can have dinner with her before the auction.

"There are two sales held per week. On Wednesday nights the better furniture, antiques and collectibles are auctioned, and on Saturday nights the locals come out for the less expensive items. I want your face to be familiar by the time the Hughes antiques go up for bid.

"I had Claudia try to find out where they're being stored, but Perry's doesn't have a record of original owners. Their acquisitions' dealers use a number of holding warehouses in different states. Unfortunately,

Mr. Threlkeld, the man who purchased Mark's antiques, passed away unexpectedly this morning, and though I'm not comfortable leaving a chest with Hughes's duplicate documents out who-knows-where, we don't have the funding and personnel to search all..." Nathan leaned forward. "Maggie, are you listening?"

"Sir?"

"You seem to be off somewhere."

"Oh, sorry, sir."

"Anyway, here are your credentials and airplane tickets." Shoemake gave her the flight information. "Your undercover name is Mary Margaret Ryan. I'm assuming Brian can stay with your Aunt the sixteen days you're in Seaton?"

"Sixteen days, sir?"

"Yes. Hughes's antiques are scheduled for auction two weeks from Wednesday. While you're in Georgia, I want you to investigate HIV/ AIDS. You're the perfect person for the job, what with your having taken all those biology, chemistry, and histology classes needed for your entomology and botany majors. You'll be able to sort through the research—understand the viral science on a cellular level. Visit AIDS Atlanta and Emory University. Emory has a hospital, and medical information is available in their library. Seaton is about an hour's drive west of Atlanta, so you can get to these facilities fairly easily from your motel.

"Rather than flying you back and forth to DC, I want you to stay in Georgia. With Reeves Sjoda still out there until D-Tech is closed, it'll be safer for you on assignment in another state."

"Okay, sir. And, oh, yes, Brian can stay with Aunt Mary. She's always glad to have him visit."

Shoemake's phone rang and he picked up the receiver. "Thank you," he said to the caller.

He turned to O'Neal. "Your limo is here."

* * * * *

Maggie enjoyed the view from her window seat on the one-hour, fifty-minute flight to Atlanta's Hartsfield-Jackson Airport. Soon after takeoff, the scenery below went from buildings to green country, and at cruising altitude, the sun's brilliance blued the sky and whitened cumulus clouds, puffed like bales of soft cotton.

O'Neal reclined her seat. She thought again of her lunch discussion with Francie, and about the sudden turn of events that were taking her to Seaton, Georgia for sixteen days.

"*Synchronicity,*" and, "*It's meant to be,*" her friend would say.

Maggie wondered if she could even get an appointment with Dr. Dansk. Probably not. According to Francie, Eli scheduled weeks in advance.

Unbidden, a scene from her childhood popped into her head. O'Neal pushed it away and kept her thoughts on present matters for the remainder of the flight.

CHAPTER THIRTY-ONE

Reeves awoke from his nap with a hard-on and thoughts of Maggie O'Neal. He got up and smoked a cigarette, poured himself a brandy, and told his chef he wanted lunch.

He'd been too sick over the weekend with his cold to talk with Julian Gundry's replacement regarding the personnel changes in D.C. Homicide. He felt better now, but took the day off from his senate duties to catch up on personal interests.

His chef brought his meal of rack of lamb, asparagus, and scalloped potatoes on a tray, and got the senator another drink. Reeves ate everything, though his stomach didn't really want food.

Afterward, he opened the package of tapes that were delivered to his home earlier in the day. He put one in the recorder and listened, stunned, to segments of conversations recently held in the Directorate of Operations' office and the voices behind them.

McKenna's back with the CIA, and the bombs didn't kill him... shit! Fuck, fuck! Maggie O'Neal's one of Shoemake's people and she's on her way to Georgia to get the duplicate documents my idiot brother hid in an antique! Fuck! And she's investigating HIV/AIDS...

Reeves Sjoda hit STOP on the recorder and dialed the phone number of Gundry's replacement.

"Belosi."

"What did you get on the people in DC Homicide?"

"The detective's name's Maggie O'Neal, the sergeant's, McClusky. Jaffey's got a photo of both."

So that sweet treat's also been working in Homicide. Why? I wonder if... He said to Belosi, "O'Neal's gone to Seaton, Georgia to get some papers my brother hid in furniture that's being sold at auction. Fly down there immediately and keep an eye on her. She's coming back to DC two weeks from Thursday." He gave his man Maggie's return flight information, undercover name, and motel accommodations. "Get on the same plane as O'Neal and snatch her and the documents when you land in Dulles. Bring her to me alive and well." He disconnected.

He called his other employee, Hackett.

The man answered, "Yeah?"

"McKenna's staying someplace called the Dungeon. Find out where that is. Also watch for his coming and going from Langley. He'll be in disguise. Look for a tall woman in a red dress. Kill him."

He hung up and placed one more call. Martina. He needed to relieve some stress. He'd listen to the rest of the tapes later.

CHAPTER THIRTY-TWO

Four subfloors below the basement of the CIA facility at Langley, McLean, Virginia, COBOL cleared a place on PASCAL'S crowded desk within his personal computer lab to make room for a pizzeria box and a couple of bottles of water.

PASCAL handed a few sheets of blank computer paper to COBOL. Shoemake understood their purpose and used them as a plate for his pizza.

McKenna presented him with another piece of paper. "Napkin," he said.

COBOL gave PASCAL a warm, just-like-old-times smile. He took a seat in McKenna's guest chair and asked, "What do you have?"

"Names. Not all, but some, of the D-Tech buyers. I'm still on it."

"Good." Shoemake took a bite of his pizza. The stringy cheese drooped a bridge from the slice to his lips and he scooped it into his mouth. He chewed slowly, as if savoring not only the taste of the food, but also the memory of having shared many moments like this with his long-time friend, PASCAL.

"Wouldn't you be better off at the safehouse, Mac? It doesn't look too comfortable here." Nathan eyed the army cot, strewn with computer printouts, on which McKenna sat.

“The Dungeon’s got more technical resources,” McKenna said, swinging his arm to take in his workspace and the adjoining computer labs, “than would be practical to set up in Great Falls.”

Shoemake nodded and took another piece of pizza from the box.

The men ate several more slices in silence. Indistinct conversations from CIA computer techs, along with muffled noises from surrounding equipment, reached inside the room.

“What did you plan to do with your teaching sabbatical from the university?” Shoemake asked. He wiped his hands on a piece of paper.

“I’m setting up a business for my nephew, Jason.” McKenna threw his pizza crust into the box and picked up a fresh slice.

“What kind?”

“Computer games. Spy games in particular. They’re popular in Japan now, and I think they’ll hit big in the US soon.”

“You mean like CIA spy games?” Shoemake grinned.

“Yeah. Well kind of.” McKenna wore a sheepish expression.

“Huh.” Nathan kept his grin. “How old is Jason now?”

“Just turned twenty. Going into his third year at Michigan State. Computer science.”

“Does he know you’re doing this for him?”

“No, it’s a surprise. I’ll start the company, get a couple of games completed, and turn it over to him.”

“What kind of computer equipment do you need for development?”

McKenna blotted some pizza oil from his chin and rattled off the hardware necessary for his spy-game endeavor.

Shoemake nodded his understanding.

PASCAL stood and removed the pizza box from his desk, empty now except for a few crusts. He tore off the top, free of grease stains, and put it in his recycling bin, tossing their spent water bottles in as well. He threw the rest in the trash. “I’m going to the cafeteria for coffee,” he said. “You want some?”

COBOL shook his head. He reached for the phone as PASCAL left the lab.

When McKenna returned to the Dungeon a while later, new equipment had been brought into the already-crowded space. "What's all this?" he asked.

"The start of what you need to develop spy games for your nephew," Shoemake said. "I'll get the rest for you tomorrow."

McKenna regarded his old friend, and a moment passed between them.

COBOL stood to leave. When he reached the door, he turned and said to McKenna, "You didn't take your flight back to Michigan. Thank you for that."

PASCAL gave a small nod and turned to face his computer.

CHAPTER THIRTY-THREE

Maggie turned the ignition key on her rental and the compact car came to life. She left the Atlanta airport and followed map directions to Seaton, noticing differences between Georgia and the D.C.-Virginia areas along the way. Here, red clay and loblolly pines with long, sturdy needles commanded the roadsides, and in places, kudzu overtook fields and trees. The sky looked faded, its gray-white washing out the landscape like an overexposed photograph. A smell of industrial pollution filled the air.

When she arrived in Seaton, O'Neal found her way to Perry's Auction House, located across from the motel, and went to the office on the chance that the Hughes antiques, under the name of Threlkeld, were stored there. Finding a closed sign on the door, she got back in her car and drove down the street to shop at a Publix Supermarket for a late lunch of yogurt, fruit, and fresh vegetables before checking into the Pine Grove.

She settled into her room and, propping pillows behind her back on the bed, opened her laptop to create a work and running schedule for the next two weeks. When completed, she put her computer aside and slumped against the pillows to think about the Mark Hughes case. Soon, her eyelids grew heavy and she fell into sleep.

Maggie awoke with a start, covered in sweat. Her heart pounded as fear and waves of nausea washed over her. She'd had that recurring nightmare again.

In it she was a little girl, lying immobile in her bed. A pain stabbed her and she wanted to cry out, but couldn't. A merry-go-round spun slowly around her bedroom, eyes of hideous-faced carousel horses glaring.

Nearby, a man held a gun. Smoke rose from its barrel, though Maggie couldn't remember hearing a shot. The man retreated through the carousel horses, naked from the waist down, his buttocks a ghastly white. He turned, and his shriveled penis dripped a viscous liquid. The man raised the gun to her, but she awakened before he pulled the trigger.

O'Neal waited until the dream paralysis dissipated before going to the sink to splash cold water on her face. After she dried her hands on a motel towel, she opened her fanny pack and took the business card Francie'd given her ages ago from her wallet.

Maggie looked at the digital clock on the bedside table. 6:07 p.m. She'd call, leave a message. She dialed.

She expected to reach a recorder, but a woman answered the phone. "Elizabeth Dansk."

O'Neal's heart thundered and her throat went dry. She tried to speak but couldn't.

"Hello?" Eli gently prompted.

Maggie cleared her throat and found her voice. "Um, Dr. Dansk? My name is Maggie O'Neal." She realized she'd given her real name. But she should, shouldn't she? "My friend Francie, ah, that is Francesca Strauss, suggested I call you."

"Hello, Maggie. How may I help you?"

"Well, I, uh, realize this is late notice and all, and I know you stay booked far in advance, but I only found out this morning I was going to be in Seaton for two weeks, and, oh, I'm from Washington, DC, and I was wondering if you would have any time to see me? For an appointment I mean."

"How about tomorrow at eight a.m.?"

"Tomorrow? You could see me tomorrow? Francie says you're really busy."

"Well, yes, normally I am. I'd planned to leave last night to teach a two-week seminar in England, but the event was rescheduled due to a fire at the facility. So, I have a fairly open calendar. How much therapy time were you hoping to have?"

"Um, I don't know."

"Why don't we meet tomorrow at eight, and we'll take it from there. I'll tell you how to get to my office."

O'Neal wrote the directions on a sheet of paper, and disconnected from Dr. Dansk.

She heaved a sigh and sat on the bed. Then, for some reason unbeknownst to her, Maggie put her face in her hands and cried.

CHAPTER THIRTY-FOUR

McKenna needed air. He'd been cooped up in the Dungeon for nearly twenty-four hours and wanted to get outside to move his body.

He borrowed a security uniform from a CIA guard he'd known in the early days, and gave the man a sixty-dollar restaurant gift certificate he'd purchased on-line and printed on his computer. He placed a short black wig on his head and topped it with a baseball cap.

After the retirement-dinner shooting, McKenna had traded his original rental car for another. He now drove this vehicle out of the gate at Langley and headed east. About an eighth of a mile down the road, he spotted a late-model green van parked on the grass, backed into the trees. Acting on instinct, he pulled a digital camera from his rucksack and snapped a series of photos of the man in the driver's seat, who, looking anxious and bored, tapped his fingers on the steering wheel as he watched each passing vehicle.

McKenna stowed his camera and continued driving to his destination, the runner's path along the Potomac River. When he arrived, he did some stretches and ran a mile in each direction at an easy pace.

Nearing his car again, he spotted a copse to his left. He entered it and performed the slow, rhythmic moves of his daily QiGong routine within the trees' clearing. Centered and energized, he headed back to the Dungeon, stopping on his way for Chinese takeout.

McKenna ate the cashew chicken and fried rice in his computer lab, the distinctive aroma of soy sauce filling the room. He drank his Chinese tea and opened the fortune cookie to read his fate before putting the crunchy almond-flavored bits in his mouth. ROMANCE IS ON THE HORIZON, the red letters mocked from the small, slightly curled strip of paper he held between his fingers.

McKenna mumbled an expletive and threw the fortune into the trash. He brushed his hands free of both the cookie grit and the taunting prediction.

Fed and caffeinated, PASCAL began working on his spy-game software, rapidly generating the necessary code. His ideas came quickly, and he entertained the possibility that his creative juices flowed so easily because he was once again involved in real-time spy situations at Langley. He wondered if he'd be so in sync with the process if he'd stayed in Michigan.

He lost awareness of time as he clicked away on the keyboard, complex code appearing on the screen. When he stopped to stretch, the clock on his desk read 1:19 a.m.

Wakeful, McKenna switched focus and got the digital camera from his rucksack, placing the photo-card in a slot in his computer. He viewed the pictures of the driver of the van that'd been parked outside Langley, and something in the middle of the first few images caught his eye. He enlarged the center portion of a photo and stared, almost disbelievingly, at what the van's occupant held in his hand.

McKenna sorted through additional pictures until he found a full-face shot of the man and ran the image though a 1,700 grid-point match, facial-identity computer program. After a few moments, he had a name to go with the face.

Eugene Hackett.

He keyed Hackett's name into his CIA resource software and a page of information appeared on the screen. He speed-read the text and printed the data.

He e-mailed COBOL at home, typing his message in code. McKenna didn't expect a reply at this hour and was surprised when he received an instant response.

WHAT'S THIS ABOUT A MAN IN A VAN? Nathan's code read.

McKenna keyed, I'VE SOME IMPORTANT THINGS TO SHOW YOU.

URGENT NOW?

NO. TOMORROW A.M. (ACTUALLY TODAY).

MY OFFICE?

PREFER THE DUNGEON.

AFFIRMATIVE.

CHAPTER THIRTY-FIVE

Reeves felt better. In fact, he felt damned good. He'd taken Viagra and Ecstasy to heighten his experience with Martina last night, his thoughts on Maggie O'Neal through it all.

He'd been rough with the whore, leaving her badly bruised and battered, but she'd probably recover. O'Neal wouldn't be so lucky. He'd keep her for days, no, weeks, then kill her when he was done.

He called Hackett. He got a busy signal, strange clicking noises, and dead air. After a few more tries, he got through. "Anything?"

"No. He hasn't left Langley."

"You sure?"

The man hesitated. "Yes."

"You find out where the Dungeon is?"

"No one seems to know."

"Well, someone has to. Keep trying."

"Yes, sir."

"What's wrong with your cell phone?"

"Dunno. It's been breaking up on me."

"Get it fixed or replaced. It took me a time to get through to you."

"Yes, sir."

"And Hackett?"

"Huh?"

"Don't screw up your hit on McKenna or you'll regret you did."

"Yes, sir."

Sjoda called Belosi next.

"You on the job keeping your eye on Maggie O'Neal?

"Yeah."

"Anything?"

"She checked into the motel yesterday."

"Make sure you snag O'Neal and those documents in two weeks. Attend the sales at Perry's Auction House in a low-profile way so your presence is familiar when my brother's antiques come up for sale. Take notice of the piece she buys so you'll recognize the chest and be able to secure the papers it contains later. Don't pay O'Neal any special interest or she might grow suspicious. Stay close to her only after she gets Mark's chest and goes to the airport."

"Yes, sir."

Reeves disconnected and lit a cigarette, watching the smoke tendril in swirls around his face.

Yes, he felt damned good.

CHAPTER THIRTY-SIX

Dr. Elizabeth Dansk extended her hand. "Hello, Maggie. It's nice to meet you."

Eli's handshake felt warm and secure and her eyes sparkled in welcome. She stood about five-feet, two-inches tall, and slightly plump. Her dark hair puffed away from her face and went into a bun at the back of her head. Maggie guessed her age to be around fifty, as her fair skin revealed laugh lines at the corners of her hazel eyes.

The therapist's office looked inviting. A plush, Arabian rug in soft hues covered the floor and enhanced the room's mauve walls. Two crème-colored club chairs facing a third, each with small tables alongside, furnished the right side of the long, rectangular space, and sunlight filtered through sheer-weave curtains at two front windows. A wood desk, filing cabinets, and shelves filled with psychology books were positioned to the left. The office, additionally lit by table and floor lamps, promoted a sense of warmth and safety, and Maggie experienced a longing to move in.

"Please have a seat," Eli said, indicating a choice of the two side-by-side chairs.

Maggie lowered herself into one and felt embraced by its comfort.

Eli sat in the chair opposite and came directly to the point of their meeting. "How may I help you today?" she asked, kindness showing in her hazel eyes as she focused on her patient.

"Oh. Uh, Francie says I'm afraid of men."

"What do you say, Maggie?"

"Um. It's more like I'm really uncomfortable around them. I also have these feelings, and I don't know what they are, but they're always with me except sometimes when I run. And I have these dreams. Francie said to tell you about my dreams." Maggie fidgeted. "I'm sorry if I'm rambling. I do that sometimes, especially when I'm nervous. And I feel guilty all the time around my mother, and I don't know why." She shifted in her chair. "That's all."

Dr. Dansk tilted her head slightly, regarding her patient.

"If you want me to tell you about my childhood, I don't remember much," Maggie said.

"That's all right," Eli said. "I won't need to take a history from you in the traditional sense. That would be a waste of your therapy time. Your past will come to light as we progress through the work on your issues. My approach is different from that of most counselors."

"I know. Francie told me. She said you use a muscle test to access a person's unconscious mind to get right to the root cause of his or her problem. It has something to do with the mind-body connection."

"That's right. Muscle testing is also called kinesiology."

Maggie nodded. "And once you discover exactly what happened to cause a patient's problem, you have a way for the individual to release the origin's impact so the issue goes away permanently and is, um, resolved. Francie said it's a breathing exercise of some sort."

"Yes, that's correct. You explained it very well."

"That's how Francie explained it to me," Maggie said. She lowered her eyes and rubbed her thumbnail. After a moment, she looked up again at Eli. "I've always been led to believe it took years to overcome a problem. But I know this works fast because I saw tremendously positive changes in Francie in a very short period of time."

"It takes only minutes, perhaps, to experience a trauma that can change your life," Eli said. "On the other side of that equation, its impact can be released in a similar amount of time."

"That makes sense," Maggie said.

"And with this therapy, you won't have to overcome the problem, or be sentenced to a lifetime in recovery having to put daily energy into coping skills. Instead, you'll remove the core cause of the problem, so it will simply no longer be there."

"Like pulling a weed up by the root instead of constantly cutting off the part that shows above ground and having it come back again and again, maybe even stronger," Maggie said, rambling a little.

"Exactly." Eli smiled. "Are you ready to begin?"

O'Neal gave a nervous nod.

"All right, let's start with your being uncomfortable around men," Eli said. "Is that the best way to describe the problem, or is there another way you'd word it?"

Maggie thought a moment. "It's kind of a combination of being discomfited and intimidated by men. And um, maybe Francie is right, being afraid of them."

"Okay, let's begin."

Maggie's heart pounded and her palms got sweaty. She reported feeling anxious to Eli.

"What do you think your anxiety is about?"

"I'm scared of what we might find."

"Your body and unconscious mind won't reveal anything you're not consciously ready to know. You will revisit what happened to you to cause your current difficulties around men, and it does take courage to access these events. But unaddressed traumas can bring about unhealthy patterns that impact your life in profoundly negative ways.

"Bringing these traumas to consciousness allows you to heal. It can get uncomfortable exploring the associated experiences and feelings, but that discomfort is transitory. You'll pass through it relatively quickly, and your problems concerning men, or any other issues you choose to address, will be gone forever."

"What if I can't remember anything? Will you make suggestions as to what might have happened?"

"No, I won't. This information has to come from you. If I suggest anything or ask you leading questions, it might influence you to 'remember' events that didn't occur. And, not only will false memories not help you, they can harm you. I'll only be asking objective questions designed to help you bring to consciousness what really did take place. We'll also double and triple blind these findings to make sure we have accurate information about the root causes of your symptoms." Eli tilted her head. "Ready?"

"Yes," Maggie said, her voice tentative.

"Okay, using muscle testing, we'll begin by finding the age of the event that either originated, or reinforced, your discomfort around men."

Maggie trembled slightly as Eli began the discovery process. Within minutes, the kinesiology test revealed that she'd experienced a contributing trauma when she was four-years', nine-months' old. O'Neal was astonished at the speed of Dr. Dansk's technique.

"When is your date of birth?" Eli asked.

"October twenty-eight. I'm thirty-two."

"What was going on in your life when you were four-years', nine-months' old. That would be, let's see..." Eli counted on her fingers, "between July 28 and August 28 of that year."

"Um." Maggie closed her eyes in concentration. "We would have been in Cape Cod with my Aunt Mary and Uncle Levy."

"Who are 'we'?" Eli asked.

"My two older brothers, Dennis and Patrick, and me. My brother Brian wasn't born yet."

"How old were Dennis and Patrick at the time?"

"Dennis would have been fourteen, and Patrick, ten."

"Were your parents with you?"

"No, they never came with us. My mom hated Uncle Levy because he was Jewish. His first name was actually Yehoyakem, but it was too hard to say, so everyone just called him Levy. I think Mother was actually glad when he died two years ago. She's never had any use for people who aren't Irish.

"My mother also didn't like the beach, and besides, she wanted Aunt Mary to take my brothers and I off her hands for the summer. And my father, well, he would have just been drunk all the time if he came to Cape Cod."

"Your father's an alcoholic?"

"Yes," Maggie said, choosing not to elaborate. She focused instead on her Cape Cod memories, keeping her eyes closed. After a moment, they opened wide.

"Oh! One summer my brother Dennis said he wanted me to learn how to swim. We were on the beach and he grabbed my arm and pulled me toward the ocean. I was afraid of the waves, so I told him, 'No!' and kicked my feet. I got away from him, but he came after me. He caught me and dragged me down to the water by my hair. There were a few other people on the beach, but nobody paid any attention."

"What happened then?"

Maggie closed her eyes.

"Dennis picked me up, carried me into the ocean, and tossed me in over my head. I sunk to the bottom. I can still feel the sand on my knees." O'Neal ran her hand over her tan slacks.

"What happened next?"

"I got my feet under me and kicked up from the ocean floor. I surfaced, but when I went to take a breath, a wave washed over me, and a lot of saltwater got into my nose and throat. I went underwater again and couldn't breathe. I struggled for a while." Maggie paused. "Then everything went peaceful."

O'Neal opened her eyes. "I came to on the beach with a lifeguard giving me mouth-to-mouth resuscitation. I threw up all over him and felt terrible about that."

"Where were your aunt and uncle when Dennis threw you into the ocean?"

"They'd gone to get us lemonade at a nearby stand. They'd instructed my brothers to take care of me.

"Dennis told Aunt Mary that I went into the water alone against his orders, and Patrick backed his story.

"When we got home to DC, I told my mother that before the lifeguard brought me around, I'd visited God and seen Kathleen. That's my baby sister who died," Maggie explained. "And Mom slapped me hard across the face and said I blasphemed."

"It appears you have three traumas to resolve here," Eli said. "The near drowning, your brothers lying about what happened and making it your fault, and your mother slapping you, accusing you of blasphemy. How did you feel when your brother dragged you down the beach and threw you in the ocean?"

"Terrified."

"How else did you feel?"

Maggie thought a minute, but nothing came to her. "I don't know," she said.

"Often, when we experience trauma, we make decisions, either on a conscious or unconscious level. Did you make any during or immediately after this event?"

Maggie considered Eli's question for a moment. "Yes," she said, "I decided boys couldn't be trusted."

"And what feelings were associated with that decision?"

"Oh." Maggie slowly nodded her understanding. "I felt betrayed... hurt...and sad." Tears welled in her eyes. "And I couldn't tell anyone what really happened because Dennis threatened if I did, he'd kill me. I forgot to tell you that part," she said in a little girl's voice. "I also felt very lonely. And Mother slapped me for seeing God."

O'Neal lowered her head. A tear ran down her cheek. She took a Kleenex from a nearby box, dabbed at her face, and balled the tissue in her fist. She shut her eyes again and sat quietly, thinking.

"Anything else?" Eli asked after a moment.

"Yes!" Maggie boomed, shocked at the force of her own voice. Her eyes popped opened. "I was angry! I *am* angry! How could anyone do that to a little child?"

"You were that little child, Maggie."

"I know," she said, her voice smaller now. "How could anyone do that to me?" O'Neal blew her nose and threw the tissue in the wastepaper basket by the chair. “I also decided that boys would treat me like that for the rest of my life, and so I'd stay away from them.”

“That's good insight. Did you set up any other defense mechanisms to help you cope with the impact of this event?”

O'Neal thought a moment, and said, “Nothing's coming to me right now.”

Eli asked, “Did you experience additional thoughts or feelings, or make any other decisions?”

“Yes, that I'd learn to run faster than any boy. And I have.” She looked at Eli and smiled. “I'm a runner.”

Eli returned the smile.

Maggie sat quietly for a minute before saying, “Perhaps the event with Dennis is why I don't like the ocean, lakes, or rivers. I hate to swim even though I know how. I like to take baths, though, because I can touch the bottom and sides of the tub. I even have this habit of slumping down until my head is underwater. It's so peaceful.” O'Neal's own words surprised her. “I wonder if I'm trying to recreate the peacefulness I experienced when I almost drowned?”

“You're very good at this, Maggie.”

O'Neal lowered her eyes.

“When you're in the presence of men,” Eli asked, “how old do you feel?”

“Not adult-aged at all.” Maggie raised her head. “Oh! I feel four- or five-years' old. The same as when Dennis threw me into the ocean.”

“Yes,” Eli said. “That's called arrested development. Mental, emotional, psychological, physical, intellectual, spiritual, and sexual growth can become stopped at the time of a trauma. Part of the individual stays stuck at the age when the event occurred, while the rest of him or her matures. In other words, a person becomes fixated at a specific age or stage of development.”

“So when I'm around men, I'm not entirely an adult? Some of me is still a little girl?”

“Yes. You're coping with adult situations as if you're still four-years', nine-months' old. And, you'll perceive and react from that age when faced with anything that consciously or unconsciously reminds you of, or triggers, this unresolved event."

"That makes sense."

Eli asked, "Do you feel ready to let go of the effect of your near-drowning incident?"

"Yes." Maggie sat up straighter. "Yes I do."

Dr. Dansk explained the breathing techniques necessary to release the trauma's impact and its associated arrested development.

O'Neal carefully followed her instructions, and afterward, experienced immediate relief. "Oh, Dr. Dansk, I feel"...Maggie tried to find the right words..."lighter. More peaceful. Like something I've been carrying around in here forever," she pointed to her heart, "is gone."

"Excellent. Now, the next step in the therapy is called reframing. We'll role-play and redo the scene with a positive outcome. I'll be Dennis, and you'll be four-year, nine-month old Maggie."

"Okay, let's see," Maggie said, moving immediately into the spirit of the exercise. "I want to stand up to Dennis and have him not throw me into the ocean."

"Good. Now speak to me assertively and as Dennis, I'll respond in an affirming way."

Maggie spoke to "Dennis" in a strong voice, and this time, he respected her request.

"And now," Maggie continued, still redoing the scene, "after we have our lemonade, Uncle Levy slowly introduces me to the ocean. First, I jump the waves at the shore with my hand in his, and I can run away if a big wave scares me. Next, I body surf the little waves close to the shoreline with my uncle by my side. Then when I'm ready, Levy carries me into the water a little deeper, and we jump the waves together with him holding me tight. And I learned to swim that summer, instead of in that awful chlorinated pool at the YWCA when I was ten."

"Good job, Maggie." Eli smiled. "How do you feel?"

"I feel great. Stronger."

"Excellent. Now let's address the impact of Dennis and Patrick lying about your going into the ocean alone, Dennis threatening to kill you if you said otherwise, and your mother slapping you when you told her you saw God and Kathleen."

"Okay."

When O'Neal finished releasing these traumas, Eli said she'd done enough therapy for one session and needed time to process.

"How soon can I come back?" Maggie asked.

"Let's not speculate on that," Eli said. "Your body has it's own wisdom and knows when it will be safe for you to resume. We'll use kinesiology to determine the appropriate time."

The muscle test revealed that O'Neal would be able to continue the next day, so an appointment was made for the following morning.

Maggie paid Dr. Elizabeth Dansk without minding the cost. As she stood to leave, she asked, "Is there a good place to run in Seaton?"

"Yes. There's a one-mile path surrounding a lake in Lee State Park." Eli smiled. "I don't think you'll mind being around large bodies of water anymore. If you want to feed the resident ducks, I suggest you give them whole wheat bread. They seem to prefer it over white."

* * * * *

Maggie exited Dr. Dansk's parking lot and drove to Perry's Auction House. She found it open and went in. A harried, white-haired woman behind a desk in a small, cluttered office told her Mr. Threlkeld's antiques couldn't possibly be in their warehouse because furniture is not delivered until immediately before it comes due for sale.

Disappointed, O'Neal got in her car and headed for Emory University.

CHAPTER THIRTY-SEVEN

"What do you want to show me?" COBOL asked PASCAL as he walked into the Dungeon, more crowded now with additional spy-game development equipment.

"Those." McKenna pointed to an array of photographs on his cot extracted from a collage that Sjoda's man, Hackett, held against the steering wheel as he sat in the van outside of Langley.

Nathan bent toward them and frowned. "What the hell?"

"Yeah. That's what I say."

The images were close-ups of McKenna wearing different-colored women's wigs in various lengths and styles.

"You're in a red dress in all of these. How could anyone have known to look for you in a red dress? The only people privy to your request for that outfit were Maggie, Claudia, you and me."

"Yes, I know." McKenna narrowed his eyes.

"No, Mac." Shoemake shook his head. "Not Claudia. She's been with us since the beginning, and I trust her completely. And not O'Neal either."

"And not you or me," McKenna said.

"No. Not you or me."

They regarded each other a moment, neither speaking.

McKenna broke the silence. "I ran one of the photos of the guy in the van through our facial recognition software and came up with a name. Also got some information on him." He handed Nathan a couple of computer printouts.

Shoemake looked at the first page. "Eugene Hackett. Doesn't sound familiar." He flipped to the second. "See he has a rap sheet, though."

"Yes. And, I finessed my way into Hackett's cell phone records and got a copy of the calls he's made in the past two days." He gave COBOL his findings.

Shoemake raised his brows. "He's telephoned Sjoda."

"Yup." McKenna passed some additional papers to Nathan. "And here are Sjoda's records. Just pulled them."

Shoemake read the list of numbers. "He contacted Hackett several times."

"Yes. Once at seven forty-three this morning. I accessed satellite images. Hackett was in position outside Langley then."

Shoemake looked at McKenna. "He must not have spotted you leaving here yesterday when you called me and said you were going for a run."

"No, I wore a security guard's uniform and a man's black wig under a baseball cap."

"Good." Shoemake pocketed the printouts. "I'll have Hackett brought in. We have to find out how he, or Sjoda more likely, knew about the red dress."

"Yup."

"How're you coming with the rest of the D-Tech buyers?"

"Slow. I thought I'd be finished by last Thursday. Whoever's setting up these buyers' routes is darned clever. When I first started the search, the ISPs involved were numerous, but static. Now they keep changing and my traces aren't yielding results. Someone's going to a lot of effort to cover his or her tracks."

"Don't worry, you'll get it," Shoemake said.

"That's not the only thing slowing me down."

"Oh? What else?" Shoemake feigned innocence.

McKenna narrowed his eyes at his old friend. “Since I’ve been here, several of the computer techs have asked me to help them with various aspects of their work. They said you told them I would.”

Shoemake grinned sheepishly.

“I came here to assist you with the Hard Placers’ investigation. These additional jobs are pulling me off task and preventing me from getting back to Michigan.”

“The other Agency projects needing your help are important, too, Mac.”

McKenna responded to Nathan’s comment with a frown. He went quiet a minute and drummed his fingers on his desk, his brow furrowing. “About this Eugene Hackett,” he said, “Sjoda’s lookout in the van. If I’m being watched, O’Neal could be too.”

Shoemake pursed his lips. “You’re right.” He went to PASCAL’s desk phone, lifted the receiver, and punched a number on the keypad. He put the call on speaker.

“Hello?”

“Maggie, it’s Nathan. Mac is here with me. Are you okay?”

“Yes, sir.”

“Where are you?”

“I’m just pulling into the parking lot near Emory’s library.”

“Have you noticed anyone watching or following you?”

Maggie hesitated. She’d seen a man sitting in a car outside the Pine Grove Motel when she checked in, but didn’t give it much importance. She said, “Nobody knows I’m in Georgia, except you, McKenna and Claudia.” *And Eli Dansk.*

“Well, be extra alert.” He told her about the photographs.

“A red dress? Who’d know about that except the three of us and Claudia?” She paused. “Could your office be bugged, sir?”

“I don’t see how. It’s swept monthly. I’ll have it rechecked today, anyway.”

“Okay, sir. I’ll e-mail you tonight with any pertinent HIV/AIDS findings from Emory’s library. I’ll copy McKenna, too.” She disconnected.

McKenna raised his eyebrows. He'd noticed Maggie hadn't stammered during her exchange with COBOL. In fact, she'd sounded confident. He mentioned this to Nathan.

Shoemake nodded. "Maybe it's because she's away from her parents." He reached for McKenna's desk phone, still on speaker, and punched a number on the keypad.

A man answered. "Security."

"It's Nathan Shoemake. I want my office swept for bugs immediately."

"Yes, sir. Right away."

CHAPTER THIRTY-EIGHT

Maggie O'Neal sat cross-legged on the motel bed in shorts and T-shirt and opened her laptop, which McKenna had programmed with an optional encryption key. She'd arranged the notes from her Emory library research, as well as those from the D.C. Health Department and articles she'd previously accessed on the Internet, in neat piles on either side of her.

She booted up, launched Outlook Express, and addressed her e-mail to Nathan with a copy to McKenna. After entering "HIV/AIDS Findings" on the subject line, she tabbed to the main window and typed:

> *The virus that causes AIDS, or Acquired Immune Deficiency Syndrome (Syndrome meaning a group of symptoms and diseases that are related) is HIV, or the Human Immunodeficiency Virus.*
>
> *An estimated 49 million people are currently infected with HIV/AIDS, 60% of whom live on the African Continent. Life expectancy in Africa has dropped from age 70 to 26 due to the disease.*
>
> *Twenty-five million people have died from AIDS thus far. Three-point-one million perished last year worldwide, and 4.9 million became infected. Children are currently dying at the rate of 1,400 per day from this disease. HIV is now thought to be spreading to ten people every minute.*

Fifty-seven percent, or 456,000 of new HIV cases, were found in African-American individuals globally, higher than other ethnic groups. African-American men's infections represent 7 times those of Caucasians, and African-American women's 21 times those of whites. HIV/AIDS rates in Asian-Americans and Native Americans are low.

Maggie felt uncomfortable relaying the next part of her report, but continued nonetheless.

HIV viruses are transmitted through contact with bodily fluids: blood, semen, vaginal secretions, and breast milk. HIV has been found in low amounts in tears and saliva, but none in urine or feces. Outside the body, the virus is fragile, i.e., it doesn't live long without a host.

HIV can be transferred from one individual to another through sexual contact, needle sharing, pregnancy and breast feeding (infected mother to baby), organ transplants (from infected donors), artificial insemination (from infected donors), needle-stick injuries to health care workers, and dental instruments if they're not sterilized both with chemicals or ultra-violet light AND autoclaved (heat treated).

The ease of HIV transmission depends upon several factors: 1) the number of HIV viruses present in the fluid (semen has much more HIV than vaginal secretions, for example), 2) WHEN the transference takes place from infected person to non-infected person (because viral numbers are different at various phases of HIV infection. Early and late stages are the most dangerous times for transmission. Early, because there is more HIV before antibodies have had a chance to reduce infection, and late, because the individual has fewer CD4 cells (so antibodies decrease and HIV numbers increase again)), and, 3) HOW the contact is made (penis to vagina more likely than vice versa, anal sex more likely than vaginal sex because the anus lining has only one layer of membrane, while the vagina is thicker, and if genital sores (such as herpes) are present, the virus can enter the body more easily).

Maggie stopped typing and leaned back on the pillows propped against her headboard, glad she didn't have to a make a report with such sexual content in person to Shoemake or McKenna.

Her cheeks were warm, so she extricated herself from her notes and laptop, hopped off the bed, and went to her in-room mini-refrigerator for bottled water. She put the cool plastic against her face before opening the cap and taking a drink.

Carrying the water with her, she placed it on the nightstand, returned to her computer, and resuming typing.

Initial symptoms of HIV infection are usually similar to that of having the flu: fever, night sweats, swollen lymph nodes, fatigue, and weight loss. Progressive symptoms include diarrhea, sore throat, and additional viral and yeast infections.

AIDS is diagnosed when people with HIV develop opportunistic infections and complications that include pneumocystis carinii pneumonia, meningitis, Kaposi's sarcoma (this is a skin cancer which causes purple blotches), lymphoma (lymph node tumor(s)), cytomegalovirus (in the herpes family), candidiasis (thrush), toxoplasmosis, and nervous system manifestations such as memory loss, seizures, and change in motor coordination. Thus, a number of diseases are grouped together and called AIDS.

There are three tests performed to diagnose the presence of HIV: 1) the ELISA test, which checks for antibodies to HIV (proteins from the virus are called "antigens." Antibodies form in response to these proteins), 2) Western blot test, which is used to confirm ELISA, and 3) Polymerase chain reaction (PCR), which detects HIV itself and does not depend on the presence of HIV antibodies.

O'Neal stopped typing to review her notes, getting her bearings amidst the volumes of medical information she'd gathered. She took a few sips of bottled water and resumed her e-mail.

HIV is not a virus, but a retrovirus (HIV belongs to a group called Lentiviruses, "lenti" meaning "slow"). Viruses convert DNA to RNA, while retroviruses convert RNA to DNA in a process called "reverse transcription" (i.e., retroviruses reverse the flow of genetic material).

Once retroviral RNA is incorporated into the host's DNA, it becomes part of the cell's genetic code. It then reproduces in each "off-spring" cell when division occurs. In this way, HIV changes the genetic composition of the cells it invades.

These (retro)viruses have several component parts. One enables the virus to gain entry into a cell. Another allows the virus to be incorporated into the host cell's genetic code. A third may (but it's not known for sure) provide a way for the identification of a particular strain.

NOTE: The terms "virus" and "retrovirus" are interchanged in the research, i.e., HIV is often referred to as a "virus," when, in fact, it is, as stated above, a "retrovirus."

There are over 3,000 known retroviruses, most of which are considered harmless. Some can, however, cause arthritis, hemolytic anemia, and lung disease.

Other retroviruses in the same group as HIV include: Simian T Lymphotropic Virus, which is found in Macaque monkeys, Feline Immunodeficiency Virus (cats), Equine Infectious Anemia Virus (horses), Parvo (dogs and humans), Bovine Leukaemia Virus (cattle), and Visna Virus (sheep).

HIV penetrates CD4 T cells. (These are the immune system cells that would normally respond by fighting and ridding the body of the virus. But HIV inserts its genetic material into these cells and actually uses them to create additional viruses.)

More specifically, the primary initial targets of HIV are the monocytes and macrophages. However, the virus doesn't destroy these cells, it simply resides in them (sometimes remaining dormant therein for years) and can then be transported to other tissues in the body and to T cells.

Monocytes and macrophages regulate lymphocytes, which are the basic cell types of the immune system. Lymphocytes are derived from bone marrow. The lymphocytes called B cells remain in the bone marrow until they mature. B cells respond to disease by producing antibodies, which are designed to destroy antigens. Lymphocytes called T cells mature in the thymus gland, which is the seat of the immune system.

There are three types of T cells: T-helper cells (these aid B cells in producing antibodies by releasing chemicals called lymphokines), T-suppressor cells (which aid in protecting the body's tissues from being destroyed by its own immune response by inhibiting B cells from making antibodies after they are no longer needed (a breakdown of this system is what causes auto-immune diseases)), and killer T cells, (which destroy antigens (viral proteins) with their own chemicals).

NOTE: Killer cells have been reduced, on average, 30% over the past 16 years in the "healthy American."

The latency period for HIV can be 2 weeks to 15 years, depending upon the strain and the health of the individual. Dormant HIV can be activated and proliferated by stress, pollutants, illness, bacterial invasion, other viruses, protozoa, fungi, alcoholism, drug use, poor diet, or diseases such as Epstein-Barr, herpes, and syphilis.

AIDS occurs when enough T-helper cells and T-suppressor cells are destroyed to create a susceptibility to infection (so diseases like Pneumocystis carinii pneumonia, the leading cause of death in AIDS patients, as well as those illnesses mentioned above, can take hold and flourish).

Normal T-helper cell numbers are 400/mm3. When these numbers fall below 50-20/mm3, death occurs.

Maggie stopped typing and drank some water. She arced her back to loosen the kinks and stretched her legs on either side of her laptop between the piles of notes. Her fingers went back to the keyboard.

HIV is not a single retrovirus, but a family of retroviruses. Each retrovirus in the HIV group has distinctive characteristics, and each can be highly mutating. One person can have many strains.

Researchers have mapped out the genetic structure of the Human Immunodeficiency Virus but have been unable to produce drugs that can kill it without killing off other tissues in the body as well. Also, an antibody that can destroy one strain of HIV may not destroy another. (These represent a couple of reasons it's been so difficult to find a vaccine.)

The infection process, and the subsequent killing of T cells by HIV, has been successfully duplicated (i.e., the virus replicated) in medical laboratories, using both in vitro and in vivo techniques.

O'Neal leaned against the pillows and looked out the motel window. The sound of children's voices and running feet accompanied a family passing by.

She returned to her laptop and typed:

Still researching. Will contact you with more findings soon.

Maggie.

O'Neal hit "send," shut down her computer, and gathered her notes into a neat pile to place on her nightstand. She called her aunt to check on Brian and O.J., put on her Nikes, and left the motel for a long evening run.

CHAPTER THIRTY-NINE

Reeves Sjoda called his security contact at the CIA. When the man answered, the senator asked, "You know where McKenna is?"

"No."

"How could you not? He's coming and going from Nathan Shoemake's office."

"I've checked with the front desk guards. No record of him signing in or out."

"Could he be using a different name?"

"Possibly."

"Do you know where the Dungeon is?"

"Sure. It's a computer area several subfloors below the basement. Why?"

"McKenna's there, you nitwit. Why would you not know that?"

"That's not my sector. I've got no reason to go there."

"Well, now that we've determined his location, I want you to eliminate him."

"How?"

"Put something in his coffee."

"Like what?"

Reeves exhaled in exasperation. "When you take your dinner break, meet me." He gave the man directions to a tavern. "I'll give you something. He'll never know what hit him."

* * * * *

"Dr. McKenna?"

PASCAL looked up from his computer. A man in a security uniform stood in the doorway to his lab. The hand that held a Styrofoam cup shook slightly.

"What is it?" McKenna asked.

"Uh, I noticed you working late. Thought I'd bring you some coffee for a pick-me-up."

McKenna regarded the man a minute before indicating a spot among some computer printouts with a nod.

The man put the coffee on the desk and left.

McKenna returned his concentration to the computer. He entered a few commands before being interrupted by the ringing of his desk phone. He lifted the receiver.

"Need a break?" Nathan.

"Sure."

"I'm working late, and Claudia's ordering sandwiches. Want one?"

"Sounds good."

"I'll come down."

"Why don't we eat outside? I could use some air."

* * * * *

When McKenna returned from dining alfresco on the grounds of Langley with Nathan Shoemake, the office had been vacuumed, the trash emptied, and the few desk and table surfaces unburdened by computer equipment and piles of paper had been dusted and polished. A faint lemon scent hung in the air.

McKenna marveled that the cleaning people managed to do this job nightly, even if he only stepped out for a few minutes to use the men's room. He appreciated the respect the housekeeping staff showed for the sanctity of his workspace.

He noticed the unopened Styrofoam cup missing from its place on the desk and left again to get a cup of coffee.

When he came back to his lab caffeinated and refreshed, he speed-read and committed O'Neal's e-mail to memory, and then settled in for a night's work.

CHAPTER FORTY

Early Wednesday, Maggie made the ten-minute drive to her second appointment with Elizabeth Dansk.

"Good morning, Maggie." Eli greeted her patient warmly. "How are you?"

"I'm feeling great, Dr. Dansk. How are you?"

"Fine, thank you. You may call me Eli, if you prefer. Most of my patients do."

Maggie nodded, and sat in the same chair as yesterday.

Eli asked, "What would you like to work on this morning?"

"Guilt. My mother."

"All right. Let's begin."

The kinesiology test revealed that Maggie's guilt originated when she was three-years', eleven-months' old.

"That's when my baby sister, Kathleen, died," O'Neal said.

"How did she die?"

"The pediatrician diagnosed SIDS, or sudden infant death syndrome."

"How old was she when she passed?"

"Two months. Kathleen wasn't a healthy baby. When she was born, Mother told me I had to help take care of her because she had my older brothers to look after."

"But you were only three-years', nine-months' old then."

"I know," Maggie closed her eyes. "And my mom blamed me for Kathleen's death. I've felt responsible and obligated to Mother ever since."

"How else did you feel at three years, nine months?"

"Guilty, like I really should have done something to prevent my sister from dying. I wanted Kathleen to sleep in bed with me so I could keep a better eye on her, but Mother wouldn't allow that and said the baby had to sleep alone in her crib.

"The doctor told me I had nothing to do with my sister's death. Intellectually, I know that's true. But in here," she pointed to her solar plexus, "I feel like it's my fault."

O'Neal continued to explore the issue of guilt with her therapist and released it before the session ended.

She gave Eli a check and made another appointment for Friday. When Maggie stood to leave, she said, "I'm doing research on AIDS. I found some material in Emory's library yesterday, but I'm looking for additional information and hoped, because you're in a healing profession and probably network with others who are as well, that you could give me some direction."

"What aspect of AIDS are you researching?"

"Well, I'm not sure." Maggie thought a moment. "Alternative causes and treatments, perhaps. Those that may not be known to mainstream medicine."

"Sounds like you mean underground information."

O'Neal nodded.

"Maggie, are you—"

"Oh, no. I'm, um, researching for someone else. But it's very important."

Eli regarded her patient a moment before going to her desk and pulling a card from a drawer. She copied something onto a piece of paper.

"I'm giving you the phone number of a doctor in North Georgia. Tell him I've recommended you contact him. He won't accept calls without a referral from someone he trusts. You must keep his name and location confidential, except for the person or persons for whom you're doing the research, and they in turn must abide by the same stipulations."

"Yes, of course."

Eli handed the doctor's information to Maggie. She smiled and said, "I'll see you on Friday."

* * * * *

Maggie left the therapist's office and slid into the driver's seat of her rental. She phoned the doctor from her cell, and he agreed to fit her in the following day. She then accessed Yahoo Maps on her laptop for directions to AIDS Atlanta, and headed east.

When she arrived at the facility, a staff member gave her a list of doctors in the area who worked with HIV/AIDS patients, along with several pamphlets, a couple of which were duplicates of what she'd received from the health department in D.C. She asked for alternative medicine leads, but none were available through this office.

While she talked with the AIDS Atlanta representative, she noticed a man watching her with interest from where he sat at a corner desk. He followed her out when she left the building.

O'Neal got quickly into her car and started the engine. She placed her hand over the cylinder of mace clipped to her fanny pack as the man approached her vehicle.

He rapped on the roof. Maggie put the gearshift in "drive" before rolling down the window a few inches.

"I heard you ask Martha about alternative medicine for AIDS."

"Yes," Maggie said.

"I can give you a phone number."

O'Neal called the contact from her cell. She reached an answering machine and left a message.

* * * * *

Maggie ate lunch in a health food co-op and drove back to Seaton. She spent the majority of the rest of the afternoon searching through alternative medical HIV/AIDS sites on her laptop.

When she'd exhausted the pertinent research, she e-mailed her findings to Nathan and McKenna, and went to Lee State Park for a nine mile run around the lake.

After, she returned to the motel, showered, and dressed to meet Betty Ann Almon for dinner.

CHAPTER FORTY-ONE

McKenna reviewed the stack of printouts on his desk, one of the many side jobs he'd been doing for the young computer techs in the surrounding labs, at Nathan's request. He'd just finished checking a page of code when his computer bleeped. Incoming from O'Neal.

He opened the e-mail and speed-read the text. Then, knowing Shoemake to be out of the office, called his cell.

"Just got something from O'Neal," McKenna said after Nathan answered his phone. "Looks interesting."

"I'm on my way back to Langley. I'll stop by the deli for sandwiches. What kind do you want?"

"Surprise me."

"Okay. I'll see you in thirty minutes."

COBOL walked into the Dungeon and handed PASCAL a bag from the delicatessen. McKenna opened it and pulled out a sandwich of rare roast beef piled high on whole wheat bread, with lettuce, tomato, horseradish sauce, and a pickle on the side. He also took out a large, soft, chocolate chip cookie, still warm to the touch and giving off a fresh-from-the-oven smell. Nathan handed him a cold Perrier, as well.

McKenna got up from his chair and moved to the cot. He nodded toward his monitor and said, "Have a read."

Shoemake sat in PASCAL'S vacated seat and leaned toward the screen. He read O'Neal's e-mail aloud.

"Nathan and McKenna: Tomorrow I have an appointment with Dr. Corgin, an M.D., Homeopath and Naturopath in Clayton, Georgia, whose name and location I can reveal only to you, and must otherwise remain undisclosed. Today, I've researched 'alternative opinions and approaches to HIV/AIDS' and have detailed my findings below:

"Not all HIV positive people get AIDS and not all people who are infected with AIDS have or ever had HIV. In fact, AIDS-related diseases have been found in all risk groups with no antibodies to, or other evidence of, HIV infection.

"Normally, when the body is invaded with an infectious agent, the presence of antibodies indicates that..." Here Nathan emphasized for McKenna the words Maggie capitalized, "THE IMMUNE SYSTEM HAS SUCCEEDED IN CONTROLLING THE VIRUS OR BACTERIA, AND HAS 'NEUTRALIZED,' OR RENDERED THE DISEASE HARMLESS. In addition, it means that the body is PROTECTED from further symptoms or disease. In fact, vaccines for other diseases are created to PURPOSELY INTRODUCE ANTIBODIES INTO THE BODY TO PROTECT THE HOST AGAINST RESPECTIVE BACTERIAL OR VIRAL INVASION.

"Yet HIV/AIDS goes against this medical standard/rule of immune system functioning, because when HIV antibodies are detected, their presence is, in mainstream medicine, used to PREDICT THE INEVITABILITY OF GETTING AIDS.

"The National Institutes of Health (NIH) states that diseases, viruses and retroviruses evolve; they don't just 'pop-up suddenly.' Yet HIV/AIDS did just 'pop up suddenly' (also called spontaneous generation).

"HIV is the only medical condition that is initially tested for ANTIBODIES, instead of FOR THE DISEASE ITSELF. This, too, is outside standard and accepted scientific procedure.

"HIV shares many similar traits to NONPATHOGENIC (non-disease causing) retroviruses and is considered by some scientists to BE a NONPATHOGENIC retrovirus. Some research indicates that there are over one hundred retroviruses in the human gene line, and HIV is not dissimilar to these, NONE OF WHICH HAS EVER BEEN *PROVEN* TO CAUSE DISEASE.

"HIV is hypothesized to invade and kill T cells. Yet research has shown that only one in ten thousand T cells are typically infected with HIV, which is too small a number to have such a devastating effect on the immune system. So what is it that is actually killing the T cells if not HIV?

"Latency for HIV is up to fifteen years. No known retrovirus or virus takes this long to cause disease, and such represents a contradiction to long-established principles of virology. For most viruses, the incubation period is only A FEW DAYS. 'Slow' viruses do not exist; there is no basis in medical precedence for them. 'Slow' is against the 'virus rule.' Viruses must replicate quickly in a host cell to survive.

"Although diseases that are normally sexually transmitted affect men and women equally, more than ninety percent of AIDS-infected people in the United States are male. This holds true even in health-care-worker groups, where, although two-thirds are female, ninety percent of the health providers who get AIDS are men.

"The risk of getting AIDS from HIV is not consistent throughout countries and gender; it varies. For example, HIV is transmitted primarily through heterosexuals in Africa, but mostly through homosexuals in the US.

"Many diseases are lumped together and called AIDS. African AIDS involves a different set of associated diseases and opportunistic infections than does AIDS in the United States. AIDS is DEFINED differently in the each of these two countries. In the US, AIDS is claimed to be present when diseases like Kaposi's sarcoma (and others named in previous e-mail) are present; in Africa, AIDS is diagnosed when 'wasting disease' symptoms appear. Malaria and parasite invasion fall into this category—the same conditions that have plagued impoverished countries for centuries. SAME (retro)viruses should cause SAME diseases. This (retro)virus doesn't; it causes DIFFERENT diseases.

"HIV is barely detectable in AIDS patients' semen.

“HIV-positive and HIV-negative intravenous drug users show the same diseases in the same frequency; the general mortality rate of the two drug-user groups is identical.

“People who have or have had malaria, tuberculosis, the flu, measles, multiple sclerosis, multiple infections, or who suffer from malnutrition can test positive for HIV.

“Forty percent of AIDS patients studied by the Center for Disease Control (CDC) were found to have ANTIBODIES to HIV, but not the retrovirus itself. In test subjects from some of our large cities such as San Francisco and New York, only seven percent of AIDS victims were HIV positive. So in these groups, NINETY-THREE PERCENT WERE HIV NEGATIVE.

“HIV has not been found to be a unique molecular entity, but instead a collection of cellular particles. There is no fixed pattern to the whole composition or to segments of the claimed HIV viral genome. The particles have different shapes and sizes. No unique microbe (that's purported to cause AIDS) has ever been isolated or cultured. What HAS been cultured (in regard to AIDS) is a large variety of particulate matter; some, but not all of which resemble retrovirus material. If one or some of these particles is/are really the retrovirus HIV, then what are the others? Viruses are normally easy to isolate; they are easily identifiable entities.

“Typically, retroviruses are virtually spherical in shape, are covered with knobs, and have a diameter of one-hundred to one-hundred-twenty nanometers. The particles that are claimed to be HIV are not spherical in shape, DO NOT have knobs, and have incorrect diameters to classify them as retroviruses. Knobs are essential for the HIV particle to 'dock' onto a cell (the first step in cell infection). If HIV has no knobs, how can it invade and replicate? And if it can't replicate, then how can it be considered 'infectious?'

“Reverse transcription is a normal process of DNA repair and is thus not PROOF of retroviral-invasion activity.

“Antibodies form in response to antigens (viral proteins). Researchers tested HIV-infected individuals and found that none of the proteins were unique to HIV, and in all cases, the presence of these viral proteins could be explained by other conditions within the test subjects.

"A high number of leprosy-infected people in Africa test HIV positive; the leprosy germ itself shows in reaction to the HIV test.

"I understand that some of these research results may be controversial, confusing, and in direct contradiction to the HIV/AIDS material provided previously, but thought the findings important to include in our investigation.

"I'll contact you after my appointment with Dr. Corgin.

"Maggie."

COBOL turned to PASCAL and said, "Interesting stuff. It sure begs some questions."

"Yes, it does."

"Maggie seems to be doing a good job investigating HIV/AIDS."

"Yup." McKenna crumpled his food wrappers and deli bag in a ball and threw them in the trash. His empty Perrier bottle went into the recycling bin.

CHAPTER FORTY-TWO

The strong scent of sweet perfume assailed Maggie's nose as she entered the lobby of the Pine Grove Motel. A thirty-something woman with teased brown hair, heavy makeup, and fire-engine-red lipstick on a large, pouty mouth, flounced forward to greet her. She wore a white-fringed, red shirt, gold-belted into jeans, and high-heeled cowboy boots.

"Mary Margaret?"

"Yes," Maggie said.

"Hey. I'm Betty Ann Almon," the woman said, talking rapidly in a strong southern accent. "You're just gonna love our little ol' auction. Why it's just across the fourlane. We'll be there in a heartbeat after we eat. You're just gonna love the buffet, too. It's always so-o-o good."

O'Neal mentally gritted her teeth at her contact's rapid chatter as she accompanied her into the Pine Grove's restaurant.

The hostess showed them to a table, took their drink orders, and directed them to the buffet.

Maggie inwardly groaned when she saw the food. The selection consisted of fried chicken, fried catfish, fried okra, fried hushpuppies, grayish roast beef, black-eyed peas with chunks of pork fat, and corn on the cob sitting in ersatz butter.

Artificially dyed cherries in a cobbler with fake whipped cream sat in the dessert section. O'Neal knew the red coloring in the cherries, called *cochineal extract,* came from ground bodies of the Dactylopius Coccus Costa insect. This small, bright-red, cactus-feeding beetle also provided color for lipstick, rouges, red liqueurs, fake crab, and strawberry ice cream. She said nothing of this, of course, to Betty Ann, who scooped some cobbler into a bowl and seemed downright pleased with the prospect of eating it.

Maggie made a face.

"What's the matter, Mary Margaret? Don't you like the buffet?" Betty Ann ladled whipped topping onto her dessert. "Oh, you're from up north. I hear you Yankees don't fry your food," she said in a good-natured way.

"No, we don't." Maggie managed a smile. "My family's Irish. We boil everything."

Dinner seemed interminable. Almon talked incessantly, and her fragrance wafted across the table. Maggie's perfume allergy kicked in, clogging her nose and causing her head to swim.

Around mid-meal, O'Neal had an epiphany. *There's a fine line between being gracious or polite, and being someone's victim.*

When supper ended, the small amount Maggie'd eaten sat uneasily in her stomach. She felt sluggish as she rode in Almon's pickup truck across the street to Perry's Auction House. She'd wanted to walk, but her companion insisted they'd get all sweaty.

"This your first auction?" Betty Ann asked. She carried on without waiting for Maggie's reply as they entered Perry's parking lot. "Doesn't this just look like an AA gatherin', with all those men standin' outside drinkin' out of Styrofoam cups 'n' smokin' cigarettes just before the meetin' starts? I used to drive my husband to AA. Of course, he'd go drunk as a skunk."

O'Neal remembered taking her father to AA meetings after he'd had a few. He only went because the priest insisted. "*You don't have to stop drinking to attend,*" her dad had said. "*You only have to have the desire to stop.*"

Betty Ann's chatter brought Maggie back to the present. "We'll have twenty minutes to look around at stuff before the auction starts. If you're lookin' for bureaus, make sure you open the drawers 'n' smell inside. You wouldn't want furniture with smelly drawers."

The women exited the pickup and walked toward a one-story, charcoal-gray building with white trim and brick-red awnings. They entered Perry's through double wood-and-glass doors and came into a large fluorescent-lit space. The lighting cast an eerie glow on the array of items available for auction and the people milling about. A stage with a microphoned podium faced five long rows of chairs, with additional bleacher-type seating behind.

"That's where you register 'n' get your biddin' number," Betty Ann said, pointing to a wide interior window in a corner near the entrance. "My number's permanent, so I get to sit in the reserved seats in the first three rows."

Maggie nodded and excused herself from Betty Ann. She walked to the far side of the room to survey items up for auction, feigning interest.

After a few minutes, Ms. Almon closed in again. "Do you have your bid number yet?"

Maggie shook her head.

Betty Ann lightly stomped her booted foot. "Well, you'd better go 'n' get it. You don't want to wait until the last minute."

"I'll go right now."

Maggie went to the registration window. Out of the corner of her eye, she saw a man wearing a cowboy hat and alligator boots sitting at the end of a row, observing her closely. It was the same man she'd seen lounging in a car outside the Pine Grove Motel. When she glanced his way now, he quickly turned his head.

The peal of the microphone followed by several reverberating taps brought the room to attention. A voice boomed from the stage fronting the rows of chairs.

"Hey hey hey! Let's go, let's go! All of my good floor help, come out where the folks can see you."

Men in tan slacks and navy polo shirts with PERRY'S AUCTION HOUSE written in beige letters over their left chest pockets spread themselves across the area between the stage and audience.

"Welcome to Perry's!" the auctioneer shouted. "Lot's of nice merchandise tonight! Go home with truckloads! All sales final! VISA, MasterCard, cash or checks! Make sure you have a number! Can't bid without a number!"

People were taking their seats and shifting around to get comfortable.

Maggie spotted an empty chair in the fourth row, one behind and over from Betty Ann. She noted the cowboy-hatted man watching her as she went to it.

The auctioneer, in full voice, commanded the room. "All right, here we go! First item! A beautiful nineteenth century Cantonese vase! How much? You tell me! Someone give me fifty! Fifty!"

"Yep!" A floor person pointed to a woman who raised her bid sign in the air.

"Now sixty!"

"Yep!"

"Now seventy!"

"Yep!"

"Now eighty! Anyone for eighty?" The man at the podium looked around the room. "No?" He pointed to the most recent bidder. "Sold at seventy! Number 134!

"Okay, next item! A McCoy cookie jar! It's the real McCoy folks!"

"Ooo, I collect those!" Betty Ann said. She bounced in her chair, her lacquered hair rising and falling in one solid piece.

The auctioneer's voice boomed, "Oh, what'll it be what'll it be what'll it be? How 'bout thirty-five? Thirty-five, thirty-five!"

"Yep!" A floor person acknowledged Betty Ann.

"Forty!"

"Yep!"

"Forty-five."

Betty Ann waved her number furiously.

"Yep!"

Maggie sat quietly, observing the different styles of bidding. Some nodded, others raised a polite forefinger, and some stabbed the air with their numbers.

"Sold for forty-five dollars!"

Betty Ann squealed with delight. She turned to Maggie while the next item came to the floor. "Ooo, I got it!" she said. A wave of perfume flooded Maggie's nose.

Ms. Almon nodded toward the floor help. "They used to be called '*Ringmen*,'" she whisper-shouted. "But that's not considered polite anymore, because it reminds people of slaves or of oxen being led around by a ring in their noses to be sold. So now they're called '*bid catchers*.'"

"That's interesting," Maggie said, being polite. She gave a small smile.

"Next item! A nineteen twenties lamp!" the auctioneer said.

The sale went on. When all the smaller goods were gone, a new caller stepped to the podium.

The door to the outside opened and latecomers entered the building. A few moths and other insects, attracted to the bright fluorescent lights, accompanied the people who came inside. Maggie identified the classification for moths in her head. *Lepidopterous.*

Betty Ann turned to her and gestured toward the individuals now taking their seats. "These are dealers coming in just for the furniture," she said.

Bidding began again as a mosquito buzzed by Maggie's ear. *Arthropoda, Mandibulata, Deptera, Culicidae,* she recited in her mind.

O'Neal paid closer attention to the furniture portion of the auction, knowing she'd be bidding on Hughes's antique African chest in two weeks.

The sale lasted another couple of hours, and Betty Ann asked her to go to a bar for a drink afterwards.

"I have to get up early tomorrow," O'Neal said, making the excuse to decline.

Betty Ann expressed disappointment, but dropped Maggie at her motel.

CHAPTER FORTY-THREE

Reeves sat in the leather recliner in his townhouse and rubbed himself. He couldn't stop thinking about Maggie O'Neal. This afternoon, he'd even masturbated to thoughts of her in the private bathroom attached to his senate office.

Martina was out of service, still healing from the injuries he'd inflicted upon her. Earlier tonight he'd used another prostitute, but it didn't alleviate his want for O'Neal. Soon. He'd have her soon.

He punched a number on his portable phone, calling Belosi.

"Anything to report on Maggie O'Neal?"

"She went to the auction."

"She spot you?"

"No."

"Keep it that way."

Reeves disconnected and dialed Hackett's number. No answer. He tried again. Nothing. He swore and slammed the handset on the table next to the recliner.

He grunted out of the leather and went to his bar. Breaking the seal on a fresh bottle of Cardinal Mendoza, he poured himself a drink.

Sjoda returned to his chair and called his security contact at the CIA. "You get the poison in the coffee and give it to McKenna?"

"Done."

"You see him drink it?"

The man hesitated. "No."

"Idiot!" Reeves slammed down the phone.

He sat back in his recliner and noticed he felt tired and achy. Probably just stress.

CHAPTER FORTY-FOUR

Maggie gratefully entered her room at the Pine Grove Motel and removed her clothes. She showered to rid herself of the stale beer and cigarette odors from Almon's pickup truck, and scrubbed off the smell of Betty Ann's perfume, which seemed to have stuck to her skin and hair. Her nose and lungs began to clear as she breathed the hot steam.

It'll only re-stick Saturday night, Maggie thought. Reluctantly, she'd agreed to meet Betty Ann for dinner again before they went to Perry's. "*No Boundaries,*" Francie would say. "*Maggie, you have no boundaries.*"

O'Neal went to bed after her shower and fell into a deep sleep. She dreamed of the auction, with a voice at the microphone reverberating in her head. The dream shifted, and she found herself in her bedroom in D.C. A gunshot resounded. A man held a smoking pistol and casually blew on it as if to cool the barrel. The gun turned into a dead mackerel.

The shooter morphed into a teenage boy, naked from waist down, who retreated backwards from her bedroom and into the dim hall light. The teen seemed familiar and Maggie strained to identify his face.

O'Neal awoke with a start, her heart pounding. The motel room felt oppressive and she struggled to breathe. She let a few moments pass before she tentatively moved her limbs.

She tried to recall the face of the boy in her dream, but the image dissipated like smoke.

CHAPTER FORTY-FIVE

Maggie's appointment with Dr. Corgin lasted forty-five minutes. Eager to pass her findings along to Shoemake, she called his office from her CIA-secured cell phone rather than waiting to e-mail.

Claudia answered.

"It's Maggie. Is Nathan there?"

"He's with McKenna in the Dungeon."

"Where *is* the Dungeon?" Maggie asked.

Claudia laughed. "It's four subfloors below the basement. I'll transfer you."

* * * * *

McKenna answered the phone. "It's O'Neal," he said to Shoemake, covering the mouthpiece with his hand.

"Put her on speaker."

McKenna punched a button on his console.

"Maggie? Go ahead," Nathan said, moving the guest chair closer to the phone.

"Okay. I just finished meeting with Dr. Corgin in Clayton, Georgia. Based on his own findings, he confirmed, as Mark Hughes said in his letter to you, that AIDS is a man-made, genetically-engineered disease, and there are several laboratories making the virus in the United States and elsewhere throughout the world.

"He also validated many of the research findings in my most recent e-mail to you, including that not all AIDS patients have HIV and not all HIV-infected individuals progress to AIDS. He clarified, saying that AIDS patients with T cell depletion don't always have either HIV or antibodies to HIV, and that some have antibodies but not the virus itself. He also confirmed that there are not always enough HIV in AIDS patients to account for the killing of the T cells. Normally, a certain number of microbes must be present before the associating disease can manifest. HIV doesn't follow this medical rule. He said, too, that there is actually no dormancy period for HIV, and that for those who contract it, the retroviruses are active and replicate within their bodies right from the start. The immune system fights the virus, but eventually becomes overcome and loses the battle.

"Did he seem to be a conspiracy theorist, or solid?" Shoemake asked.

"He seemed solid, sir. He's a regular M.D., but also practices alternative medicine, homeopathy and naturopathy, for which he's not only been condemned by the established medical community, but also harassed by the FBI. He said he treats AIDS patients and has had some success using a Royal Rife machine and homeopathic remedies."

"Royal Raymond Rife," McKenna said. "His machine works on the theory that disease can be targeted by electromagnetic waves pulsed in exact opposition to the frequency of a virus or bacteria, thus canceling it out."

"Yes. He showed me the unit and gave me a similar explanation of how it worked. He explained that every virus has a signature in the form of a sine wave. His machine projects a mirror image of the virus back through the body destroying, say, HIV, or other viruses, similar to what you just described, McKenna.

"But recently he's been testing a different machine that uses electrification to prevent viruses from attaching to the receptor sites of lymphocytes, so they can't bind to the host cell. This technology, he said, is designed to alter the outer protein layers of HIV by emitting fifty to one hundred microampheres, which inhibits these viruses from being able to produce an enzyme necessary for their reproduction.

"Dr. Corgin also said he's had success with Nosodes, as well as with mega doses of vitamin C. A nosode is a remedy that's made up of the patient's own disease material, which is then rendered down to a minute amount, or an echo of the disease. So when taken, the patient's body builds up it's own immunity and cures itself of the condition."

"Did he say he's cured AIDS patients, or only 'had success' with these therapies?" Nathan asked.

"His exact words were, 'I've had success.' He told me he's aware there are 'standard' medical cures available for AIDS, but only for the 'very rich and very well connected.'"

"As in a famous basketball player?" McKenna asked.

"Yes, he specifically mentioned a basketball player. He also told me that the anti-retroviral medicines, or ARVs, don't always work, and patients can become immune to their effect because the viruses are becoming stronger and more drug resistant. Also, ARVs only keep HIV at bay. The viruses stay alive in the body. If ARVs are not taken exactly on schedule, consistently, for the rest of the infected person's life, HIV will replicate and flourish again. He said he has a better chance keeping AIDS patients alive if they haven't taken the anti-retrovirals."

"That's interesting data on ARVs," McKenna said.

"Yes. Corgin mentioned, too, that HIV/AIDS is *not* a fragile virus. It can stay alive outside the body, on surfaces such as tables and doorknobs, for up to three weeks."

"That differs from the information the public's been given for years," Shoemake said.

"Yes, sir. Dr. Corgin also said he's familiar with a study done by the CDC years ago where frozen sera from twenty AIDS patients who died showed they had active syphilis at the time of death. So he started testing his AIDS patients for syphilis, and sure enough, one hundred percent of them were positive. The syphilis, however, didn't show up in standard tests, so more sophisticated ones had to be performed. Now he uses aggressive penicillin therapy administered intravenously for twenty days during the initial phases of treatment, then different oral antibiotics for a year to eighteen months after that to cure the STD."

"That's a long time to be on antibiotics," McKenna said.

"It is, but the doctor explained that because syphilis has reproductive cycles, it's necessary to target each phase to rid the patient's body completely of the disease. And, oral antibiotics can't always penetrate into the central nervous system and the brain, and that's where the Spirochete bacteria which causes syphilis hides. Some patients showed a complete resolution of all AIDS-related symptoms using this antibiotic treatment."

"That's impressive," Shoemake said.

"Yes, sir. The doctor also told me that California researchers gave the Morning After drug to over four hundred people who'd engaged in risky, um, behavior, and to healthcare workers who'd been accidentally exposed to HIV, and not one of them developed an HIV infection.

"Also, there are now two drugs, called tenofovir and emtricitabine, or FTC, which are being combined under the name Truvada and given to people who admit to partaking in unsafe...behavior. These drugs seem to be effective in keeping the virus from reproducing, both in previous trials with monkeys, and now in humans.

"And, studies are currently being performed on microbial gels which prevent the virus from entering the female's body if the male is infected."

"That sounds promising," Shoemake said. "Did you discuss any connection between HIV/AIDS and Parvo with Dr. Corgin?"

"Yes, sir. He said he's heard of one. Both are in the same family of retroviruses.

"The doctor mentioned, too, that everything he related to me about HIV/AIDS is validated in articles in medical journals, some of which are mainstream and some of which are not. He gave me copies, and I'll pass them along to you.

"Dr. Corgin also stressed that I should talk to a virologist. He knew of one and went into another room to make a phone call. A few minutes later he came back and handed me a piece of paper. On it he'd written the same number a man outside AIDS Atlanta gave me. No name, just a number.

“I mentioned to Dr. Corgin that I’d already phoned this contact and left a message, but haven’t yet received a returned call. He said that’s because the virologist would most likely only talk with a man, and asked if I had a male colleague.”

“Okay, Maggie. Give us the contact. Mac can do the interview.”

“Yes, sir.” Maggie recited the virologist’s number. She asked, “Nathan, did you have your office swept for bugs?”

“Yes, but security didn’t find anything.”

“Oh.”

“So we still don’t know how the McKenna-red-dress information got out,” Shoemake said.

“No, sir.”

They said their goodbyes and disconnected.

Afterward, Shoemake said, “O’Neal sounds increasingly more confident.”

“Yes. She does.”

“She’s doing a good job with the investigation.”

“Yes, she is. She’s a thorough researcher, and good at archery, and knows about botany and entomology. But all that does not necessarily make her a good CIA officer,” McKenna said. “I don’t see much use for bows and arrows or plant and bug expertise in our field.”

Nathan narrowed his eyes at his friend. “You forgot being top of her class at Camp P.”

“Yes, well, there’s that too.”

“Indeed, there is.” Shoemake shifted in his chair. “And speaking of O’Neal,” he said, “I altered her records.”

“Meaning?”

“After the retirement dinner, I modified her personnel file to show she left the CIA following her training at Camp P, then got a job in the same DC police precinct her father worked in—he was a cop before he retired. From there, according to her new information, she transferred briefly to Homicide, found it not to her liking, and returned to the CIA. So if Sjoda went digging—”

“It's credible, especially since her father was a DC cop.”

"Yup."

"You do that to cover the part of your anatomy you sit on for sending her into Homicide using her real name?"

"We don't always change the names of our undercover officers, and you know it," Shoemake said, a hard edge to his voice. "We just don't let it be known they work for the Agency."

"That's not it," McKenna said, his voice steely. "You doubted her too. You didn't think she'd even make it through D-Tech, much less be assigned to another op."

COBOL looked at PASCAL, but didn't respond.

CHAPTER FORTY-SIX

Maggie left the motel at 7:45 Friday morning, eager to work again with Eli. During the night she'd been startled awake once more by her recurring dream. This time, she'd seen a face.

"What would you like to work on today?" Eli asked.

"Two things. First, boundaries. Francie explained to me what they are and said I don't have any, and I agree with her. I do what other people want me to do when I don't want to do it. And second, I have a recurring dream."

"Tell me about the dream."

Maggie did. "Sometimes the man with the gun is older, and sometimes he's a teenager. I've never been able to identify either one, until last night."

"Who did you see?"

O'Neal looked out the window. After a moment, she turned again to Eli. "My brother, Dennis." Maggie brought her legs together in a knock-kneed position. "In my dream he's about sixteen."

"You mentioned during our first session that Dennis is ten years older than you. That would make him forty-two now."

"Yes. And my other brother, Patrick, is six years my senior. My mother lost one baby between Dennis and Patrick, and another between Patrick and me.

"Patrick is dead. He was a cop, and my parents think he got killed in the line of duty, and they're so proud of that. They never found out, but he actually died of a heroin overdose."

"I'm sorry to hear about Patrick, Maggie. What about Dennis? Where is he now?"

Maggie lowered her head. "In prison," she said just above a whisper. "He was a parish priest in Arizona and got sentenced for child molestation."

O'Neal lapsed into silence, chin down and rubbing her thumbnail. After a moment, she raised her head and asked in a pained voice, "Do you think he did that to me? Is that what my dream is about?"

"I don't know, Maggie. Your dream is telling you something, but we'll have to ask your body and unconscious mind what that something is. If anything of that nature is there for us to find, it'll take courage to look at it. Do you feel ready to explore this as a possibility?"

Maggie gave herself a moment to gather her strength. She took in a breath. "Yes," she said, a bit shakily. "I'm ready."

Using kinesiology and the dream as an access, Eli asked O'Neal's body for an event-year and month. The muscle test yielded the age of six.

"My birthday comes to mind," Maggie said. "I've always dreaded it. It's not that I'm afraid of getting older, I just don't like the day."

"Okay." Eli waited a bit before asking, "Is anything else coming to you?"

O'Neal closed her eyes and sat quietly. Minutes passed. Finally, she stirred and said in a small voice, "I'm remembering something." Tears slid down her face. She left them unattended.

"What do you remember?" Eli asked.

Maggie spoke in a whisper. "Dennis came into my room on my birthday after I went to bed. He said he was giving me a special present, and that I couldn't tell any one. If I did, Satan would come for me.

"After, there was blood on the sheets and mattress pad. I felt ashamed, and I cut the stains out with scissors. The next day, my mother beat me for ruining her linens."

Eli gently encouraged Maggie to explore the long-term impact of her brother's sexual abuse, and the feelings, thoughts, defense mechanisms, and conscious or unconscious decisions she'd made at the time.

"I felt so violated," Maggie said. "And dirty." She looked out the window. "I only dated a few times when I was in high school, but I stopped going out with boys because I didn't want them to touch me. I guess this is another reason why I've been so uncomfortable around men. And why I have no boundaries. He took away my boundaries, making me do something I didn't want to do."

Maggie turned to Eli. "So why, now, would I sometimes let people do things to me I don't want them to do? It seems I'd react the opposite way."

Dr. Dansk explained. "It's common to repeat patterns in an attempt to resolve old wounds. You might unconsciously attract or set up similar situations in hopes that *this* time either someone wouldn't trample your boundaries, or they would try, but you'd stand up to them and protect yourself. Either way, you'd be trying to make it come out all right."

Maggie nodded her understanding.

"Are you ready to release the impact and arrested development of the sexual abuse, and address your mother's beating you for ruining the bedding?"

Maggie took in a deep breath and said, "Yes."

* * * * *

After leaving Eli's office, O'Neal spent the rest of the workday in her motel room reviewing the materials Dr. Corgin gave her. She had trouble concentrating and gave in to bouts of crying. At 6:00 p.m. she washed her face, put on running clothes, and went to the park for a few laps around the lake.

It all fits, she thought as she ran. She put the puzzle pieces of her emotions together and realized, with clarity, that these were the feelings she'd been trying to outrun.

Maggie slowed her pace after several miles, walked a final turn around the lake, and left the path for the parking lot. As she neared her car, she saw an old man sitting on a bench. He put his hand to his fly as if checking to make sure it were zipped. Even though he looked to be over eighty years of age, his gesture generated in her a wave of fear.

O'Neal went back to the motel and showered, staying under the stream of water a long time, having trouble getting to the place of feeling clean. Skipping supper for lack of appetite, she got in bed and fell into a fitful sleep.

CHAPTER FORTY-SEVEN

McKenna squeezed his eyes shut and put the heel of his hand to his forehead. Surely, he should have succeeded in finding all the D-Tech buyers by now. His traces, instead, resulted in nothing but endless loops.

I missed something, he thought.

You mean missed something again.

The words came unbidden. He must have overlooked what'd been right in front of him eight years ago, too, or his wife and son would not have been killed. Matthew would be fifteen now, a little older than Brian O'Neal.

His shoulders drooped, and he sat staring blankly at his monitor.

Maybe he'd been unable to run down the defense technology buyers because he'd simply become too technically out-of-date while teaching at the university, or, as a professor of basic and mid-level computer science, had grown stale in his field. He felt like an antique. Or, worse still, a fossil.

In the past many days, McKenna'd had too little sleep, not enough exercise, and too much caffeine. He attempted to re-focus on his computer screen, but it seemed a blur. He needed to get out of the Dungeon.

Minutes later, he left Langley wearing his security uniform and drove to the runners' path along the Potomac. The trail, empty on this mid-morning Friday, afforded him solitude.

McKenna stripped to his running shorts and T-shirt, ran a few miles at a moderate pace, and went through his QiGong routine in the same copse as before. When finished, he found a forested area overlooking the Potomac. Here, he sat under a tree and brought himself into a lotus position.

He closed his eyes and took a few deep breaths. Relaxing and drawing upon a Mind Management technique he'd learned during his early CIA years, he entered an Alpha brainwave state that matched the pulse, or Hertz level, of the earth.

Staying in Alpha, McKenna envisioned himself descending ten stairs and approaching a room he'd designated years ago as his "Solutions Place." In his mind's eye, he took a large key from a leather cord around his neck, unlocked the door, and entered. The empty space welcomed him home, and stress fell away from his body and mind. Here in his Solutions Place, he set the intention of solving his block to finding the remainder of the D-Tech buyers.

The noise of the Potomac flowing below played at the edge of his awareness. In his imagery, McKenna walked to the window of his Solutions Room and gazed upon a similar body of water. He tuned to its coursing, and the thought came, *Don't push the river. Let it flow.* Something else about the river seemed important, but he couldn't yet access its gist.

He inhaled deeply and went further into relaxation. In his mind, he moved from the window to sit in the middle of his Solutions Room, cross-legged on a mat. He placed a giant child's block, about six-feet cubed, in front of him, and gave the toy texture and color. He imaged a raised number three painted in yellow on one side of the cube. On another, he saw a green triangle. A red letter "E" appeared on a third, a brown bear on the fourth. He left the remaining sides blank.

The block sat immobile in front of him. He planned to use his will to move it out of the way, a few inches at a time to the right until it disappeared, and to have symbolic images pertinent to identifying all the D-Tech buyers appear behind where the block had been when he'd accomplished this goal.

McKenna sat alert but relaxed, and concentrated. The wooden cube shifted slightly to the right. He willed it further along, and in a few minutes, it was gone.

Several objects lay manifest behind the space the block had occupied, the first a container of brake fluid. He gave thought to its significance. *Brakes. Yes, I've been stopped. The brakes need fluid? Maybe. Perhaps the fluid has another meaning. But if so, what?* The river appeared in his consciousness once again, and this time, it flowed over the container of brake fluid. He gave these symbols a few more moments of attention, then put each on a shelf in his mind for later access.

He inhaled and cleared his head.

Soon, a new scene came into his awareness: Four men playing bridge. He accessed the image, thinking, *Bridge. Bridging the ISPs, perhaps?* He focused on the card game and heard each member of the foursome say, "Pass," when it came his turn to bid.

Nothing more transpired, so McKenna put the bridge game on his mind's shelf with the brake fluid and river.

He gently willed the next symbol into view. A computer monitor filled with code appeared. He scanned the screen and shelved it with the other objects.

McKenna waited, but no further images came, so he mentally removed all the symbols from his shelf and arranged them in order. Brake fluid, river, men playing bridge saying, "Pass," a screen full of code. He reviewed each separately, then strung them together.

In a moment, he had his answer.

McKenna counted himself up from one to seven to a fully awake state. Feeling refreshed and resolved, he headed back to Langley to implement his discoveries.

* * * * *

You look busy and in your zone," Shoemake said, poking his head into PASCAL's room in the Dungeon. "Are you disturbable, or should I come back later?"

"No, it's okay," McKenna said. "Come on in." He cleared a stack of computer printouts from his guest chair. "I'm writing a new program for D-Tech."

"Oh?"

"It'd been taking me too long to wrap up the buyer traces, and I got stuck trying to figure why. So I went into Alpha and visited my Solutions Place to get an answer."

Shoemake nodded his understanding. He and McKenna had taken the same Mind Management class years ago. "I've not visited my Solutions Place in a while. I'm glad you reminded me of it."

"Yes, it'd been a while for me, too."

"So, what'd you discover?"

"Brake fluid, a river, bridge players saying, 'Pass,' and a computer screen full of code."

Shoemake raised his eyebrows, a smile playing at his lips. "Meaning?"

"Meaning, that whoever set up the D-Tech buyers' route learned that someone's been tracing through the ISPs, and wrote a complex counter program to create bridges to false servers. The valid routes actually bump to new servers every four minutes. Also, a purchaser must now have a pass-code to enter into a buy. The pass-code changes every four hours."

"In other words, the *brake* in the brake fluid symbol suggests you've been discovered and stopped. The continuously changing routes and pass-codes means they're *fluid,* just like in the brake fluid and the river images."

"Exactly. So I'm writing a counter-counter program for the ISP routes and another program to reveal each pass-code. This way, I can stay *current,* like the river image, with the buys."

"Pass-code. As in the bridge players saying, *'Pass,'* and the *code* that appeared on the computer screen in your Solutions Place visualization. And *four* card players, possibly pointing to *four* minutes and *four* hours for the server and pass-code changes."

"Yes."

"That's great." Shoemake grinned.

He regarded McKenna a moment and his smile faded. He leaned forward. "What's wrong, Mac?"

"I should have figured out these fluid ISPs and pass-code set-ups earlier," McKenna said. He shook his head. "I think—"

"You figured them out soon enough," COBOL said. He moved his chair closer to PASCAL and looked him straight in the eye. "You've been experiencing self doubt since Iraq, Dr. McKenna. It's time you got over it."

McKenna glanced away for a minute. He opened his mouth to speak, but Shoemake cut him short.

"I've never doubted you, Mac. Don't you doubt you, either."

CHAPTER FORTY-EIGHT

Maggie arose Saturday morning with new resolve. She phoned Betty Ann and told her she wouldn't be joining her at the Pine Grove Motel Restaurant after all, but would meet her at the auction at seven o'clock. Almon protested and pressed to keep their dinner plans, but O'Neal held her ground.

Maggie disconnected and went for a morning run in Lee State Park. After, she sat under a tree by the lake reading through more of Dr. Corgin's HIV/AIDS materials.

At 12:00, she got take-out from the Lazy Burro, a Latino restaurant in town Eli recommended, and returned to the motel room to eat her meal. Feeling emotionally spent from yesterday's session with Eli, she got into bed and fell into a dreamless sleep.

She awoke refreshed an hour later, and spent the rest of the afternoon reviewing AIDS information.

* * * * *

Perry's Auction House appeared to be crowded with locals looking for something to do in a small town on Saturday night. Maggie, having already picked up her bidding number, was reviewing items for sale when Betty Ann flounced in.

She greeted Maggie in a swirl of fluff and ruffles, her teased hair stiff with spray. Her perfume seemed even stronger than it did on their first meeting.

"How do you like my new dress, Mary Margaret? My husband bought it for me. He's so good to me."

Betty Ann sported a bruise on her upper cheek not there on Wednesday night, and Maggie wondered just how well Almon's husband, in fact, treated her.

"Your dress is pretty," Maggie said, being polite. "The auction's about to start." She gestured toward the man taking his place at the microphone. "I'm going to find a seat."

Maggie extricated herself from Betty Ann and located an empty chair. The man who'd observed her Wednesday night sat at the end of the row. He glanced at her sideways.

The sale lasted three hours. Betty Ann walked out to the parking lot with Maggie afterward.

"My husband's pickin' me up. Will you wait with me until he gets here, Mary Margaret? He took the truck 'n' went out with the boys tonight."

Maggie didn't want to leave Betty Ann alone in the lot, so she agreed.

Auction attendees were streaming out of the building, loading goods into their cars and trucks. The cowboy-hatted man exited Perry's and gave O'Neal a covert look as he walked to his car. Maggie memorized the license plate number and make of the vehicle.

Betty Ann chatted non-stop as they waited for her husband. Forty minutes passed, and Mr. Almon still hadn't shown. All the other people attending the auction were now gone, and the last of the employees turned off the building's interior lights, locked up, and left.

The two women stood in the gravel parking lot, dark now except for a security light, which attracted bugs. O'Neal identified them in her mind as they flew in a circle overhead.

"Would you like me to take you home?" Maggie asked.

"Oh, no. My husband would kill me if I wasn't here when he came." Betty Ann stared into the distance and became uncharacteristically quiet.

Maggie made conversation. "Did you bid on any items tonight?"

"No. My husband said I couldn't get a thing. Did you?"

"No."

"What are you interested in?" Betty Ann asked. "You didn't buy anythin' Wednesday night either."

"I'm looking for something specific. An antique chest from a person's estate. His furniture is scheduled for sale one week from Wednesday. In the meantime, I'm observing and learning about auctions."

"Do you know the dealer's name 'n' the state the antiques came from?

"Yes, Mr. Threlkeld from Virginia."

"Well, now, that sounds familiar. Jus' wait a little minute." Betty Ann opened an oversized, glittered purse and took out a flyer. Maggie saw "PERRY'S AUCTION HOUSE DEALERS' PREVIEW" written across the top.

Ms. Almon ran a brightly-lacquered fingernail down a column, and said, "Yes, here it is. The Threlkeld antiques from Virginia are comin' in tomorrow."

"But the woman in the office said—"

"Well, now, Mary Margaret, that's the owner's mother, 'n' bless her heart, she went 'n' had herself a stroke a few months ago, so she's not firin' on all cylinders anymore. Besides, she's just fillin' in for the office manager who's on vacation. Antiques always come in more than a week before a sale, delivered on Sunday, after the Wednesday 'n' Saturday before's auctions have cleared out the warehouse. It's so the dealers can get first pickin's. You don't have to wait to bid for somethin', you can jus' offer them a good price for the piece you want 'n' they'll sure enough sell it to you. They won't let anybody in tomorrow, but they'll be open again on Monday mornin' at ten o'clock."

A pickup ripped into the parking lot and came to an abrupt halt in front of the women. A man rolled down the window and leaned out with a tattooed arm.

"Get in."

The husband.

"Bye, Mary Margaret." Betty Ann ran to get in the truck.

Mr. Almon hurled an empty Budweiser can into the parking lot. Maggie heard anger in his voice as he peeled away, spewing gravel at her feet.

CHAPTER FORTY-NINE

Reeves Sjoda'd just gotten over his cold when he became achy and developed a fever. He'd taken leave from his senate duties once more last Thursday, too sick again to do much of anything except lay in bed. Most likely the flu.

Then on Friday, his breathing became labored and his chauffeur drove him to the doctor for a chest X-ray, blood work, and antibiotics.

By late Sunday the senator's fever broke, but he didn't have the strength to check on his men or listen to more tapes recorded in Nathan Shoemake's office.

Not a big deal. O'Neal would be in Seaton until Mark's antiques came up for auction more than a week hence. When she returned to D.C., he'd be fully recovered from his illness, and she'd be his.

With what little energy Sjoda could muster, he took a knife and slit open an envelope containing O'Neal's employment records. He reviewed the few sentences and tossed the papers on the table beside his chair.

He thought about McKenna. *He's like a cockroach. You can't kill him with a stick.* Well, perhaps his security snitch had succeeded in eliminating PASCAL this time.

Neither Belosi nor Hackett had called in lately. Hackett probably didn't have a clue his cell phone wasn't working. That idiot sat on his brains. Belosi would come through. He was too afraid of what Sjoda would do if he didn't.

The senator poured himself a drink, lit a cigarette, and popped another antibiotic.

CHAPTER FIFTY

McKenna approached a man who appeared to be in his mid-sixties, sitting on a bench. "Does this park have a rose garden?" he asked, using prearranged code words.

"No. You must be thinking of another park. Perhaps the Atlanta Chamber of Commerce could help you," the man responded, his accent German.

"I'm flying back to Washington today and won't have time to explore other locations," McKenna said.

The man nodded. "How may I help you—Mr. Browning, is it?"

"Yes." McKenna sat beside the German, a newspaper separating them. "First of all, who are you?"

"My name is not important. I'm a virologist retiring from the Center for Disease Control. Before the CDC, I worked for The National Institutes of Health and a laboratory in Zambia, Africa, and previous to that, a facility in Germany."

The man sounded tired. He paused, and McKenna waited for him to continue.

"My parents were Nazis, and my father, a medical scientist, worked in the death camps performing experiments on Jewish prisoners. After, Neo-Nazi scientists recruited him to develop biological agents for mass destruction. When I finished my education, I went to work for him. He retired, and I took his place as lead virologist in a secret German laboratory. Seven years later, I immigrated to the United States."

McKenna asked, "Is it true that HIV/AIDS is a man-made disease?"

"Oh yes. I participated in its development. Very ingenious, actually." He gave a small smile. "We succeeded in creating a virus that destroys the human immune system."

McKenna stared at the German, who seemed perversely pleased with himself.

"You see," the virologist said, "the genes of HIV didn't initially exist in humans. We took viruses from other animals and created new diseases in man. Not too difficult, since human genes are in DNA form. Retroviruses turn RNA into DNA in a process called reverse transcription. So, retroviruses can invade man's genetic material, alter the DNA, and replicate."

The German looked at McKenna as if to discern his level of understanding. McKenna nodded for him to continue.

"In a petri dish, we could, for example, insert bovine leukaemia from cows and visna virus from sheep into human tissue, and have these diseases proliferate in human DNA.

"By this process, we were able to make a DNA-specific strain of HIV to target African Blacks. There are many tissues that bacteria and viruses can infect. HIV and the Yersina Pestis, or Bubonic plague, which caused the Black Death, attack the same cell tissue within the body. There is a mutant form of a gene called CCRF that is present in those whose ancestors survived the bubonic plague. CCRF provides protection against HIV, and this mutant gene is absent in Africans. So, we put DNA-specific HIV serum in a Hepatitis B vaccine and injected it into thousands of individuals in Zambia, Zimbabwe, Botswana...well, you get the picture.

"Around the same time and unbeknownst to some in our association, several of our virologists also developed a gender-specific HIV strain and placed it into the Hep B vaccine that was injected into male homosexuals in New York, Chicago, Los Angeles, San Francisco, and other major cities. We experimented with a third strain in Thailand."

McKenna kept his face neutral, not allowing the disgust he felt to become evident. "So, you're telling me that this virus didn't, in fact, come from monkeys?"

"This virus didn't start from a monkey biting one man, or by one gay airline steward having sex with several men, as the masses have been led to think." The virologist scoffed. "Humans so gullible, so ignorant. All we had to do was plant those stories in corporate media to get the news coverage we wanted. People will believe anything and repeat the lies to each other all over the planet.

"We made up those preposterous stories over coffee and pastries one morning. The truth is, we infected thousands of people simultaneously. The first outbreaks of HIV/AIDS were numerous and occurred at the same time, on three continents far removed from one another, in diverse cultures, with unique populations. How could that possibly be explained?"

"I thought monkeys carried the HIV/AIDS virus."

"Monkeys carry a similar retrovirus, and some have HIV/AIDS because we injected them with it. We infected hundreds of these primates and shipped them to research labs all over the world, including one in Reston, Virginia.

"And don't you find it significant, Mr. Browning, that while the AIDS virus in Africa affects men and women equally, the majority of those affected by AIDS in the US are men? We designed it that way."

"Why?"

"One reason, some of my colleagues and I are present-day Nazis and eugenicists. Instead of rounding up ethnically inferior races or unacceptable behavioral groups and putting them in concentration camps to be gassed in ovens, we created diseases that specifically target the individuals we want exterminated. And the second reason, we were asked to."

"By whom?"

"The US Government, of course, as well as others. The Department of Defense requested ten million dollars in 1969 to bioengineer viruses to destroy the human immune system. The United States Army contracted two major drug companies, Worth and Bromm Biomedics and Draybough Pharmaceuticals, to manufacture these viruses. It's all been overseen by your very own CIA. The National Institutes of Health is involved, as is the World Health Organization. Don't forget, the NIH, the CDC, and other such organizations are funded with federal dollars. Many high-level government officials worldwide are participating. Many laboratories."

"Again, why?"

"Hate, power, greed. Different reasons for different people. Some individuals involved in this plan want the land and resources in Africa. Oil, and uranium, diamond, and gold mines are plentiful there. Others see this as a way to control the world's peoples. Some want these viruses and other diseases for biological weaponry. Others simply want to do it because they can.

"Nazis despise members of races they don't consider pure. The religious right and homophobes abhor homosexuals. They see them as detestable and expendable. It's another holocaust, but one that's less obvious. Anyway, our world is overpopulated and needs to be culled in order for the rest to survive.

"And the money, of course. HIV/AIDS is a billions-of-dollars-per-year industry. The pharmaceutical companies create a disease, then sell the drugs to control it at great profit. It's a perfect system."

Two women pushing baby strollers passed McKenna and his contact. The virologist waited until they rounded a bend in the path before continuing.

"We're working on airborne viruses now. Some of our people are oncogenic specialists and have created an oncological, or cancer, virus that spreads like flu. We've been experimenting in small pockets of populations around the world.

"As an aside, you might also want to investigate the similarities between the bovine, or cattle, leukaemia, and the HTLV human T cell virus-two."

McKenna struggled to keep the anger out of his voice. "What about people contracting avian flu? Is that your handiwork too?"

"We're hoping the human form of the H-five-N-one strain becomes fast and deadly. Right now, it hides deep within the lungs so it can't be easily spread by coughing or sneezing. We're working to speed things up to make it the perfect illness by inserting the bird flu virus into the common flu virus that visits populations annually. We all know how easily the common flu spreads, Mr. Browning. Likewise, we're engineering an H-one-N-one, or swine flu. We feel HIV/AIDS has been somewhat of a failure because it's been too slow.

"We also created Ebola from the Marburg virus, which shares a close similarity to the Rhabdovirus Simian, but we decided that even though it has the contagion speed and high death rate we're looking for, it's too exotic and would not, shall we say, 'play well in Peoria.' We were concerned it would pique suspicion and invite investigation.

"The avian and swine influenzas jumping species and marrying the common influenza virus is much more acceptable to the ignorant minds of the masses. We started a media blitz to heighten awareness and fears of the bird flu, and to prepare the populace for what's coming."

The virologist smiled. "There's a laboratory in the Panama Canal Zone and its top floor is dedicated to hemorrhagic fever. Only those people who've gotten the disease and survived are allowed access. We infected them, you see, and if they lived, they earned the privilege of working for us at a very low wage."

Some joggers passed the bench on which the men were sitting. McKenna waited until the runners were out of earshot before asking, "Why did you agree to meet with me?"

"Ah." The German gazed across the park and sat in silence for a moment before he responded. "Because I know what it's like to be dying and not to be able to do anything about it. Last week, my doctors gave me four months. I've done many bad things in my life, hurt and killed many people. In the little time I have left, I want to try to make a few things right. It's amazing how you change when faced with your own death and the possibility that hell exists."

McKenna gave only a few seconds pause to the virologist's disclosure before asking, "Is Parvo connected to AIDS?"

"Parvo is in the same family of retroviruses as HIV. We have many veterinarians working with us at the laboratories. We created Parvo and put it in vaccines at the same time and in the same place as one of our HIV trials. Retroviruses are known to jump species. We've heard of cases where AIDS patients' dogs ended up getting Parvo. Anecdotally, of course."

"Are there vaccines effective against HIV/AIDS?" McKenna asked.

"Oh yes. We've developed those too. Different sera for different strains. Unfortunately, there's no vaccine for what's killing me."

"Who are the people involved and where are the labs?"

"Between us on this bench there is a newspaper."

McKenna glanced at the Sunday Edition of the Atlanta Journal Constitution next to him.

"I think you'll find the Entertainment section interesting. Good day, Mr. Browning."

McKenna left the virologist and returned to his car. He opened the newspaper and found, on a single sheet of paper, a list of laboratories worldwide. Two were highlighted with yellow marker: The United States Army Medical Research Institute for Infectious Diseases, or USAMRIID, and a facility in Zambia, Africa.

A notation appeared under the Zambia listing. "You'll find viral strains, vaccines, and the names of people involved in the depopulation plan in an offline computer in the underground office of this laboratory complex. Visit USAMRIID first."

CHAPTER FIFTY-ONE

Reeves awoke Monday morning still feeling like crap. Now a whopping hangover added to his misery of having the flu. He got out of bed, lit a cigarette, and poured a shot of brandy in his coffee. After the mixture of alcohol and caffeine took effect, he called his senatorial aide and said he'd not be coming in.

He finished his cigarette and ate what breakfast his stomach could tolerate. He phoned Hackett, and once again got no response.

Reeves made another drink and sat in his recliner. His eyes fell on Maggie O'Neal's personnel records on the table next to him. *So, she'd transferred into Homicide from a precinct where her father'd been a cop. She'd quit the CIA after her training and went back to the Agency after a short time doing police work. Why? Because she started dating McKenna? Why'd he reappear in DC? Because he met O'Neal and wanted to be near her? Maybe they were in love.*

Reeves snorted.

Julian told me Jaffey described O'Neal as a mouse of a thing. So what'd that shithead know? He had no taste in women, obviously.

And this Sergeant McClouski was reported to be in only a temporary position awaiting retirement. So perhaps both O'Neal and McClouski were coincidental to Homicide and not there to investigate the defense technology relays. Maybe I'm just being paranoid. He took a swallow of his brandy. *Then again, maybe not.*

He ejected a cassette from his recorder and put another one in to listen to more taped conversations from Nathan Shoemake's office.

CHAPTER FIFTY-TWO

On Monday morning Maggie went to Perry's Auction House and bought the African chest that'd belonged to Mark Hughes. Being relatively small, it fit nicely into the trunk of her rental, along with a shipping box she'd purchased for the flight home.

She checked out of the Pine Grove Motel and ate an early lunch at the Lazy Burro. After, she phoned her boss's office and left a message with Claudia that she'd already secured Hughes's antique and would be coming back to D.C. tonight.

O'Neal arrived ten minutes early for her final appointment with Eli before heading to the airport. She wanted to review the documents from Mark's chest in the relative privacy of Dr. Dansk's tree-lined parking lot prior to her therapy session. She popped open the trunk of her car and removed a manila envelope from the false bottom of the antique.

Her cell phone rang and she unclipped it from her fanny pack to answer. "Hello?"

"Maggie?" Her aunt. Her voice sounded strained.

"What's wrong, Aunt Mary?"

"Oh, I'm afraid I have very bad news, dear..."

"Are you okay? Is Brian? O.J.?" O'Neal's pitch rose in panic.

"It's your mother and father. I'm so sorry, dear, they were both killed this morning."

A moment of shocked silence passed. Maggie felt herself going numb. "How?" she asked, her voice sounding distant and hollow. She tossed the envelope back into the chest and shut the trunk.

"The gas furnace in your brownstone exploded. Your parents were directly above it in the kitchen when it happened."

"Does Brian know?"

"Yes. I told him."

"Is he okay?"

"He seems to be."

"How are you, Aunt Mary? Mom was your sister, after all."

"I'm all right, dear."

"Okay," Maggie said. "I'm coming back to DC tonight and I'll head straight to your house from the airport." Her voice sounded tinny. "My job here finished early, and I've already booked my flight."

"All right, dear. I'll see you when you get back."

O'Neal hit the END CALL button and leaned against the car, stunned. She stayed there, unmoving, for several minutes. Then, like a switch being thrown, memories surged. She doubled over in emotional pain, and violent sobs erupted from a place deep within.

Someone appeared before her. Eli. She must have seen her crying through the windows that fronted her therapy room.

"Maggie? What's wrong?"

"My p-parents. My p-parents are...d-dead."

"Oh, I'm so sorry."

"No. No, it's not...it's...I-I'm remembering something."

Dr. Dansk put her arm around her patient. "Come with me," she said. She guided Maggie inside the office to one of the side-by-side chairs, and sat next to her. O'Neal rocked back and forth, trembling, tears flooding down her cheeks. Eli stayed with her until she calmed.

"What do you remember?" Dr. Dansk asked. She handed O'Neal a Kleenex and moved to the seat opposite.

"My father." Maggie wiped her eyes and blew her nose. She threw the Kleenex in the wastebasket and took another. "It wasn't just Dennis. My dad came into my room, too.

"It went on for years, I think," Maggie said, dabbing her face with a clean tissue. "I'm remembering now that one time, my mother looked in and saw it happening. She simply walked away and did nothing."

For the rest of the session, Eli helped Maggie wade through the pain and grief of her father's sexual abuse and her mother's conspiracy of silence. After O'Neal released the impact of these traumas, Eli asked, "What are you feeling about the death of your parents?"

"Nothing. Nothing about their deaths. Just rage over what they did to me as a child."

Eli looked at her patient with compassion in her eyes.

"I wonder why I remembered my father's abuse today, right after I got the call from my aunt about the explosion?" Maggie asked.

Eli explained. "It's not uncommon for events to come to consciousness after the death of one's mother or father. It's as if there is an unwritten contract that these memories will remain buried while parents are still alive, and may surface only after they're gone. Ties with parents can be very strong, even if those bonds are unhealthy."

Maggie nodded her understanding.

"You may continue to feel rage toward your father and mother in the weeks ahead as you process your emotions from uncovering the abuse," Eli said. "Then, grief over their deaths may ensue. Call me, Maggie. Don't go through this alone."

Both women stood and said their goodbyes. Maggie thanked Eli for her help, and gave her a warm hug before leaving for the airport.

* * * * *

O'Neal landed at Dulles and, after a few minutes of conversation with a D.C. official, called Shoemake on his cell.

"Sir? It's Maggie."

"How are things going?"

O'Neal paused. "Well, sir, my parents were killed this morning."

"What? Oh, no. I'm so sorry, Maggie. How did it happen?"

"Our furnace exploded. They were in the kitchen, right above it."

"Do you think it was sabotage? I can send an investigative team to your home immediately."

"Oh, that won't be necessary, sir. The fire marshal already deemed it an accident. I just got off the phone with her. She said something faulty in our heating unit caused the explosion, even though the system was not in use. My dad always left the pilot light on through the summer because the heater was old and too hard to restart again in the fall."

"How are you doing, Maggie? Are you all right?"

O'Neal hesitated. "I'm okay, sir. I'm at Dulles."

"Claudia told me you were coming back tonight. She said you got Hughes's chest. But she didn't tell me about your parents."

"She didn't know. My aunt called with the news after I talked with Claudia."

"Where are you headed now?"

"I'm on my way to Aunt Mary's."

"I'll put security guards on your aunt's house immediately. Claudia said you gave her a license plate number to run. Some man at the auction?"

"Yes, sir. He seemed to be keeping an eye on me both Wednesday and Saturday night. I also spotted him when I arrived in Seaton in the Pine Grove parking lot, but didn't grow suspicious until I saw him those subsequent times at Perry's."

"When are you planning on going to your brownstone?"

"Tomorrow. I'll have to assess the damage and make funeral arrangements. My parents' last wishes are in a box in their bedroom closet."

"All right. I'll provide guards for both the front and back doors of your home, too. They'll be there first thing in the morning."

"Thank you, sir. I found a manila envelope in Hughes's chest. It's still sealed. I've not had a chance to read the contents."

"I'm having dinner with Zann in Georgetown right now. I'll swing by your aunt's house tonight when we're finished eating and pick it up, if that's all right with you."

"Yes, sir."

"Again, Maggie, I'm so sorry about your parents."

"Thank you, sir."

CHAPTER FIFTY-THREE

The dank smell of cigarette smoke, old paste, and years of living assaulted Maggie's nose as she desperately pounded a wet sponge on the bathroom wallpaper and scraped it off with a putty knife in rapid, furious strokes.

O.J., who she'd brought home for the day, sat with furrowed brow behind the toilet seat, mostly out of range of pieces of sopping paper that were being flung in all directions from the blade.

Maggie gritted her teeth as she worked, and guttural, angry sounds emanated from her throat.

* * * * *

The tall, silver-haired priest exited his car, parked about a half a block from Maggie O'Neal's brownstone. He walked slowly up the street, stooped slightly with age, past construction trucks that punctuated the vehicles parked curbside. A neighborhood under renewal, he noted. Shiny SUVs and a Mercedes Benz sat positioned nose-to-tail with the faded Fords and Chevys of the dwindling poorer residents.

Arriving at his destination, the priest saw a young man leaning against the brownstone's wall at the top of the stoop. He expected the man to be here, sent by Nathan Shoemake to guard Maggie O'Neal. The cleric climbed the stairs with seeming difficulty and nodded to the sentry.

The young man came away from the wall and said, "Hello, Father."

"I'm here to comfort Miss O'Neal."

"Of course, Father."

The priest entered the home through the screened door, closing it silently behind him. He stood in the entry and noticed a flower arrangement on the table next to a black, rotary-dial telephone. He crossed the hall noiselessly and read the card tucked inside the bouquet. MAGGIE, SO SORRY FOR YOUR LOSS. NATHAN SHOEMAKE AND SUZANNE CINQUE.

He walked to the kitchen doorway and peered around the jamb, his knee touching a pet gate. Blood and bits of human flesh, bone, and hair were splattered over what remained in the space. A large section of floor was missing, with pieces of table, chairs, and kitchenware strewn around the perimeter. The charred walls were wet, no doubt from fire hoses. An area of wallpaper, patterned in ivy climbing a green trellis, was surprisingly unaffected. A camera sat on a jagged piece of countertop, most likely containing pictures for the insurance company. The room smelled of death and smoke.

The priest retraced his steps through the hall and looked into the living room and adjoining dining room. The furniture and curtains were dated and spare, but clean.

He turned and went to the bottom of the stairs that led to the second floor. He listened.

An odd, rhythmic noise came from above. Thud, swish swish, scrape, scrape, scrape. Slosh. Thud. Swish swish. Scrape scrape scrape.

The robed cleric quietly climbed the stairs, no longer feigning age. For this was not an old man, and he was certainly no priest.

He arrived at the top of the steps and followed the sounds to a bathroom. He paused in the doorway to take in the scene.

Maggie O'Neal stood on a stool in the bathtub scraping old wallpaper, the same pattern, he noted, as in the kitchen. A bucket of water sat atop a tray table, and as he watched, O'Neal plunged her sponge into the water and slammed it on the wall above the tub's tiles. Her reddish-blond twin ponytails swung back and forth intensely as she worked.

She wore a tank top and shorts, showing toned arms and shapely legs. Her body, littered with pieces of wet ivy, trellis, and yellow-white, looked both comical and sad. Corrugated strips of wallpaper were piled at her bare feet and covered her toes.

An ancient orange cat sat crouched behind the toilet, watching the scene with a mixture of curiosity and alarm.

The man dressed in priest's robes spoke. "Maggie?"

O'Neal whirled around, almost losing her balance on the stool. Bits of wet wallpaper flew off the putty knife, and a piece of green ivy landed on the cat's head. He gyrated to flick it off.

Maggie gasped and stood with eyes wide, shoulders up, putty knife held out in defense. After a beat, she relaxed and brought her eyes into a squint.

"McKenna."

"I heard about your parents. Are you all right?"

Maggie bit her lip and shook her head, her ponytails moving back and forth.

McKenna regarded her a minute. She didn't appear grief-stricken, she seemed...*furious.* He looked a question at her.

Maggie shook her head again. Tears welled in her eyes, and she turned from McKenna and faced the tub wall. She dipped her sponge in the bucket and pounded it on the paper above the tile.

McKenna glanced around and spotted a toolbox on the floor. Bending down, he reached into it, removed a hammer and a couple of screwdrivers, and found another putty knife.

Then, in priest's robes, he stepped into the tub beside O'Neal. He picked up a nearby washcloth, sloshed it around in the bucket of water, wet a section of wallpaper, and started scraping.

CHAPTER FIFTY-FOUR

Maggie, Brian, and Aunt Mary stood at graveside, Maggie's right arm around her brother's shoulders. Nathan Shoemake and Suzanne Cinque were standing behind. The group waited for the O'Neal's family priest to begin the final portion of the funeral ceremony.

A large woman in an ebony dress, gray hair, and a black pillbox hat and veil stepped up to Maggie's left side and took her elbow. She looked up into the face and smiled.

McKenna.

He leaned down and spoke softly in her ear. "You okay?"

She nodded.

Brian peeked around Maggie and gave McKenna the once-over. His eyes went big.

"Aunt Mary, Brian," Maggie whispered, "This is McKenna."

"You're in drag!" Brian said.

"He's in *disguise,*" Maggie said, keeping her voice low. She felt smiles coming from Nathan and Zann behind.

The priest raised his arm and a hush fell over the gatherers. He intoned his final words for Patrick and Maureen O'Neal, conscripting their bodies to earth, souls to heaven.

Maggie leaned slightly into McKenna. He gave her elbow a gentle squeeze.

* * * * *

After the service, McKenna walked Maggie, Brian, and Mrs. Levy to the funeral home's limousine.

He pulled O'Neal aside. "Where are you going now?"

"First, to pick up my aunt's car, then to the brownsto...." She cleared her throat. "Um, home." She shifted her feet. "My house."

McKenna regarded her.

"Just for the afternoon. Aunt Mary and I have some estate papers to review. Nathan has a couple of security men posted there."

McKenna nodded.

"Nathan told me you ran the license plate number I gave Claudia from the man at the auction," Maggie said.

"Yes. It's a rental, leased to a thug named Salvador Belosi. His phone records show contact with Sjoda.

"Oh, my gosh."

"Yes." McKenna kept his voice low. "As we suspected might happen, Sjoda's having someone keep an eye on you."

Maggie nodded her acknowledgement and said, "I'll keep on the alert."

"All right." McKenna looked at O'Neal's brother, standing about twenty feet away, and called to him. "Hey, Brian, do you like baseball?"

"Yeah!"

"Want to shag some flies?"

"Yeah!"

McKenna turned to O'Neal. "Okay, I'll meet you at your house."

Maggie didn't protest.

* * * * *

Words like, "Nice catch!" and "Great hit!" and "Here comes a grounder!" punctuated by bursts of Brian's fourteen-year-old laughter cannoned through the screened door as Maggie and her aunt stood watching McKenna, still in black dress and wig, practicing softball with Brian in the brownstone's backyard.

"He seems like a nice man," Aunt Mary said.

Maggie nodded.

"Nathan and Zann, too."

"Yes, they really are," Maggie said.

Her aunt smiled, kindness showing in warm brown eyes that crinkled at the corners. Her wavy, thick, auburn hair fell to the shoulders of her black dress.

Mary put an arm around her niece. "Let's go into the dining room. I want to discuss some estate matters with you."

"Okay."

They walked through the kitchen, the room now free of debris and scrubbed clean, compliments of a crew sent by Nathan Shoemake after the insurance adjuster's visit. A temporary plywood floor covered the blast hole.

The dining room, amazingly unscathed by the explosion, had been set up with a coffee urn and cold beverages in an ice-filled cooler. Platters of chocolate éclairs from Zarelli's Bakery and diced fruit stood ready, in case anyone stopped by to offer condolences. No one did. Francie, out of town on business, had phoned her support to Maggie earlier from New York.

Aunt Mary poured herself a cup of coffee and took an éclair from the platter. Maggie got a Perrier and fruit for herself.

The women sat in silence a few moments, listening to the sounds coming from the backyard, laughter interwoven with cracks of the bat and smacks of a ball landing mitt-center.

Mary Levy went to the sideboard to refill her coffee and came back to the table, sitting cater-corner to her niece. She looked directly at Maggie and said matter-of-factly, "Your mother and father were very difficult people."

O'Neal nodded. Tears threatened, so she stood and busied herself cutting an éclair in two, putting half on a plate.

When she returned to her seat, Mary put a hand on Maggie's arm and said, "There's something I have to tell you, dear."

O'Neal pushed the éclaired plate aside to give full attention to her aunt.

"When your Uncle Levy died, he left me well off."

Maggie acknowledged her aunt's statement with a nod.

Mary patted her niece's arm. "He left you well off, too."

Maggie looked at her in question.

"Levy established a trust fund for you, and one for Brian as well. They were to become activated only upon the death of both of your parents. He understood that your mother and father, would, by whatever means possible, get their hands on any money you or Brian had that they knew about, and you'd never see it again."

Maggie considered this disclosure a moment.

"You have a savings account you kept secret from your parents, don't you?"

"Yes, Aunt Mary, I do."

"Good for you."

Mary stood and went to her purse, sitting open on the other end of the dining table. She reached into it, removed a folded piece of paper, and returned to her seat. She handed the paper to her niece.

Maggie unfolded the document and read its contents. "Oh, my," she said, stunned at the large sums of money Levy left to her and to her brother.

"Some of Brian's money is held in trust until he's graduated from high school. That's for his college fund. And more for graduate school, if he chooses to continue his education.

"The majority of his funds will be released to him when he turns thirty. Levy wanted him to inherit when he reached a certain level of maturity so he'd be sensible with the money. The rest is available to him now through you as trustee, for whatever he needs."

"That was extremely generous of Uncle Levy," Maggie said, her voice quivering.

Her aunt smiled. "We couldn't have children, as you know. We've loved you and Brian as our own."

Maggie looked at her aunt through moist eyes. "I've always been so grateful to you and Uncle Levy for paying for my college and graduate school, and for taking care of Brian while I went to classes. Were it not for you, I wouldn't have been able to get my education."

Mary squeezed her niece's hand. "We were more than glad to help you both financially, and with Brian. You did an excellent job raising him, Maggie."

"Thank you, Aunt Mary."

"I remember the day your mother brought Brian home from the hospital," Mary said. "She put him in a crib in his room and went to bed. He started crying and she didn't attend to him, so I went to see if she was all right. I stood in the doorway to her room, shocked to see her just lying there staring at the ceiling. You were at her bedside saying, *"The baby's crying, Mom. He won't stop. He needs something."* Your mother rolled on her side and turned her back on you. You walked into Brian's room, picked him up, and held him to you. From that moment on, you loved him and cared for him as if he were your own." Mary smiled, her eyes tearing. "I'm so grateful you did."

Maggie returned her aunt's smile. "Me, too."

Mary wiped her eyes with a napkin and, after a moment, brought the conversation back to the O'Neal estate. "As you already know, because your parents felt Dennis brought disgrace upon them, and because Patrick is deceased, they left you the brownstone, on which the mortgage has been paid. Also, their Ford Taurus and personal items. No money, however. They did leave a small amount to the church—"

The clamor of Brian and McKenna bursting through the back door, all energy and testosterone, interrupted Maggie's aunt. O.J., who'd been asleep on a chair near the sideboard, pricked his ears and came to attention. Maggie went to him to give him a few reassuring strokes on the head.

Mary said, "Well, that's all I had to tell you about the estate."

Maggie returned to the table. "Thank you," she said, touching her aunt's arm. "For everything."

Aunt Mary smiled. "You're welcome, dear."

Brian came into the dining room, grabbed a bottle of water and two éclairs, and plopped in a chair at the table. McKenna followed, choosing a beer and éclair and sitting across from Maggie. His wig was askew, and a five o'clock shadow showed through his makeup. O'Neal looked at him and the corners of her mouth turned upward.

After he and Brian had their snacks and spent some additional time engaging in baseball talk, McKenna stood to leave. He took the pillbox hat from his large dress pocket and put it on top of his wig.

Maggie walked him to the entry.

As McKenna opened the screened door to the front stoop, Brian called out, "Hey Mac! You hit pretty good, for a girl...."

CHAPTER FIFTY-FIVE

Ten o'clock Monday morning a few days after the O'Neal funeral, Maggie and McKenna sat in front of Nathan Shoemake's desk in the CIA building in McLean, Virginia.

"How close are you to locating and identifying all the buyers of the defense secrets being passed through DC Homicide, Mac?"

"Close." He turned to O'Neal and explained. "The traces have taken me longer than I anticipated because the buyers' ISP routes kept changing, and the program designer set up a pass-code scheme."

"What's a pass-code scheme?" Maggie asked.

"Something needed to enter into a buy. It's a number-letter sequence that allows a purchaser access to still another progression. One pass-code changes every four minutes, another every four hours. I also found the trace pattern and wrote a program called *Leap Frog* that will allow me to get one step ahead, instead of staying one step behind, the changing ISP configuration. The scheme is complex. Whoever set it up has connections bouncing all over the globe like a game of pin ball."

"Sounds like things are going well," Shoemake said, studying PASCAL for a moment. He then turned his attention to an opened file on his desk. "I've reviewed the documents Maggie got from Mark Hughes's antique chest." He pushed the folder containing two stapled sheets of paper across to his officers.

McKenna asked O'Neal, "Have you seen these yet?"

"No, I was just about to look at them when I got the call about my parents."

McKenna nodded and reached for the file.

Maggie moved her chair close to him and peered over his arm while he held the document. McKenna speed-read the text and let out a low whistle.

When Maggie finished reading, she said, "The governments involved in the depopulation plan are named here."

"Yes," Shoemake said.

"Hughes also states that he saw, but was unable to remove from the laboratory in Zambia, a roster of the specific individuals involved within each of these governments, as well as locations of other labs," McKenna said.

"Yes. We'll move to confirm the validity of Hughes's information," Shoemake said. He took back the file folder. "Mac, why don't you tell Maggie about your interview with the virologist in Atlanta."

McKenna did. He finished by relating that this contact, like Hughes, said that the names of the depopulation plan's participants within each of the governments were kept in an underground lab in Zambia, and that this facility also housed both HIV/AIDS viral strains and vaccines. He said the man highlighted USAMRIID as important to their investigation.

"Looks like that's your next order of business," Nathan said to McKenna. "After all the D-Tech buyers are identified."

"Actually, I could multitask—that is, set up USAMRIID while my traces run, finish D-Tech, then pay the lab a visit."

"Sounds like a good plan. I know the defense technology being passed now is false, and Maggie is being guarded and you only leave Langley in disguise, but I still want to bring Sjoda and Jaffey in—"

"All the buyers should be identified soon," McKenna said.

"Excellent," Shoemake said.

Nathan turned to O'Neal. "Maggie, I didn't tell you at the time, but you did a great job at the retirement dinner hooking Senator Sjoda. He made a play for you, just as we hoped he would. I'm glad we've been able to determine Sjoda's involvement in all this without the need for your getting close to him, as we first anticipated you might."

"Yes, sir."

"I want you to attend to things at home for a few days. You have a lot on your plate with the death of your parents and the repair of your brownstone. We can call you in if we need to.

"If any further HIV/AIDS research is required, you can do it from your laptop. For now, Mac can fly solo on the next part of this investigation." Shoemake paused before speaking again to O'Neal. "Have you found contractors yet?"

"Yes. I talked with the people at Georgetown Renovations. They've just finished a place down the street and another job they'd lined up is postponed pending financing, so they can start tomorrow."

"Good. I'll keep the guards in place during the day while you're there with the contractors. But I don't want you sleeping at home until we wrap up D-Tech and bring Sjoda in. He found out you were in Seaton and had a man watching you. For the time being, spend the night at your aunt's. I know Brian needs you now. The guards will continue to stay on duty there. And I trust you'll be alert at all times to the possibility of anyone following you."

"Yes, sir. And thank you for the security."

Shoemake nodded. "We picked up Sjoda's man, Hackett, and he's in our custody. He doesn't know how the senator found out about the red dress, so that's still a puzzle. He said Sjoda just gave him those photographs of McKenna."

Nathan put Hughes's file in his briefcase and turned again to his officers. "Mac, after you've finished D-Tech and return from USAMRIID, and Maggie, after you get the contractors going, I want you both to take a trip."

"Let me guess," McKenna said, a sourness creeping into his voice. "You want us to go to Zambia."

"Yes," COBOL said, giving PASCAL a no-argument look. "Zambia."

CHAPTER FIFTY-SIX

Two o'clock Tuesday afternoon, Reeves, still at home with now mitigated flu symptoms, lit a cigarette and switched on the tape player to listen to more of the recordings from the CIA's Directorate of Operation's office.

Shoemake's voice came to life. Nothing of interest. He fast-forwarded. Nothing. Fast forward. Shoemake's voice again.

"How close are you to locating and identifying all the buyers of—"

Reeves's phone rang. He hit PAUSE on the recorder and lifted the receiver. "Senator Sjoda."

"Senator?" His doctor. "I have the results of your blood tests."

"And?"

The doctor hesitated. He breathed an audible sigh and said, "You're HIV positive."

"You're sure."

"I had the tests run three times. You need to come in so we can plan a course of drug treatment for you."

"That won't be necessary."

"Senator—?"

Reeves disconnected. He fixed himself a drink, downed it, poured another, and sat in his chair. He lit a second cigarette, the first still burning in the ashtray. Taking a drag, he inhaled deeply, feeling that odd combination of warmth and coolness reach his lungs.

Sjoda thought about the news he'd just received from his doctor. *HIV. How? From the whores? No. He'd always been smart enough to use condoms. Still....*

An image of his brother came to mind. His too-loose clothing on an emaciated body. *Did Mark have the disease? He said his lover, Phillip had died. From AIDS?*

Reeves ran the scene of the last moments he'd spent with Hughes in his head. Stabbing his brother, the gash on his own hand, Mark's blood mixing with his....

The senator took another drag on his cigarette and finished his drink. He heaved himself out of the chair and went to the computer to e-mail a lab in Zambia.

That done and a fresh drink in hand, he returned to his recliner and got comfortable. He hit PLAY on the recorder.

"... the defense secrets that are being passed through DC Homicide, Mac?"

What? Fuck!

"Close...The traces have taken me longer...Pass-codes...."

McKenna! When was this recorded? He looked at the date and time written on the tape's cover. *Yesterday. The bastard's still alive. He's figured out the buyers' pass-code scheme....* Sjoda continued to listen.

"Sounds like things are going well. I've reviewed the documents Maggie retrieved from Mark Hughes's chest."

O'Neal got the documents! Shit!

Papers rustling, chair sliding across carpet. Silence.

"Oh my gosh. The governments..." *Maggie O'Neal. She's back in D.C!*

Impatient, Reeves hit FAST FORWARD.

Shoemake's voice again. "We'll move to confirm the validity of Hughes's information. Mac, why don't you tell Maggie about your interview with the virologist in Atlanta."

Virologist? Shit! Reeves continued listening. *USAMRIID! Crap. They know....*

Shoemake again. "Maggie, I didn't tell you at the time, but you did a great job at the retirement dinner hooking Senator Sjoda. He made a play for you, just as we'd hoped he would...."

What? She was a plant? Just doing a job to lure me? Fuck. Fuck fuck fuck!

Sjoda pitched himself from the chair and threw his brandy glass against a mirrored-door cabinet, breaking both and sending shards everywhere. He swung his girth around and roared. The recorder played on....

Shoemake to O'Neal, "...and want you to be free to tend to things at home for a few days. You have a lot on your plate...."

O'Neal's at home! The bitch. I'll get her....

The recorded conversation continued.

Bring me in? Never! They have Hackett....

Zambia. The lab in Zambia. Fuck fuck fuck!

Reeves thundered around his townhouse, bellowing, until he spent his energy and collapsed in the recliner. When his breathing calmed, he speed-dialed a phone number.

"Vice President Serling's office."

"Put him on. It's Senator Sjoda."

Serling came on the line. Reeves told him about the taped conversations in Shoemake's office. There was a long silence on the other end of the phone, and a click as the VP disconnected.

The senator got up and poured another drink. He gulped it and, anger rising in him again, slammed the glass on the bar. He balled his fists and exploded.

Sjoda stormed back to his phone and speed-dialed another number. When the man answered, he said, "Find Belosi in Seaton, Georgia. Eliminate him. Maggie O'Neal's at home. Send three men there and kill her. Make sure she's dead."

The man on the other end of the line asked a question.

"What? No. I don't want her brought to me. I want her dead."

CHAPTER FIFTY-SEVEN

It took McKenna forty minutes to hack into USAMRIID's mainframe. It took him an hour and a half to learn all he needed, and a few more hours to set up his plan.

First, he accessed and photo-memorized the building's layout, taking particular note of the locations of the various laboratories on each floor, including Biohazard Level 4, the most dangerous part of USAMRIID. Next, he reviewed the security procedures in place for entering the facility and biohazard areas, so his movements could be planned and rehearsed. Then he studied personnel records, learning names, occupations, job descriptions, years of service, vacation schedules, and routines.

He asked Claudia to get a biohazard suit from the Office of Technical Service, the department within the CIA responsible for outfitting disguises and providing other equipment for covert missions, to allow him to practice getting in and, especially out of, the suit in a hurry, as if he'd spent a career doing so.

He sent memos to various USAMRIID staff members, routing these through the Center for Disease Control's computer, and printed and laminated his own official identification, using the rather generic and non-memorable name of General John Anderson. He then hacked into the CDC's personnel records and embedded his undercover name and credentials within the database.

That done, McKenna checked on his D-Tech traces. Two hours later, he completed identifying and profiling all the buyers.

As if on cue, Shoemake walked into the Dungeon, bringing with him a welcomed cup of coffee.

"Got it," PASCAL said to COBOL, giving him a list of purchasers' names and locations in exchange for the coffee.

Nathan took a seat in the guest chair, read the list, and arched his silver brows. "Wow."

McKenna nodded and opened the lid on the Styrofoam cup. He sipped the steaming coffee. "I've put together profiles for each of these defense tech buyers," he said. He handed COBOL a stack of printouts containing information on individuals within China, North Korea, Iran, Pakistan, and other countries.

Nathan scanned the material. "Great job," he said. He looked at PASCAL. "And Mac?"

"Hmm?" McKenna peered over the rim of his coffee cup.

"Thanks."

"Sure." PASCAL gave a small grin, though it was hidden from COBOL's view behind the Styrofoam.

"I'll have Jaffey brought in. Sjoda, too," COBOL said, reaching for McKenna's phone.

"Wait," PASCAL said, his smile gone. "I want a half hour alone with the senator before you do."

CHAPTER FIFTY-EIGHT

Drunk and calmer now, Reeves landed in his chair and hit PLAY on his tape machine. He put lighter to cigarette and inhaled, smoke trailing in a spiral above his balding head.

The doorbell rang.

Sjoda pushed PAUSE. He swore over his chef and maid having their day off, and heaved his bulk out of the leather, knocking over the remainder of his drink in the process. He wove a path to the door and cracked it open to find Vice President Serling standing there.

"You didn't have to come," the senator said, slurring his words.

"Yes, I did." The Vice President walked into Sjoda's townhouse.

"Want a drink?"

"No." Serling followed the senator into the den.

"What should we do about Shoemake?" Sjoda asked, his voice thick. "And that oh-so-clever Jonathan McKenna. Nothing I've done has worked to kill the bastard who seems to have nine lives. I've got O'Neal covered."

"I'll take care of Shoemake and McKenna. That's not why I'm here. You e-mailed Zambia."

"So?"

"The rule was no contact."

“There are extenuating circumstances. And besides, those three at the CIA know about the lab anyway. We’ll have to make sure they don’t live to—”

“No contact.” Vice President Serling gave the Senator a steely look. “You've become a liability.”

Reeves scoffed.

It was the last sound he ever made.

CHAPTER FIFTY-NINE

McKenna approached the front door to Senator Sjoda's townhouse and found it ajar. He entered the home and listened, hearing only the whir of a central air conditioner. He walked through the living room, dining room, and kitchen, and found nothing. He went into the den.

Reeves Sjoda lay facedown on the floor, blood pooling from an area under his chest.

McKenna stared at the senator's unmoving form. *Grotesque in death as in life,* he thought.

Four letters on the hardwood floor appeared to have been written in Sjoda's blood by his own hand. The last letter ended in a serif and trailed red liquid to the senator's forefinger.

McKenna squinted at the message, trying to discern its meaning. It read,

M O S Q

He stared at the letters a moment longer, and lifted his head to look around the room. He saw Outlook Express opened on Sjoda's computer and he went to it. Taking a handkerchief from his pocket, he covered his finger before accessing the senator's most recently sent e-mail.

He scanned the addressee and text.

McKenna turned from the monitor and noticed Sjoda's tape recorder with the PAUSE button in the down position. He walked to it and, using his handkerchief, hit PLAY. The audio came to life with shuffling noises, his voice, O'Neal's.

Shoemake's office.

He hit REWIND and listened.

The whole conversation.

Everything.

He handkerchiefed the senator's phone and pushed the REDIAL button with a covered finger. A man answered, traffic noise in the background.

McKenna made his voice low and gravelly. "Repeat my last instructions to you."

The man did.

Maggie.

McKenna dropped the handset and ran out of the townhouse, stuffing his handkerchief in one pocket and pulling his cell phone from another. He dialed 911.

Static, then dead air.

He got into his car, screeched out of the driveway, and steered one-handed for several blocks, repeatedly dialing 911. He came to a stop in rush hour traffic and looked at the cell's screen. No service. He crawled a few more vehicle lengths and tried his phone again. Nothing. Spotting an opening at the curb, he angled into it and shut down the engine.

McKenna grabbed the CIA-issued Glock he kept with him and, exiting his car, ran the remaining four miles to Maggie's brownstone.

CHAPTER SIXTY

The arrow sang through the air and hit target-center. O'Neal grabbed another from her back quiver, pulled the bowstring, and sent it to its mark. At 5:00 p.m., the contractors left for the day and Maggie decided to take some time for her archery in her brownstone's backyard.

She'd sent the rear-door guard home earlier when he reported feeling ill. The front-door sentry, still on duty, would leave at 6:00 when she headed to her aunt's house.

O'Neal took a third arrow from her quiver, nocked it, and raised her bow. She heard a footfall in the grass behind her and spun.

A man stood pointing a gun at her.

Reacting, she loosed the arrow.

A cry of agony came from the gunman. The pistol flew from his hand and landed on the lawn.

In one smooth movement, O'Neal loosed a second shaft.

The man wailed.

Maggie left him incapacitated and ran into the brownstone. The smell of cheap cologne assailed her as she reached the hall telephone. Its wire dangled, pulled from the jack.

She hurried to the front stoop to alert the guard. He lay face up, eyes open in visionless death.

Cell phone. Upstairs.

O'Neal took the steps two at a time. She entered her bedroom and freed the phone from its holder clipped to her fanny pack.

She heard loud sounds below. Unfamiliar footsteps coming rapidly up the stairs.

O.J. jumped from the bed where he'd been sleeping. He rubbed his thin body against her legs as she punched 9-1- on her cell.

Maggie never got to finish the call.

CHAPTER SIXTY-ONE

McKenna bolted up O'Neal's front steps. A young man lay dead on the stoop.

He drew his Glock and, catlike, quickly entered the home. His eyes went to a large man climbing the stairs to the second floor, a gun held ready in his left hand.

A loud crash and the sound of items skittering across the floor came from overhead.

Maggie.

An orange blur streaked down the stairs and got tangled in legs, causing the ascending man to lose his footing. The intruder fell backwards and went head first down the steps. The cat maneuvered safely out of his way and fled into a partly opened closet door at the landing.

The floor shook underneath McKenna's feet as the gunman crashed to a stop, hitting his temple on the sharp corner of a contractor's metal tool chest stowed below. Blood flowed from his hairline.

McKenna leapt over the body and raced up the stairs, following sounds to a room. He arrived at the doorway to see a man standing cater-corner to Maggie across a queen-sized bed, his revolver pointed at her head, his finger on the trigger.

A gunshot sounded, followed by an explosion of red and a thud as a body hit the floor.

McKenna lowered his Glock and looked at O'Neal. "Are you all right?"

She closed her eyes, pressed her lips together, and nodded.

McKenna went to her and sat her on the bed. He stayed with her a moment before taking stock of the carnage.

His bullet had blown the intruder's head apart. Splatters of blood and bits of brain and bone matter covered parts of the floor, bedspread, and dresser on the entry side of the room. An open toolbox lay on its side near the man, its contents strewn over the floor.

The crash. Maggie had thrown the box at the gunman.

"There were supposed to be three men," McKenna said.

"One's in the backyard."

"Dead?"

She shook her head. "I heard loud noises. It sounded like they came from the stairs."

"O.J. tripped one of the men. The guy's dead, I'm sure, on the landing."

McKenna reached for Maggie's cell phone, flipped open on the bed. "I'm going out to the backyard. I'll call this in."

"Okay." Her throat sounded dry. "Is O.J. all right?"

"I saw him go into the closet at the bottom of the stairs."

"That's his hiding place. He always went there when my parents fought." She looked at McKenna as if she regretted what she'd just revealed. "Loud noises frighten him," she said, embarrassment in her voice.

McKenna extended his hand to her, and she took it and stood. They left the bedroom and descended the stairs.

Maggie stepped over the body on the landing and called to her cat. "O.J.? It's okay now, you can come out. It's over." She opened the closet.

McKenna headed for the backyard. As he pushed through the screened door, he heard moaning. He alighted the back steps and saw a man with his right hand pinned by an arrow to the yard's wooden tool shed. His left hand, partially covering his right, had been skewered with a second shaft.

McKenna dialed 911. When he finished his report, he called COBOL.

His boss came on the line. “Nathan Shoemake.”

“Go to a phone in another room and call me back. I’m on O’Neal’s cell.”

Two minutes later, Shoemake did.

“What’s up?” COBOL asked.

“Your office is bugged.”

“It’s been swept.”

“Yeah, well, I expect Sjoda put one of our security people in his pocket.”

McKenna told Nathan about the tape recordings in the senator’s townhouse and of what’d just transpired at Maggie’s.

“You both all right?”

“Yes. We’ll have to stay here until the police come and assess the crime scene. It may take awhile. I’ll let the aunt know.”

“All right. I’ll have a couple of our CIA officers contact the police detectives to apprise them in a bare bones, need-to-know way of our investigation. I’ll also send Zach Ellis over for extra security.”

“Ellis is a good idea, in case this isn’t over,” McKenna said. “And by the way, when your guys pick up Sjoda, they’ll need a body bag.”

“Did you—”

“No. He was already dead when I got there. And, he'd sent an e-mail forty minutes before I arrived.”

“To?”

“A lab in Zambia.”

CHAPTER SIXTY-TWO

McKenna reentered the brownstone after his phone conversation with COBOL. He heard O'Neal's deep sobbing and followed the sound to the living room. Police sirens wailed in the distance.

Maggie sat on the couch, a lifeless orange cat across her knees. Her head was bent over O.J.'s body, tears dripping onto the ancient fur.

McKenna went to her. He stood for a moment, looking down on her shiny desert-sunset hair, her grief painful to witness. He kneeled and touched her arm.

"I'm so sorry, Maggie." He tried to think of what else to say. "His age," he said gently, "probably a heart attack from the loud noises…the fright."

She continued crying.

After a few minutes, McKenna left O'Neal and went upstairs to her bedroom where the man lay dead on the floor. He opened some dresser drawers and found an old T-shirt among a small stack of neatly folded clothing.

He returned to Maggie and knelt in front of her. "I think he'd like this," he said, laying the T-shirt gently over the orange cat, leaving its head exposed.

Maggie sniffed and nodded.

McKenna stood and went to the dining room. He took a roll of paper towels from a holder and brought it back to O'Neal. He tore off a sheet and handed it to her.

She absently took it, wiped her face and blew her nose.

Sirens blared up the street and wound to a halt in front of the brownstone. Sounds of footsteps on the stoop and police radios were followed by a banging on the door.

"I'll take care of this," McKenna said.

CHAPTER SIXTY-THREE

Sjoda's men were removed, two dead and one alive, and McKenna gave the detectives a statement. He made arrangements to postpone O'Neal's report until morning.

Through all of the police activity, Maggie remained on the couch, rocking back and forth, O.J. in her lap.

The detectives left and darkness fell. McKenna accessed Mary Levy's phone number on O'Neal's cell and dialed. He held a brief conversation with the aunt and disconnected.

McKenna checked briefly on Maggie and went in search of a flashlight, locating one in a drawer. He then turned on the backyard spotlight by the rear door and walked down the back stairs and to the tool shed outside. Rooting through its contents, he found a shovel, saw, and some old lumber, and made a twelve-by-twenty-four-inch cross, which he carved into a staked point at the bottom. He took a waterproof pen from among a box of plant-identification sticks—Maggie's, he assumed—and wrote O.J. O'NEAL in block letters on the grave marker.

Carrying flashlight, shovel, and cross, he reconnoitered a spot at the back of the yard and dug a three-and-a-half-foot-deep hole, cat-sized in length and width, and pounded the grave marker into the ground behind.

McKenna reentered the brownstone and went to O.J.'s hiding place in the closet. He fished around inside until he found a well-used toy mouse, then walked into the dining room, still set up as a temporary kitchen, and took an unopened can of cat food from the sideboard. He put the cat toy and food in his pocket.

He went into the living room and approached O'Neal, sitting quietly now, stroking O.J.'s head with her thumb.

"Maggie?"

She raised her head, her eyes red-rimmed and hollow.

He touched her shoulder. "It's time to let him go," McKenna said gently. He worried the cat would go into rigor and add to O'Neal's distress.

Maggie looked at O.J. and sniffed. She continued to stroke his head.

"Come on now," he said softly. He reached for O'Neal's elbow and helped her stand.

She pulled O.J. to her chest in a hug.

McKenna coaxed Maggie to the backyard. He aimed the flashlight's beam a few feet in front of them as he guided her to the gravesite.

Maggie held her cat close.

McKenna watched her in the moonlight. A shadow crossed her face as her eyes went first to the hole, then to the grave marker.

"Oh," she said, tears welling again.

McKenna placed the flashlight on the ground, its beam directed toward the grave. He waited. After a moment, he said gently, "It's time."

Maggie clutched O.J. to her a minute longer, then loosened her grip and kissed the top of his ancient head.

McKenna took the cat from her arms and wrapped its orange body in the T-shirt. He kneeled in the dirt and lowered O.J. into the grave. Taking the two items he'd gathered earlier from his pocket, he placed the can of food and play-mouse next to the animal.

Maggie knelt and looked into the hole. She turned her head and met McKenna's eyes.

"The food is so he won't get hungry on his journey. The toy is so he'll have something to play with along the way."

She nodded, her face wet with tears.

McKenna took a fistful of dirt and handed it to Maggie. She sprinkled the soil gently on O.J.'s remains. McKenna scooped another handful and did the same.

"Oh, O.J.," Maggie whispered. She hiccupped back a sob.

McKenna gave her a moment before he stood and reached for the shovel. "I'll finish this," he said. "Would you like to go inside?"

Maggie shook her head. She got to her feet.

McKenna began covering the cat with small shovelfuls of dirt. While he worked, he wove a story to occupy O'Neal's mind.

"Once there was a prince," he said. "He was...um..."twenty-one years old. He was a nice young man, not spoiled at all, and everybody liked him. He had a beautiful white horse, named...ah...Snow."

Maggie sniffed as the grave filled with dirt.

"The prince was very fond of all animals," McKenna said, "but particularly of Snow. In fact, he and the horse were almost never apart. He loved Snow so much he even often slept in the barn with him."

McKenna stopped filling the grave and leaned on the shovel. He looked at Maggie, her head down, eyes on O.J.'s resting place. He stayed still for a moment before continuing.

"Sadly, one morning the prince awoke to find that Snow had passed away during the night. The young man was grief-stricken and inconsolable for months."

"Oh," Maggie said.

McKenna hurriedly resumed his story. "But one evening as the moon came to full light, the prince saw a beautiful white filly, a magical creature really, descending the hillside. The horse looked just like Snow, and strangely, she came right over to him and nuzzled his neck as if she knew him. The young man felt an immediate love for the animal, and threw his arms around her.

"Then the prince heard another horse's hooves, and turned his head to see a magical golden-orange colt come toward him from atop the same hill. The colt approached and nuzzled his neck, too, just like the filly had done. The young man hugged his mane, sensing something very familiar about the animal as he did, and experiencing, once again, an intense love."

Maggie looked at McKenna, a flash of interest in her eyes.

"The next morning, the prince sent his servants to all the local villages to find the owners of the young horses, but no one set any claim to them. So he kept both, loving them as much as he did Snow.

"What did he name the horses?" Maggie asked, just above a whisper.

"Oh. Well, let's see. He named the white filly...uh... Moonlight, and the golden-orange colt...Mango.

"In time, the prince became king, and the horses lived a very long time with him."

"Did he ever marry?" Maggie asked in a small voice.

The question surprised McKenna. He leaned on the shovel and regarded her a moment.

"Yes," he said. "He married and had two wonderful children. A boy and a girl. The queen and his children loved the horses just as much as did the king."

Maggie nodded, seemingly satisfied.

When McKenna finished filling the hole, Maggie knelt and smoothed the dirt. She rested her hand on top of the grave.

"Goodbye, O.J," she whispered. "Thank you for being my cat."

* * * * *

McKenna helped O'Neal to her feet and walked her into the brownstone, sitting her on the couch in the living room. She shivered even though the night was warm, so he took an afghan from the back of the sofa and wrapped it around her shoulders.

"Would you like me to fix you something to eat?" he asked.

She shook her head.

McKenna went into the dining room and found a bottle of Merlot in the sideboard, the same brand, he noted, as what Maggie'd had in the limousine the night of the retirement dinner. He opened it with a nearby corkscrew and, taking two clean coffee mugs from a tray, poured a good measure of wine into each.

He returned to O'Neal, sat beside her, and handed her a mug of wine. She accepted it and brought it to her lips.

They drank in silence.

When the cups were drained, McKenna refilled hers and gave it to her before going out to the front stoop to speak with Zach Ellis, who'd just arrived for guard duty.

McKenna looked at the CIA officer. Late twenties, height about five foot eight, broad, athletic build, intelligent brown-black eyes, skin the color of coffee beans. "Don't let anybody in," he said. "Not even a priest."

Zach nodded his understanding.

McKenna came back into the living room and found O'Neal lying on her side, her feet on the floor, her head on the arm of the couch, asleep. Her fingers were entwined in the handle of the mug of wine. He extricated the cup from her hand and put it on a table.

He went upstairs and got a pillow from the room he easily identified as Brian's from the baseball posters on the walls.

When McKenna returned to O'Neal, he gently lifted her head and slid the pillow underneath. He slipped off her shoes, moved her feet to the couch and took the afghan, which had fallen to the floor, and placed it over her.

He walked into the dining room, removed the cat's used dish, and went upstairs to wash it in the bathroom sink, drying it with a towel. When he came back downstairs, he put the dish away in the sideboard and refilled his mug.

McKenna returned to the living room and eased himself into a chair. He sipped his wine, watching over O'Neal as she slept.

CHAPTER SIXTY-FOUR

"Mac told me everything," Nathan said to Maggie. "I'm so sorry about O.J. I know how much he meant to you."

O'Neal looked at Shoemake through red eyes and nodded. She and McKenna sat in front of his desk at the CIA.

"I had my office swept this morning by a new-hire," COBOL said. "The bugs were found and removed. The security guy confessed to being in Sjoda's pocket. And speaking of the senator, Mac, have you told O'Neal?"

McKenna shook his head and turned to Maggie. "Reeves Sjoda is dead," he said.

She raised her eyebrows. "How?"

"Murdered. I finished D-Tech yesterday and went to see Sjoda before our guys picked him up. The door to his townhouse was open when I got there. I found him on the floor in his den. He'd written 'M-O-S-Q' on the hardwood in his own blood.

"MOSQ?" COBOL asked. "You didn't tell me that part."

"Yes, well. A lot happened last night."

"I've not gotten the scene-of-crime photos yet," Shoemake said. "I wonder what the significance of MOSQ is? Either of you have any ideas?"

His officers shook their heads.

"We claimed national security jurisdiction over the police in this investigation, and our guys dusted for prints in the Senator's townhouse," Nathan said. "Mostly Sjoda's, of course. Some of the prints belonged to his housekeeper and chef, as is to be expected. Others to prostitutes with arrest records. None of yours though, Mac."

"Didn't need to touch the doorknob. Used a handkerchief for his computer keys, tape recorder, and telephone."

"Good," Shoemake said. "On my request, our men worked through the night on this. They got perfect thumb, index and ring finger prints on the inner doorknob."

McKenna asked, "Belonging to...?"

"Vice President Serling," Shoemake said.

His officers raised their brows.

"We also pulled Sjoda's telephone records detailing the calls made since you last checked them, Mac. The senator phoned Serling approximately a half hour before being killed, according to the time you arrived at his home and found him dead."

"He e-mailed the lab in Zambia about ten minutes before he called the VP, then," McKenna said.

Claudia buzzed. "The senator's crime-scene photos just arrived, sir."

"Bring them right in," Shoemake said.

Claudia came into the office and gave Nathan a manila envelope. She patted Maggie on the shoulder before she left.

Shoemake quickly reviewed the photographs and handed them to his officers.

O'Neal and McKenna studied several images of Reeves's murder scene. Each showed MOSQ written clearly in blood letters.

Maggie looked up from the photos. "Serling could have visited that townhouse another time. Other than the fingerprints on the inner doorknob, is there additional evidence implicating the vice president in the senator's homicide?" she asked Nathan.

"Yes," he said. "Our guys reviewed Sjoda's surveillance tapes. He had outdoor security cameras—well hidden, I'm told—and at the approximate time of death, Serling visited the senator's home, stayed five minutes, eighteen seconds, and left. A canvass of the neighborhood revealed that a limousine pulled up to Sjoda's townhouse, and the VP stepped out of the vehicle and went inside. So we have the fingerprints, surveillance tapes, and eyewitnesses.

"Serling didn't disguise himself or his movements," McKenna said. "He even had a chauffeur drive him to the senator's. Pretty cocky of him. It amazes me that people of power seem to think they are immune to getting caught for their crimes."

Nathan agreed. "You were on the security camera tapes, too, Mac. Seems the record of your visit's been erased, though," he said, wearing a sly expression. "You showed at Sjoda's about seven minutes after the vice president left."

"We don't know when the senator listened to the taped conversations from this office," McKenna said. "He could have heard them before he phoned Serling and told the VP about the contents of the recordings."

"Yes. In fact—"

Claudia buzzed in again. "Urgent call for you, sir."

Shoemake picked up the receiver and listened. He hung up the phone, his face ashen.

"Someone just took a shot at my wife coming out of our Foreign Resources Branch building."

Maggie drew in a breath. "Is she—"

"She's okay. She's on her way to the safehouse in Great Falls. I'll join her there later. I want you to spend the remaining nights before your trip to Africa at the safehouse, too, Maggie. I'll have your aunt and Brian relocated to a secure place as well." He turned to McKenna. "Mac, when are you going to USAMRIID?"

"Tomorrow morning."

"All right. You should come to the safehouse with us this evening."

"I'll stay in the Dungeon for now, and move to Great Falls after I come back from USAMRIID."

"I don't think that's the wisest decision."

"I do," McKenna said, his face set.

COBOL gave PASCAL a displeasured look, but didn't pursue the conversation. He spoke instead to O'Neal. "Maggie, can you be ready to leave for Zambia a week from Monday? That'll give Claudia and I time to get all the arrangements made for your trip."

"Yes. "I'll turn some of the brownstone renovations over to Derek Weisner. He's offered to help. I'll give him my aunt's phone number, and leave him my list of wall color and cabinet choices and such. I just want to make sure he's kept safe."

"I'll see to it," Shoemake said. "Give Derek my telephone number as well." He turned to PASCAL. "You'll be ready to leave for Africa then, too, Mac?"

"Looks that way," McKenna said, sounding none-too-happy about it.

"Good," COBOL said, ignoring PASCAL's mood. "From here on in, we'll call this investigation Operation MOSQ."

CHAPTER SIXTY-FIVE

McKenna pulled up to the guardhouse at the entrance to USAMRIID, the United States Army Medical Research Institute of Infectious Diseases at Fort Detrick, Maryland. He rolled down the window.

A man in army fatigues approached his vehicle, and, noting the four-star general's uniform on the gray-haired driver, saluted crisply. McKenna handed the young man his credentials, and the guard checked his name against a clip-boarded roster.

"Thank you, General Anderson," the man said, returning the papers. "Have a nice day." He saluted again.

The gate opened and McKenna entered the compound. He turned right, heading to a parking lot next to a yellow concrete building, the size of which approximated his sister-in-law's ten-acre farm in Michigan. The structure had only two windows on the front side; one serviced a stairwell, the other a lobby. Ventilation pipes rose from the building's roof to emit heat-sterilized, biohazard air.

He parked his car and went into the facility. A front desk guard checked his credentials and allowed him through.

Playing the role of General Anderson, McKenna headed down a corridor of USAMRIID, the military's institute of medical defense. Here microbiologists, biochemists, entomologists and veterinary pathologists studied the characteristics of bacteria, viruses, and toxins that could threaten American troops, and developed antidotes against infectious diseases and biological weaponry.

The Institute's charter did not include creating lethal strains of bacteria and viruses. Such offensive uses of microorganisms against America's enemies had been outlawed in 1969 by Executive Order, signed by President Nixon.

McKenna reached the end of the corridor and turned a corner. He paused and went quickly into an Alpha brainwave state to withdraw his energy, making himself as if invisible to those around him, a technique he learned in the Mind Management class he and Nathan took in their early CIA years. He continued his trek through the photo-memorized halls, passing by technicians in lab coats and soldiers in fatigues, none of whom acknowledged his presence.

He walked into a centralized laboratory housing white-coated men and women sitting at microscopes, some observing cellular activity on computer monitors. Enlarged photographs of viruses and bacterium were taped to tan, cement-blocked walls. A machine enclosed in a beige metal casing about nine-feet long by four high and wide hummed in the center of the room. On the unit's side were the words BIO-GUARD BLOOD.

McKenna continued on, exiting the area opposite to where he'd entered, and came to another corridor with glass-windowed laboratories on either side. As he passed these rooms, he saw lab-coated workers within injecting liquids into vials or hovering over centrifuges.

Toward the end of the hall, he stopped at an office on the right. He ran his general's identification through the door's side scanner and heard the lock click open. Still in Alpha, he took Latex gloves from his pocket, snapped them on, and went into the room.

McKenna stood in the office of Colonel Wheeler, head of the Institute's Infectious Diseases Division, currently out of country.

He stepped to the colonel's computer and checked for cables. The system was a stand-alone, used for internal records only with no Internet connection. He booted up and input several password possibilities gleaned from information he'd obtained from the man's home computer and dossier: his birthday, his wife's name, those of his children. No access. He keyed the moniker for the colonel's German shepherd dog, "Shogun," and the screen came to life.

McKenna opened files, scanning and photo-memorizing their contents. Twenty minutes later, he shut down the system and left the office.

He checked his watch. 12:10 p.m. Lunch hour. His plan held; the labs would be mostly empty.

McKenna walked a maze of corridors and entered a room that housed a bank of refrigerators. Blue panels with control dials were set into the left front of each white unit. Biohazard symbols, red background with three black rings joined at the middle and another black ring centered behind, were pasted on several doors.

He opened a refrigerator and saw a second door made of glass. He peered through. Clear flasks, about eight inches in height, occupied the interior. Pulling the inside door open, he removed a flask with his Latex-gloved hand. He swirled the red liquid contained within, and bits of what he knew to be viral tissue rose from the bottom. McKenna read the number written in black on the container and checked it against the list of memorized sequences from the colonel's computer to learn its contents. He replaced the flask and shut the inner and outer doors.

He went to a neighboring refrigerator and removed several more vials, noting their numbers. He put each back and closed the unit.

Still in Alpha, he left the area and descended a set of stairs to a lower maze of corridors, heading for Bio-containment Level 4.

* * * * *

McKenna scanned his identification, keyed a code, and entered a small changing room. He removed his Latex gloves and everything else he wore, including underwear, watch, and ID, and placed it all in a locker, careful not to leave fingerprints. He took a green surgical suit, cap, and white socks from a shelf, and put on the clothing.

Dressed in scrubs, he elbowed through a door into Bio-Safety Level 2, feeling the immediate difference of a room kept under negative pressure. If a leak occurred, he knew, air would flow in against the bio-hazardous material rather than out into the surrounding area.

McKenna next went into a shower stall containing the soap and shampoo he'd use later. Ultra violet light flooded the space, and he stood in its glow. In preparation for his visit to the Institute, he'd learned that UV kills viruses by bursting their genetic materials, rendering the microorganisms unable to replicate.

After UV decontamination, he pushed through a door on the other side of the shower into Bio-Safety Level 3, a room housing a desk, chair, telephone, and a shelf holding protective supplies needed for entering Biohazard Level 4.

He took Latex gloves from the shelf and put them on before sliding his hands into yellow surgical ones. He then got tape from the desk and wrapped his cuffs, sealing shirt to gloves, pants to socks.

Taking a blue biohazard "spacesuit" from a rack, McKenna stepped into it and pulled it up around his chest. He put his arms into the sleeves and slid his rubber-gloved hands into the thick green ones attached to the suit. He slipped his socked feet into green rubber boots. Next, he placed a helmet with a clear plastic faceplate over his head and closed the zipper, connecting the bonnet to the suit.

His breath fogged the plastic, and he reached for a coiled yellow hose on the wall, plugging it into a valve on the right side of the spacesuit at the waist. Air roared in his ears and his faceplate cleared. The suit inflated to stiff.

McKenna turned to the stainless steel door that separated him from Level 4. He noted the red and black biohazard symbol pasted there, and the words, CAUTION, BIOHAZARD, DO NOT ENTER WITHOUT WEARING VENTILATED SUIT.

He unplugged the air hose, went through the steel entry, and with fogged faceplate, stepped into a second shower. He pulled a chain and wall nozzles spewed germicidal disinfectant onto his spacesuit.

After de-con, McKenna entered Bio-Level 4 through the shower's back door. He connected an air hose to his waist valve and walked an epoxy-sprayed, cement-blocked corridor, its electrical outlets puttied with a gluey substance.

He came to a glass-windowed door and peered inside at dozens of caged chimpanzees. He went into the room, unhooking and reattaching his air coil. The chimps became excited at his presence and moved around within their wire-mesh enclosures, hooting and chittering.

McKenna remembered what he'd seen on Colonel Wheeler's database. *Chimpanzees have a 98.6% genetic similarity to humans, but don't get AIDS*. He scanned the cages looking for evidence of illness. He didn't see any and left the room, disconnecting and reconnecting air hoses.

He walked the hall to the length of the coil and peered into a thick-glassed laboratory. A woman in a blue spacesuit sat within, her arm inserted into a rubber tunnel inside a large aquarium-like glass cage. She held a spray can, aiming it at two beige-faced monkeys who looked at her curiously.

McKenna glanced above the doorway to read the sign that indicated the infectious agent being tested, then brought his attention back to the activity in the laboratory.

The researcher now sprayed the aerosol into the glassed enclosure. The monkeys backed into a corner. They clung to each other, their eyes wide.

McKenna recalled his conversation with the virologist in Roswell Park and put the scene in front of him together with that interview and what he'd found on the colonel's computer. *Airborne*. He shook his head.

He investigated the remainder of this section of Biohazard Level 4, reading the signs posted over each door to validate the German virologist's claims.

Afterward, McKenna exited the area into the disinfectant shower. He pulled the chain and stood while chemicals sprayed him for seven minutes. He left de-con and removed the spacesuit and surgical scrubs, putting them into marked stainless steel receptacles before stepping through another door into a second shower. He soaped his body and shampooed his hair. Exiting the shower, he dried himself, redressed in the general's uniform, and put on a fresh pair of Latex gloves.

Still in Alpha, McKenna came out of the changing room, retraced his route through the Institute's corridors and stairs, and left the building.

He got into his car and drove away from USAMRIID, his findings weighing heavily on his mind.

CHAPTER SIXTY-SIX

Zann carried bowls of shrimp sautéed in wine sauce, fettuccine noodles, and broccoli to the safehouse's kitchen table. "Isn't Mac coming to dinner?" she asked.

"He's accessing satellite images of Zambia." Nathan uncorked a bottle of Albarino wine, a Spanish white. "He said to start without him."

Maggie put the salad she'd made onto plates while Shoemake poured the wine. The three sat down to dinner and engaged in companionable conversation.

Fifteen minutes later, McKenna came in and joined his colleagues. He helped himself to food, but ate his meal in relative silence.

* * * * *

After the berries-and-cream dessert, McKenna stood and cleared the dishes. He began rinsing and putting them in the dishwasher.

"Why don't I finish cleaning up while you three have your meeting?" Zann said. "I'll put coffee on."

McKenna accepted her offer and left the kitchen. He returned a couple minutes later with satellite images of the laboratory in Zambia, and took a seat at the cleared table across from O'Neal and Shoemake. He pushed a photograph toward his co-workers.

Maggie and Nathan studied it.

"The lab appears well secured," O'Neal said, pointing to the six guards outside the facility.

"Doesn't seem much of a place," Shoemake said.

"No. That might support Mark Hughes's claim that part of it is underground," McKenna said.

Shoemake agreed.

"I wonder what these are?" Maggie pointed to six large round objects on the north side of the building.

Shoemake peered at the photo. "Mac, do you have a closer shot of these?"

McKenna picked an image from the stack and handed it across to Nathan and O'Neal.

"They look like covered swimming pools," Maggie said, "with some sort of ductwork coming out from the top and then leading underground."

"Certainly worth investigating when you're there," Shoemake said. "The lab seems to be located in a tropical area of Zambia. I'm assuming you've both begun taking your anti-malaria meds? The drug has to get into your bloodstream a few days before exposure to malaria-carrying mosquitoes."

His officers nodded.

"Good." Nathan got up from the table and went to his open briefcase. He removed some envelopes and came back to his seat.

"I have the details of your trip," he said. "You're flying commercial." He slid airline tickets to O'Neal and McKenna. "Monday, a car will pick you up at Langley and take you to Dulles. Your Glocks are being sent to the American Embassy in Lusaka, Zambia, by diplomatic pouch. I have a substantial amount of cash for both of you for any contingencies, and credit cards. Also undercover passports and other documentation supporting your aliases, of which you have several." He gave each of his operatives a packet.

"Claudia has you booked into the Holiday Inn in Lusaka for Tuesday and Wednesday night under your primary cover names, which are Kate Winters and Alistair McCrae. The Holiday Inn has a courtesy bus that'll transport you from the airport to the hotel.

"You'll have a day in the city before meeting with Cecil Pearson, the American Embassy attaché, at seven o'clock Thursday morning. That'll give you a chance to exchange currency, pick up supplies, and adjust to the six-hour time difference.

"Pearson's arranged a charter flight to take you from Lusaka to Mbala, and a four-wheel-drive rental from there. You should be able to get in and out of the lab in a couple of hours and back to Lusaka by the next day. Claudia left the time of your return flights open." Nathan looked from Maggie to McKenna. "Any questions?"

His officers shook their heads.

"Okay," Shoemake said. He leaned back in his seat. "You want to fill us in on your trip to USAMRIID, Mac?"

McKenna gave a short nod.

Zann brought coffee and tea, and placed cream, sugar and lemon on the table. She patted her husband on the shoulder and smiled to the group before exiting the room.

McKenna poured himself a cup of coffee and left it black. He glanced across the table at O'Neal, who bobbed a teabag in a cup of hot water, looking at him expectantly. He drank some of his beverage before relating his visit to USAMRIID.

"So what you saw in Level Four validated the claims the German virologist made?" Shoemake asked.

"Yes." McKenna told them about the airborne virus test. For Maggie's sake, he omitted the detail of the monkeys being on the business end of the aerosol.

"I also accessed Colonel Wheeler's computer for HIV/AIDS vaccines, and there were several listed. I checked refrigerated vials against the numbered references in his closed system."

"And?" Shoemake asked.

"One vaccine appears to contain live attenuated viruses, or LAVs, from blood of non-progressors."

"Non-progressors are people who contract HIV but don't advance to AIDS," O'Neal said. "Normally an HIV LAV wouldn't be safe, according to the widely accepted medical belief, because injecting the retrovirus into humans would cause an attack on the immune system, the very thing that a typical live attenuated virus is designed to stimulate. But if the LAVs are from non-progressors—"

"They might stop HIV from proliferating," Shoemake said. He looked out the kitchen window for a moment. He turned back to his officers and asked, "I wonder who the human test subjects are for the non-progressor live attenuated viruses?"

"There was a reference on Wheeler's computer to test subjects in Zambia."

"So that's something else to look into when you get there."

"Yes," McKenna said. "And, according to the data on the colonel's system, the non-progressor vaccine is cheap and easy to make."

"But it's not being distributed," Shoemake said.

"No." McKenna drained his coffee. He reached for the pot and poured more into his cup. "They're also extracting something from Chimpanzees at USAMRIID." He told Shoemake and O'Neal what he'd found on the Institute's computer about chimps.

"The animals are ninety-eight-point-six percent like us genetically, and they don't get the disease?" Shoemake asked.

"That's right," McKenna said.

"Interesting. Okay, what else?"

"They're doing something with the CCRF gene."

O'Neal added hot water to her cup and re-dunked her teabag. "The mutant gene from ancestors who survived the black plague. Those who have it don't get AIDS," she said.

"Yes," McKenna said. "The virologist told me the same."

"Were there any cure-rate statistics in Wheeler's database?" Nathan asked.

"Yes. Cross-referenced by number only, but showing results of ninety through ninety-eight percent."

"Impressive," Shoemake said.

"Yup." McKenna gathered the reviewed satellite images into a pile.

"Anything else you have to tell us about USAMRIID?" COBOL asked.

"No, that about sums it," PASCAL said.

"All right."

The men went silent and sat drinking their coffee.

"What's happening in regard to Vice President Serling being charged with the murder of Reeves Sjoda?" O'Neal asked. She squeezed lemon into her tea.

"He's out on bond," Nathan said. "He hired a top notch attorney, of course, and disclosed nothing when questioned. The evidence against him is overwhelming, though."

"Which means squat with him being the VP," McKenna said. "This administration's seen to it before that its staff avoided indictment for criminal activity. It seems quite adept at breaking laws and getting away with it."

"True," Shoemake said.

"So, we know nothing further about why Serling killed Sjoda," McKenna said. "The senator e-mailed the lab in Zambia and made a call to the VP right before he was murdered. And, since I found the pause button engaged on his tape machine as I mentioned before, Sjoda most likely had just been listening to the recorded conversations from your office, Nathan."

"The content of which covered D-Tech, the HIV/AIDS depopulation terrorist plan, and the lab in Africa," Shoemake said.

"Yes. We can probably assume, therefore, Sjoda did talk with Serling about those tapes, which may implicate the VP in the passing of our defense technology, or in an involvement in the HIV/AIDS infection plan, or both," McKenna said.

"And Zann was targeted with a bullet right after Vice President Serling visited the senator," Maggie said. "Unless it was random, we might presume that either Sjoda ordered her killed before he died, or Serling took over the job of eliminating those who know about D-Tech, or the

HIV/AIDS depopulation scheme and the lab in Zambia, or are associated with people who do."

"Yes," Shoemake said. "And if Serling did take over, it means your safety in Zambia could be compromised."

His operatives exchanged a glance.

"Because," COBOL continued, "according to Sjoda's phone records, the senator didn't make any other calls after he e-mailed Zambia and called Serling, except the one you redialed, Mac, to learn of his men going after Maggie."

"True," McKenna said. "So it is most likely Serling's become our nemesis. And, he'll probably alert his people to expect a breach at the lab in northern Zambia."

"Yes. He might also have someone keeping a lookout for your arrival in Lusaka, though only Claudia and I, you two, and Cecil Pearson know your undercover names."

"Right," McKenna said.

"So watch your backs while you're in Africa. It could get nasty."

Maggie and McKenna agreed.

"Any other comments or questions?" Shoemake asked.

His officers shook their heads.

"Okay, then, Operation MOSQ is a go."

PART II
ZAMBIA, AFRICA
AUGUST

CHAPTER SIXTY-SEVEN

The plane leaving Dulles Airport reached cruising altitude and the pilot turned off the seatbelt sign. The two-legged flight to Lusaka, Zambia would take twenty-one hours, with a twelve-hour stopover in London.

McKenna made sure he didn't get a seat assignment next to O'Neal, and to his relief, she didn't question him about it. Being on his way to Africa with this woman, instead of his wife, darkened his already uncivilized mood.

His thoughts drifted back to his honeymoon with Grace in Kenya. A picture-taking safari, his gift to her. She'd been a freelance photojournalist and wanted to capture on film the Continent's wild animals in their natural habitat.

McKenna caught himself reminiscing and brought his mind to present. He looked across the aisle at O'Neal, who seemed engrossed in a book titled *Plants of Africa*. Two more volumes sat on the empty seat next to her, one on Zambian insects, the other a guidebook. A couple of maps lay there as well, and occasionally she referenced them and made a penned notation.

He issued a sigh and opened his laptop to key in code. After a few minutes his concentration waned, and he looked once more at his co-worker.

She'd changed markedly since her trip to Seaton, and he wondered why. She'd been annoyingly self-assured of late, seeming to stand taller within herself.

He had no intention of asking her about it or attempting to get to know her on a personal level. They'd kept their distance at the safehouse in Great Falls, McKenna spending most of his time with his computer, Maggie with Zann or Nathan. And, this was only to be a quick trip in and out of Zambia before getting back to his life in Michigan.

A flight attendant interrupted his thoughts, offering him a choice of beverages. He waved her off.

McKenna tried entering a few more lines of code, but became agitated and stopped. He slumped in his seat and attempted to sleep, but his mind refused him.

CHAPTER SIXTY-EIGHT

Maggie O'Neal and Jonathan McKenna arrived in Lusaka, Zambia, on Tuesday at 7:15 p.m., and took the courtesy bus to the Holiday Inn Garden Court, a 155-room white stucco building with beautiful landscaping, on the corner of Independence Avenue.

They'd spoken little to each other since leaving D.C., and now barely mumbled a "good night" as they headed to their separate rooms.

* * * * *

The next morning, O'Neal rented a car at the Holiday Inn's Avis and toured the city, surprised to find the center of Lusaka so modern and metropolitan.

She stopped at a Barclay's bank to exchange her U.S. money for Zambian currency at the rate of 3.486 Kwacha per American dollar, then went to the crowded South Cairo Road Market to browse through indigenous crafts of intricate baskets, bright cotton clothes, and pottery. She lunched at the Polo Grill and visited the Namwane Art Gallery to look at Zambian paintings and sculpture.

After the museum, Maggie located a Checker's Supermarket and bought bottled water, coffee and tea, and canned goods. She finished her afternoon at The Cathedral of the Holy Cross, where she lit votive candles and said prayers for Brian, Aunt Mary, and for her mission to the north of this country.

Upon returning to her room at the Holiday Inn, Maggie e-mailed her brother and aunt before going downstairs to McGintry's Irish Pub for dinner.

She entered the hotel's restaurant and saw McKenna sitting in a corner eating a burger, a bottle of beer next to his open laptop. He didn't acknowledge her presence, and O'Neal left him to his meal.

Maggie dined alone, looking through her guidebook.

CHAPTER SIXTY-NINE

McKenna and O'Neal were picked up from the Holiday Inn at 6:45 the next morning and brought to the United States Embassy on the corner of Independence and United Nations Avenues.

Cecil Pearson, Attaché, greeted the CIA operatives in his office with a limp handshake and glances to the floor. "I'm afraid there's been a change of plans," he said. He tattooed the fingers of his right hand against his thigh. "The pilot's been delayed in Livingstone and—"

"We'll fly commercial," McKenna said.

"That's not possible." Pearson shifted his slight frame and looked sideways. "All flights have been grounded. Something about the ozone layer being too thin to fly."

"Grounded for how long?" McKenna asked.

The attaché shrugged. "Indefinitely, I'm told."

McKenna glared at him.

"However," Pearson said, "we've provided you with a car."

McKenna scowled. "We have to *drive*?"

"It's nothing really, only two days. You can overnight in Mpika. We've secured a reservation for you at the Malashi Executive Guesthouse. It's quite nice. I've already had your bags put in the vehicle."

"You've made alternative arrangements very quickly," McKenna said. "Efficient of you by seven o'clock in the morning."

The attaché's eyes flitted briefly to the CIA officers.

"I need to use your computer to e-mail Nathan Shoemake," McKenna said. "My laptop's in my rucksack."

"I'm afraid our systems are down at the moment."

"A lot of glitches in Lusaka today," McKenna said. "The phone, then."

Pearson frowned, but gestured toward his desk. "I'm late for a meeting. Your Glocks are in there," he said, pointing to a pouch on his blotter, " and your vehicle's in the lot. It's a jeep." He handed McKenna a car key on a chain. The license plate number showed through the orange plastic tag. "Have a nice trip." The attaché turned on his heel and left the room.

McKenna glowered after him and went to the phone to place an overseas call to Nathan's office. He'd leave a message, knowing Shoemake wouldn't be there at that hour because of the time difference.

A digitalized voice came on the line. "The number you have reached has been disconnected."

"What the—?"

Maggie looked at him in question, but he ignored her.

He called Langley again and got the same result.

He tried Nathan's cell. "We're sorry, but this cellular number is no longer in service."

McKenna did a slow burn. He picked up the diplomatic pouch from the desk and opened it, satisfied at least over seeing the two Glocks and extra ammo inside. "Let's go," he said.

CHAPTER SEVENTY

A decade-old army Jeep sat by itself in the corner of the embassy parking lot. The license plate number matched the one on the orange key chain.

"No top," McKenna said.

His olive-green rucksack and O'Neal's tan suitcase were on the backseat, hers about five-and-a-half feet long by two-and-a-half wide by ten inches deep. McKenna frowned at its strange shape.

He put the diplomatic pouch containing the Glocks on the floor by the passenger seat and went around to the front of the vehicle. He opened the Jeep's hood and did a quick but thorough inspection.

"Checking for a car bomb?" O'Neal asked.

"Yes, and a tracking device."

Maggie pulled a working flashlight from the glove compartment and looked beneath the dash. She reported finding nothing suspicious, and gave the light to McKenna.

He got on the ground and surveyed the undercarriage. After a few moments, he slid behind the steering wheel and returned the light to O'Neal, who stowed it back in the glove compartment before settling into the passenger's side.

Maggie secured her seatbelt and squinted at the sky. She took a pair of sunglasses and a canvas hat from her vest pocket.

McKenna did the same.

"At least we're wearing long sleeves and pants," Maggie said. "I have sunscreen in my suitcase."

"Later."

McKenna started the Jeep and drove from the embassy lot, heading toward the Big North Road. He didn't need to consult a map; he'd photo-memorized the entire country from topography charts and satellite images. Major and minor roads, lakes, rivers, elevations, towns, villages, and even connecting footpaths were stored in his mind.

* * * * *

A bank's marquee displayed the temperature in Celsius, and Maggie converted it in her head. Fifty-nine degrees. She crossed her arms against the chill of riding in the open air and watched the modern buildings of central Lusaka give way to dilapidated hovels on the outskirts of the city. Small, often windowless shacks made of corrugated metal, plywood, plastic tarps, and board remnants fit together like mismatched puzzle pieces. Scrawny chickens and rib-thin dogs roamed the dusty yards, while women shucked corn or squatted outside washing dishes in shallow pans of water.

Billboards with HIV/AIDS messages appeared every mile or so. *Use Condoms to Prevent AIDS. People with AIDS Deserve Compassion. Follow the ABCs of Sex: Abstinence, Be Faithful, Condoms.*

Away from the city the landscape turned to dried grasses the color of khaki, broken by islands of green scrub and stunted acacia trees. The smooth road gave way to potholed pavement, and McKenna, with set jaw, downshifted and swerved around the ruts.

They passed occasional villages, and O'Neal saw clotheslines drooped with frayed T-shirts and faded dresses. Here and there barefooted children stood in doorways with big eyes, sucking dirty thumbs and clinging to women's skirts. Others played listlessly with rocks and sticks in the dirt.

The poverty tugged at Maggie's heart.

Alongside every village, O'Neal saw dozens of rectangular dirt mounds spreading into the countryside. She presumed these were graves, filled, most likely, with victims of AIDS.

They traveled on.

Maggie pulled her hat lower on her forehead. "Ready for sunscreen?" she asked.

McKenna waved her off.

"Want me to drive a while?"

He shook his head.

The distances between villages increased. McKenna slowed for pedestrians and livestock in the road as they neared a cluster of round, thatched-roofed mud huts. Women worked in surrounding fields while men sat in groups, looking glaze-eyed as they passed around leaves they put into their mouths and chewed.

Cat leaves, Maggie surmised, from the compound Cathinone, found in certain East African evergreens and having addictive properties similar to Methamphetamine. She sighed and looked away from the scene.

They drove on.

Three hours north of Lusaka, McKenna tapped the petrol gauge and made a sound of disgust.

"What's the matter?"

"The gauge seems stuck. It hasn't moved since it read half full. I've no idea how much fuel's left in the tank."

O'Neal knit her brow.

"There should be a petrol station about thirty-five kilometers up the road just south of Chifwefwe," McKenna said.

"Are you hungry?"

"Yes."

"I have some canned food in my suitcase."

"Okay. I could use a stretch, too."

Maggie nodded.

McKenna pulled off the road and parked under a mopane tree, its butterfly-shaped leaves providing shade from Zambia's unyielding sun. He turned off the ignition. The Jeep shuddered for a moment before quitting.

After the CIA officers walked around for a few minutes, Maggie leaned into the backseat and unzipped her suitcase to get sunscreen and food. She pulled back the top, wrinkled her brow, and moved some things around.

"McKenna? My laptop's missing."

"What?"

"My laptop. It's not here."

McKenna came closer to the Jeep and looked into the backseat at O'Neal's opened suitcase. "You brought your bow and arrows."

"Yes."

He let out a sigh.

"Do you have your computer?" Maggie asked. She re-zipped her luggage.

McKenna lifted his rucksack out of the vehicle and put it on the ground. Squatting, he opened the flap and slid his hand inside. He removed some clothing, stacking it on his thighs, and fished around the bottom of the bag. He looked at O'Neal and shook his head.

They regarded each other a moment.

McKenna repacked his bag and returned it to the backseat. He went to the passenger side for the Glocks, opened the pouch, and inspected the guns. "These have been tampered with," he said, a hard disgust in his voice. "They're useless to us."

O'Neal gave a deep frown.

"Let's get out of here," McKenna said. "We can eat later. We'll rent another vehicle in Serenje and leave the Jeep there."

He turned the ignition key and the engine whirred but didn't catch. He let the vehicle sit a minute, working his jaw muscles.

A plane flew overhead. McKenna looked up. "Thin ozone layer, my foot." He switched the key and the Jeep sputtered to life. He pulled out onto the road.

A short time later, the CIA officers stopped for gas and applied sunscreen. They didn't take time to eat.

When they got back into the Jeep, McKenna made several attempts to start the engine before it caught. The vehicle bucked a few times and stalled.

He shook his head. "At this rate, we'll be lucky if we make it to Serenje by the end of the day."

They didn't make it at all.

CHAPTER SEVENTY-ONE

The black pickup seemed to come out of nowhere. It sped alongside the Jeep, and two men in the cab glared at McKenna and O'Neal. The truck backed off and moved behind.

McKenna kept an eye on the rearview mirror. A few seconds later, he shouted to O'Neal, "They're going to ram us!"

The truck hit their bumper, jolting them forward.

Maggie turned and saw two more men lean over the sides of the pickup's bed, taking aim with firearms. "Guns!" she shouted.

"I'm going into the ravine! Get ready to jump!"

O'Neal released her belt and held on, putting one hand on the seat, the other on the window ledge.

McKenna floored the Jeep and made a hard right toward the embankment. They cleared the top, becoming airborne.

Maggie's stomach did a flip.

The Jeep slammed to the ground and nosed toward a riverbed.

"Jump!" McKenna said. "Now!"

Maggie pushed herself up and over the vehicle's side. She hit the earth hard and rolled down the hill, coming to a stop on the topside of a large shrub.

She took a few seconds to regain her wind, then scrambled to an upcropping of tall grass and tucked herself into it, blending her khaki clothing with the dry vegetation.

The Jeep crashed into a boulder below. It flipped, pounded on the ground, and burst into flames, fueled by a full tank of gas.

Maggie remained still, listening to the crackling of the fire and feeling the heat from its blaze. The smell of burning fluids, upholstery and plastics assailed her nose.

A few clumps of dirt rolled by her hiding place. She heard voices above and carefully parted the grass.

Four men, three with AK-47's, stood looking at the upside-down Jeep burning at the bottom of the ravine. They stayed until the flames reduced the vehicle to a skeleton of metal.

O'Neal watched them walk away. She heard truck doors open and close and the start of an engine. The pickup appeared briefly at the edge of the ravine as it U-turned back toward Lusaka.

The sounds of the departing vehicle faded and Maggie slowly climbed the hill, looking around for McKenna but keeping low to the ground within the scrub in case any of the men stayed behind. When she neared the top, she raised her head just enough to see the road. Only potholed pavement, and field grasses dotted with sparse trees and bushes, remained.

She heard a rustle behind her and turned. McKenna stood about thirty feet below. O'Neal issued a sigh of relief and called to him, "They're gone."

"I figured." He climbed the embankment. When he got within a few yards of her, he asked, "You okay?"

Maggie rolled over and slid toward him. "Yes. You?" His left side was soaked with water.

"Yes." McKenna followed her eyes and said, "I ended up halfway in the river."

He sat next to her and brushed grass from his shirt. He had a small cut on the back of his right hand and a few scrapes on the same side of his face.

O'Neal surveyed his wounds. "That blood will attract mosquitoes." She pointed to his cut. "I've got some salve in my suitcase. Also herbal pills to prevent parasites from taking hold in your body. These rivers can be full of amoebas, protozoa and microscopic worms." She paused and frowned at the smoldering Jeep. "Oh, well," she said, waving a hand. "I guess our bags are toast."

McKenna shook his head and indicated a spot about forty feet down. Maggie's suitcase lay at the bottom of the ravine, its corner in the shallow stream of water.

"Oh, good," she said. "What about yours?"

He shrugged.

"Let's see if we can find it," Maggie said.

They first walked down the hill to O'Neal's bag.

McKenna pulled it out of the water and inspected it. "It looks okay," he said. "It's still closed, anyway."

Maggie unzipped the top, rooted around, and found everything inside dry and unbroken. She removed a small round container and handed it to McKenna.

He unscrewed the cap and dipped the tip of his left pinky into the salve. He rubbed it on his cut hand.

"Your face, too."

"Where?"

O'Neal passed him a compact. He dabbed his scrapes with cream, closed the container, and gave the items back to her.

She pulled two more bottles from her suitcase.

"What are those?" McKenna asked.

"A couple of things I mixed up before we left DC. One is swamp-strength mosquito lotion. The other is insect repellent for our boots."

"I have Deet. In my rucksack."

"Let's see if we can find your rucksack. But in the meantime, use these repellents." She handed him a bottle.

He opened it and drew back. "Whew!" he said. "This smells strong. What's in it?"

"Herbs and such. Rosemary, lemongrass, cedar, geranium mint, cloves, sweet almond oil—"

He narrowed his eyes.

She stopped her recitation. "You can put it on over the sunscreen. It's all natural. Healthier than Deet."

McKenna appeared doubtful, but squeezed a little into his palm and returned the bottle to Maggie. He spread the concoction on his face, neck, and hands.

O'Neal did the same and recapped the lotion.

She handed him the second bottle and he cautiously gave it a sniff test, looking at her in question.

"It's similar to Neat's-foot oil. It has eucalyptus, citronella and orange oils—"

He cut her off with a nod.

"It'll keep the ticks and such from crawling up your legs," she said.

"I'm for that." He rubbed the repellent on his footwear before giving it back to her.

Maggie treated her boots and tightly replaced the cap. She returned the bottles to her luggage and took elastic bands from a Ziploc bag. She handed him four.

Understanding their purpose, he put one around each of his ankles and wrists to secure his pants and shirtsleeves against insects.

Maggie rubber-banded her own clothing and said, "Okay, let's search for your rucksack."

They went in separate directions.

After a few minutes, O'Neal spotted McKenna's olive-green bag bumped up against a stunted shrub. She called to him.

McKenna came over and looked at a four-inch tear in the side of his rucksack with a frown. He opened a flap, pulled out a roll of duct tape and a Leatherman tool, and repaired the rip. When he finished, he hitched his pack onto his back and started climbing the ravine.

O'Neal retrieved her suitcase and tugged it up the embankment behind her, its wheels bumping over the uneven terrain. When she joined McKenna at the top, he pointed to a mopane tree among the scrub about thirty feet beyond the other side of the road. They crossed to it and sat underneath, the surrounding vegetation hiding them from any passing traffic.

"Hell of a situation," McKenna said. He picked up a rock and pitched it into the bush.

O'Neal turned to him with a creased brow.

A muscle moved within the hard set of his jaw.

"That wasn't random," Maggie said.

"No. They got a good look at us before they acted."

"I wonder who—?"

"Whoever made sure we didn't fly to Mbala. Whoever took our laptops." He tossed another rock.

"Serling via Cecil Pearson?"

"That'd be my guess."

Neither spoke for a moment. Flies buzzed their faces and McKenna waved his off.

"They'll presume us dead," Maggie said.

McKenna shook his head. "Those gunmen were just grunts. Whoever hired them will send others to confirm our remains. When that evidence isn't found, they'll come looking for us again."

"And make sure we're killed this time."

"Yes," he said.

Maggie gave a frown. She checked her watch, still intact after her roll down the ravine. "We're a little more than three and a half hours driving distance from Lusaka."

McKenna reached into his pants pocket, took out a satellite phone, and flipped it open. Pieces fell into his hand. He swore under his breath.

He put the disabled phone parts inside one flap of his rucksack and pulled out a small padded case from another. He removed a hand-held Global Positioning System Device from its encasement and pressed the ON button. "At least this isn't damaged," he said, taking a reading. He put the GPS back in his pack and glanced southward. "Chances are high those who are after us will be looking for us to hitch back to Lusaka and get on a plane, or go on to Serenje to rent a vehicle, or catch a train in one of the upcoming towns."

"What if we go forward but avoid Serenje and the train stations?"

"Maybe not quite as expected."

A truck approached from a distance.

"That's the only traffic since we went into the ravine," McKenna said.

"Yes." Maggie paused. She turned to him. "Forward or back?"

McKenna sat for a moment, tossing stones into the African bush. He seemed to be adjusting his mood. "I say forward. You?"

She thought a minute. "Yes, if we stay off the road."

"There are secondary footpaths that connect smaller villages." He looked at O'Neal's luggage.

Maggie followed his gaze. "I know you've got duct tape in your rucksack. Any chance you have rope in there, too?"

McKenna offered something like a smile. "Just so happens, I do. I'll fix shoulder loops for you and tie the ends to the handle so you can drag your suitcase behind you."

"That sounds good."

"First," McKenna said, "let's open a couple of those cans of food."

CHAPTER SEVENTY-TWO

McKenna and O'Neal walked through the Zambian bush, staying on a path about a sixteenth of a mile from the road. They didn't talk, so the only sounds keeping them company were the buzzing of insects and the bumping of O'Neal's suitcase behind, kicking up caramel-colored dust.

They trekked along drying riverbeds and came upon dambos, low plateaus that flooded in the wet season. Knee-high termite mounds populated the area, and McKenna gave them wide berth.

The sun reached its zenith and Maggie, having lost her sunglasses in the tumble down the ravine, squinted against its glare. The weather held around the mid-sixties, the humidity low.

The operatives traveled for a couple more hours, drinking bottled water as they went. The path veered right and came close to T2, the main road to Mbala. A train passed nearby.

O'Neal stopped and put her hand to her brow to shield her eyes. She pointed ahead.

"Looks like an encampment of some kind," McKenna said. "We're going to have to seek shelter for the night anyway, so let's see what that is, but approach with caution. Even though we may have bought some time with those grunts thinking we're dead, they could have called their boss by sat phone and been instructed to go back immediately to confirm our remains. Not finding any…well, we need to watch for signs of anyone awaiting us."

Maggie agreed. "I'll carry my suitcase when we get close to avoid the noise of dragging it."

"Good idea."

They arrived at the outskirts of the compound ten minutes later. The encampment consisted of five tents in two different sizes, and a low, white, cinderblock building with a gray-tin roof. Behind the tents were eight outhouses, and about thirty feet to the left of the building, a cistern-type shower stall.

Chickens pecked in the dirt inside a wire enclosure. A rooster strutted the perimeter of the cage, his beady eyes watching the strangers.

Only a red pickup with dust on the windshield sat in the small lot; there were no fresh tire tracks, and no people in sight. Shoeprints indicated light foot traffic between the structures.

The CIA officers entered the compound and stopped in front of a wooden sign that read MKUSHI RIVER CLINIC. WARD A and WARD B were posted over the entries of the two largest tents.

They walked silently toward the first. Low moans emanated from within.

McKenna waited as Maggie eased her suitcase to the ground, then went to the wooden-framed entry and pushed the door slowly open. He stepped inside and smelled air thick with sweat and sickness. It took a moment for his eyes to adjust to the interior's low light.

A tall, slender, Caucasian man wearing dusty-green-colored shirt and pants and a stethoscope around his neck came toward McKenna between two rows of twelve cots, all filled with men and women with sunken faces and large, hopeless eyes. Each was extremely thin and seemed lethargic.

McKenna backed out of the tent.

The man followed him outside. A nametag on his shirt read Dr. Ian Covington.

"What can I do for you?" the doctor asked, his accent British.

McKenna kept his voiced hushed. "What is this place?"

"An AIDS clinic," Covington said. The doctor's eyes assessed the travelers and he raised his brows.

"We had a vehicle accident," McKenna said.

"Where?"

McKenna told him.

"And you walked from there, carrying that?" He pointed to Maggie's suitcase.

"I mostly dragged it," O'Neal said, indicating the ropes attached to the handle.

The doctor regarded them a moment before seeming to come to some decision. "I'm Ian Covington," he said, extending his hand to the officers.

McKenna and Maggie introduced themselves using their undercover names, Alistair McCrae and Kate Winters.

"You both look done in," the doctor said. " How about some tea?"

CHAPTER SEVENTY-THREE

McKenna, O'Neal and Covington sat at a metal folding table in the kitchen of the cinderblock building having a late afternoon tea of canned chicken, vegetables, and fruit. The men drank warm Rhino beer, and Maggie, bottled water. The clinic had no electricity, except, the doctor said, when he ran the generator to autoclave hospital instruments.

After the civilities of the meal, Covington looked at the officers pointedly. "Are you two running from the law?"

"No," McKenna said. "Not from the law."

The doctor met his eyes. After a moment's appraisal, Covington gave a slight nod and asked, "You're needing a place to stay for the night, I take it?"

"We'd be grateful for the lodging," Maggie said.

He looked from McKenna to O'Neal. "Are you a couple?"

"No!" the CIA operatives said in unison.

"Then, Ms. Winters, it's the women's staff tent for you. And," he said to McKenna, "you can share the men's tent with me. There are extra cots."

"Thank you, Dr. Covington," O'Neal said.

"Call me Ian, please. No need for formality in the bush."

"Kate, then," she said, using her undercover name.

"Appreciate the meal," McKenna said. "We have some canned goods to contribute."

"Not necessary," Covington said. "We have plenty of food, and a storeroom full of donated tents and other supplies. What we sorely need is medicine. And more staff."

"How many staff do you have?" Maggie asked. "I don't see anyone else around."

"I'm the only one here right now. Local aides come in every three days on foot to bathe the patients. They were here yesterday. Two nurses are due in on Saturday to help with clinic. That's when the ambulatory patients come for checkups and medications. The examination tent is next door."

"How short of medicine are you?" O'Neal asked.

"Only three anti-retrovirals are available in Zambia," Covington said. "Other countries offer a choice of twenty-six. Anti-retrovirals are highly toxic, and if our HIV/AIDS patients are intolerant of any of the three drugs, worst luck. And, we are poorly supplied with even those ARVs."

"Doesn't the United States contribute large sums of money to the AIDS effort here?" Maggie asked.

"Yes, they do. But in order to be eligible for funds, the US imposes strict moral standards on any participating Zambians."

"Such as?" McKenna asked.

"Abstinence, for one. The program doesn't advocate the use of condoms. Those of us receiving American funding aren't allowed to recommend them, either. We miss a huge opportunity to educate these people in disease prevention. It's bloody criminal. Also, the AIDS funds are due to expire in about a year."

"How many patients do you have here?" O'Neal asked.

"Forty-eight, currently, and our bed capacity is well below what's needed. We service towns and villages from Kapiri Mposhi to Serenje and beyond. We're the only such facility in the area."

They spoke for a few more minutes about the AIDS situation in Zambia before McKenna excused himself to the latrine. When he returned to the kitchen, Covington stood at the sink alone washing dishes.

"Where's Ms. Winters?" McKenna asked.

"She put her luggage in her lodging and went to Ward A."

"Ward A? Why, is she sick?"

"No, she's with the patients."

McKenna gave Ian a puzzled look and left the building to head for the hospital. Stepping inside, he saw O'Neal sitting in the center of the tent. He tilted his head and listened a moment. She was reading a story to the men and women lying on the cots.

He walked over to her and kept his voice low. "O'Neal?"

She stopped reading. "Yes?"

"I was hoping to get more salve. I seem to have...well, perspired it off."

"It's in my suitcase in the women's staff tent. Help yourself."

McKenna thanked her and left the ward.

* * * * *

The women's tent held four cots, two on either side, with small rectangular tables separating each.

O'Neal's odd-shaped luggage lay open on a bed to the immediate right of the door, the bow and quiver of arrows alongside. Her books on Africa were on the table at the head of her pillow. He picked up the one on insects, turned to a book-marked page, and shuddered. A large, hideously hairy creature stared back at him. He quickly closed the book and returned it to the stack.

He selected the one titled *Plants of Africa,* and thumbed the pages of ornamental, edible and medicinal plants, flowers, and herbs with hard-to-pronounce Latin names. Midway through the book, he found a photo of Brian holding O.J. He looked at it a moment and thought of O'Neal. Her mom, dad, and obviously-beloved cat, all gone. Like his own family. Something stirred in his gut, and he pressed his lips together and bowed his head until the feeling passed. He replaced the picture and the book.

McKenna found the salve and tended to his cut and scratches. He put the container back and glanced at the contents of Maggie's suitcase. She'd packed a minimal amount of clothing, all khaki or white. She would have known not to wear dark clothes in Africa, especially blue, which would attract tsetse flies, potential carriers of sleeping sickness.

A pair of running shoes, several clear bags of what looked like twigs and leaves, and an opaque-yellow zippered bag about nine inches rectangular lay among her things. The simplicity of her packing tugged at him.

An image of her reading to the AIDS patients flashed in his mind.

McKenna noticed dusk gathering outside the screened window of the women's tent door, and saw a lantern on the table next to the books. He found a lighter, lifted the lamp's globe, and torched the wick. The flame rose. He turned it low and replaced the glass.

He left the tent, closing the door tightly behind to keep out the bugs.

CHAPTER SEVENTY-FOUR

McKenna went into the men's tent and sat on the cot across from Dr. Covington, who, looking exhausted, sipped a bottle of Rhino beer.

"Want one?" Ian asked, indicating the half-full case on the floor.

"Sure." McKenna leaned over and pulled a beer from a slot in the box. "I see you have a laptop, " he said, nodding to one sitting on a small table.

"Yes," Ian said. "Satellite."

"We lost ours. Mind if I send an e-mail?"

"Help yourself." The doctor got up from his cot. "Log on as 'User Two.' I'm going to check on the patients before turning in. I'll have some questions for you when I get back."

He left the tent.

McKenna scooted a folding chair to the table and powered up the laptop. He sent one encrypted message to Langley and another to Shoemake's personal e-mail address, hoping COBOL would respond immediately.

He drank his warm beer and waited. After twenty minutes, the computer bleeped twice in succession. Both e-mails came back as undeliverable.

What the hell?

Covington returned to the tent, grabbed a beer, and sat on his bed.

McKenna deleted the e-mails and moved to the cot opposite, anticipating Ian's questions.

The doctor got right to the point. "Where were you headed when you had the accident?"

"Northern Zambia."

"Coming from?"

"Lusaka."

"What's your story?"

McKenna looked at the man.

"You and Ms. Winters came here on foot. Why didn't you stop for help in Chifwefwe? Try to hitch? Hop the train at Mkushi Boma? Make any calls for assistance from the petrol station you would have passed on your way?"

McKenna leaned over and put his elbows on his thighs, holding the beer bottle in both hands. He studied the floor between his legs.

"You came here covered in dust. You didn't walk the main road, did you?"

McKenna looked up at Covington and narrowed his eyes.

The doctor seemed to be making an assessment. "You have a reason to travel undetected, yet you told me you're not running from the law."

The CIA operative took a sip of beer, his eyes still on the doctor, Covington's on him.

After a minute, Ian got up and went to a steamer trunk. He opened it and reached inside.

McKenna came to high alert, eyes sharp in the lamplight.

Covington walked back to him and flipped open a wallet. MI6. British Intelligence.

McKenna regarded the Brit a moment before reaching into his pocket and pulling out his CIA identification.

"Thought you were," Ian said. "This business gives one instincts for such, does it not?"

McKenna gave a noncommittal nod.

Both men put away their badges.

"Where in north Zambia?" Covington asked.

"Outside Mbala."

"West?"

"Yes."

"Tell me about the accident."

McKenna did.

"They go on, or turn around and head back to Lusaka?"

"Turned around."

Covington drank some beer, looking at McKenna in the dim light.

"You planning on walking to Mbala?"

"Any way we can get there undetected."

"You have nothing but your luggage? No shelter, no supplies except for some water and a few tins of food?"

"That about sums it."

Ian waved his hand in the direction of the cinderblock building. "I've got a storeroom full. Tents, cots, sheets, blankets, tinned food—"

"Guns?"

"Yes. You may take a couple of Glocks." Covington paused, looking pensive. "You have multiple fake passports, other documentation?"

McKenna passed over the doctor's question and took a swig of beer. He swirled the contents around in the bottle for a moment before asking, "Any chance you could get us a vehicle?"

"Sorry, old chap, no. But there's a supply truck coming tomorrow from Lusaka. Two lads along with it. One's quite handy and could fix you up a pull-cart of some sort. There are a couple of motorbikes beyond salvage here, but the tires probably only need minor patching. I've got lumber; they're bringing more."

"Sounds good." McKenna stood and put his empty beer bottle in the case. "Why is MI6 in Zambia? You a real physician?"

"A real M.D., yes. I'm part of a team investigating a pharmaceutical company in Lusaka. We have a man inside. A matter of national security."

"Are the men who're coming tomorrow part of your op?"

"Yes. They're updating me as well as bringing supplies."

"Anything further you want to tell me about your mission?" McKenna asked.

"Not at this time. You?"

"No."

McKenna put his hand on the tent door. "I'd like to catch Ms. Winters before she goes to bed. Okay if I tell her you're MI6?"

"I'm assuming she's CIA also?"

"Yes."

"Go ahead, then."

McKenna looked at the doctor, seeing again the fatigue on his face. "What can I do to help?"

"In the morning, you can bring water up from what's left of the river. This dry season.... Rain won't come again until November."

"No well?"

"Not yet. Not enough funding. Soon, hopefully. The river water has to be boiled. We've a propane stove in the kitchen. Large pots."

"Anything else?"

"Yes. The supply truck's due about noon. You could help the chaps unload and erect a new tent. That'll free up my man to build you a pull-cart."

"Sounds good. I'll take care of things in the morning. You sleep in."

CHAPTER SEVENTY-FIVE

Maggie stopped reading when McKenna came into the ward a second time. He walked over to her and said in a low voice, "I wanted to speak with you before you went to bed."

O'Neal closed her book, stood, and followed him outside. She noticed the lantern on in the women's tent and turned toward McKenna with raised eyebrows.

He looked at the ground.

They stood silently for a moment.

Maggie rubbed her arms. "We should get away from the mosquitoes. I didn't reapply lotion. Did you?"

He shook his head and went with O'Neal to her lodging.

Once inside, Maggie rolled the lantern wick higher and sat on her cot. McKenna went to the bed opposite.

"You wanted to speak with me?" O'Neal asked, keeping her voice low so as not to be heard outside the tent.

"Covington's MI6," McKenna said just above a whisper.

O'Neal's eyes widened.

"He knows we're CIA and in Zambia on assignment, but not the nature of our op. He said he'd give us a tent and some supplies for our trip north. No vehicle, but a couple of men are coming in from Lusaka tomorrow at noon, and one of them can build us a wheeled cart of some kind."

"How long will it take to build the cart?"

"Don't know. Covington's guys are going to erect another hospital ward. I said I'd help. We're right near the main road north. Staying here another day would give us time to see if anyone comes looking for us."

"It would, yes. And I could help with the new ward construction, too."

"All right, then," McKenna said. "By the way, I tried sending an e-mailing to Nathan at Langley and his personal address. Both came back as undeliverable. I expect you'd like to send a note to your brother and aunt, but I'm not sure it's a good idea. I've got a hunch about my mail not getting through. I'm going to investigate and attempt communicating to Shoemake again, routing through several servers."

"If you do get through, depending on how you word your correspondence, he'll know to contact Brian and Aunt Mary."

"He will, yes."

Maggie got the bottle of insect lotion from her suitcase and handed it to McKenna. "Put more on. It gets sweated off easily. Even though our cots have mosquito netting, this offers double protection."

McKenna nodded in the lamplight.

She smiled at him. "And you know to check your boots for spiders and scorpions before you put them on in the morning."

"Wouldn't have it any other way," McKenna said, applying lotion to his exposed skin.

He gave the bottle back to Maggie and left the tent.

She listened to his footfalls as he walked away.

CHAPTER SEVENTY-SIX

McKenna arose at first light and hauled water from the river to the kitchen, putting it on to boil before he went to get more.

When he returned with the second two buckets, he made coffee in a stovetop percolator using yesterday's clean water. He found oatmeal and a can of Spam, and with plates from a shelf and silverware from a drawer, set the table.

After the first of the water boiled long enough to kill parasites and bacteria, McKenna set it aside to cool. The coffee perked and he poured himself a cup.

He went to the river and came back with two more full buckets. The first batch had cooled to an acceptable level of hot, and he brought one of the pots outside and poured the contents into the shower cistern from atop a ladder leaning against the side.

When he reentered the kitchen, Ian stood at the counter holding a cup of coffee. McKenna noticed six eggs in a basket on the table.

"The chickens were good to us this morning," Covington said. "I see you've found the oatmeal and Spam. I'll start cooking breakfast if you'll fetch Ms. Winters. She's in Ward B."

McKenna nodded and left the building. He intercepted Maggie leaving the hospital. "There's a warm shower waiting for you," he said. "And breakfast should be ready soon."

"Thanks."

McKenna returned to the kitchen and helped Ian make the meal.

A short time later, Maggie came in with wet hair and joined the men at the table.

McKenna reached for the coffee pot. He refilled his cup and poured one for O'Neal.

She took a small sip.

McKenna noticed her face. "Do you drink coffee?"

"Tea usually, but this is fine. Really."

He regarded her a minute before starting on his oatmeal.

When the three finished breakfast, McKenna volunteered to wash the dishes. "All right if I use your laptop again when I'm done here?" he asked Ian.

"Feel free," Covington said. He left to attend to his patients.

Maggie followed.

CHAPTER SEVENTY-SEVEN

After McKenna showered and changed into fresh clothing, he sat at the doctor's laptop, booted up, and opened Outlook Express. He typed commands and waited for results. Data filled the screen.

Damn.

He bolted from the chair and ran to the hospital wards. As he entered the first, he saw Ian hanging an IV drip, talking quietly with O'Neal.

He went to them and, keeping his vice low, said, "It's important I speak with you both as soon as possible."

"All right," Covington said.

McKenna walked outside with Ian and Maggie, leading them away from the tent. He said, "My e-mails came back as undeliverable last night. I investigated and found the recipient's server's been compromised, which means someone may have traced the origination of those messages to this location, even though I routed them through several ISPs."

Ian frowned. "We could have company," he said. "Pack up all your personal items, and we'll store them in the locked medicine cabinets in the laboratory—the room behind the kitchen. We'll hear a vehicle approaching from a distance. You'll have time to hide at the edge of the ravine to the side of the building. I'll do my best to keep anyone from searching there." He turned to McKenna. "Tell me the name of the person you e-mailed."

"Nathan Shoemake, Directorate of Operations, CIA." McKenna gave Covington the addresses. "The messages were encrypted. I'll tell you what they said, in case you need to know."

O'Neal and McKenna brought their belongings to the laboratory and the doctor stowed the luggage. As he locked the cabinet doors, the sound of a vehicle coming up the road reached inside the lab. McKenna looked out the window and saw a black pickup heading their way. He nodded to the doctor.

"Follow me," Covington said. He led them to the rear room where the supplies were kept. He pulled two loaded Glocks with holsters from a drawer and handed them to the CIA operatives.

McKenna and O'Neal strapped on the firearms and went quickly through the backdoor. They hurried over the edge of the riverbank and blended their khaki clothes with the tall grasses. They watched the compound, Glocks at the ready.

Moments later, the truck pulled into the clinic's small parking area. The same four men than ran McKenna and O'Neal off the road spilled out of the vehicle, three holding AK-47s. All wore camouflage pants, light brown T-shirts, and army boots.

The men walked to the cinderblock building where Ian stood in the doorway.

From his vantage point on the riverbank, McKenna clearly heard Covington's voice. "This is a hospital, gentlemen. Put your firearms away."

The men sneered in answer.

"Now," the doctor said, his tone demanding compliance.

The three gunmen went to the pickup and put their weapons on the passenger seat. They left the vehicle door open.

"We're chasing two fugitives," the driver said. A man and a woman. American. Names are Kate Winters and Alistair McCrae. We have reason to believe they're here."

"Other than the patients, I'm the only one here at the moment. What makes you think they'd be at this clinic?"

"E-mails."

"E-mails?" Covington asked, his voice incredulous.

"Yes."

"Why would anyone be monitoring the hospital's computer transmissions?"

The driver ignored the question. "Who'd you send messages to in the past twenty-four hours?"

"Not that it's any of your business, but if it will speed your departure so I can get back to my patients...my sister Sara in London, and Nathan Shoemake in the United States."

"How do you know Nathan Shoemake?"

"We did a summer at Oxford together. We're old friends."

"What did you write?"

"Words to the effect, 'Dry season here in Zambia, but the weather's okay. Overscheduled and under-resourced at the Mkushi River AIDS Clinic. Looking forward to getting together with you on vacation, but I may have to postpone the trip a few weeks.'"

"The e-mails were encrypted. Why?"

"It's a game we play. Keeps our minds sharp. Like solving Sudoku puzzles."

The driver didn't respond.

"You haven't answered my question," Covington said. "Why is someone reading my correspondence?"

"These fugitives work for Nathan Shoemake."

Ian folded his arms across his chest and said nothing.

"Search," the leader told his men.

The doctor held up his hand.

"Quickly and quietly, without scaring the patients. They're suffering enough."

The man regarded Covington. After a few seconds, he jutted his chin toward the hospital tents. His three men left and entered Ward B. A moment later, they burst from the tent and exhaled. The searchers stood breathing deeply before going into Ward A. They emerged in less than a minute, let the air out of their lungs, and shook their heads.

The leader gestured toward the examination and staff tents. The gunmen conducted a brief search.

"Look in here," the driver shouted, indicating the cinderblock building.

The men pushed past Ian. McKenna could see them go by the kitchen window, aiming for the middle-room laboratory. The driver and the doctor followed. Their heads reappeared in the lab's opened window near the locked medicine cabinets.

The leader said something McKenna couldn't hear.

Covington raised his voice. "These cabinets contain live AIDS cultures. You must put on a biohazard suit before opening them. You're welcome to borrow mine, but it has a tear in it. I, of course, will leave while you expose these viruses."

McKenna saw the men turn quickly away and go toward the supply area in the back. Moments later they retraced their steps and walked outside.

"The outhouses," the driver said to his men, "and over there," indicating the riverbank where the CIA operatives hid.

"You may investigate those areas, of course," Ian said. "But you should know that the latrines are used by the AIDS patients, and the embankment is where we keep medical waste and dead bodies until a crew comes in biohazard suits to bury everything. They're due in about noon today. It's been awhile...."

The searchers looked at their leader and took a few steps backward. The driver's eyes scanned the area. He ordered his men into the truck.

"You see or hear from the two fugitives, you contact this person," the man said, pulling something from his pants and handing it to Covington. "Immediately."

The driver slid behind the wheel of the pickup and slammed the door. He started the engine and headed back toward Lusaka.

After the truck disappeared over the horizon, the CIA operatives emerged from the bush and walked over to Ian.

"One of the men just gave me this," the doctor said. He handed McKenna a business card. It belonged to a vice president of Draybough Pharmaceuticals, Lusaka branch office, Zambia.

McKenna passed it to O'Neal, who read it and frowned.

CHAPTER SEVENTY-EIGHT

The supply truck came early. Mid-morning, two trim, fit men about six-feet tall, with short, blondish hair, alit from the vehicle and greeted the doctor.

Ian introduced McKenna and O'Neal—Alistair McCrae and Kate Winters—to Travis Raines and Michael Allard, and the four shook hands.

"Let's go inside," Covington said.

Allard sat at the kitchen table and placed a thick manila envelope in front of him.

Ian made coffee.

"I thought you Brits drank tea," McKenna said good-naturedly, getting mugs from a shelf.

"Coffee in the morning, tea in the afternoon," Raines said, opening a bag of fresh scones and sliding them onto a plate. We stop everything promptly at ten a.m., and again at three p.m., and have a sit down."

"Ah." McKenna found a tin of tea in an overhead cabinet. He filled a pot with clean water and put it on to boil.

Maggie got napkins and dishes for the scones.

When the coffee was ready, Ian brought it to the table and each man helped himself.

O'Neal sat next to Covington.

McKenna put a mug of tea in front of her, and she looked at him with gratitude in her eyes.

His face softened.

"I want you lads to show our guests your MI6 ID's," Covington said.

His men expressed surprise, but complied.

"CIA," McKenna said, indicating himself and O'Neal. He reached into his pants' pocket. The Brits waved him off in a no-need gesture.

"What do you have?" Covington asked Allard and Raines.

"Our chap inside Draybough found a connection between the pharmaceutical company and a lab in northern Zambia, outside Mbala," Raines said.

Covington looked at the CIA operatives.

Neither responded.

"We've been monitoring the activities around the laboratory by satellite for over a week," Allard said, opening the manila envelope. He spread photos on the table amid the mugs and plates.

"Initially, the facility had one guard with a shotgun. For some reason, though, that number increased to two men with shotguns and four local-type archers—with poisoned arrows, no doubt—on duty from eight a.m. to midnight. Then a shift change with only two gunmen on guard until eight in the morning. Lab employees stagger in between seven-fifty and nine a.m., and leave between five and six fifteen p.m. No overnight workers."

"They've upped their security coverage," Ian said, looking at McKenna. "Seems they're expecting a breach."

McKenna didn't respond.

"An American came through here several months ago," Covington said to the CIA officers. "Name of Mark Hughes. He had AIDS and wanted an update on his T-four count. Told me he was an agricultural engineer just back from an area west of Mbala."

McKenna and O'Neal stayed silent.

Covington studied them a moment. "This chap said he uncovered an HIV/AIDS depopulation plan involving Draybough Pharmaceuticals and other drug companies, along with individuals within multiple governments, including those of Great Britain and the United States. Also someone in your CIA. Claimed it to be terrorism."

McKenna drank his coffee, looking at the doctor over the rim of the cup.

"I didn't give credence to his story at first," Ian said, "but we were looking into this pharmaceutical company anyway, and our luck, pieces of what this Hughes bloke said started coming to light. We're not investigating through official channels, you understand. Too sensitive considering the parties allegedly involved."

"Anything you want to tell me about your Draybough findings?" McKenna asked, putting down his cup.

"Only what I already have—the connection between this company and the lab in northern Zambia."

Raines pointed to a satellite photo. "This seems too small a facility to be of much importance."

McKenna and O'Neal said nothing.

"I'm guessing you two are going in alone, with just the Glocks I gave you," Ian said, making the assumptive leap. "I can give you ammo, but no personnel. Sorry. Even though this investigation isn't official, we're still going by the book. I've no authorization to send operatives into the lab right now."

McKenna nodded.

Raines said, "We've established another connection between the men we're investigating in Draybough and someone on the outside in Lusaka, but we don't yet know who that person is."

"Try Cecil Pearson," McKenna said.

Ian raised his eyebrows. "The Embassy attaché?"

"Yes."

"Look into it, lads," Covington said to his men.

The doctor explained the CIA operatives' need for a pull-cart, and Allard agreed to build it.

Maggie finished her tea and scone and went to the sink. She washed the available spoons, cups, and plates, and excused herself.

Covington followed.

The three remaining helped themselves to more coffee and pastries. Afterward, McKenna stood and said to Allard and Raines, "I'll clean up the rest of the dishes, then help you unload the supplies."

The MI6 men offered their thanks and left the kitchen.

CHAPTER SEVENTY-NINE

At 4:45 p.m., Dr. Covington walked into the newly-erected Ward C and expressed his appreciation to Raines and the CIA operatives for a job well done. Allard was off constructing the pull-cart.

The three acknowledged the thanks and McKenna and Raines left to go to the supply truck. A few minutes later, they came back in with a carton and cut it open with a knife. They removed six of the twelve enclosed folded cots.

"They're so small," O'Neal said.

"This new unit is for children with AIDS," Covington said.

"Oh, no," Maggie said.

"Yes, it's heartbreaking," Ian said. "The villages simply cannot handle all the sick, and there's no other place for them to go." He opened a cot and started a row. "Pediatric wards in hospitals are filled. There are about one hundred fifty thousand people in Zambia under the age of fifteen with AIDS. And unfortunately, the problem is growing. Infected mothers are passing the disease to their babies during childbirth or when breastfeeding, because they don't always know they're HIV positive. There are medications to prevent childbirth transmission, but these are in short supply in this country."

McKenna went to the box and got the remaining beds.

Ian continued describing the AIDS situation in Zambia. "Eighty-four percent of the HIV positive population is between the ages of twenty and twenty-nine, and many parents have died or are dying from AIDS.

"About thirty percent of the individuals in this country are known to be HIV positive," Covington said, snapping open a cot and adding it to the row, "but above that number, only nine-point-four percent have been tested for the disease."

"Women are getting infected from their husbands, many of whom work in the mines and are gone from home for months at a time. They seek relief from the sex workers that frequent mining camps."

Raines wheeled in a dolly holding another carton of cots.

"And there's the other problem causing the children to get HIV/AIDS."

"The other problem?" McKenna asked, bringing two more beds.

"It's believed by many Africans that if an HIV/AIDS infected adult male has sex with a virgin, he'll be cured of the disease. So these men are having sex with—"

"Don't say children," McKenna said, his face turning ashen.

"I'm afraid so," the doctor said. "Sometimes very young ones. Babies, even."

"Oh, no..." Maggie bit her lip and looked away.

"That's unconscionable," McKenna said.

"Right you are," Covington said. "We're trying to reverse this belief through education, of course, but we're not trusted."

"Why?" McKenna asked.

"Africans believe it's the white people who are making them sick. We inoculate them and they get ill. If they refuse the vaccinations, we withhold supplies necessary for their survival."

"That's awful," O'Neal said.

"Yes, it is," Ian said. He momentarily stopped working and looked around the tent. "Let's finish this row and call it a day. We could all do with a meal."

* * * * *

Allard and Raines were spending the night. After dinner, they played cards and drank Lion beer at the kitchen table with McKenna.

Maggie and Ian sat outside talking long after sunset, burning citronella candles to keep the mosquitoes away.

McKenna couldn't make out their words through the window over the noise of the card game, but it surprised and irked him that O'Neal, normally reticent, now had so much to say.

He finished his second beer and got another, slicing his finger yanking at the bottle cap before he twisted it free. He tried playing a few more hands with the MI6 men, but was too distracted and excused himself to go to the men's tent.

He used Covington's laptop to e-mail Nathan, routing through servers in London, New York and Virginia. He didn't encrypt the message, trusting that Shoemake would glean the importance of why he chose not to.

He typed: DEAR NATE: IRAQ. HARD PLACE. IT HAS BUGS. I HATE BUGS.

YOUR FRIEND, IAN.

CHAPTER EIGHTY

McKenna lay on his cot staring at the canvas ceiling, listening to O'Neal and Covington carrying on their conversation, punctuated occasionally by soft laughter. He rolled on his side and tried to sleep, but couldn't.

He got up and went to the supply room with a lantern.

Covington had told him to take anything he and O'Neal needed for their trip north, and he'd planned to gather those items in the morning. But now wide awake, he rooted through cartons and culled a large military-style camouflage tarp, a nine-by-seven-by-six-foot camouflage tent, two cots, two camp chairs, sheets, blankets, pillows, mosquito netting, towels, flashlights, batteries, lanterns and fuel, lighters, a shovel, two mess kits, cooking pots and utensils, a coffee pot, buckets, canned and boxed goods, bottled water, sunglasses, and ammo. He put it all aside for loading on the cart Allard had built for them.

McKenna returned to the men's tent and flopped on his bed, putting wrist over forehead.

A half hour later, he heard O'Neal and Covington say goodnight, and the women's tent door ease closed.

Ian came into the men's lodging and sat on his cot. "You awake?" he asked McKenna.

"Yes."

"A fine lady, Ms. Winters. I'll be very sorry to see her leave. She has qualities one doesn't find often in a woman."

McKenna grunted a response and rolled on his side, his back to Covington.

CHAPTER EIGHTY-ONE

McKenna arose at first light and started loading the pull-cart. Allard had constructed a sturdy conveyance made of scrap lumber and patched tires from the beyond-use motorbikes. The MI6 man also fashioned two sets of padded rope pulls for looping around his and O'Neal's shoulders.

The cart measured six feet long by four-and-half wide, with eight-inch headers, footers and sidepieces. The footer board was hinged like a pickup tailgate for easy access.

McKenna finished packing the conveyance and covered it with the camouflage tarp. He looked around the compound, his eyes falling on the newly erected Ward C. He was glad they'd be leaving before the AIDS children arrived, so O'Neal wouldn't have to witness their plight and have it endure in her memory.

* * * * *

McKenna and O'Neal stood next to the loaded pull-cart, the padded loops around their shoulders.

Allard and Raines shook hands with them and took their leave.

The remaining three watched the supply truck head back toward Lusaka.

Covington turned to O'Neal and his eyes lingered on her face. He took her hand and held it.

McKenna worked his jaw muscles.

The doctor released Maggie's hand and removed a folded sheet of paper from his shirt pocket. He gave it to McKenna and said to the CIA officers, "I've suggested a route for you to follow. You will intermittently come upon tribal villages. English is the official language of Zambia, and the people are generally warm and friendly. They'll share any food they have with you. Always ask permission to camp on or near their properties.

"Be sure to keep everything in your tent, because hyenas are known to steal. Tightly pack away all your food and clean up even crumbs, or you'll encourage rodents and thus attract snakes."

Ian reached into his pants pocket and removed the business card the driver of the black pickup had given him. He stuck out his palm and said, "Hand over your passports and any documentation containing the undercover names, Kate Winters and Alistair McCrae."

Maggie and McKenna raised their brows.

"I'm going to call this VP of Draybough Pharmaceuticals and tell him that the bodies of two Americans were found near the Jeep's crash site. I'll say animals ate most of the remains but locals found identification at the scene and gave it to me because, as the area's doctor, I represent a kind of authority to them. I'll tell him for sanitation purposes, I advised the natives to bury your bodies in one of the many unmarked graves dug for AIDS victims. I'll rough up your documentation to make it look dirty and chewed. That should keep these Draybough chaps from searching for you—give you breathing room until you get to your destination, which I'm presuming, though you've never confirmed, is the lab west of Mbala. I imagine security will continue being high there, however, because they'll believe someone will be sent to replace you. I'm certain you have alternative undercover ID for the continuation of your mission."

The CIA operatives confirmed they did and gave Covington their spent identifications.

McKenna unfolded Ian's ink-drawn map, glanced at it, and handed it to O'Neal.

"Photo memory?" the doctor asked.

"Yes." McKenna reached into his pocket and brought out folded American bills. He offered them to the doctor. "For your clinic," he said. "I'll send more when I return to the States."

"Thank you. This is generous and much appreciated."

"We're grateful for your help," Maggie said.

McKenna shook the doctor's hand.

Covington looked again at O'Neal. After a long moment, he let go his gaze, sighed audibly, and said to both operatives, "I do hope you'll let me know what you find in northern Zambia."

McKenna gave a noncommittal nod and jerked his side of the ropes to get the conveyance rolling.

O'Neal had to move quickly to keep from being run over.

CHAPTER EIGHTY-TWO

McKenna and O'Neal traveled on foot for three days heading north along the route suggested by Covington, the pull-cart bumping behind, kicking up camel-colored dust. The path ran through sparse dried grasses, punctuated by the green of an occasional stunted flat-crowned tree.

Every now and then they'd pass a small herd of antelope or zebras grazing in the distance, and O'Neal would smile and point to them.

McKenna acknowledged the grazers with a curt nod.

Once, they came to within a hundred feet of a pride of lions lazing in the distance, washing themselves as if after a meal. "Oh, look, McKenna," O'Neal said, keeping her voice low. Her face beamed.

"I see them," he hissed.

A shadow crossed Maggie's brow and she turned abruptly away. She tugged the cart's ropes and moved forward quickly.

McKenna jogged a few steps to match her pace. He looked to the ground. He'd been snarling at O'Neal since they'd left Covington's, and he couldn't get a handle on his attitude.

While he'd been at the clinic, he'd kept busy and distracted with the men from MI6 and the work he'd done there. But traveling alone with O'Neal, with the sights, sounds, and feel of Africa, brought painful reminders of his wife. He grew increasingly heavy.

He felt helpless, too, as he trekked along in the Zambian bush, like an over-the-hill operative unable to accomplish his mission with dispatch. He wondered, and not for the first time, why he'd agreed to let Nathan recall him to the Agency. He mentally shook his head, and kept walking.

* * * * *

The CIA had operatives developed a routine as they went along on their journey. Each day they rested at noon to eat a lunch of canned chicken, tuna, or beans, with vegetables or fruit. When evening came, McKenna and O'Neal stopped before sunset and pitched their camouflage tent about a hundred feet from a river so they wouldn't get in the way of the wild creatures that came to drink at night. They ate a silent campfire-heated meal, took turns cleaning the mess kits, and rinsed and buried the tin cans to prevent animals from cutting their mouths on the sharp lids. They refilled their plastic water bottles with cooled boiled water.

Afterward, they typically separated for the evening, McKenna sitting in his camp chair by the fire drinking coffee, O'Neal about fifty feet from the river, sipping chamomile tea and watching the animals arrive at dusk. When darkness fell they'd slip into their separate cots without conversation.

The officers had also worked out a privacy plan for their shared camp. Maggie would bathe and locate a "restroom" to the right of the tent, McKenna to the left.

* * * * *

On the fifth day they sat having their noon meal in the shade of an acacia tree, its thorns as prickly as the tension between them.

They then resumed traveling, McKenna's mood as unyielding as the sun.

Maggie walked next to him, pulling her side of the cart without speaking.

A movement on the path ahead caught McKenna's attention and he put out a hand to stop O'Neal. A coiled cobra hissed a threat, its puffed head swaying. The officers stood still, letting the snake settle. After a few moments, the serpent stopped posturing, lowered itself to the ground, and slithered into the scrub. They waited a minute before proceeding.

After their supper that night, Maggie went to the river to wash the mess kits. She returned a few minutes later to stow them inside.

McKenna took the shovel and buried the cans. He was headed back to the camp when he saw O'Neal walking toward him with a purposed stride.

She stopped three feet in front of him, her feet planted flat and wide on the ground, eyes narrowed.

"Have I done something to offend you?" she asked.

"What? No—"

"Look, McKenna, we have a long way to go. And your moodiness, this..." she flapped a hand, "*snapping* at me, is unacceptable."

McKenna's eyes went wide.

She put her hands on her hips. "Is it contempt? Do you feel contemptuous of me?"

"No...honestly. I...."

Maggie breathed heavily.

McKenna stood there, dumbfounded.

"Is it because you're traveling with me and not your wife?"

McKenna swallowed.

"I am not your wife, and I can't help that. I am not—"

McKenna's shoulders slumped. "Grace. Her name was Grace."

"I am not Grace," she said, her tone heated. "I am Magdalene Reilly O'Neal!"

McKenna detected a foot-stomp in her voice.

Maggie crossed her arms and looked toward the river. She took a breath and turned back to him. "And...I am not your enemy."

McKenna opened his mouth to speak, but she went on.

"You can like me or not like me. But if you feel disdain for me—"

"I don't, Maggie—"

"If you feel disdain for me," she said, "then keep it to yourself. I don't know what awaits us ahead," she waved northward, "but if it means the end for me, I don't want to have to spend my last days with someone who..." She paused. "Well, you're just like that hissing cobra we came across on the path before."

"O'Neal...."

Maggie spun on her heel and marched into camp. She grabbed a chair and walked with long strides toward the river. She thumped the chair on the ground and sat, crossing her arms.

Head down, McKenna walked to the tent, went inside, and closed the flap behind him.

* * * * *

About ten minutes later, McKenna lifted the tent flap and saw Maggie still sitting with folded arms facing the river. He pursed his lips and stepped outside.

Taking a deep breath, he walked in her direction and tentatively approached. He stood for a moment, noting her feet hooked inside the rung of the camp chair.

She kept her eyes on the water.

McKenna waited.

She ignored him.

"I do like you," he said, his voice throaty.

She didn't respond.

He cleared his throat. "I do like you, O'Neal."

Maggie rocked her heels back and forth on the chair rung. She looked at him, her eyes slits.

He took a breath and gave her a smile. "Waiting for the animals to come drink in the river?"

She turned back toward the water and nodded once.

He sat on the grass about six feet away and put his hands on the ground.

Maggie's head swiveled. "McKenna, you may not want to sit directly on the grou—"

"Yow!" he howled, leaping up and slapping his left knuckles. "Ow, ouch, damn." He danced around, whacking and shaking his hand, which felt partly on fire.

Maggie rocketed out of her chair and ran toward camp, shouting something over her shoulder that sounded like "TIE-FOO."

"What?" He rubbed his skin, but it didn't help the burning.

O'Neal disappeared into the tent and, re-emerging, raced back to McKenna. She opened the cap on a tiny vial of clear liquid and tipped the bottle on her forefinger. She dabbed an oily substance on the raised red bumps on his hand.

A strong smell assailed his nose, but the stinging stopped immediately.

"What is that stuff?" he asked. "It smells like toothpaste on steroids."

"Tei-Fu," she said, showing him the vial so he could read the label.

"It's amazing."

"Yes, it is." She surveyed his hands and wrists. "Any other places?"

McKenna shook his head. "What bit me, anyway?"

"*Formicidae Hymenoptera Solenopsis*—"

"What?"

"Stinging ants." She replaced the cap on the Tei-Fu and put it in her pocket.

"Ugh."

Maggie looked at him a moment. "If you're going to sit out here, you'd better get a chair and keep your feet off the ground. In fact," she said, "let's move a few yards."

"More than a few yards," McKenna said with a grimace. He left to get a camp chair.

Maggie relocated closer to the tent.

McKenna joined her and sat, lifting his feet to inspect the ground underneath before hooking his boots on the wooden rung. His long legs made the position uncomfortable.

He touched his welts, though they didn't hurt anymore, then brought his hand to his nose and sniffed. "Spearmint?"

"Wintergreen oil."

"You have something in that suitcase for everything?"

"No. Many things can be obtained along the way."

McKenna craned his head left and right. He put on a stupid face. "I don't see a plethora of stores around here."

"In nature, I mean. Nature provides. For any bad, there's usually good. A cure for almost everything."

McKenna looked at her questioningly.

She waved a hand. "Take poison ivy, for example—"

"I'd rather not—"

"Wherever there's poison ivy, you'll find *Impatiens capensis*, or jewelweed, close by. It's also called forget-me-not, and blooms orange flowers in the shape of upside-down cups."

"Uh-huh. So?"

"So, if you take the jewelweed leaves and mush them between your fingers, you'll release a gooey compound that's an antidote to poison ivy. You just rub it on the exposed areas, and it'll keep the itchy rash from erupting."

"Huh."

"Unfortunately, our natural habitats are being destroyed. Acres and acres a day. And with it, medicinal plants and insects. We're losing our cures."

"Bugs cure?"

"Not bugs. Insects."

"Okay."

"There's a difference."

"Okay...so, tell me something about...insects."

She looked his way and creased her brow.

"Seriously."

Maggie narrowed her eyes. "You're 'handling' me."

McKenna grinned sheepishly. "How'm I doing?"

She pursed her lips and studied him a beat. "Not bad."

"Okay, so insects—"

"Yes." Maggie moved around in her seat as if to get comfortable for a long lecture. "They belong to a specific phylum of invertebrate animals called Arthropoda," she said. "Lobsters and crabs are also Arthropods."

"Lobsters and crabs are bugs?"

"No. They just belong to the same phylum. Insecta is the largest class within this category."

"And, invertebrate, meaning they have no spine?"

"Right. Also, their bodies are comprised of three parts: head, thorax, and abdomen. They usually have one pair of antennae. And they have certain mouth parts, like mandibles, maxillae with palpi, which are small feeler-type sensory organs, a tongue-like part called a hypopharynx, and a labium—"

"Lips?"

"Well, sort of. But that's kind of an over-simplification."

"Hmm." McKenna stifled a yawn.

"Insects have three pairs of legs on the thorax, and usually two pair of wings, or just one pair of actual wings and one vestigial. Although *Ectoparasitic* insects usually lack wings.

"Insects also have an exoskeleton, so their hard structure is on the outside—"

"While ours is on the inside."

"That's right," she said, her enthusiasm showing. "We're of the phylum Chordata, and class Mammalia, order Primates, family Hominidae, genus Homo, and species H sapiens."

McKenna felt his eyes glaze over. He struggled to pay attention. "And bugs, I mean insects, have all those classifications too?" he asked.

"Yes, they do."

"Impressive." He lost the battle with a yawn.

"Yes, they are."

And that ended O'Neal's recitation on insects. She sat silently facing the river.

McKenna drummed his fingers on the arm of his chair. He shifted around in the canvas. Time passed. Finally, he turned to her and said, "I'm sorry, O'Neal."

She nodded.

Silence.

McKenna opened his mouth to speak and closed it again. He waited another minute.

"My wife. Grace." He paused. "We came to Africa on our honeymoon."

Maggie angled in her seat toward McKenna, giving him her full attention.

"Grace was a photojournalist. Liked to take pictures of animals and got so excited seeing them in the wild."

McKenna looked away. After a moment, he turned back and said, his voice throaty, "She was very good. Sold her pictures to *National Geographic*."

Maggie sat still, watching McKenna.

He moved in his chair. "My son, Matthew…." He cleared his throat. "He'd be fifteen now."

"Oh, McKenna, I'm so sorry you lost them."

He nodded and stared at the water. "I missed something," he said, pain in his voice.

Maggie asked, her tone gentle, "What do you mean, 'you missed something?'"

* * * * *

McKenna kept his eyes on the river. "Something I should have seen or anticipated…." He shook his head.

Maggie suddenly understood. She leaned toward McKenna with a wrinkled brow. "So you've been blaming yourself." She made it a statement.

He worked the muscles in his jaw.

She studied him a moment. "And you've been over and over it in your mind, searching for what you could have missed."

He nodded slightly.

"And you've found nothing."

An almost imperceptible headshake.

Maggie turned her chair to face him.

"McKenna, what if there's nothing *to* find, *nothing* you could have done? *What if you're not to blame* for the deaths of your wife and son?"

He looked at her with hollow eyes and shook his head. "I was the target."

"You don't know that."

No response.

She reached across the space between them and touched his arm. "Maybe it was random. Americans in Iraq."

McKenna shook his head.

"Who would have been targeting you?"

"Tuh."

"Reeves Sjoda?"

"Certainly a possibility. He's hated me from day one."

"Why?"

McKenna shrugged.

"Too good an operative?" she asked. "Talented, smart, a threat to his illegal activities? He was overweight, you're athletic; he was repulsive, you're handsome?"

McKenna raised his eyebrows at the last word. He shrugged again.

"It may not have been your fault," she said. "You shouldn't decide it was."

"It's not that easy, O'Neal."

She waited a few seconds before responding. "It could be," she said.

McKenna shook his head.

Maggie sighed and moved her chair to face the river again.

They both watched the water as silhouettes of animals appeared. The sun descended behind the horizon, painting the sky in reds and purples.

Maggie took in an audible breath and turned to McKenna in the fading light. "Your wife, Grace."

He knit his brow and looked a question at her.

"What would she say about your eight-year-long reaction to her death and that of your son's?"

McKenna narrowed his eyes.

"Would she say, 'Go ahead and shut down for the rest of your life, Jonathan? Only hover in a subterranean level of human existence?'"

"O'Neal—"

Maggie held sternness in her eyes. "Or would she say, 'Stop carrying guilt that doesn't belong to you. Loved ones die, Jonathan, and those left behind must go on living.'"

He clenched his teeth. "O'Neal, stop."

"No, McKenna, I won't. Tell me, would Grace want you to isolate yourself and be so ill tempered, hissing at people like that snake in the path? Or would she want you to heal?"

He cut her a look, a hard set to his jaw.

"You can heal this," Maggie said.

McKenna made a sudden roaring sound and flew out of his seat. He spun, grabbed the canvas chair, and thundered toward camp. He flung the chair on the ground and stormed inside the tent.

When O'Neal came in about twenty minutes later, he ignored her. He breathed heavily on his cot, the mosquito net closed tightly around his space.

CHAPTER EIGHTY-THREE

Embassy attaché Cecil Pearson stood looking out his office window at the sliver of sunlight remaining on the horizon. He drummed his fingers on his thigh and, heaving an impatient sigh, glanced again at his watch.

The man, as usual, was late.

Pearson moved to his desk, grabbed his now-cold decaf, and headed to the lavatory adjacent to the room. He tossed the mug's contents into the sink, watching the coffee splash brown droplets on the white marble. He thought about getting a refill, this time adding a little something extra to help him through the after-hours meeting.

The attaché heard someone clearing his throat and left the bathroom to find the Vice President of Draybough Pharmaceuticals standing in the office, a large, bulldog of a man, with gray, crew-cut hair. His arms bulged underneath his expensive shirt, his tie loosened around his generous neck.

The VP gestured for Pearson to sit, and in an act of obedience, the attaché went to the chair behind the desk and shrunk into it. The Draybough man commanded the seat opposite.

"Have you heard from Nathan Shoemake?" the VP asked. His thunderous voice matched his height and bulk.

"No," Pearson said, sounding weak in comparison. "Surprising, since we blocked his officers' ability to reach him to confirm their arrival."

"Well, I came to tell you a doctor at an AIDS clinic north of Chifwefwe contacted me. He'd been instructed to call if he heard anything about the two Americans. It seems locals brought him identifications belonging to a couple of bodies found near the Jeep's crash site."

"Shoemake's operatives, I assume."

"Kate Winters and Alistair McCrae, yes."

"Did your men get a look at the remains?" Pearson kept his voice deferential.

"No. According to the doctor, villagers buried the bodies in some unmarked AIDS graves, for sanitation purposes. Supposedly, animals made a handsome meal of most of their flesh."

"Sounds like a story to me."

"I agree," the Draybough man said.

"Did you investigate the doctor?" the attaché asked.

"Yes. Name's Ian Covington. He appears to be just what he is, an M.D. running an AIDS clinic. But we intercepted an e-mail sent to Nathan Shoemake from his hospital."

Pearson raised his eyebrows.

The VP of Draybough continued. "When my men interviewed Covington, he denied the Americans being at the clinic and claimed he'd sent the e-mail. Said he knew Nathan Shoemake from doing a summer with him at Oxford. My people searched the premises, but didn't find any evidence of the officers' presence."

"And the content of the e-mail?"

"Encrypted, but innocuous. There was a second one sent, too, but it didn't say much."

"My guess is that the Americans are still alive and made their way to the AIDS clinic," Pearson said. "They used the hospital computer and worded their e-mails in code. That would explain why I haven't heard from Shoemake. It means he got their messages and knows they're still on mission." The attaché looked out the window at the now-dark sky. After a few seconds he returned his attention to the Draybough VP. "I think it's odd that McCrae and Winters would be continuing on to Mbala after the Jeep incident. They must suspect they're being hunted and all the major transportation routes are monitored. Surely they're not walking? They have no guns, no supplies."

"Seems far fetched, I know. But just in case, I'm sending another team to search for them north of the AIDS clinic, this time by helicopter." The VP of Draybough grew pensive. After a moment, he said, "Phone Nathan Shoemake and tell him his operatives were involved in a road accident and lost their lives. Give him details about their ID's being found and their bodies buried. Garner his reaction, and see if he discusses sending replacements."

"That ought to tell us something."

"That's what I'm hoping." The big man rose from his chair and moved to the door. He stopped partway through the entry and turned to Pearson before taking his leave. "I'll contact you again in a few days."

After saying his goodbye the attaché waited, and when he heard the VP's footsteps fade, he went to the coffee urn to put hot decaf in his cup. He returned to his desk and added a shot from the expensive bottle of cognac he kept hidden from the staff.

CHAPTER EIGHTY-FOUR

The day after their spat, the CIA operatives continued their journey in relative silence, McKenna remaining distant. Maggie let him be, not bothering to point out a small herd of buffalo about two hundred feet to their left, which he didn't seem to notice.

They made several water crossings over the days, stepping over stones, their conveyance rocking and splashing through rivulets as small fish darted away.

One afternoon, they arrived south of a river too deep to navigate with their pull-cart. A young Zambian male sat idly on a pontoon boat made of long pieces of board tied atop empty oil drums. To keep the boat from drifting, a steel cord was attached to an eyebolt on the right side of the raft's floorboards and looped around an overhead cable that spanned the water.

The man came to attention at their approach.

McKenna handed him the few Kwacha the Zambian quoted, and the CIA officers towed their cart onboard. The boatman first studied the Americans, then walked around their conveyance inspecting its construction. He broke into a broad smile of approval and gave McKenna and O'Neal a pumping handshake before pushing off the bank with a long pole.

When they reached the opposite side of the river, the young man shook their hands again and helped push the cart off the pontoon.

O'Neal and McKenna continued their trek.

Later in the afternoon, Maggie noticed buzzards circling the air in the distance, waiting, no doubt, for an animal to die before alighting to earth. The birds erupted into a cacophony of screeches, and immediately thereafter flew northward on hard-flapping wings.

Maggie heard a helicopter a second later and saw McKenna look sharply to the sky. They both whipped off their sunglasses to prevent sending a flash of glare to the chopper that came ever closer, and yanked on the cords of the pull-cart to move it quickly under a mopane tree. They dove under the camouflaged tarp-covered cart and withdrew the padded ropes just as the aircraft flew over their position. It hovered, moved away, and came back again.

Maggie's heart thundered to the "thwap thwap thwap" beat of copter's rotor. She looked sideways at McKenna and watched him close his eyes and inhale deeply. Unlike hers, his breathing now seemed calm and steady.

The helicopter circled and hovered twice more over their hiding place, then banked to the right and flew away.

Maggie's heartbeat slowed as the sound of the aircraft faded to silence.

The CIA officers belly-crawled from under the pull-cart, stood, and brushed dust from their clothing. McKenna seemed to be surveying his body for bugs, and slapped at his arms and legs a few times as if attempting to rid himself of any adhering insects.

"Close call," he said.

"Yes. I wonder if they were looking for us."

"Very possibly. Maybe the riverboat man sat-phoned our whereabouts."

"I'm sure Ian followed through on phoning the Vice President of Draybough to tell him we were dead."

"Yes, I trust that he did. Perhaps the VP didn't buy it." McKenna pulled the padded ropes from underneath the cart and handed a pair to Maggie. He looped his around his shoulders.

Maggie shouldered her ropes, listening for noise from a helicopter, hearing none.

They rolled the conveyance out from under the mopane tree and back onto the path.

"Another possibility," she said.

"What's that?"

"Rangers looking for poachers."

"Maybe. We may never know."

They put on their sunglasses and continued their journey, alert for sounds of aircraft.

CHAPTER EIGHTY-FIVE

The helicopter didn't return, but McKenna's foul mood came back in spades.

After another tense dinner that evening, Maggie sat in her chair by the campfire.

McKenna stood at the river, waving his arms to dry the mess kits he'd washed. He returned to the tent and stowed the cooking gear inside. He re-emerged and took a seat by the fire.

Fog rose from the river and crept up the trunks of surrounding trees. Nature went quiet, and the landscape took on an ethereal look.

Neither spoke.

McKenna sat with his feet flat on the ground, legs spread, elbows on knees. He picked up a blade of dry grass and twisted it around his finger. He unwound it and rolled it again.

"McKenna...."

He didn't respond. He unrolled the grass and tied it into a knot.

Maggie took a breath. "McKenna, a good friend of mine went through some...well, difficulty in her teen years. A family matter, but it was horrific, and it dominoed into a series of painful events."

The campfire crackled.

"The school counselor suggested she go into therapy. She went to several psychologists in the DC area, but they didn't help."

McKenna tossed the blade of grass into the fire. It ignited and burned brightly for a few seconds before fading into extinction. He pulled another from the ground.

"My friend became...bitter. Angry and distant. It was as if a part of her went missing. Then about five years ago, someone told her about a counselor who'd developed a unique and particularly effective method of therapy."

McKenna knotted the grass and tossed it into the flames. It caught and the brightness reflected in his eyes.

"My friend went to this therapist," O'Neal said. "Just a few times."

Maggie added a piece of wood to the fire.

McKenna leaned forward and rubbed his palms together. He stared into the flames.

"In a very short period of time...well, my friend came back to her old self. She recovered, as though she'd never been through those terrible events as a teenager. She's been happy ever since."

McKenna sat unmoving.

"The therapist is still in practice," Maggie said. She paused. "In Seaton, Georgia."

McKenna continued to stare at the campfire. A minute passed before he stirred, his expression shifting. He turned his head slowly to O'Neal.

"Seaton?"

"Yes, McKenna."

He studied her a moment. "You went to Seaton."

"Yes."

"You saw the same therapist your friend went to."

"I did."

He narrowed his eyes. "You changed."

She gave a little smile. "You noticed."

McKenna kept his eyes on her. "Your e-mails, your phone call to Nathan and me. You were...bold."

O'Neal arched her brows. "Bold?"

"Yes. Confident. Self-assured. You stopped—"

"Um-ing and ah-ing?"

"Yes." He paused. "You changed in other ways, too."

Maggie tilted her head.

McKenna's attitude made a sudden shift, anger appearing his face. "You're not suggesting I go for therapy...."

Maggie put up a hand. "No. No, I'm not." She chose her words carefully. "It's the technique."

McKenna's eyes darkened. A muscle twitched in his jaw.

She picked up a stick and poked the fire. Its glow increased and illuminated the surrounding fog. Their campsite took on the appearance of a cocoon.

Maggie continued, speaking slowly. "This therapist, Dr. Dansk. She developed a method that completely releases the impact of a trauma, of any horrific event, so that her clients get back to who they were, and would now still be, as if the trauma had never taken place."

McKenna crossed his arms and stared into the fog. "No, O'Neal."

"Dr. Dansk uses a muscle test to determine the exact age and content of the unresolved experience."

McKenna shot her a look.

She ignored it and went on. "But you already know your exact age when Grace and Matthew—"

"O'Neal. I said no."

"Why not, McKenna?"

He glared at her.

She narrowed her eyes. "Is it because you feel you would be betraying your wife and son to let go of the pain of their deaths?"

"O'Neal...." His voice had a hard edge.

She pushed on. "You wouldn't be. You'd be honoring them. By living a full life again. By being happy. By *feeling*—"

"No!" McKenna came partway out of his chair and flung his arms. He thumped down hard in his seat and let go a growl.

Maggie stood and faced him, her tone heated. "It's not just you, McKenna. You want to wallow in your misery, fine. But your pain flies over everybody else. Everybody you come in contact—"

"E-R-G-H-H!" McKenna pitched from his seat, sending it backwards. He turned around, kicked it, and stormed off into the fog.

Maggie dropped into her chair, crossed her legs, and heaved a sigh. She stared into the fire.

McKenna didn't return.

After a while, O'Neal put another log on the fire. She attended to her toilet and went to bed.

Some time in the night, McKenna came into the tent. She heard him sit heavily on his cot and whip the mosquito net closed.

CHAPTER EIGHTY-SIX

Cecil Pearson, with two shots of cognac warming his belly, looked across his desk at the Vice President of Draybough. He said, “I called Nathan Shoemake and was told by his administrative assistant, Claudia, he'd be out of the office for a period of time. I left a message with her but haven't heard back from the Directorate. What about the helicopter search for his officers?”

“My men didn't find them.”

“I've been wondering about this Dr. Covington, and if he might actually be suspect. Who'd he have working with him at the clinic?”

“Just some locals who come to bathe the patients every few days and two nurses who work the ambulatory clinic on Saturdays. Also a couple of supply truck drivers. They help with construction jobs at the hospital when needed.”

“We had a couple of construction workers here at the embassy the other day. They did some repairs and routine maintenance,” Pearson said.

“What'd they look like?”

“I didn't see them, but they were cleared by my staff before being accepted to work on the premises.”

“Your staff isn't privy to our operation, and you need to be more vigilant,” the Draybough man said, anger in his voice. “With your position here at the embassy and your contacts in Zambia, you're important to our group's endeavors. Make sure you check for bugs."

"The offices were routinely swept for electronic listening devices this morning. None were found," Pearson said, liking the boldness the cognac provided. "Who else does Dr. Covington have coming from or going to the AIDS clinic?"

"Only a lot of sick people, which is good for us. The more sick people, the more meds we can sell on their behalf. My wife just added something else to her 'must-have' list—a villa in France."

"Yeah, and mine wants a vacation home in Roatan, wherever that is."

The men shared a brief laugh.

The Draybough VP turned serious again. "I've put extra security at the laboratory to backup our usual guards, hidden from view a short distance from the facility on the north side. I'm also sending the helicopter search team out again to look for the CIA operatives. If we don't find them beforehand and they make it to the lab, they'll be eliminated there. We've a lot riding on this. We've come too far and planned this for too long to let anyone ruin it now."

"What about Nathan Shoemake?"

"Shoemake won't be a problem."

Pearson raised his brows, but the Draybough man didn't explain.

CHAPTER EIGHTY-SEVEN

McKenna continued to remain withdrawn for the next few days. He seemed to be trying to work something out.

One evening after the CIA operatives made camp, Maggie brought her chair halfway to the river, leaving him alone to stare into the fire and drink his coffee.

She watched the animals arrive at dusk, two giraffes first, spreading their feet wide and bending long necks to reach the water. A small herd of antelopes came later.

When the sky turned magenta and slipped into darkness, she went back to camp. McKenna was gone, but he'd put a pot of water on the campfire rocks to heat. Strange, considering the late hour.

O'Neal brushed her teeth and entered the tent. She lit the lantern and, after settling into her cot, picked up her book on African plants and began to read.

She heard McKenna return to camp. A few minutes later, he opened the flap and entered the tent backwards, carrying something in each hand. Maggie smelled a combination of coffee and chamomile.

He turned and held out a mug to her. "Tea?"

O'Neal looked at him in surprise, but sat up cross-legged and took the cup. She placed her opened book upside down on the cot.

McKenna seated himself on the bed opposite. He swirled his mug in small circles and focused on the contents, his denim-blue eyes looking soft in the lantern light.

Outside, the campfire crackled.

Maggie held her tea but didn't drink, letting it cool. She looked at him and waited.

McKenna took a sip of coffee and resumed swirling, keeping his eyes on the mug. After a moment he said, "This technique…."

Maggie raised her brows.

He stilled his cup but didn't look up. "Tell me about it."

O'Neal responded quickly. "It involves focusing on different parts of the body, breathing, and verbalizing the trauma in a specific way."

McKenna raised his head, a pained expression on his face.

"I'll give you an example. An event I released." She related her near drowning incident to him.

"Oh, O'Neal."

"No, McKenna, it's all right." She leaned forward. "That's what I tried to tell you. It no longer has any charge. There's no impact or energy left from it now. It's like, I have the memory, but the memory doesn't have me."

He looked briefly into her eyes.

"I'll show you how I released my Cape Cod ocean trauma." Maggie put her feet and tea on the tent floor and demonstrated the breathing exercise.

McKenna held his coffee cup and concentrated his attention.

When O'Neal finished, she said, "See?"

He nodded.

Maggie pressed on. "How old were you, year and month, when your wife and son were killed in Iraq?"

He turned his head toward the tent's window and stared into the fogged darkness, softened by the glow of the campfire. It took several minutes before he whispered the answer.

"The age is important for addressing arrested development." Maggie said. She went on to explain the concept of fixations.

Afterward, McKenna nodded his understanding.

“Is there anything you want to say about how you felt, or what you thought, or decided at the time? Or about any belief systems or coping mechanisms you put in place?”

McKenna looked into his cup and shook his head.

Maggie regarded him. “No, I expect you’ve been going over much of that in your mind for the last eight years.”

McKenna gave a slight nod, keeping his chin down.

“Do you have any questions about the release technique?”

“No,” he said, the word barely audible.

She took in a breath. “Ready to do it now?”

He put his cup on the floor and raised his head. He seemed so lost.

Maggie kept her voice gentle. “Perhaps the best way to verbalize the event would be—”

McKenna said the words for her, his voice hollow.

“Yes,” O’Neal said softly. “I think that’s good wording.”

McKenna looked at her, his pain hard to witness. He waited a moment. Then, seeming to find resolve, he took a deep breath, and did the release.

Afterward, he wore a strange, far-away expression.

They both remained silent on their cots. Outside, the bush stayed quiet.

McKenna sat unmoving, and Maggie studied him in the lantern’s light. His eyes looked cloudy.

Twenty minutes went by.

He stirred, seeming to come back from a distant place.

“You okay?” Maggie asked, her voice soft.

He nodded almost imperceptibly.

She waited.

McKenna shifted on his cot.

“Ready to free yourself of your arrested development?”

He nodded.

Maggie gave him the wording, and he let go of his fixation. When he completed the release, he sat staring straight ahead, his face impassive.

O’Neal heard the ticking of her watch as moments passed.

Then, like a volcano coming to eruption, energy seemed to rise through McKenna's body. He opened his mouth, but no sounds came. His face showed great turmoil.

Maggie put on her shoes, picked up her mug of tea, and stood. She touched him briefly on the shoulder before leaving the tent.

Outside, the air had cooled and the fog began to lift. O'Neal took a chair and went halfway to the river. She sat in the moonlight, her brow furrowed, her head turned toward camp.

A moment later, she heard McKenna erupt into a resounding agony that seemed to shake the earth.

* * * * *

O'Neal watched the animals at the water by the moon's light. Distant hyenas laughed, and frogs and crickets offered their songs to the Zambian night.

She sipped her cold chamomile tea. Occasionally, Maggie looked toward the tent where inside, she knew, McKenna processed years of grief.

The moon rose further in the sky. From its light, she saw the outline of a bull buffalo eyeing her with interest. He gave a snort.

Maggie rose and, careful not to make any sudden movements, lifted the camp chair and walked slowly backwards. The bull snorted again, but turned his attention to the river.

When she reached the campfire, O'Neal added a log and sat in its warmth until the flames burned to low.

A mosquito whined in her ear, and she waved it away and stood.

Maggie entered the tent, easing the door flap closed. McKenna had been quiet for some time, and she saw him in the low light of the lantern, lying on his side, knees partway to his chest. He stared at nothing through half-closed lids.

O'Neal gently sat on his cot, lifted his head, and slid her lap underneath. She put an arm around McKenna's shoulder, and stayed with him until he fell into sleep.

* * * * *

Maggie arose at first light and left McKenna sleeping in the tent. She got the morning campfire going, put water on, and waited for it to boil.

When she heard McKenna stir, she fixed coffee and brought it in to him.

He sat on the edge of his cot, head in hands, fingers separating the waves of his muted-red hair.

She handed him the coffee. He took it without looking up.

O'Neal went back outside and heated a can of beans.

Moments later, McKenna came out of the tent and attended to his morning toilet. When he returned, Maggie spooned warmed beans onto a plate and handed it to him.

A struggle still raged behind his eyes, but it had lessened.

They ate breakfast in silence.

O'Neal gathered the dishes to wash, and McKenna began packing the pull-cart. Before she went to the river, she said, "It's important, now, to reframe the event."

He gave her a haunted look and continued loading the cart.

"Wait, McKenna."

He stopped and turned to her.

"Do you understand?"

He nodded.

CHAPTER EIGHTY-EIGHT

Mid-afternoon a couple of days later the pull-cart developed a squeak. McKenna looked over his shoulder and gave a small grimace. "Not very stealth, are we?"

Maggie smiled and shook her head.

They'd skipped lunch and O'Neal's stomach growled. The corn they'd had for breakfast was the last of their canned food.

"You hungry?" she asked.

"Very," McKenna said. "The river's beginning to widen." He gestured toward the water on their right. "There might be a spot up ahead with fish. We can tickle some for supper."

"Tickle?"

"Yes, I'll show you."

They stopped an hour later and pitched the tent. Maggie got a fire going before they went to the river.

There were fish, though small and not plentiful.

"Maybe two each for dinner?" McKenna asked.

"Okay," Maggie said. "And after we finish here, I'll look around for side dishes. I saw groundnuts just south of camp. Some edible flowers, too."

He looked at her dubiously.

She grinned.

McKenna stepped out onto some rocks and squatted over a small school of fish. "Watch," he said in a whisper.

Maggie came closer.

He took in a breath, exhaled, and eased his hands into the water, one on each side of a fish. He began moving his fingers as if playing a flute. The creature remained still. Slowly, he brought his hands in closer, continually fluting his fingers. Maggie could see why he called it "tickling."

McKenna made a sudden grab and flipped the fish onto the bank.

Maggie's eyes went wide. "Where'd you learn to do that?"

"My uncle taught me. But I later learned it helps to go into Alpha."

"Alpha?"

"It's a brainwave state. I'll explain more about it later if you want."

"Yes, I'd like that."

"Okay." He put his hands back into the water and caught another fish.

CHAPTER EIGHTY-NINE

"Humans sequence through four brainwave states daily: Alpha, Beta, Theta, and Delta," McKenna said. He sat with O'Neal in their camp chairs by the fire. "Alpha ranges from seven to fourteen cycles-per-second. Within that range is ten CPS which represents the Hertz level of the earth. Beta, at fourteen to twenty-one beats-per-second, is the normal activity brainwave state of most adults. Theta is the frequency of hypnosis at seven, and Delta, or deep sleep, is below that. If you reach a level of ten cycles-per-second within Alpha, you can tap into universal energy, and in this state, you can restore to normal what is abnormal, and do much, much more.

O'Neal raised her eyebrows.

"Plants and animals operate at fewer beats per second than people. Children's brainwave frequencies are lower than adults. As humans develop, their brainwave activity increases."

"Is that why children seem more in tune with nature?"

"Yes. They're literally on the same wavelength as the natural world. It's also why they're so magical."

Maggie smiled. "So what's the benefit to tapping into universal energy, and what's the 'much, much more' you can do in Alpha?"

McKenna poured water into a pot and set it on the campfire rocks to boil. "Well, you can help your body heal an injury or illness, slow your pulse, and stop bleeding. You can also make yourself invisible to others, find solutions to problems, manifest what you need or want, and enter objects with your mind—"

"Seriously?"

"Yes. Say you have a plumbing leak behind a wall, but don't know exactly where. You can go through the wall with your mind and find the leak."

Maggie looked at him incredulously.

He grinned. "You can also enter someone's body and find out what's wrong with them. Medically, I mean."

"No kidding?"

"No kidding. And, you can remote view."

O'Neal looked at him in question.

"In remote viewing, a part of you stays where you are and a part of you leaves and visits somewhere else. The part that travels can go to another continent, enter a building, eavesdrop on conversations, observe technology, and things like that. The military uses remote viewers for spying. Not just our military, but others as well.

Maggie lifted her brows.

McKenna stood and got two mugs from the mess kit sacks. He put a chamomile tea bag in one and coffee granules in the other. He poured hot water into Maggie's cup and handed it to her.

"It can be dangerous, though," he said. "Militaries expect spying from remote viewers. So experts, familiar with the technique, stand guard. If the spies are caught by these 'watchers,' the traveling parts of them can be snatched and may never get back."

"Sounds 'out there,' pardon the pun," Maggie said.

McKenna smiled. "Indeed." He filled his mug.

"Do you know how to remote view?"

"I know how to. Learned it in class. Flew over Colorado once. I felt like an eagle looking down on some river rafters. I never pursued it because it's not my thing. I'd rather use computer hacking to spy."

Maggie nodded and sipped her chamomile.

"After we clean up from dinner, would you like me to show you how to go into Alpha?"

"Oh, yes."

* * * * *

"Just sit comfortably," McKenna said.

O'Neal did a side-to-side wiggle in her chair.

"Now close your eyes and take a deep breath in."

Maggie did.

McKenna guided O'Neal into Alpha. He gave her a few minutes in the lowered-brainwave state and counted her up from one to seven, bringing her back to Beta.

"How did it feel?" he asked.

"Wonderful. I felt relaxed, but at the same time, had a heightened state of awareness. My senses were extra keen."

"That's great, O'Neal," McKenna said. "Now, close your eyes again. I'm going to bring you in and out of Alpha a few more times."

He did, and during one of Maggie's lowered-brainwave cycles, he said, "This time I want you to put your thumbs and forefingers together to anchor the method and create a touchstone gesture. The touchstone can, from this point on, bring you instantly into Alpha."

Maggie put her fingers together as McKenna suggested.

He gave her a minute before counting her up to Beta.

"Now go into Alpha on your own, using your touchstone. It helps to defocus your eyes on the in-breath. When you want, simply count yourself up from one to seven."

O'Neal followed his instructions and in a few moments, opened her eyes.

"That was great, Maggie. I could tell from your breathing you were at about ten cycles per second. Tomorrow night I'll teach you some things to do while in Alpha."

Maggie grinned. "It's so pleasant, I'd like to stay in Alpha all the time."

"My Mind Management teacher did just that. He could accomplish anything, and in fact, became a great healer. He said Beta is 'the state of the walking dead.'"

Maggie smiled at the image McKenna's comment conjured for her. She then grew thoughtful.

"McKenna?"

"Hmm?"

"When we were under the pull-cart with the helicopter hovering above us, you went into Alpha, didn't you?"

"Yes."

"Why?"

"I didn't trust the camouflage tarp to be good enough to hide our entire conveyance, so I lowered my brainwaves to make the cart, with us underneath it, invisible to those in the aircraft. I also used imagery to send the copter away."

"That's impressive."

"Thanks." McKenna smiled. He drained his coffee and glanced at her. "You look exhausted."

"No worse than you."

"Sometimes going forward is less productive than standing still. How about we don't travel tomorrow. Let's stay in one place for two nights."

"Sounds like a great idea."

CHAPTER NINETY

The next morning McKenna and O'Neal washed sheets and clothes and put the wet laundry over bushes to dry in the sun. They tickled fish and gathered edibles for lunch.

After their noon meal, Maggie wove dry grasses together and, using fallen branches as poles, tied her crude weavings in between to use as archery targets. Moments later, she stood with her bow, nocked a series of arrows, and let them fly. She saw McKenna in her peripheral vision, watching.

"You're darned good at that," he said.

She turned to him. "Want to shoot a few?"

"Sure," he said, "but I've never done it before." He walked over to her.

"It's okay, I can teach you." Maggie handed him her bow with an arrow already nocked, and launched right into instructions.

"There are six steps used in archery: standing, nocking, drawing, holding and aiming, releasing, and follow through."

McKenna lifted his eyebrows.

"First, stand at a right angle to the target and raise the bow, holding the arrow like so." She showed him.

He followed her directions, and Maggie checked his stance. She put her hands on his waist and twisted him slightly. She stood back, looked him over, and pursed her lips.

"Keep your left arm straight, or it can get injured." She adjusted McKenna's arm. "Okay. Pull back to full draw. Good. Now pause a second and take aim. Don't look at the arrow, focus on the center of the target."

McKenna took aim. He moved the arrow left, right, and slightly up, then left and right again.

"McKenna, loose the arrow."

"I'm aiming."

"I think you're trying too hard."

He made another few adjustments. His right arm began to quaver.

"McKenna—"

"I'm aiming."

"Let the arrow go."

He did. It went wide of the target.

He made a sound of disgust. "This is a lot harder than it looks."

Maggie acknowledged his comment and handed him another arrow.

He pulled the bowstring back and held position, taking his time adjusting his sight.

"McKenna, you're over-aiming. Loose the arrow."

He sighed and eased his draw. "I want to hit the target."

"You'll have a better chance of doing so if you let your instincts take over." She regarded him a moment. "Why don't you go into Alpha?"

He raised his eyebrows. "Good idea."

McKenna took a deep breath in and exhaled, defocusing his eyes. His whole body relaxed. He drew, aimed, and let the arrow fly. It hit the target low and right.

"That's very good," Maggie said. She handed him another arrow. "Try again."

He did. The shaft caught the target on the upper left side.

He continued shooting. A few arced wide, but he gradually improved his aim.

When the arrows were spent, they gathered and returned them to O'Neal's quiver.

McKenna watched as Maggie shot a few.

"You're so fluid," he said. "I bet you can loose an arrow a second."

She smiled at him. "It just takes practice. You'll be doing the same in no time."

* * * * *

After their evening meal, McKenna offered to teach Maggie how to enter objects with her mind while in Alpha.

She eagerly accepted.

"Breathe in, use your touchstone, and defocus your eyes."

She did.

"I'm going to hand you the shovel. I want you to hold it in your lap and go inside the wooden shaft first, then the metal spade."

It took Maggie a few minutes to enter the object. Once inside, she said, "This is interesting. The wood is striated. And not completely dry. It's kind of warm, spacious and light. I can move around easily in here."

"Good job, O'Neal. Now, go into the metal part."

Maggie did and reported it to be dense, dark, and cold, not as nice a place to be as the wood.

"Okay, wait a minute. I'll get something else."

McKenna went to a shrub and broke off a small branch. He returned and handed it to O'Neal.

She entered it. "It's coursing. Alive. But it's traumatized from being separated from the bush."

"Apologize to it and thank it for sacrificing itself to teach you more about plants."

She did and waited a moment. "Oh, that's better. It's calmer."

"Good. Now I want you to enter the tent with your mind and look around."

Maggie stayed quiet for a brief time, after which she reported finding six stitches loose in the canvas's seam, forming a small gap near the floor.

"All right," McKenna said. "The next thing to do is to go inside someone's body. Ask their permission first. They'll let you know if it's okay."

O'Neal sat in silence a moment. She stirred and said, "Aunt Mary."

"Good. Tell me what you see inside your aunt."

"She's got plaque built up in her arteries. I want to vacuum it out."

"That's good instinct, O'Neal. You've already moved into the healing phase of the exercise. Go ahead and take care of the plaque."

She did and told McKenna the results.

"Excellent," he said. "When you're ready, count yourself up and open your eyes."

"...six, seven." Maggie blinked and looked at McKenna.

He wore a wide smile. "How was that?"

"Amazing. I saw everything so clearly."

"That was impressive, O'Neal. Now, if you'll show me where the stitches are loose in the tent, I'll get the duct tape and fix it."

CHAPTER NINETY-ONE

Cecil Pearson added a shot of cognac to his morning coffee in preparation for the ridiculously early meeting with the Vice President of Draybough Pharmaceuticals. He looked out his window at the still-dark sky and drummed his fingers on the desk.

At 6:00 a.m., the Draybough man, a half hour late, walked into the attachés office offering no apology. He helped himself to coffee, leaving it black.

"The second helicopter search got delayed," he said, lowering himself into the seat opposite Pearson. "Mechanical problems. The crew's going out this morning to look for Winters and McCrae. You hear from Shoemake?" He took a sip from his mug, not bothering to let the brew cool.

"No. I phoned Langley again and talked to his administrative assistant. He's still out of the office."

"Those construction workers come back to the embassy?"

"I hired two new ones to do maintenance. Met with them directly. Couple of Brits."

"What'd they look like?"

"Tall, fit, short blond hair. Could almost pass for twins."

The Draybough man opened his mouth to speak, but Pearson continued.

"Don't worry, I checked them out myself."

The VP looked unsure, but nodded.

"How's the swine flu program going?" the attaché asked.

"It's going well." The man gave a short laugh. "My wife really wants that villa in France."

Pearson joined him in a chuckle. "Yes, and mine wants a—"

The VP held up a hand. "I know, a vacation home in Roatan." With that he got up and left the room, taking his coffee, and yet another embassy mug, with him.

CHAPTER NINETY-TWO

The morning after Maggie learned to enter objects with her mind while in Alpha, the CIA operatives breakfasted on a stew of fish and vegetables, and roasted groundnuts to eat for lunch.

"You're not having coffee this morning," Maggie said.

"I'm out. You're not drinking tea, either. You have any left?"

"Only medicinal ones." She looked into the distance for a moment. She turned back to him and asked, "McKenna, where are we?"

He raised his eyebrows in question.

"Where are we? How far have we come from Lusaka, and what's the distance yet to the lab? You seem to be keeping dibs on the GPS and not reporting our progress. Are you trying to keep me from getting discouraged?"

"Yes."

"Well, don't. We're a team."

"You're right," he said. He doused the fire with water. It hissed and sent up smoky steam. "What with us dragging the pull-cart, we're not making very good time. Maybe twenty-two miles a day."

"Obviously, walking is taking much too long," Maggie said. "Why don't we both go into Alpha and manifest a safe, undetected ride to northern Zambia?"

McKenna grinned. "That's a darned good idea, O'Neal," he said, and wondered, with a fading smile, why he hadn't thought of it earlier. He then reminded himself of the impaired state he'd been in up until a few days ago when he released the trauma of his wife and son's deaths. Before that he'd felt trapped in some grayness that dulled his senses and compromised his abilities.

Shaking his head slightly, he came back to present and leaned forward in his chair, elbows on knees. "Okay, I'm going into Alpha, now." He took a breath in and lowered his brainwave. "It's better if we see the same image," he said. "What does the vehicle look like, for instance?"

O'Neal went into Alpha, too. "How about a pickup? Four-wheel drive."

"Okay," McKenna said. "We need to agree on a color. How about navy blue?"

"All right."

"What make?"

"I see a Toyota," Maggie said. "Older model. It's listing slightly to the driver's side. Rust on the back fender."

"Yes, and the tailgate's missing. The owner has ropes crisscrossed to keep things from falling out."

"What does the driver look like?" Maggie asked.

"He's a Zambian man," McKenna said. "About thirty-five. Big toothy grin. We're riding in the bed of the truck, on top of our pull-cart, which is taking up the entire width and length of the cargo space. Boxes and other items are stored underneath."

"Someone's sitting in the passenger seat," Maggie said. "A woman. I'm moving my awareness around to get a look at her. Okay. I'm there. She's plump and pleasant looking."

"I see her too. Broad face, big smile."

Maggie paused. "That's all I'm seeing."

McKenna waited a moment. "Yes. Me, too."

They came out of Alpha, looked at each other, and smiled.

"How long do you think it'll take to get our ride?" O'Neal asked.

"Maybe a day, maybe several." McKenna grinned. "But I bet we get it."

* * * *

After breakfast, they struck the tent, packed the pull-cart, and resumed travel.

A couple of miles up the path, the helicopter returned. The CIA operatives moved their conveyance under a tree and dove beneath it, just as the rotor blades sounded loudly overhead. McKenna and Maggie went into Alpha, and moments later, the aircraft moved on.

They came out from under the cart, re-shouldered their pull ropes, and walked for some time without talking.

A distance up the trail, McKenna turned to O'Neal and started a conversation. "How long have you known your friend?" he asked.

Maggie gave him a puzzled look.

"The one who went to the therapist in Seaton."

"Oh. We met in first grade."

"Nice."

They walked along for a while.

"Do you have any other friends?" McKenna asked.

Maggie slid him a look.

"It's a serious question, O'Neal."

"Oh." She walked some steps before answering. "My brother, Brian. And Aunt Mary." She paused. "O.J. was."

"I'm really sorry about O.J., Maggie."

She nodded.

They walked for a few minutes in silence.

"But do you have any other friends?" McKenna asked.

Maggie turned her head to him. "Why do you ask?"

"Well, when you worked in DC Homicide, you seemed such a loner."

"Oh."

"I didn't mean that in a negative way," McKenna rushed to say. "Just an observation."

Crows cawed in stunted trees on both sides of the path as the operatives passed beneath them with their cart bumping and squeaking. The shiny black birds rose up from branches and settled again, looking indignant.

"I'm an introvert," Maggie said. "I get my batteries recharged spending time alone. Extroverts get their batteries charged being around other people."

"Hmm. I must be an introvert, too."

"That would be my guess."

He cut her a look.

Maggie's lips turned up at the corners.

McKenna "hrrumphed" before joining her in a smile.

Maggie said, "And I'm very discerning about friends. It's a quality-not-quantity kind of thing. You?"

"Me, what?" He waved a fly from his face.

"Any friends?"

He walked silently for a moment. "My sister-in-law, Constance. Grace's sister," he said. "And my nephew, Jason." He pursed his lips. "That's about it."

"What about Nathan and Zann, aren't they your friends?"

McKenna went quiet for a minute. "Yes," he said, "I suppose they are again."

"And me. Don't forget about me."

McKenna looked at her.

"I'm your friend, too."

* * * * *

A female's singing voice floated in the air, originating a short distance behind them on the path. The CIA operatives stopped and waited until the women came into view. O'Neal left McKenna with the pull-cart to greet her.

Maggie walked back up the trail with the Zambian, and introduced Mrs. Mudenda to her traveling companion. They shook hands.

"Please call me McKenna, or Mac if you'd like." He and Maggie had decided to save their remaining two aliases and do the unexpected thing—use their real names with the natives in the bush.

"Kiki," the woman said, offering her first name and smiling broadly. Her round face was the color of coffee left black, and the corners of her brown-black eyes crinkled beneath her short-cropped hair. She stood about five feet, four inches tall and carried ample weight. She wore a simple green-print cotton dress and had a bulging canvas sack slung over her shoulder. Trail dust covered her sandaled feet.

"Mrs. Mudenda is going to her cousin's village, about forty kilometers ahead," Maggie said. "She's come from Lusaka."

"I got a ride with an acquaintance most of the way," Kiki said. "I'm on foot just for two days. It gives me a chance for exercise and fresh air."

Maggie and McKenna invited Mrs. Mudenda to walk with them, and the woman, promoting a fast friendship, started talking as soon as they were underway.

"I'm actually only stopping at my cousin's village for a few days," Kiki said. "My final destination is an AIDS orphan day care facility outside of Mbala. Normally, I work for a couple in Lusaka, home-schooling their two children. Every year the family goes to America for three months, and I spend that time helping at the center."

"How are you getting to Mbala?" McKenna asked.

"My cousin, Sunday Ndoba, will drive me in his pickup truck."

Maggie looked at McKenna and smiled.

He gave a small nod.

CHAPTER NINETY-THREE

As the trio walked along, Mrs. Mudenda taught Maggie and McKenna the history and politics of Zambia, about its seventy different tribes, its Christian, Muslim, Hindu and tribal religions, and its resources, which included copper, lead, cobalt, coal, gold, silver, uranium, and emeralds.

"Most of our eleven and a half million citizens are subsistence farmers," the Zambian said, "with the remaining working in manufacturing and mining jobs. The income per capita is around four-hundred-thirty American dollars a year."

"What do the farmers grow?" Maggie asked.

"Well, let's see. There's coffee, sugarcane, soybeans, rice, groundnuts, sunflower seeds, sorghum, vegetables, especially maize, or corn. But we are having a problem with insects ruining the maize crop. We are being coerced by the United States government to plant genetically modified corn. We are resisting because we do not believe it is safe to eat. However, unless we accept this maize seed, funding, which we desperately need, is withheld."

Maggie knew there were three different families of insects in Africa that attacked both rice and maize, *Crambidae*, *Pyralidae*, and *Noctuidae*, with a total of fourteen genus and species groups divided among these, including *Chilo aleniellus*, *Eldana saccarina*, and *Sesamia calamistis* and *nonagrioides*. She turned to the Zambian woman and said simply, "Stemborers."

"Yes," Kiki said, sounding surprised. "How do you know that?"

"Maggie knows insects," McKenna said, smiling. "And plants, too. She studied entomology and botany at university."

"Well, if you know plants, perhaps you would like me to point out some of interest along the way. A few are highly poisonous, but there are delicious edibles, and I can tell you how to prepare them."

"Oh, I'd like that," Maggie said.

A few kilometers up the path, Kiki stopped and pointed to some foliage with clusters of stiff, oblong green leaves, about an inch in length, with dark-blue berries. "There," she said. "We call that plant Bushman's poison."

Acokanthera oblongifolia, Maggie thought. She said, "It's a variety of dogbane."

"Yes," Kiki said. "Hunters put it on their arrows. They also use poison beetles."

"*Diamphidia nigroornata*," Maggie said. "The bushman find the beetle larvae in cocoons in *Commiphora* plants."

"Why, that is true," Kiki said. "The hunters gather black mamba venom for their arrows, too. The black mamba is one of the deadliest snakes in the world. Its venom causes paralysis to the prey's muscles and organs, resulting in death."

The Zambian woman continued, "The archers drill a hole in the tip of the arrow shaft and insert the hollow foreleg bone of a small animal. They put venom into the bone and rub the arrow tip with either the milky sap of Bushman's poison or beetle larvae. Both speed the action of the black mamba toxin by making the victim's heart race to pump the venom through the body faster."

"Often in the wild there are natural antidotes," Maggie said to Kiki. She related the example of jewelweed for poison ivy. "Do you know of any anodynes in nature for arrow toxins?"

"For the Bushman's poison and black mamba venom, yes. A berried-clustered plant we call *shinganga*. There is no known antidote for the beetle larvae, though. In fact, *shinganga* actually speeds that toxin's effect, so when one is treating arrow wounds, one must be certain what poisons were used. There is an anti-venom serum available for black mamba poisoning, too, but most people do not carry it with them."

"I'm not familiar with *shinganga*," Maggie said. "I didn't see it included in my book on African plants. Does it grow around here?"

"It used to. But with so much deforestation, it has become rare because it hangs on the upper branches of trees. Some grew last year near my cousin's village. If I see any *shinganga* while we are walking, I will point it out to you. Perhaps we will also come upon other things that are not in your African plant book."

The three continued traveling a river trail linking lesser Zambian villages. Tropical birds cawed from the banks, and on either side of the path, monkeys chattered and swung in trees.

Maggie took note of them.

"We haven't come across as many animals as I'd expected," she said to Mrs. Mudenda.

"They have been hunted out, so their numbers have dwindled severely," the Zambian said. "Even in parks where they are supposed to be protected, there are poachers."

"Oh," Maggie frowned.

Kiki regarded her a moment. "It is a shame, I know. But we are a poor nation, and hunting animals is how we feed our families. Everywhere there is human development, there is loss of animals and their habitat. Even in your own country, no?"

"Yes. That's true."

"It is the same all over. In Asia, Europe, and here in Africa. It is sad," Kiki said. "We humans are hard on the earth."

CHAPTER NINETY-FOUR

The three travelers found a suitable camping site along the river and pitched the tent.

Kiki squatted by the fire and showed Maggie how to prepare the *bowa*, and *chipama*, *mayabe*, *ndiya*, and *hauhye* roots they'd collected, most of which were unfamiliar to O'Neal.

When it came time for supper, McKenna gave his camp chair to Kiki and sat on an overturned bucket. The Zambian chatted while they ate as if her companions were old friends. After the meal, Maggie and Kiki drank "bush tea," a strong brew of leaves and twigs that Mrs. Mudenda brought from Lusaka.

"I am afraid I have done most of the talking," Kiki said. "I have a tendency to do that, for which I apologize."

"Oh, not at all," Maggie said.

"I have not asked you anything about yourselves. What are you doing in Zambia?"

"We're going to the north of your country," McKenna said.

"On foot?"

"We had a car, but we had a mishap," he said.

"What part of northern Zambia?" Kiki asked.

"Just west of Mbala," McKenna said.

"Why, that is where I am going! My cousin Sunday could drive you there as well."

"We'd appreciate the ride," McKenna said. "And if it won't offend your cousin, we'll pay him for transporting the extra passengers and gear."

"It is not necessary, but I am sure the money will be gratefully accepted."

"How did you learn about the day care center near Mbala?" Maggie asked.

"I was born in the village nearby. Part of my reason for returning every year is to see some of my family. I met my husband and left the village to move south when I was eighteen. He was very good to me. I was able to go to school and get my teaching certificate. We have a son, who is now at university."

The Zambian woman looked off into the distance. "My husband died two years ago," she said, sadness in her voice. "Later in our marriage, his business fell into difficulties and he had to find work as a mining supervisor. He was absent from home for months at a time, but sent me most of the money he earned. I was careful with it and saved enough for our son to go to school.

"He—" Kiki's throat caught. "He went with the prostitutes who always have their mats ready in the bushes near the mines. He got AIDS." She sat quietly for a moment. "Fortunately, he did not give it to me. My son also does not have the disease."

"I'm so sorry about your husband," Maggie said.

Kiki nodded.

The campfire crackled, and McKenna put another log on to keep the evening's chill at bay.

Mrs. Mudenda poured herself more tea and sighed. "Outside my village there is a laboratory. If only we'd had the money...."

The CIA operatives locked eyes.

McKenna turned to Kiki. "A laboratory?"

"Yes. It is supposed to be a secret, but some in my village know of it. My brother's wife worked there, but she died. Now my niece has taken her mother's job at Mosquito Lab."

McKenna raised his eyebrows. "Mosquito Lab?"

"Yes, that is what it is called. My sister-in-law told me that this laboratory has cures for HIV/AIDS. If you are well connected and have a great deal of money.... But, it is too late for my husband."

"How did your brother's wife die?" Maggie asked.

"It is my belief she was murdered, although I cannot prove it. She had come to know an American who had the disease. He came to Mosquito Lab for a cure, but something happened, and he was denied. My sister-in-law told me she showed this man something on a computer and was afraid for both of their lives because of it. All this she said to me in a letter. The day after I received her correspondence, her body was found in the weeds near the facility."

"Oh," Maggie said.

"Yes. Our family is very sad," the Zambian woman said.

The three shared a moment of silence.

Kiki sighed and stirred. "And now I must excuse myself. All this tea." She got up and went toward the right side of the camp.

"Mosquito Lab," McKenna said in a low voice. "Interesting name."

"*Culicidae, Diptera*," Maggie said.

"What?"

"Mosquitoes." O'Neal wrinkled her brow in concentration and looked toward the river. "There's something about mosquitoes...."

McKenna watched her. "Maggie?"

"Huh?"

"You seem off somewhere."

"I'm trying to think of what it is about mosquitoes." She frowned. "It's on the tip of my brain but I can't seem to pull it in."

The corners of McKenna's mouth curved upward. "When you concentrate like that you look like a constipated rhino."

"What?" She turned to see a grin on his face.

"Well," he said, keeping his smile, "you compared me to a hissing cobra."

Maggie grinned. "True."

Kiki came back and took her seat in the camp chair. She resumed drinking tea.

"Is your niece in danger working at Mosquito Lab?" McKenna asked her.

"She believes so and is terrified. She also thinks her mother was murdered and will now say nothing about what goes on in the laboratory. My niece stays there only because she needs the money to support her family. They do not pay her well, either. She just took a second job working nights at the Sunnyvale Day Care Center, where I am headed.

"Sunnyvale hired her because they are expanding their facilities to house children full-time. The number of AIDS orphans is growing. There are currently seven hundred fifty thousand in Zambia alone. Children as young as eight or nine are becoming heads of households. And grandmothers take care of so many youngsters. They are overwhelmed."

Kiki shook her head. "I don't know of any families who have not been affected by HIV/AIDS. This disease has had a huge impact on our economy as well. The young and productive work force is being decimated by the illness, leaving mostly parentless children and old people who are not strong enough to work. And a laboratory right outside Mbala has a cure that is not being given to the people. It is criminal."

The Zambian woman lapsed into silence.

Darkness fell, and McKenna added another log to the fire. He asked Kiki, "How far is the day care center from Mosquito Lab?"

"Eight kilometers. My niece rides a bicycle from one job to the other."

* * * * *

Mrs. Mudenda, being too large a woman to double up on a cot, was given Maggie's bed for the night. O'Neal shared McKenna's, their backs touching.

Maggie felt the heat from his body, and its warmth filled her own. A sensation never before experienced arose in her, and her breath quickened.

McKenna stirred too, and swallowed often. Eventually, he took in a deep breath and exhaled, going, she presumed, into Alpha. Soon after, he fell into the rhythm of slumber.

Sleep didn't come so easily for Maggie.

CHAPTER NINETY-FIVE

McKenna, O'Neal and Mrs. Mudenda resumed their journey early the next morning.

That afternoon, McKenna pointed out a herd of gazelle in the distance. O'Neal looked at the animals a moment, then into McKenna's face.

He beamed.

Kiki glanced from Maggie to McKenna, and a sparkle came into her eyes.

They continued traveling and went about another kilometer before Mrs. Mudenda said, "We are approaching my cousin's village."

Moments later, they rounded a bend and stopped before a clean-swept yard with eight round, thatched-roofed dwellings. Several women squatted before pots that hung on iron rods over a fire pit in a community cooking area.

Chickens scratched in a large wire enclosure toward the rear of the village, and four cattle grazed in an adjacent pasture.

A couple of dogs barked at the incoming visitors, and the females tending the cooking pots stood and put hands over brows. Kiki called a greeting to them.

Recognition registered and the women ran forward, alerting other tribe members.

Men emerged from huts and bush, and children left their studies in an open-air school. Within seconds, excited Zambians surrounded the travelers with smiles, their curious faces falling on the strangers and the conveyance they pulled. The villagers exchanged hugs with Kiki and were introduced to McKenna and Maggie, who greeted each member warmly.

"This is Tasila Ndoba, my cousin Sunday's wife," Kiki said, singling out a woman of about twenty-four. She explained to Tasila that she'd offered a ride to the Americans in her husband's truck.

"Oh, he will be happy to have these extra passengers. You were right to offer them a ride, Kiki." Tasila smiled. "He will be back in two or three days. He is out on one of his sales trips."

McKenna and Maggie exchanged looks of disappointment at having to wait for Sunday's arrival.

Kiki said, "My cousin is a tradesman and travels from village to village exchanging hand-made goods. He then drives great distances to towns and cities and sells these items for cash before bringing supplies back here. Because of his job, Sunday's people are luckier than most. They are, for example, well stocked with books to better educate their children."

The villagers beamed.

The CIA operatives received permission to camp on tribal property, and the men showed the couple where to pitch the tent. One asked Maggie if he could take her place pulling the cart to the campsite. He shouldered the padded ropes, grinning broadly.

After settling in, O'Neal and McKenna were invited to join the villagers in their evening meal of *nshima*, the Zambian porridge-like staple cooked from maize flour and tasting like grits.

Maggie and McKenna sat with the tribe members on hardened earth around the cooking pots, where Kiki, as usual, did most of the talking.

"*Nshima* is eaten three times a day," she said. "It is usually served with *ununani*, or 'relish.' *Ununani* consists of one or more side dishes, which can be of fish, beef, goat, buffalo, deer, elephant, warthog, wild pig, mice or rabbit, antelope, turtle, frog, alligator, monkey, chicken, or eggs. Also green vegetables like rape, which is added to the stew tonight. I believe you call this vegetable 'collard greens.' Other things that can make up a relish are cabbage, squash, pumpkin, peas or beans, groundnuts, mushrooms, peanuts, or peanut butter."

Kiki's recitation left her breathless and she gulped in air, causing the villagers to burst into laughter.

After the *nshima* and relish were eaten, Maggie offered a pail of dried Mopani caterpillars to her hosts. She'd purchased them earlier from two young Zambian men heading south on the path to market the insects in Serenje.

The villagers clapped their hands in excitement.

"Dried Mopani caterpillars are such a delicacy," Mrs. Mudenda said, looking very pleased. "So tasty. And they are full of vitamins, minerals, protein and fat. The villagers who gather the Mopani do not keep them for themselves because they can get such a good price when they sell them in the towns."

The caterpillars were eaten with delight by all but McKenna, who endured the sound of crunchy chewing with a grimace.

CHAPTER NINETY-SIX

Maggie and McKenna spent the next two days with Sunday Ndoba's tribe.

Since all chores were done in groups in African villages, Maggie got up at 4:00 a.m. and worked side by side with the adult females, performing the physically demanding task of pounding corn kernels into maize with mortar and pestle. She also learned how to prepare the resulting *nshima* with relishes.

The women taught her how to weave vines and dried grasses properly, and giggled at her first attempt at making a fishing basket. Maggie joined in their laughter.

Because she didn't grow up carrying heavy loads on her head and to do so now would crush her neck bones, O'Neal used the pull-cart to help the women fetch water from a well over a kilometer away.

Mrs. Mudenda strolled alongside talking.

A few minutes into their journey, Kiki stopped and shielded her eyes, looking into a tree.

"There," she said, pointing. "*Shinganga* berries. The antidote to Bushman's poison and black mamba venom."

"It looks a little like mistletoe," Maggie said, "except the berries are purplish-brown, and mistletoe's are a translucent white."

"Is mistletoe toxic?"

"Yes, but it can also be used in low doses in a tea to treat epilepsy, headaches, lung diseases and parasites."

"It is similar with *shinganga* berries," Kiki said. "They are toxic, but in the right dose, medicinal. Perhaps the plants are related."

"Maybe so," Maggie said. "How is *shinganga* prepared as an antidote?"

"The berries are crushed between rocks, because they are too hard to squash with fingers, then put into water to make a hot or cold tea."

"How many are typically used?"

"Well, for a woman your size, about six berries. For a person my size, about ten. If too many berries are ingested, the individual will die. If too few, the *shinganga* will not help as an anodyne."

Maggie glanced at Kiki and calculated about one berry per twenty pounds.

"How long can a person who's been shot with Bushman's poison and black mamba venom live before the *shinganga* berries have to be administered?"

"Usually less than twenty minutes," Kiki said.

* * * * *

When the women returned to the village with full jugs of water, Maggie scanned the area for McKenna.

Kiki followed her eyes. "If you are searching for Mr. McKenna, he is over there, helping the men build a new hut," the Zambian woman said, nodding to the right. "The tribe has a couple getting married in two weeks, and are providing them a home."

O'Neal watched McKenna for a moment. He worked with his shirt off, mudding the sides of the round hut, his skin covered in wet gray-brown clay.

Kiki turned to Maggie with dancing eyes and gave her a broad smile.

Around 4:00 p.m. that day, the tribesmen ceased their construction and went into the bush. McKenna, being invited to go with them, asked O'Neal if he could use her bow and arrows, and she agreed.

Maggie saw him return in an hour, going through what seemed like a great deal of effort to keep something hidden from her view. She later noticed him washing an arrow in a shallow pan of water.

That evening, the group shared a meat relish with their *nshima*. The village men looked at McKenna, nodding and smiling with approval.

CHAPTER NINETY-SEVEN

At sunset, a vehicle entered the village trailed by a cloud of dust. A man got out, and Tasila rushed into his arms. They hurriedly entered a hut and closed the door. Giggling erupted from within the structure, and the tribespeople looked at each other with smiles.

"My cousin Sunday," Kiki said. "After he has had some time alone with his wife, I will introduce you."

McKenna and Maggie looked at Ndoba's vehicle. A navy-blue pickup. The truck listed slightly to the driver's side, and the tailgate, above a rusting bumper, was missing. Ropes crisscrossed the space. Maggie's eyes went wide. McKenna glanced at her and grinned.

* * * * *

Later that evening, Sunday expressed his delight at having the two additional passengers. "You wish to travel incognito?" He gave a toothy smile, as if proud of knowing the word.

McKenna gave a small nod.

"I have driven others who wished to remain incognito."

Sunday studied Maggie. "You could pass for a 'white African.' They come from ancestors who mixed with the colonists."

McKenna looked at Maggie. It was true. She'd become quite tan.

"You should wrap your head in a scarf and pretend you are Muslim," Sunday said to O'Neal. "I have just such a scarf, and also a matching outfit." He turned to McKenna. "I'll supply you with something, too. Perhaps a park ranger's uniform."

McKenna thanked him, and offered the man a sum of money. The Zambian accepted with a smile.

"Where do you want me to drop you?" Sunday asked McKenna.

"The day care center where your cousin is going is fine."

"Before we go to Sunnyvale we must first stop overnight in Mbala, because I have something to attend to there that cannot wait. However, when we are in that city, I will get for you whatever supplies you need while I hide you where no one will know. As we travel, there may be police roadblocks. They are common. I will provide the necessary bribes so you do not have to show identification."

CHAPTER NINETY-EIGHT

At 7:00 the next morning, the Zambian women presented Maggie with a sack of cornmeal. Kiki, McKenna, and O'Neal thanked the villagers for their hospitality and went on their way.

Mid-afternoon the following day, Sunday Ndoba pulled his pickup into the driveway of the Sunnyvale AIDS orphan facility. O'Neal and McKenna removed their pull-cart from the back of the truck, and Sunday helped load the canned goods and bottled water he'd bought for them in Mbala. The conveyance no longer squeaked, compliments of a villager with an oil can.

Kiki got out of the passenger seat. She pointed to a cement-block structure. "That is the new orphanage," she said. "It has just been completed."

In front of the building, two women in black mid-calf dresses and gray wimples supervised children sitting under a tree, writing on tablets.

"For those who are not living here full time," Mrs. Mudenda said, "Sunnyvale gives young ones a place to come during the day. They are fed a meal at noon, and for many, it is the only food they get. There is a regular school here, and in addition, children are taught things they would normally learn from their mothers and fathers, like cooking, sewing, weaving, farming, mechanics, handling personal finances, hygiene and child care."

Kiki glanced at Sunday, who was re-securing the ropes across his tailgate. She pulled O'Neal and McKenna aside and said in a low voice, "You have not given me any details regarding your purpose for coming to this part of my country. And because you have not, I believe it is none of my business. When I leave to greet the nuns and children soon, my back will be turned so I will not see in which direction you head.

"Mosquito Lab is eight kilometers up this path," Kiki pointed north, "in case you need to use that facility as a reference point. Avoid the river that flows by the laboratory. This close to Lake Tanganyika, such water would have leeches and crocodiles. There will also be rhino, and these animals can be mean when disturbed. The river is filled with parasites which can eat away at your intestines, or cause blindness."

The three returned to the truck and stood next to Mrs. Mudenda's cousin. The CIA operatives thanked the Zambians for their help, and McKenna shook hands and said his goodbyes. Sunday hugged Maggie and Kiki before getting into his pickup and driving away.

McKenna went to the pull-cart, and O'Neal's eyes followed him.

"Mr. McKenna," Kiki said to Maggie in a whispered voice. "You look at him often."

O'Neal registered surprise.

Kiki smiled. "He looks at you often, too."

CHAPTER NINETY-NINE

McKenna and O'Neal traveled up the trail from Sunnyvale, still dressed in the outfits Sunday provided, their cart in tow. They walked quietly, staying alert to being observed, though no one passed them on the path. They stopped to assess their progress.

"We're about three-quarters of a mile from the laboratory," McKenna said, consulting the GPS. "This looks like a good place to spend the night. We'll be well concealed here."

Maggie agreed.

They went off-path and found a campsite under a canopy of tall trees, pitching the tent within sublevels of vegetation. Not far from their camping area, they could hear the rushing sounds of the same river that ran past the lab.

This area in the rift valley of northern Zambia was more tropical, with higher heat and humidity. Rivers were deeper and flora more plentiful. Maggie had even noticed a bunch of *shinganga* berries about a quarter mile south of their camp, atop a tree in a small clearing.

Leaving their gear in the camp, the CIA operatives walked the remaining distance to Mosquito Lab, staying slightly left of the trail. When the low, white-cement building came into view, they stopped and hid within the foliage above the bank of the deep water flowing south from

Lake Tanganyika, its noise enough to cover any sounds they might have made on their approach, though they'd come with stealth.

As they squatted at the top of the ravine about thirty-five feet west of the facility, O'Neal felt a vibration coming through the ground, most likely from a large generator not visible from her vantage point. She scanned the area and saw a pile of rubble and something large under a couple of brown tarpaulins on the south side of the lab.

Six guards stood in a group toward the front of the building, drinking from cups and eating food wrapped in paper. Two wore shotguns slung over their shoulders, and four had bows and arrows.

After twenty minutes, a group of twelve men and women came out from the far side of the facility, some in white lab coats looking like scientists or medical personnel, others like local villagers. They each passed by the armed men and walked to a parking lot about thirty feet to the east, got on a bicycle or into a vehicle, and drove away. One pickup truck needed a muffler, it's rumble loud enough to be heard over the coursing river.

Maggie checked her watch. 5:05 p.m. The guards remained in place.

The operatives stayed in the bush, and after an hour, they watched another, smaller group of people leave. They waited, but no one else came out of the lab. It seemed all but the guards had gone for the evening.

McKenna and O'Neal returned to their campsite and ate a cold canned dinner. They didn't build a fire; the smell of burning might raise suspicion and alert others to their presence. After the meal, they sat outside the tent and talked in low voices about plans for the following day.

"The satellite images Covington's men provided showed only the presence of two guards on duty from midnight until eight in the morning, at which time a shift change takes place, and six, like we saw today, replace them," McKenna said. "Allard reported that lab personnel stagger in between seven-fifty and nine, and leave between five and six-fifteen."

"That matches the time we saw the employees coming out of the building this evening."

"Yes. Allard also said there are no overnight workers. It seems the best time to enter the lab is around five forty-five a.m. That would give us time to investigate the facility and get out before the first employees report for work. It's also when the fewest guards are on duty."

"Yes, and if we need to go back in, we can the following morning," O'Neal said. "But let's hope that's not necessary."

"I'll second that."

"You said the virologist in Atlanta told you the information regarding the HIV/AIDS depopulation terrorist plot is on an offline computer. So while you investigate what's there, I can look through any hardcopy files."

"It must be offline, because I hacked into their system from the safehouse, securing the location from the e-mail Sjoda sent to the lab before he died, and found nothing incriminating."

"Yes, Nathan briefed me." Maggie drummed her fingers on her knees. "We'll have to get past the two guards. How can we best do that?"

"I'll take care of it," McKenna said. He reached over and touched a spot on her neck, applying very light pressure.

Maggie nodded her understanding. "You'll put them unconscious for a while."

"Long enough for us to get in and out. We'll bring our Glocks, but hope we don't have to use them."

"Yes, shots fired at the lab might bring a legion down on us. We don't want to call attention to our presence."

McKenna barked a laugh. "They'll probably smell us coming with all the mosquito lotion we put on. We'd better be sure to stay down wind of the guards. I'm glad there was no breeze when we were there today."

Maggie smiled. She looked at her quiver of twelve arrows resting against the tent pole. "It's too bad we don't have another bow."

"Why?"

"You've become proficient enough to hit someone in the chest."

"I'm still slow, O'Neal. I take it you're bringing your bow and arrows tomorrow morning?"

"Yes."

"Good." He fell quiet a moment. "Isn't your equipment bulky? Doesn't it get in the way of your movements?"

"No, not unless I have to run with it. It's almost as if it's become a part of me."

McKenna regarded her a moment, then nodded.

Maggie said, "Sunday offered us a ride to wherever we want to go next, as long as it doesn't delay his sales travel schedule. He said we could go to the orphanage when our business is completed and sat phone him."

"Yes, and I'm hoping that'll work out for us. But we don't know what'll occur tomorrow, and we may even have to revisit the lab the day after. Also, I don't want us to jeopardize his safety, or that of the orphanage residents by our further presence there."

"I agree. We'll have to see what happens."

CHAPTER ONE HUNDRED

McKenna and O'Neal crouched in the vegetation on top of the embankment outside of Mosquito Lab, and stayed in position until the sun began to rise over its entry, which they knew from the satellite photos to be on the opposite side of the building. There were two guards on duty, both with shotguns, standing about thirty feet from each other, their backs to the water.

The CIA officers slid their hands into Latex gloves, locked eyes and nodded to one another.

On whispered feet, McKenna approached the first man while Maggie covered him, arrow at the ready. He quietly choke-held the sentry with his left arm, pressed his right thumb into a point on his neck, and eased the man's body to the ground. A minute later, he downed the second guard and towed him into the bush on the north side of the facility.

Maggie replaced her arrow in her back quiver and shouldered her bow. She dragged the other gunman into the vegetation next to the first.

The operatives looked left and right. All clear. They emerged from the weeds and went toward the lab's entrance. Six large, round, swimming-pool-like structures with screening on top were located next to the north side of white-cement structure, each emitting a high-pitched whining. They'd investigate them after they'd searched the interior of the laboratory.

The officers slipped into the facility through the unlocked door, closing it behind them. Inside, a single bare light bulb hanging from a low thatched ceiling illuminated the space. A picnic table with two attached benches centered the room, an opened case of bottled water on top, a six-by-nine foot sisal rug underneath. A cabinet, between a sink and camp stove, sat along the left wall beneath a shelf holding mismatched mugs and dishes, coffee, tea, sugar and powdered creamer.

A bank of army-green lockers lined the right wall. Men and women's facilities were across from the room's only exit, the door through which they'd entered.

They saw no obvious entry to a basement, so the CIA operatives moved the picnic table and sisal rug, exposing a trap door.

McKenna quietly pulled it open. An eerie light flooded the stairs leading to the lower level. He drew his Glock.

Maggie unshouldered her bow and took an arrow from her quiver.

Alert for signs of threat, they descended the steps to a room below. Four desks with chairs, three filing cabinets, four computers, and a printer occupied the space.

The operatives spoke in low voices.

"I'll start looking through the files," O'Neal said. She replaced her bow and arrow.

"You might not have to," McKenna said, going to a computer and checking for cables. "I'll fire up this off-line unit and see what I can find."

He sat at a desk, put the Glock in his holster, and booted up the hardware. He pushed the power button on the printer. When the computer monitor to came to life, he typed a few commands.

"Not very secure," he said, turning to his co-worker.

Maggie rifled through papers on a desk. "A facility out in the middle of nowhere, guarded, someone allegedly getting killed for snooping, probably doesn't need to be," she said. "The door wasn't even locked."

"Yes, well..." His fingers flew over the keyboard and data appeared on the screen. He scanned and closed the file, then accessed another. He speed-read, aborted it, and opened a third.

"O'Neal, look at this."

Maggie came to his side and bent toward the monitor. "Oh, my gosh. Those are the names of the HIV/AIDS depopulation participants Mark Hughes wrote about in his letter to Nathan."

"Yup." McKenna scrolled down the page. "And look at this."

"Oh, no."

"At least we know who at the CIA is involved."

They regarded at each other a moment, neither speaking.

"I'll hardcopy the list," McKenna said. He tasked the print icon, but nothing happened. He stood and rigged a cable to a nearby on-line computer, booted it up, and keyed some commands.

McKenna returned to his seat, opened screens, entered text, and mouse-clicked a box. He hit PRINT again, but the peripheral remained unresponsive. "I'll come back to it." He opened another file.

He looked to his left. "What's that noise? It's the same as we heard coming from those round things outside. It sounds like…" He shook his head.

Maggie's interest seemed to go to a desktop about two yards away.

McKenna focused on the computer again, his fingers keying commands. He stopped as information filled the monitor.

"Got it," he said, intensity in his voice. "Separate strains of HIV, one injected into Africans, another into homosexuals, and a third into victims in Thailand. Nothing on this page about the actual manufacturing of the sera, but I see a link to another file. I want to look at something else, first." He clicked an icon and opened other data. "Yes, here. This information's similar to what I found at USAMRIID. They're also researching an inhibitor of HIV derived from bananas. It's called lectin."

O'Neal turned back to the computer and peered at the screen. "Oh, yes. Lectins are chemicals found naturally in bananas and other plants. They halt the progression of certain infectious agents," she said. "And look at the vaccines on file here." She nodded toward the monitor. "Some from live attenuated viruses of non-progressors."

"Yup."

Maggie leaned closer. "These LAVs seem DNA specific. Designer LAVs?"

McKenna scrolled to another page. "They're also using ultra violet against HIV," he said. "There was a UV light in the decon shower at USAMRIID."

"Yes, and look." O'Neal pointed to a line of data. "They're working on CCRF gene modification to provide protection against the virus."

"Just like at USAMRIID." McKenna leaned forward. "There's more." He furrowed his brow. "Huh? This is strange."

"What?" Maggie turned to him.

"It seems..." He raised his head. "What *is* that noise? It sounds like buzzing. High-pitched, whiney buzzing. Like a whole bunch of..."

Maggie walked about six feet to the left and pinpointed the source of the noise. One of several baby monitors. She picked up the unit emitting the sound in her Latexed hand. "It's labeled 'Room Four.'"

McKenna scanned the room and his eyes landed on a camouflaged rectangle. He stood and went to a hidden door.

Maggie joined him, and they cautiously pushed through the entry into a laboratory measuring about forty-feet long and sixteen wide. Stations with microscopes, computer monitors, autoclaves, centrifuges, vials, and injectors lined both sides of the room. A Blood-Guard machine, like the one at USAMRIID, centered the space.

McKenna pointed to a door on the left. A sign read, ROOM 3 BIOHAZARD LEVEL 4. Pasted underneath was the accompanying black-ringed symbol on a red background.

A door to the right, labeled ROOM 4, held no biohazard warning. The CIA operatives walked over and slowly opened it. A piercing, high-pitched whining sound assaulted their ears.

"What the hell?" McKenna asked as they stepped inside.

Double-stacked screened cages, each about twenty-feet long, five deep, and three high lined both sides of the long rectangular room. Ductwork ran from the backs of the enclosures through the ceiling.

McKenna raised his voice above the buzzing. "Those ducts connect to the round things we saw outside."

"These cages contain mosquitoes," Maggie said.

"Millions and millions of them."

"They're breeding them." O'Neal furrowed her brow and looked at the insects. "*Culicidae, Diptera*," she said, more to herself than McKenna.

"What?"

"*Culicidae, Diptera*," she said, louder now. "Mosquitoes." She frowned. "There's something..."

"You're making your constipated-rhino face," McKenna said. "Lets get out of this room and return to the computer. I saw a file on mosquitoes." He tugged her sleeve.

Maggie followed him back to the office, replaced the baby monitor, and went to stand next to the computer.

McKenna sat in front of it again and scrolled down the page. "Before we look at the information on mosquitoes," he said, "let's first open this file on test subjects." He accessed a folder and data appeared on the screen.

Maggie peered at it. "They're using Zambian sex workers to test the live attenuated HIV virus."

"The mine prostitutes," McKenna said. "They're also using test subjects in Thailand, but let's come back to that."

O'Neal seemed deep in thought. McKenna saw her momentarily look toward the noise coming from the baby monitor.

He returned his eyes to the computer, keyed in commands, and mouse-clicked a box. He tabbed to the line that read "mosquitoes," and readied to open the file, but glanced at O'Neal again and saw her frowning.

"Maggie? What's—"

"Mosquitoes! That's it!" She grabbed his arm. "McKenna! I remember—"

A deafening sound erupted and the computer exploded, pitching McKenna and Maggie backwards to the floor. Monitor shards fell around them.

McKenna quickly gained his feet. A man in army fatigues and wearing a gas mask stood about five yards away, aiming a shotgun at his chest. McKenna dove and Jujitsu rolled to the gunman. He scissor-kicked the intruder's legs and the man twisted, falling on top of him, back to belly. The shotgun dropped to the ground. McKenna jerked the gunman's neck with a sickening crack.

O'Neal, now standing, unshouldered her bow.

"Let's go!" McKenna shouted. He jumped to his feet.

They scrambled up the steps, McKenna's Glock at the ready.

Maggie nocked an arrow in her bowstring. Her gun remained tucked in its holster.

They scanned the first-floor before stepping clear of the stairs.

The operatives went to the door and peeked out the small window. Four men, one with a shotgun and three with bows and arrows, had their weapons trained on the lab's only exit.

Behind them a timer dinged and a canister on the floor hissed. A bitter almond smell filled the air.

Cyanide chloride!

"Don't inhale!" McKenna said, holding his breath. "We have to get out now! I'll go left and you go right." He kicked open the door.

CHAPTER ONE HUNDRED ONE

A blast from a shotgun went between them and arrows flew wide. McKenna fired and hit the gunman in the chest. The man pitched backwards, a pink mist erupting from the area of his heart.

O'Neal's arrow entered the throat hollow of one of the archers.

McKenna head-shot another bowman.

Maggie's next shaft pierced the neck of the fourth man.

The CIA operatives took off running.

"*Iminina!* Halt!"

McKenna and O'Neal spun around to face two more archers coming toward them from the parking lot, bows drawn.

Maggie pulled an arrow from her quiver, nocking and loosing it in a single movement. Her victim made a guttural noise and dropped into the dirt.

McKenna fired his Glock and missed. He pulled the trigger again and chest-shot his target.

Another archer stepped out of the bushes and loosed an arrow. It pierced Maggie's opened vest, missing her body by a fraction. She shot back, hitting the man in the area of his heart. He went backwards and hit his head on a boulder. She reloaded her bow and waited.

Seconds later, another bowman appeared from the bush. He fired, and the missile breezed her hair.

Maggie reacted and loosed her arrow. It entered the man's throat, and he made a gurgling sound as he fell to his death.

The air around the laboratory went still, leaving only the hum of the generator. O'Neal removed the shaft hanging from her clothing and dropped it on the ground. She spun 360 degrees looking for McKenna, but didn't see him anywhere. She heard a moan off to her right and rushed to the sound.

McKenna lay on the riverbank, an arrow hanging loosely from his neck, his eyes open and cloudy.

Maggie knelt and gently but quickly removed the shaft. She peered into it. A thin bone was embedded in the center of the arrowhead. She smelled it.

Blood. And something else.

Poison.

She sniffed it again. She had to be sure.

She checked it a third time and knew.

O'Neal threw the arrow in the dirt and sprang to her feet. She shouldered her bow and took off at a full run, leaving McKenna hidden where he lay in the vegetation. The bow and half-full quiver of arrows bumped hard against her back as she flew down the path. She ignored the pain.

Shinganga *berries. One mile back. At my best time, I can make it in... No, I have hiking boots on, my bow, quiver, the Glock. They'll slow me. The path's uneven. Full of sharp turns. McKenna has less than twenty minutes....*

She ran faster than she ever had in her life.

CHAPTER ONE HUNDRED TWO

Maggie reached the tree, distinctive as a singleton in the clearing. Shielding her eyes against the rising sun, she scanned its branches until she spotted the purple-brown plant.

She pulled an arrow from her quiver, nocked it, drew, and let it fly. It severed a stem and a clump of *shinganga* berries fell to the ground.

She scooped them up and began her race back to Mosquito Lab, calculating as she ran. *One berry per twenty pounds. McKenna's about one-seventy. No, more. He's toned. Muscle weighs more than fat. One-eighty maybe. It can't be maybe. It must be exact. This clump is small. Are there enough berries? There have to be enough....*

* * * * *

Maggie reached McKenna and dropped to the ground by his side. She combed the area for the rocks she'd need, one concave to hold the berry juice like a mortar, one round to fit in her hand as a pestle.

She spotted the round, picked it up, and searched for the other. No concave stones. She looked at her hands, McKenna's. Latex gloves! Stripping off one of his, she pulled the berries from their stems and counted nine into the glove, leaving only one on the clump. She squashed them inside the Latex between two round rocks and placed the glove on the ground, propped so the *shinganga* juice wouldn't leak.

O'Neal left McKenna on the riverbank and ran through the open door of the lab, noticing the bitter smell from the canister had dissipated. She grabbed a bottle of water from the case on the table.

She rushed back to him, unscrewed the bottle cap, and dumped three-fourths of the water on the ground. She poured the remainder into the Latex, sloshed it around with the crushed berries, and fit the glove's opening into the plastic's neck, carefully draining the purple-brown liquid into the bottle.

Maggie slipped her hand under McKenna's head and lifted him. She put the *shinganga* tea to his lips.

"McKenna!"

He groaned.

"McKenna!"

His lids fluttered.

"Jonathan!"

McKenna opened his eyes. His pupils dilated, went clear for a second, and clouded again. She witnessed his struggle to stay conscious.

"Drink this!"

McKenna strained to take a few swallows. His eyes rolled back in his head.

"Jonathan! Drink!"

He focused and took a few more mouthfuls.

His eyes closed.

"Jonathan! Stay alert!"

He opened his lids.

"Go into Alpha!"

McKenna's eyes momentarily cleared. She saw the effort it took him to breathe in, defocus, and exhale.

CHAPTER ONE HUNDRED THREE

O'Neal looked at her watch. 7:19 a.m. I have to move McKenna. In about thirty minutes the first of the Mosquito Lab employees will arrive and find the carnage.

Maggie jumped to her feet and ran to the pile of rubble next to the cement building. She undid bungee cords from ground hooks that held one of the heavy brown tarpaulins in place. She flipped the tarp off an American-manufactured backhoe and dropped it to the ground.

Rummaging through the rubble, O'Neal found several long, four-inch-wide pieces of lumber. She scrounged sections of rope and gathered the bungees. She threw the lumber and cords onto the plastic cover and dragged it to the riverbank.

Working quickly, she wound rope and bungees around the lumber and threaded the cords through several of the tarp's grommets, making a bottom frame. She gently slid the now-unconscious McKenna onto the makeshift raft, loosely tying him to the tarp at his chest and ankles through unused grommets.

She put two additional ropes through holes at the bottom of the plastic and joined them in a knot around her chest, just under her armpits. Then carefully, she towed the raft down the embankment to the river and entered its coldness, pulling McKenna behind. Over the noise of the rushing water, she heard the rumble of a vehicle in need of a muffler.

Maggie breast-stroked downstream, greatly concerned about the effect the move and the water's chill would have on McKenna, but she saw no other choice. Those weren't her only worries. Kiki'd told her to avoid this river because of all the dangers it held. She kicked up her pace.

The parasites didn't concern her. She and McKenna had been taking herbs to kill any before they could take hold in their bodies. There'd be leeches in the water, and she hoped that several would attach themselves to her. They'd be needed.

She continued to swim downstream, and an image of Elizabeth Dansk came into her mind. She gave silent thanks for Eli's help in healing her fear of oceans, lakes, and rivers.

O'Neal sensed danger to her left and turned her head. A rhino studied her with interest. She remembered what McKenna'd said about the brainwaves of children pulsing more slowly, matching those of animals.

Maggie took a deep breath and went into Alpha.

CHAPTER ONE HUNDRED FOUR

Maggie sat in her chair under a tree in the miombo woodlands, the new red foliage shading her as she wove a fishing basket, her third in the past two days. She inspected her work, turning the rectangular object around in her hands, making some adjustments to the weave.

The shout took her by surprise. Her eyes went wide and she jerked her head. She threw down the basket and ran.

A second shout came.

"O'Neal!"

"Coming!"

She entered the tent.

"WHAT-IS-ON-MY-NECK!"

"They're helping you, McKenna."

"GET THEM OFF GET THEM OFF GET THEM OFF!"

"Oh, for goodness sakes." Maggie knelt and gently removed the leeches from his wound, putting them in a cup by his cot.

"O'Neal.... Leaches." He sounded disgusted. He raised his head a few inches and looked at her. His eyes were cloudy. He moaned and put his head back on the pillow. "I hate creepy, crawly things."

"Well, you're feeling better." She put her hand on his chest. "This is the first time you've come fully awake."

"I have to use the men's restroom area."

"Okay, but I don't think you'll be able to walk yet. I could wheel you in the pull-cart."

"I'd like to try to make it on my own."

"Why don't you start by seeing if you can sit?"

McKenna attempted to lift his torso, but fell back again. "Ock," he said. He waited a minute and blinked his eyes. "I feel like crap."

"Yes, well."

He lay still.

"McKenna?"

He turned his head slightly toward her and she saw his eyes trying to focus. After a few seconds, they cleared a little. "Okay," he said. "Alley oop."

He made a monumental effort to raise his body, and O'Neal reached behind his back to help him up.

McKenna sat, his head hunched over his lap. "Oh, geez."

"Give it a few minutes," Maggie said.

"I can't. I really have to use the men's area. But you're right, I don't think I can make it on my own."

"Okay. I'll help you stand, then wheel you."

Maggie assisted as McKenna got to his feet. He swayed, and leaned on her for support. O'Neal held him tightly as he stood still, took a step, and stopped. He repeated the process, and, after a couple of minutes of steps and stops, they made it out of the tent.

McKenna put his hand up to shield against the bright sun.

"Close your eyes to slits," Maggie said. "Or, I could get your sunglasses."

"No. I don't want to take the time."

"Okay." She led the unsteady McKenna to the nearby cart, helped him sit, and wheeled him to a copse of trees. "You may want to stay seated while you—"

He shook his head and slowly stood on uncertain legs, reaching a hand out to lean against a tree.

"Give me a shout when you've finished," O'Neal said. She walked back to camp to give him privacy.

Maggie waited by the tent for McKenna's call, but it didn't come. After a few moments, she walked tentatively to where she'd left him.

He sat on the open-back edge of the pull-cart, elbows on knees, head in hands.

"Are you all right?" She slid in beside him and put her palm on his back.

McKenna raised his head and gave her a pained look. He reached just under his waistband, much looser now, and tugged on something. "What's this?"

Maggie feigned innocence. "What?"

He tugged again. "This woven grass thing."

"Oh. It's a...."

He looked at her dully. "A diaper?"

She nodded.

He stared at her.

"Well, you see—"

He searched her face. "How long have I been out?"

"Uh—"

"O'Neal...."

She hesitated before answering. "Twelve days."

"Twelve days?" He slumped forward. "What the hell happened?"

She told him.

"I don't remember anything," he said.

"I think that's normal."

"Normal?"

"For the poisons, I mean." She sighed. "What's the last thing you do remember?"

He put his head in his hands once again. After a moment, he said, "Mosquitoes. Lots and lots of mosquitoes."

"Yes. About that—"

"Is it permanent, this memory loss?"

"I'm not sure. I know about Bushman's poison, but not about black mamba venom."

He turned his head in his hands and peered through his fingers at her.

"Your memory has to come back, McKenna."

She saw an eyebrow lift between the fingers.

"You photo-scanned a list of important names and other vital data. We didn't get a hardcopy. The information's only in your head."

"Which feels like it's mud-filled."

Maggie knit her brow. "Do you remember anything about our mission?"

A minute passed. He shook his head.

"We were to go to a lab in northern Zambia, investigate its activities, and get the list of HIV/AIDS depopulation plan participants," Maggie said.

McKenna stared blankly at first. After a few moments, he nodded slowly and said, "Yes. I'm remembering now."

"Do you recall any specific names?"

He shook his head. He stayed quiet a while. "Wait," he said, sitting straighter. "Yes."

"Yes?"

"Vice President Serling."

"Good, McKenna!"

"Reeves Sjoda."

"Yes!"

He took a minute. "Ex-German Chancellor Otto Vetterman."

"Excellent! Your memory's coming back fast."

She gave him time to think, and then turned to him, her head tilted. "Any more?"

"Someone at the CIA." He shook his head. "I don't remember."

She told him.

He lay back on the cart, his feet still on the ground. He put a hand over his forehead. "Geez."

"Yes."

"COBOL—"

Maggie waited, but McKenna didn't finish his sentence. He'd fallen asleep.

CHAPTER ONE HUNDRED FIVE

"O'Neal?"

Maggie left the campfire and went into the tent to find McKenna sitting on his cot.

"You look a little better," she said. "How are you feeling?"

"Like crap." He put his head in his hands. "I have to pee again."

"That's good. It means you're flushing—"

He looked at her, his forehead creased.

"Getting rid of the poison, I mean. I'll help you up."

"All right, but I'd like to try to walk all the way to the men's restroom area this time."

"Okay. I'll go with you in case you get too tired to move on your own."

McKenna stood with Maggie's assistance. She stayed alongside as he took a few tentative independent steps.

Once outside the tent, it took them five minutes to get to the men's area, and McKenna leaned his hand against a tree, his breathing labored.

"Are you okay?"

He nodded.

"All right. Call me for the trip back." She left him alone.

After a few minutes, O'Neal saw McKenna returning on his own. He slowly made his way to a tree, rested, and moved to another. He paused.

Maggie looked to where he'd stopped and saw a mound of dirt near his feet. Her eyes widened. "Oh, no, McKenna! There's a stinging anthill there!"

"Ouch! Ow!" He hopped from foot to foot all the way to the campsite. Breathing hard, he sat heavily in a chair by the fire and rubbed his ankle.

Maggie went into the tent for Tei-Fu. She came back out and handed McKenna the vial. He opened it and dabbed the oil on his bites, the smell of wintergreen filling the air.

She smiled. "Well, the ants got you moving again at least."

He grimaced and capped the Tei-Fu.

She took it and put it in her pocket. She noticed his breathing returning to normal. "You hungry?"

"I am. Yes."

"That's a good sign. I've got *nshima* cooking. I've thinned it out so you can eat more easily. I know it's still difficult for you to swallow."

He nodded, and slid down in the camp chair. He put his head back, looking toward the sky.

Maggie dished some maize porridge onto a plate and added a spoon. She nudged his knee.

McKenna sat up and took the *nshima.* He scooped a small amount into his mouth, rolled it around, and swallowed. After a minute, he spooned another bite and worked to get it down his throat. He rested.

"That's good," Maggie said.

He tried another mouthful.

"If you're okay," O'Neal said, "I'll go to the river to see if there're any fish in my basket. I don't want to leave them in there too long after they've been caught."

McKenna nodded and put the spoon on his plate.

When Maggie returned, he was asleep in the chair, his partly eaten plate of *nshima* on his lap.

CHAPTER ONE HUNDRED SIX

Maggie stirred the breakfast in a pot over the fire. She heard noise behind her and turned to see McKenna standing in the doorway of the tent.

"You're up."

"I think so." He scratched his chin, now exhibiting over two weeks of beard.

He exited the tent and went slowly to the left. A few minutes later, he returned. "Do you think I could lose this diaper now?" he asked, sitting in the canvas chair.

Maggie ladled *nshima* onto a plate and handed it to him.

"Yes. You seem to be able to...well, take care of yourself now."

She spooned some maize porridge for herself and pulled her chair next to McKenna's. He sat unmoving with the plate in his lap. O'Neal looked at him and raised an eyebrow.

"I'm trying to get the strength."

Maggie nodded and ate some of her breakfast.

After a couple of minutes McKenna dipped his spoon into the porridge and brought it to his mouth. He rolled it around for a few seconds and swallowed.

"You okay?" Maggie asked.

"It seems like nothing in my body is working right."

"It'll get better." She watched him a moment.

He took another bite, waited to work it down his throat. McKenna put his plate on his lap and rested. He glanced at his waistband and turned to Maggie. "So, you wove these diapers and have been changing me?" He sounded disheartened.

Maggie nodded.

"Oh, O'Neal—"

"It's okay. I did it for Brian when he was a baby." She slid McKenna a glance.

He looked at her with a pained expression.

"Your eyes seem much clearer today," she said.

"You're changing the subject." He paused, his forehead furrowed. "You've been bathing me, too."

"Yes."

He raised his brows and a small smile broke on his face. "Did you peek?"

"What? No! Honest!" She told the truth. "I covered you. With a towel." She looked away from him now.

"I would have," McKenna said.

She turned back and saw his mischievous grin.

He let a moment pass before eating more *nshima*. He put down his spoon and lowered his plate to his lap. "I can't eat anymore."

"That's okay. You did well." She took his porridge.

"But I am thirsty."

"I have herb tea ready for you." She poured a tan liquid into a mug and handed it to him.

He raised the cup slowly to his lips, sipped, and swallowed. "This tea." He swirled the cup a little. "You've been giving me this tea."

She nodded.

"And feeding me."

"Yes, very watery *nshima*, fish and vegetable broth."

"You massaged my throat to help me get the food down."

"I used to do that with O.J. when I had to give him a pill, to help him swallow it."

McKenna drank his herbal brew, silent for a while.

"O'Neal, this diaper business—"

"I didn't peek."

"No, but…you must have had to…clean up my...you know, also?"

She shook her head. "No, not that. You didn't do that."

"For fourteen days, now?"

"No, well, you weren't eating much. And Kiki said black mamba poison causes paralysis, so it slows everything down." She gestured toward his cup. "I put something in your tea today for that."

"Not bug related, I hope."

"No. Turkey rhubarb. It's an herb. It will really work."

It did.

CHAPTER ONE HUNDRED SEVEN

McKenna slid his hand inside a pocket of his rucksack. "O'Neal, where's my GPS?"

"I have it."

"I know we've moved a distance from Mosquito Lab because the terrain is different. But where are we?"

"About twenty-two miles southwest. I wanted to get us far enough away and hidden, but not make you travel any more than you had to."

"Have you seen or heard anyone since we left the lab?"

"No. I figured anybody looking for who killed the guards would follow the M2 road east or west, or the trail south, or would think the intruders crossed the border into Tanzania. I stayed off the path and stuck to the woodlands. I'm glad we struck camp and packed our cart before we went to the laboratory so we could make a quick exit."

"How did you get the pull-cart through the trees?"

"Thank deforestation."

He regarded her a minute. "You're a wonder, O'Neal."

She looked at him in question.

"When I first worked with you, I thought you were a vanilla wafer. But you turned out to be a ginger snap."

"Ginger snap?"

McKenna nodded.

She smiled. “Good, I like ginger snaps.”

He returned her smile. “Me, too.”

CHAPTER ONE HUNDRED EIGHT

After staying another week in the encampment, McKenna said he felt strong enough to attempt travel, so early the next morning Maggie struck the tent and packed the pull-cart.

McKenna walked a little, but mostly had to ride the conveyance.

The CIA operatives headed south, intermittently traveling for several days at a time, resting for one, then resuming their journey.

Eventually, McKenna could walk greater distances with O'Neal pulling the cart alone. His ability to swallow increased and he ate more solid meals.

They'd agreed on a destination, and McKenna again assumed navigational duties, using the GPS. His mind improved daily, but his memory remained impaired.

One night after dinner, they sat in front of the tent in their canvas chairs, listening to the crackle of the campfire. McKenna had been silent for a long time and Maggie left him to his thoughts. He seemed to be trying to work something out.

She heard sounds by the waterhole below their camp and looked to see a small herd of elephants entering the pool. They drank, then sat and rolled around until their bodies were covered in mud. A few minutes later they hosed themselves off, spurting water from their trunks. Maggie smiled as the giant mammals lumbered out of the pool and walked away.

McKenna didn't seem to notice the elephants. He sat leaned over, forearms on knees. His toes tapped on the ground and he moved his mouth back and forth as if exercising his jaw muscles.

He stopped tapping his toes. "British Parliament," he said, "Bennington Childers, and—"

Maggie looked at him in surprise. "Wait, McKenna. I'll get a pen and paper." She went into the tent.

O'Neal returned to her chair and said, "Okay, go ahead."

"Henri Valois, France. Philip Devereau, France. Cardinal Garrone, the Vatican, Colonel Wheeler, USAMRIID, General Larken, US Army. CEOs from four drug companies, Draybough Pharmaceuticals, Worth and Bromm Biomedics, Quimbel and Frost, and Burgess." McKenna continued to dictate the HIV/AIDS depopulation plot members to O'Neal. He also named the CIA participant. When he finished, he sat quietly for a moment.

McKenna shook his head. "Nathan. I wonder how he did it."

Maggie looked at him, firelight bouncing off his longish hair, beard, and now-clear eyes. "Did what?"

"Got us here. He would have had to get approval and funding for Operation MOSQ from the very people who were involved in the scheme."

"Yes," Maggie said. "From the CIA's Director, Kenneth Berns, who we learned at the lab is the HIV/AIDS depopulation plot's participant in the Agency, and from the Senate Select Committee of which Sjoda was a member."

McKenna nodded. "I'm sure at some point COBOL suspected DCI Berns."

"Probably. And it could have been the DCI, or Serling, who had someone take a shot at Zann."

"Yes," McKenna said. "I imagine Serling relayed the content of the conversations Sjoda taped in COBOL's office to Berns, and also told him the senator e-mailed Mosquito Lab."

"I hope Nathan and Zann are all right," Maggie said. "DCI Berns would know the location of the safehouse where we all stayed."

“I don’t think we need to worry,” McKenna said, looking like something just occurred to him. “COBOL has excellent instincts and, he’s a survivor. My strong sense is that they’re safe.”

Maggie’s shoulders relaxed.

McKenna resumed tapping his feet on the ground. After a few beats he said, “I’m thinking about the mosquitoes at the lab. About why they could be breeding them. We never got to open that file on their computer.”

Maggie smiled. “I know why.”

McKenna looked at her in surprise.

She grinned. “That’s what I remembered at the laboratory right before the shotgun blast. Mosquitoes manufacture a digestive enzyme within their bodies that kills the HIV virus.”

“No kidding?” McKenna gave her a broad smile. “Geez, O’Neal, you’re brilliant.”

“Thanks.” She beamed. She clipped the pen onto the paper containing the list of names he’d just dictated to her, and placed it on her lap.

McKenna lapsed into silence for a short time. He shifted his weight in his chair and said, “I’ve been putting some puzzle pieces together.”

“Like?”

“Like us flying to Zambia by commercial airline. Not unheard of, but on previous overseas ops my fellow officers and I flew military. Also, the anti-malaria meds Nathan gave us were not prescribed by our CIA doctor, but by another physician.”

“And Nathan gave us money himself. We didn’t get vouchers from the finance office,” Maggie said.

“Yup. And no agency credit cards.”

“Yes, and also a private charter flight to take us to Mbala.”

“COBOL probably hired the pilot himself—well, through Cecil Pearson—so we wouldn’t leave a trail once we landed in Lusaka.”

“Nathan didn’t know of Pearson’s involvement,” Maggie said.

McKenna shook his head.

“Do you recall if the attaché’s name was on the HIV/AIDS depopulation participant list?”

“Yes. Near the bottom.”

"Any other names coming to you."

"No. But it doesn't matter."

"Huh?"

McKenna grinned. "I don't have to remember any more."

"Why not?"

"Because of what I do remember. When we were at Mosquito Laboratory, I e-mailed the list and other data to you, and to myself, and to Nathan's personal computer, through server routes I set up at Covington's. That's why I rigged the cable from the off-line computer to an Internet-connected one."

"Oh, good job, McKenna!"

"So, Nathan will know we made it to the lab, and take steps to secure the information I sent for evidence."

"Yes, he will." Maggie got quiet for a moment and looked off into the distance. She turned back with a creased brow. "McKenna?"

"Hmm?"

"I'm assuming the shotgun blast that took out the lab's offline computer would have also disabled the online one because you hooked cables to it?"

"Oh, definitely. The electronics couldn't have survived that jolt. Why? Are you worried someone might have traced the e-mails I routed through servers to you, Nathan, and me, compromising our safety in the States?"

"Yes."

"No need. I'm positive both computers are toast."

"Oh, good." She let go a sigh. A minute later, her brow knit again. "Jonathan?"

"Hmm?"

"Did you ever suspect Nathan to be the CIA person involved in the HIV/AIDS terrorist plot?"

McKenna took a moment before responding. He spoke slowly, as if measuring his words. "I've known COBOL a long time. I don't always agree with his methods…but…I do know he's a good man. He's always been true…so…my answer is 'no.'" He looked at Maggie. "You?"

She hesitated. "My instincts told me to trust him, and, well, he seems to genuinely care about his people…so, no… I couldn't believe he was involved."

They both sighed as if relieved they'd held that conversation, and sat in silence for a while.

Darkness fell, and the Zambian night sounds came to life.

Maggie leaned over and removed the teapot from the coals alongside the fire. She poured the brewed herbs into a cup and handed it to McKenna.

He took it, blew on it, and drank. "I'm getting used to this stuff, O'Neal. Starting to enjoy the taste."

"Good. It's helping you heal. It's got a variety of herbs in it, like—"

"I'll take your word for it," he said, sliding her a look and grinning.

She smiled back at him.

They fell quiet again.

McKenna faced the waterhole, appearing deep in thought. After a few minutes, he turned to O'Neal and said, "Alpha. You told me to go into Alpha. I slipped in and out of consciousness. Mostly out of, I expect, since I didn't come fully awake for twelve days."

"Yes." She leaned over and picked up the pot of tea. She lifted it in question toward McKenna.

He nodded and extended his cup toward her. She poured, and replaced the pot on the fire rocks.

"You went into Alpha, too," McKenna said. "You sat by me and went inside my body, imaged me being healed."

"Yes, and other than what the poison did to you, you looked pretty healthy." She smiled.

"Good. That's good."

He drank his tea quietly for a while. He shifted in his chair and said, "You gave me something bitter tasting immediately after I was shot with an arrow."

"Yes. *Shinganga* berry juice."

"How did you know what poisons were in the arrow?"

"I smelled the arrowhead. I know what dogbane, which is Bushman's poison, and beetles smell like. Dogbane was there, but not beetle larvae. I couldn't identify the odor of black mamba venom, but Kiki said that didn't matter, because *shinganga* reverses the affect of mamba toxin, too, if it's used with Bushman's poison, but not if it's used with the insect larvae."

"You sure are a wonder, O'Neal." McKenna drained his tea, put his empty mug on the ground, and sat back in his chair. He rubbed his chin, then rolled his eyes up and pulled down a lock of longish hair, now gone to curl. "I guess I'm pretty hippy looking," he said.

"I like it," Maggie said. "It suits you."

"Huh." He looked at her, a glean in his eye. "Maybe I'll keep it this way for a while, then."

"Good." She gave him a wide smile.

They sat in companionable silence for a time.

Maggie turned to him. "McKenna?"

"Hmm?"

"Grace."

He looked at her in question.

"Was she a vanilla wafer or a ginger snap?"

"Oh, she was a ginger snap, all right."

"I'm sorry I didn't have the chance to know her."

"Yes. You would have liked her." He paused, looking into the fire. After a moment he turned to O'Neal and said, "She would have liked you, too."

CHAPTER ONE HUNDRED NINE

Two weeks later, they arrived at Sunday Ndoba's village, their return warmly welcomed. They stayed four days before the navy-blue Toyota pickup came into the compound trailing a cloud of dust.

Sunday got out of the truck all toothy-smile, and gently squeezed his wife Tasila, her belly now protruding in pregnancy. He spotted the CIA officers and his face showed a mixture of surprise and happiness as he came to greet them.

After the evening meal, McKenna asked the Zambian tradesman, "Would you be willing to drive us all the way to Lusaka, no stops? I'll pay you very well."

"I will be very glad to drive you," Sunday said, grinning. "No stops. But I must first spend tonight with my wife, or she will chop me up and serve me with the *nshima* as relish."

CHAPTER ONE HUNDRED TEN

"Where would you like me to drop you?" Sunday asked as they approached Lusaka.

O'Neal and McKenna wore Muslim headdress. They'd been detained at a roadblock by police, but the men knew Sunday and let him through with a payoff of eight Lion beers, giving the tradesman's passengers only a disinterested glance.

"Right to the airport," McKenna said.

"No. We should make one stop first," Maggie said.

* * * * *

Sunday Ndoba got a bag of gifts, Maggie's suitcase, and McKenna's rucksack from the back of the pickup and set the items on the cathedral stairs. The operatives had donated their pull-cart and the rest of its contents to the tradesman's village.

McKenna handed the Zambian a large sum of Kwacha. "For your growing family," he said.

Sunday rewarded McKenna with a large smile.

After warm but hasty goodbyes, the CIA officers hurried up the steps with their luggage and entered the church. Maggie dipped her hand in the holy water at the door, made the sign of the cross, and genuflected. She brought the bearded McKenna to a pew.

"Sit here," she whispered. "I shouldn't be long."

McKenna slid into the bench with their belongings. He removed his Muslim turban and adopted a posture of prayer.

Maggie rearranged her headscarf and waited in a short line outside a confessional. When it came her turn, she entered the booth and spoke through the screen to the priest. "Bless me Father, for I have sinned. It's been almost three months since my last confession."

"Yes, my child. You may begin."

"I've had uncharitable thoughts about my parents and though it's been awhile, about my colleague sitting outside in a pew." She took a deep breath and said, "I've also killed five men."

She explained.

The priest listened to her confession and gave her penitence before saying a prayer of atonement, absolving Magdalene Reilly O'Neal of her sins.

Maggie thanked the priest and said, "There's something else, Father."

"Yes, my child?"

"I need your assistance in a professional matter."

Maggie and the cleric left the confessional. The robed man held a brief conversation with a younger priest, who then went to the booth to hear the confessions of those waiting in line.

Maggie signaled to McKenna.

He rose from the pew and followed her and the older priest through a door on the right side of the altar.

Once inside the rectory, the robed man turned to McKenna and ran his eyes over his longish hair and beard. He pursed his lips. "Well, if this is going to work," he said, "we'll need to make a few adjustments."

* * * * *

When the ticket agent saw the nun and priest, she leaned over the counter and said to them just above a whisper, "The flight isn't full." She smiled. "I can bump you up to first class at no extra charge."

"Bless you," the clerics said.

They entered the jetway with upgraded tickets.

* * * * *

The plane left Lusaka and with altitude gained, the attendants served dinner. The priest and nun were offered, and accepted, a glass of wine with their meal.

This being a late-night flight, no movie was shown. One by one the passengers turned off overhead lights and slumped in their seats, leaning their heads against whatever was handy. Their breathing soon turned to soft snores.

The flight attendants, too, sat and dozed, though most likely not too deeply, in case a passenger needed their assistance.

No one did, for all were asleep.

Had anyone been awake they may have noticed, however unseemly, a nun with her head on the shoulder of a priest, one who, not hours before, was bearded with longish hair, the hue of muted red.

They might also have been shocked to see the priest's head resting atop the nun's wimple, under which was shiny hair, the color of a desert sunset.

PART III
THE UNITED STATES OF AMERICA
OCTOBER, 2007

CHAPTER ONE HUNDRED ELEVEN

O'Neal looked up from her paperwork at her brother, who sat across the dining room table doing homework.

He pushed his algebra book aside and blew out a sigh. "All done," he said, his voice deeper now than when his sister left for Africa. "You?"

"Almost." Maggie returned to completing the necessary forms to have wells drilled in both Sunday's village and at the Mkushi River Clinic. Near her left elbow lay three envelopes containing substantial checks, one made out to Covington's AIDS clinic, another to the Sunnyvale Day Care Center and Orphanage, and a third to The Cathedral of the Holy Cross in Lusaka.

Her brother closed his notebook and gave another sigh. "I missed you, Mags."

Maggie stopped writing and raised her head. "I missed you, too, Brian. Two months was a long time to go without contact. I didn't mean to worry you."

"I was only a little worried."

Maggie lifted an eyebrow. "Only a little?" She smiled.

"Uh-huh. I figured if something happened to you, I'd *know*, you know?"

"Yes." She reached across the table and squeezed his hand.

"I still think it's awesome you worked for the CIA, and not just some bogus criminal justice temp agency."

"Sorry I couldn't tell you about that before, Brian. I wasn't allowed to divulge it to anyone."

"That's okay. I understand." He paused. "Nobody knew? Really? Not even Aunt Mary or Francie?"

"No. Nobody except Derek, because I interviewed him as a witness."

"Cool."

Brian's eyes moved around the brownstone. "This place looks great. You did an awesome job decorating it. And I like how Derek did my bedroom, too. Especially the table he made with legs out of baseball bats and the chair that's like a big catcher's mitt."

Maggie smiled. "He had fun doing it. He said you didn't want to move into Mom and Dad's room?"

"No." Brian shook his head vigorously. "You didn't either?"

"No."

"What should we do with it?

"We could turn it into an office or guestroom, or maybe a combination of the two."

"That's cool." Her brother picked up a homemade chocolate chip cookie from a plate. "You decide not to run in the New York marathon after all?"

"Yes. I want to stay home for a while instead of traveling again right now. I'll go next year."

"Good." He took a bite of the cookie. "Are you going out with Mac tonight? He hasn't seen our finished brownstone yet. In fact, it's been almost a week since he's stopped by."

"He's busy completing some computer work for Mr. Shoemake. And tonight, I'm meeting Francie for dinner, because she's only going to be in town for a few days."

"Oh." Brian gave a slight frown. "It's been nice of Mac to come over and help me with my pitching. That wrist adjustment he suggested made all the difference."

"I'm glad."

"And with your help, he's really getting good in archery, though not as good as you."

Brian looked at his sister from under his red-blond lashes, his expression hopeful. "You like him a lot, don't you?"

"Yes," Maggie said with a sparkle in her eyes. "I do."

Her brother inspected the chocolate chips in his cookie. "Good," he said, relief in his voice. "Because I like him a lot, too."

* * * * *

Fourteen-year-old Brian left the brownstone to have pizza with a friend, one named Amber, Maggie noted. She smiled through a sigh.

She gathered her papers, brought them into a pile to stow in her briefcase, and reached for the portable phone lying on the dining room table. She had two calls to make before getting ready for dinner. She dialed a number.

A woman's gentle voice came on the line. "Dr. Dansk."

"Eli, this is Maggie O'Neal...."

* * * * *

Maggie dialed the second number.

"Hello?"

"Betty Ann?"

"Yes?"

"This is Mary Margaret Ryan."

"Mary Margaret! Hey! How are you?"

"I'm fine, thank you. Listen, I've made arrangements with a very good counselor in Seaton for you to have several sessions with her if you choose to. Her name is Dr. Dansk."

"Oh, no. My husband would never give me money for that."

"It won't cost you anything. The fee's been covered."

Ms. Almon went silent.

"Betty Ann?"

"Why would anyone do that for me?" she asked in a small voice.

"Because you're worth it."

Betty Ann's breath caught, and she burst out crying.

O'Neal waited. When the sobs subsided, she asked, "Betty Ann, will you go?"

"Yes," the woman said through her tears. "I'll go."

CHAPTER ONE HUNDRED TWELVE

Several weeks after McKenna and Maggie's return from Africa, they met with Nathan and Zann in a small, private dining room within a five-star restaurant in Washington D.C., a SECS placed on the edge of the table to keep their conversations private.

Nathan's eyes twinkled above his navy wool suit, white shirt and paisley tie. He was seated next to Zann, beautiful in a black Vera Wang evening dress, her shiny dark hair falling to a shoulder-length straight line.

McKenna's light blue shirt, under a medium charcoal-gray wool suit and coordinating silk tie, enhanced his faded-denim eyes.

Maggie sat next to him in a long skirt of raw silk the color of burnt-orange, with a matching mandarin-collared jacket, its round buttons covered in the same knubby fabric. The opening at the neck formed a rectangle that dipped to a laced-linen camisole across the swell of her bosom.

A wine steward uncorked a bottle of Dom Perignon and poured a taste for Nathan. After Shoemake accepted the champagne, the server filled four flutes to half and put the bottle in a chilled bucket. He left the room.

Nathan lifted his glass. "To the four of us and all our reasons for celebration."

"We're celebrating you, O'Neal, and I being forced to leave the CIA for using Agency credentials, resources and time to perform an unauthorized op?" McKenna asked.

Zann grinned. "Along with my resigning."

"Yes, that too," Shoemake said, his blue eyes dancing. "And also, Maggie's birthday tomorrow."

O'Neal's dinner companions raised their glasses and wished her good cheer.

She thanked them, looking happy.

"And here's to the successful conclusion of both Operations D-Tech and MOSQ." Nathan toasted his former officers.

Everyone took a sip of champagne.

COBOL put his flute on the table and reached inside his jacket pocket. He removed several folded sheets of newspaper and, opening them, handed the stack across the table to Maggie and McKenna. "Some souvenirs," he said.

They read the copies of the front page news items from the New York Times, Washington Post, The Atlanta Journal Constitution, Los Angeles Times, London Times, and other national and world publications, all touting similar headlines: "EFFECTIVE VACCINES DEVELOPED FOR HIV/AIDS."

The articles reported that a cooperative effort between Draybough Pharmaceuticals, Worth and Bromm Biomedics, and the United States military resulted in the successful creation of three new HIV/AIDS vaccines.

"Our government's taking the credit for spear-heading the research and providing the funding, I see," McKenna said.

COBOL nodded.

"Incredible."

"Yup. And Draybough and Worth and Bromm will get very rich on those vaccines," Shoemake said.

McKenna shook his head in disgust. He picked up the bottle of Dom Perignon and put a little in each of his companion's glasses before adding some to his own. "What's the latest on the death of Vice President Serling?"

"I don't believe Serling took his own life, as the reports suggest. I knew the man. He wasn't the type. The suicide angle's a cover-up, I'm sure," Shoemake said.

The waiter came in and took their dinner orders. Fish all around.

"What about the other participants on the HIV/AIDS depopulation plan list?" Maggie asked when the restaurant employee left. "I haven't seen anything in the news."

"It's all been hushed in exchange for a cease-and-desist on any such future activities."

"That's it?" McKenna asked.

"No. Part of the deal is that the guilty heads-of-state provide adequate financing to pay for vaccinating all individuals infected with HIV/AIDS."

"So no one's being exposed or brought up on criminal charges?" O'Neal asked.

"No. It actually works better this way. If the depop plan participants were prosecuted, we wouldn't have the leverage or opportunity to get billions in funding. The involved world leaders are in a perfect position and have the power to get all the money needed not only for vaccines, but also to set up AIDS orphanages and academies along the lines of a certain talk show host's leadership schools for girls in Africa. And besides, they'd get the best defense attorneys, so many, if not all, would be acquitted anyway."

"So now they all look like heroes instead of the bad guys they are?" McKenna asked.

"Yes," Shoemake said.

"And faith is restored in our heads-of-state instead of learning that so many of them are evil?" Zann asked.

"Yes."

"What's to prevent the pharmaceutical companies from putting something else unholy in the vaccines?" McKenna asked.

"There will be a private oversight company," Nathan said.

"What's to prevent this oversight company from becoming corrupted, paid to look the other way?" McKenna asked.

Shoemake grinned. "I'll tell you more about that later."

The waiter came with dinner rolls and salads. He stood ready with a pepper grinder, but the foursome declined.

"At least the Director of Central Intelligence, Kenneth Berns, resigned," Maggie said when the waiter left.

"Yes, and with no explanation. His reason for leaving was simply reported as 'mysterious.'" Nathan said.

"Did anyone in this HIV/AIDS depop group admit to the US President's involvement?" McKenna asked.

"No admissions, but strong indications," Nathan said.

"His name wasn't on the list," Maggie said.

"Not everybody's was," Shoemake said. "Known members spilled the beans on some who weren't listed, many of whom, when interrogated, confessed their involvement."

"Yes," McKenna said. "Like another president, and a prime minister or two."

"Exactly," COBOL said.

"We failed to get final proof of both the manufacture of the viral strains and actual cures, because we didn't finish looking into the lab's files before the shotgun blasted the computer," McKenna said to Nathan. "How'd you make the guilty parties think we did?"

"I showed them what you e-mailed me about the specific strains of sera injected into different target groups—and that in itself was enough for criminal investigation—and also the information on the live-attenuated virus vaccine from non-progressors, the banana lectin and CCRF gene research, the ultra violet light results, the Zambian sex-worker test subjects, and the other lab locations. I told them you discovered they were breeding mosquitoes and that these insects have a digestive enzyme that destroys the HIV/AIDS virus."

McKenna looked at Maggie and smiled. "O'Neal figured that one out."

Shoemake gave her an approving nod. "So," he said, "when I presented the HIV/AIDS depop plan members with what we did have, they surmised we'd obtained the rest. I let them think we had the remaining evidence and threatened to expose everything. That's when we brokered a deal."

"When did you know about DCI Berns's involvement?" Maggie asked.

"I suspected it when he vehemently denied any funding, red-lighted the investigation, and didn't pass Hughes's information on to Homeland Security or the FBI's Counter Terrorist Group. I never liked the guy and already had reasons not to trust him. So I started looking into things myself."

"Yourself," McKenna said, frowning.

"You had enough on your platters. And besides, as you recall, I was pretty good at hacking into databases in the early years, too." Shoemake smiled. "Not as good as you, PASCAL, but darned decent nonetheless."

"Yes." McKenna grinned. "You were. I remember the time you hacked into—"

The waiter entered the room, checked on the foursome who weren't quite finished with their salads, and left.

"Speaking of databases," McKenna said, "I'm glad you secured Sjoda's computer in a location not connected to Langley."

"Yes, well, I wanted to make sure we got access."

"It amazes me how men implicate themselves by keeping self-incriminating information on their PCs," Zann said.

"Ego," McKenna said in disgust. He turned to Nathan and asked, "How'd you pull off getting Serling's computer after you no longer worked for the CIA?"

"I employed some people.... But I'll tell you about that later." Shoemake put his salad fork on his plate. "Mac, did you tell Maggie that you found proof on Sjoda's database regarding his involvement in the biological and chemical weapons' deals in Iraq?"

"He did, yes," Maggie said. "And also that the senator was responsible for the murder of the Hard Placers."

"And," McKenna said, his voice a little thick, "that he had my wife and son killed. He wasn't targeting me at the time. He wanted me to live with grief for a while and terminate me later."

Maggie touched his arm. "I'm so sorry, Jonathan," she said.

Nathan and Zann raised their eyebrows.

McKenna cleared his throat. "Sjoda. What a piece of work."

"Yes," COBOL said. "The man killed his own brother. His DNA matched that in the smudges found in Mark Hughes's wallet."

McKenna shook his head in disgust.

"I've been giving some thought to the senator spelling MOSQ in his own blood before he died," Nathan said.

"I have, too," McKenna said. "M-O-S-Q are the first four letters of 'mosquito,' so maybe Sjoda, angry at being betrayed by Serling and whoever told the VP he e-mailed the laboratory in Zambia, wanted to leave a clue pointing to Mosquito Lab as having the list of HIV/AIDS depopulation plan participants—"

"Or to the research into the use of mosquito enzyme as an HIV/AIDS cure—" Maggie said.

"But only had enough life left in him to get the initial part of 'mosquito' written," McKenna said.

"Makes sense," Nathan said. He looked at the two operatives. "Did you both get your courtesy reports-to-date sent off to Ian Covington at MI6?"

"Yes," they answered in unison.

"Excellent," COBOL said.

"What happened to the defense technology buyers, Ahmed Yousef, Detective Jaffey, Eugene Hackett and Salvador Belosi?" McKenna asked.

"The D-Tech buyers are being handled through diplomatic channels," Shoemake said. "Yousef and Jaffey are detained awaiting trial, and Hackett, who was in the van outside Langley watching out for you, Mac, was charged with stalking and is serving time. He already had a record. Belosi, who was keeping an eye on Maggie in Seaton and ordered killed by Sjoda, went missing.

"Oh," Maggie said.

The four sat quietly for a few minutes

McKenna broke the silence. "Something occurred to me while we were in Africa," he said, addressing Shoemake. "That safehouse in Great Falls didn't belong to the CIA, did it?"

"No," COBOL said. "In fact, we were the only four from the Agency who knew about it. I leased it as a contingency, because I grew to suspect we might need refuge in a location undisclosed to Central Intelligence personnel. I didn't even tell Claudia, because I felt it might compromise her safety."

A restaurant employee came in to the dining room to remove their salad plates, followed by a waiter serving their fish entrées. The group suspended conversation until the staff made their exit.

"How did you manage to get us to Zambia, if you didn't get approval from the DCI and the Senate Select Committee?" Maggie asked.

"Private funding," Nathan said.

McKenna narrowed his eyes. "Private funding?"

"Uh-huh." Shoemake grinned, but didn't elaborate. He tucked into his entrée.

The four friends talked amiably while they ate their meals. When they finished, one of the restaurant workers cleared the plates and removed the champagne bucket.

The waiter took their orders for dessert, coffee and tea.

"You said you'd tell us some things later," McKenna said to COBOL when the server left. "It's later."

Shoemake put his tongue on the inside of his cheek.

"I know that look," McKenna said. "It means you're up to something and enjoying it immensely. Spill."

"All right." Nathan's eyes twinkled as he reached into his suit pocket. He handed a business card across the table to PASCAL.

McKenna scanned the card and arched his eyebrows. "The MOSC Group?"

COBOL beamed. "Yup."

"Let me guess," PASCAL said. "McKenna, O'Neal, Shoemake, and Cinque."

"Yup." COBOL's grin filled his face.

"Oh, no." McKenna held up his hand. "You'll have to count me out. I'm flying back to Michigan Sunday. I've got my teaching job waiting, and Jason's spy-game business. And, living in a hotel for the past few weeks while finishing the computer work has gotten old."

A shadow crossed Maggie's face and she turned away.

The group lapsed into an uncomfortable silence.

McKenna moved around in his seat and cleared his throat. “Here, O’Neal.” He nudged her and handed her the business card.

She glanced at it, absently at first, then stared. Her eyes widened.

“This address...it’s on the same street as my brownstone.”

“Yup. Three blocks away.” Shoemake smiled. “I like your neighborhood. It’s undergoing accelerated gentrification.”

“It really is. It’s amazing how quickly it’s changed since we left for Zambia.”

“Yes,” Nathan said. “I bought a brownstone for a reasonable price. It needs a lot of work, but Georgetown Renovations agreed to take the job upon completion of yours, Maggie. Zann’s overseeing the remodeling and decorating.”

Shoemake’s wife grinned. “Yes, and I’m very excited about it.”

Nathan smiled and put his hand over hers, giving it a squeeze. “And that’s not all,” he said. “Zann’s in charge of The MOSC Group’s first project.”

“Which is?” McKenna asked.

“Monitoring the activities of the depopulation plot members, all their involved laboratories, the HIV/AIDS vaccine production and distribution, and the AIDS orphanages and schools projects,” Zann said.

Shoemake wore a wide grin.

“Huh. And what other ventures do you have planned for The MOSC Group?” McKenna asked.

“Privately-funded investigations similar to Operation MOSQ,” Shoemake said, keeping his broad smile.

Maggie and McKenna looked at each other and lifted their brows.

CHAPTER ONE HUNDRED THIRTEEN

Before dessert and coffee were served, Maggie and Zann excused themselves to go to the ladies' lounge. McKenna watched the women walk through the door of the private dining room.

As soon as they left, COBOL said, "I'd really like to have you on board at The MOSC Group, PASCAL."

McKenna shook his head. "My teaching job, my nephew—"

"The university can get another computer science professor, Mac. And, you can do all the spy-game development from here. You'll have your own office, and all the latest computer equipment available to you. Heck, you can even live on the third floor of The MOSC Group's brownstone. The place has plenty of room."

McKenna lowered his eyes to the table. He pushed a spoon back and forth over the white cloth. After a moment, he raised his head to Nathan.

Shoemake regarded him. He said, "That was some op you experienced in Zambia. I'm glad you got your memory back."

"Yeah, it was like having pea soup for brains. And a body, too, for that matter."

"I'm glad *you* came back," Nathan said.

"I am too." PASCAL paused. "I wouldn't have, if it hadn't been for O'Neal." He'd told COBOL the whole story when he and Maggie returned from Africa.

Shoemake put his tongue on the inside of his cheek. His eyes sparkled. "You still think she's not CIA material?"

"You're going to make me eat my bugs, plants, and bow and arrow words, aren't you?"

COBOL smiled broadly. "Yup."

McKenna looked pointedly at Shoemake. "You doubted her too, Nathan."

"When she didn't fulfill her assignment of cozying up to the men in DC Homicide who might be relaying our defense technology, well.... She seems all right now, though." Shoemake grinned. "Especially around you."

"Yup," McKenna said, smiling. "She's a ginger snap."

PASCAL's smile faded. He resumed pushing the spoon around on the table. After a moment, he looked up again at COBOL. "But," he said, "you also saw O'Neal's potential."

Nathan gave a nod.

"And you recalled me to the Agency. Why, really?" McKenna knit his brow. "Another officer could have worked Operation D-Tech."

"I called you back because I believed in you. And it was time."

PASCAL regarded his old friend, and a moment passed between them.

McKenna stopped fiddling with the silverware. "Nathan, why'd you pursue the HIV/AIDS depopulation investigation anyway? Operation MOSQ cost you your position, and it didn't seem --"

Shoemake held up his hand. "In working for the CIA, particularly as Directorate of Operations, I'd seen enough corruption and evil in our government and in that of other countries to last lifetimes. Things going on in our own nation and in the world about which the general population is blissfully ignorant. What transpires in meetings behind closed doors.... And, though at first I didn't believe it, I'd heard rumblings about the HIV/AIDS terrorist plot—even about some of the individuals who might be involved and their reasons why. With Operation MOSQ, I saw the potential to get on the right side of things. That's going to be the mission, the charter if you will, of The MOSC Group."

"Maverick crusading?"

"Something like that."

"Why'd you choose O'Neal and I for Operation MOSQ instead of any of your other officers?

"Because both of you are above the rest. And I knew you could, and would, do the job."

PASCAL looked at COBOL a moment, and shook his head slightly. "I've got to hand it to you, Nathan," he said.

Shoemake gave a small smile. "In what regard?"

"Getting what you want from people."

COBOL's smile widened, his blue eyes twinkling under silver brows.

CHAPTER ONE HUNDRED FOURTEEN

McKenna found a parking spot among the high-end vehicles lining the curb. He exited his rental and walked up the steps to O'Neal's brownstone. Yellow, white, and rust-colored chrysanthemums bloomed in large terra cotta pots on either side of her stoop.

He wore a tweed jacket against the chill of the crisp late October air, and carried a medium-sized paper bag in his left hand.

He rang the bell.

Maggie opened the door, and her eyes widened. "McKenna!"

He gave a little grin.

"Come in."

McKenna entered the brownstone and stood in the hall. He smelled coffee.

"You just missed Francie and Aunt Mary. But Derek—"

As if on cue, a tall man with graying, light-brown hair sashayed from the kitchen. Derek stopped mid-hall and appraised Maggie's visitor. He put his hand over his heart and said, "Oh."

O'Neal introduced the two men, and Derek shook McKenna's hand, letting his grasp linger a moment before letting go. He leaned to Maggie's ear and said in a stage whisper, "Why are all the delicious one's hetero?" He let out a heavy sigh and grinned at both of them.

They returned the smile, one showing amusement, the other mild embarrassment.

"Nice fashion statement," Derek said, gesturing to a denim cloth pouch hanging sling-like from McKenna's neck to his belly.

"Yes, McKenna, what is that?" Maggie asked. "Did I just see something moving in there?"

McKenna ignored her and rocked back and forth on his feet. He surveyed the brownstone.

"Your home looks really great, O'Neal."

"Derek helped—"

"Derek only did Brian's room, and Derek is just leaving," the tall man said. "Derek knows when three's a crowd." He bent to give Maggie's cheek an air kiss before saying, "Ta," and slipping out the front door.

"Well, someone has great taste," McKenna said. He peered into the living room, simply decorated in a palate of caramel, camel, and creams, punctuated by a few muted-brick accessories. Three African baskets were well situated on the buffed hardwood floor, two round in a medium-dark shade of brown, and one rectangular in a natural dried-grass weave.

"Those are the baskets the women in Sunday's village gave you as gifts," McKenna said, pointing to the brown ones. "And a fishing basket you made while I was recovering."

"Yes."

He looked at a framed watercolor of a mother giraffe leaning down to kiss her baby on the top of its head. The picture, propped up against a new couch, had a red ribbon with a bow over one corner. "Weisner" was inked in the lower right. "Did Derek paint that for you?"

"Yes, for my birthday."

McKenna gestured to a piece of furniture. "Is that Mark Hughes's antique African chest?"

"Uh-huh." She turned to him, eyes going to the sack against his stomach. "McKenna, something *is* moving in there."

"It's nice you lit the fire." He nodded toward the fireplace. "It feels good on such a cool fall day."

"McKenna...."

He sighed theatrically. "Okay." He grinned, and, reaching inside the denim pouch, pulled out a tiny orange kitten. The ball of fur mewed in his hand and looked at him with blue eyes. He gave it to O'Neal.

"Happy birthday, Maggie." He beamed.

"Oh, McKenna." Her eyes pooled.

"I've named him Mango. Temporarily, of course." He cleared his throat. "You could change it."

"No," she said, wiping her eyes with her free hand and surveying the cat with a pleased expression, "I like Mango. It suits him."

She put the kitten to her cheek and it broke into a loud purr.

McKenna stood there awkwardly. "Lots of volume for such a little tyke."

Maggie smiled and nodded. She brought the kitten to her chest and held it in one hand, petting it gently on its head with a finger.

Her eyes darted to McKenna's belly. "There's still something moving in that pouch."

"Is there?" McKenna feigned innocence for a few beats before reaching into the denim and pulling out a little white kitten. "Mango's sister. I named her—"

"Moonlight." Maggie's eyes welled again.

"Yes," he whispered. He handed O'Neal the tiny cat. It immediately began sucking on her finger, joining her brother in a purr.

"She's hungry," Maggie said, sniffing a little.

"I brought kitten food." He lifted the bag he carried in his left hand. "To get you started. I got the kittens at the shelter. I thought you'd like that, especially."

"Oh, Jonathan, thank you." Her face shone.

"Sure," he said. He stood there, uncertain for a moment. He took a tentative step toward her.

The front door burst open.

"Mac!"

McKenna stepped back from O'Neal and turned to Brian. "Hi, there." He eyed the teen up and down. "I swear you're getting taller every week," he said with a smile.

"Yeah!" Brian did an air punch. "You here to shag some flies?"

"That, and other things." He looked at O'Neal, keeping his smile. After a few seconds, he turned back to her brother and asked, "Do you suppose there's any birthday cake left?"

"Oh, yeah. That cake is *huge*. I'll cut some for us."

Brian spotted the kittens. "Oh, cool!"

Maggie tenderly handed Mango to her brother.

He held the little orange ball of fur in his hand and nuzzled his nose to the kitten's head. "He looks like O.J.," he said, his voice a little throaty.

The kitten purred.

"Way cool," he whispered.

"This one's hungry," O'Neal said, petting Moonlight softly. "They probably both are."

"I'll feed them," her brother said, his face eager. "Oh, we don't have any kitten food. I'll run to the store."

"No need," McKenna said. "I brought some."

He handed over the bag, and Brian tucked it under his arm. The fourteen-year-old scooped Moonlight up with his free hand and headed for the kitchen.

"And don't forget the cake!" McKenna called after him good-naturedly.

"Gotcha covered, Mac." Brian turned his head over his shoulder and flashed a grin.

Maggie wiped her eyes.

McKenna removed the sling from around his neck. He took a step toward O'Neal and put the denim over her head, lifting her hair gently. His fingers lingered a moment on her nape.

They looked at each other and their eyes held.

McKenna moved closer. He slid his hand under Maggie's chin and raised her face to his. He leaned forward.

The loud jangle of the hall phone startled them, and they jumped back. Maggie sighed as the ringing persisted, and moved to answer the call, turning the ringer to low as she did.

She lifted the receiver and said, "Maggie O'Neal." She listened. "Yes. He's here." She covered the mouthpiece. "It's Nathan."

McKenna arched his brows.

O'Neal returned her attention to Shoemake and said, "All right. I'll put you on speaker phone." She pushed a button on the new unit's console.

"Listen, you two," COBOL said. "Something's just come across my desk here at The MOSC Group. It's big. I need you both to come in."

McKenna put his hand up and opened his mouth to speak.

Maggie looked at him, tilted her head, and gave him a smile.

She turned to the phone. "Yes, sir."

"All right, then," Shoemake said. "My office, Monday morning, ten o'clock."

ACKNOWLEDGEMENTS

Much gratitude goes to my extraordinary editor, Kaye Coppersmith of Wordsworth Editing, without whom this book would not be this book.

I also thank the Washington D.C. Metro Police Department, The United States Embassy, Lusaka, Zambia, Smokey Mountain Hobbies of North Carolina, and the confidential medical, veterinary, veterinary pathology, and computer research sources who helped with this novel.

Additionally, my appreciation goes to members of the Florida Writers Association for their gentle critiques and nudging, Ronda Birtha and Ellen Schofield of Galactic Publishing (www.galacticpublishing.com) and Writers Hub of the Mountains (www.hubofthemountains.com), Gerald Carlin, Maggie Ferriera, Linda Girard, Raymon Grace, Founder and President of Raymon Grace Foundation, Chrissy Jackson, President of Florida Writers Association, Linda Leineke, Scott Moss, Annette Rawlings, Antonia Tarto, Mark Weber of Sound Specialist Inc., Miami, and Barbara Wheeler, for their contributions to MOSQ.

LaVergne, TN USA
03 August 2010
191910LV00006B/2/P